HYDE PARK
DECEPTION

★ BOOK 2 IN THE DECEPTION SERIES ★

RICHARD LYNTTON

**MALCHIK
MEDIA**

www.richardlynttonbooks.com

Published by Malchik Media

ISBNs: 978-1-7354905-4-0 (paperback)
         978-1-7354905-7-1 (hardback)
         978-1-7354905-5-7 (audiobook)
         978-1-7354905-9-5 (ebook)

Library of Congress Control Number: 2020921974

Cover and map design by Jae Song
Interior design by Gary A. Rosenberg • thebookcouple.com
Editing by Candace Johnson • Change It Up Editing, Inc.

Thanks in advance for reading

HYDE PARK DECEPTION

The audio book is also available.

✪ ✪ ✪

For more information, to download FREE chapters of **North Korea Deception,** *or to sign up for our* *FREE Reader Regiment newsletter, CLICK on the richardlynttonbooks website link:*

https://richardlynttonbooks.com/

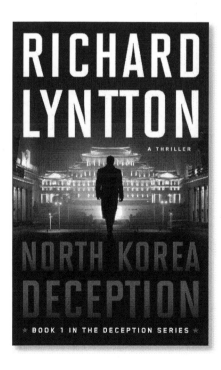

Rather Use Than Fame

—William Ellis School
Highgate, London

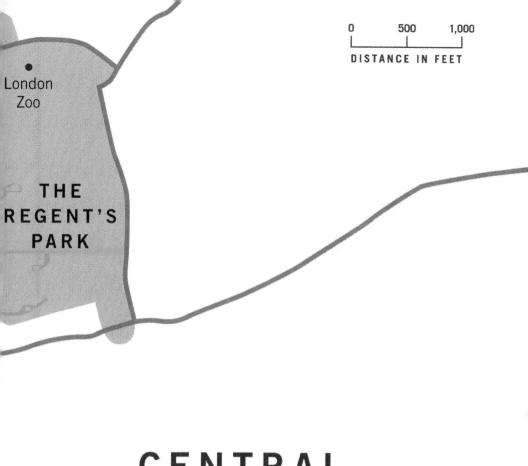

London
Zoo

**THE
REGENT'S
PARK**

0   500   1,000
DISTANCE IN FEET

CENTRAL
LONDON

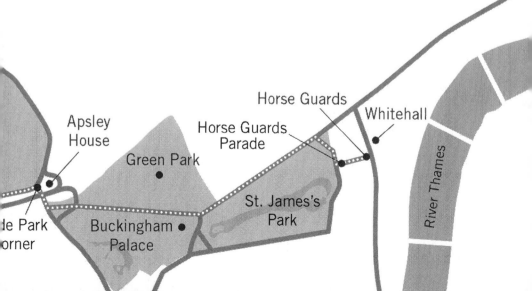

Horse Guards
Apsley
House
Horse Guards
Parade
Whitehall
Green Park
St. James's
Park
River Thames
de Park
orner
Buckingham
Palace

SARAJEVO

Pale

Rogatica

Goražde

8 MILES

N

JAHORINA MOUNTAIN

Front line encirclement

SARAJEVO

Cemetery

UN HQ

Market Massacre

Sniper Alley

Airport

Tunnel

1 MILE

FOREWORD

I n December 1991, at a Brussels meeting of the EC Foreign
Ministers, German Foreign Minister Hans Dietrich Genscher
threatened to break ranks and unilaterally recognize Croatia,
one of the former Yugoslav republics. This was a bitter blow to
European unity and the spirit of the imminent Maastricht Treaty
of 1992.

Britain—to the astonishment and irritation of former Foreign
Secretary Lord Carrington—did not send its senior foreign minister, Douglas Hurd, to the summit in Brussels. Lord Carrington
attended in his capacity as first European Community peace
envoy. Later he recorded his reaction to Foreign Ministers at the
summit in an interview.

> I said very strongly that I felt that the timing of this
> was wrong. I pointed out that early recognition would
> torpedo the conference. There was no way in which the
> conference would continue after that. It would make no
> sense at all. And that if they recognized Croatia and Slo-
> venia then they would have to ask all the others whether
> they wanted their independence. And that if they asked
> the Bosnians whether they wanted their independence,
> they inevitably would have to say yes, and that this would
> mean a civil war [in Bosnia]. And I put this as strongly as
> I could.[1]

---

1 Laura Silber and Allan Little, Yugoslavia, Death of a Nation (New York: Penguin
Group, 1997), 199.

Two months later, on March 1, 1992, Bosnia and Herzegovina organized a referendum on independence. The Bosnian Serb assembly members, however, urged their Serb population to boycott. There was a 67% turnout of Muslims and Croats, and, without the Serb vote, 99% favored the proposal. The Muslim-dominated Parliament of Bosnia and Herzegovina thus declared independence on March 5, 1992. The March referendum was the initial "reason" given by the Bosnian Serbs for setting up roadblocks in and around Sarajevo, which swiftly led to bloody conflict and all-out war.

PROLOGUE

February 1, 1994 ~ Island of Korčula, Croatia

The old gentleman sported a healthy shock of white hair and a goatee. He sipped away at a heavy tumbler half-filled with Teacher's, a mildly decent Scotch. It was a gift from a British blue beret from the Navy, Army, Airforce Institutes (NAAFI) at Divulje Barracks in Split.

He sat in a wheelchair on the veranda of the Villa Mare overlooking the Adriatic Sea. There were no other houses near the white stucco villa with pea-green shutters; the isolation would work in his favor. Regrettably, he would have to shoot his visitor—shoot to kill. He was expecting company because Boško the fisherman had telephoned, and Sir Lawrence Fitzgerald, 1st Baronet of Strachur and Glensluain, had listened carefully to the warning.

"Yes, thank you, Boško," he said. "I'll send him your regards." His final words decoded: message understood—come immediately.

Now he waited, his breathing steady. "Come on, old boy," he muttered. He had been in these situations a hundred times. But at his age, life was fragile; any loss of life—any violence—was to be avoided at all costs. Alas, not on this occasion.

After a time, he turned to go inside, propelling his wheelchair across the terrace. Its tires squeaked on the terracotta tiles. He looked at the portrait hanging above the fireplace and exchanged a nod with his old friend Josip Broz, known to the rest of the world as Marshal Tito, or just good old Tito.

The portrait, and the villa itself, had been a gift half a century before—a thank-you, the enigmatic leader had told Fitzgerald—from a grateful nation fighting fascist Nazi Germany and the Ustaša—Croatian fascist forces. After the war, Fitzgerald and his wife, Alice, had taken up residence on the island, living comfortably for decades until strangers came hunting. Hatred filled his heart now more than any other time during his many years undercover carrying out deadly operations for Secret Intelligence Service (SIS)—known more commonly as MI6. The forces trying to destroy this country had murdered Alice, his wife and best friend of forty years.

He reached the fireplace, applied the wheelchair brake, and heaved himself up. He stretched out his arm and pressed the stud that opened the hidden compartment underneath the mantelpiece. He retrieved the pistol and closed the door.

"Come on you buggers," he said flopping into his wheelchair. "Come on you blighters, let's have yer ..." Over the years, he had learned to turn fear into venom, a skill that had saved his life on several occasions.

The weight of the Browning 9mm—so much more solid than a Luger—suggested it was fully loaded. He wiped away a bead of oil next to the safety catch. The smell of lubricant confirmed the weapon was primed. *Make ready!* Even after all these years, the Sandhurst instructors barking their gunnery range orders remained with him: "Prior planning and preparation prevents piss-poor performance, gentlemen!"

Fitzgerald pulled back the working parts, checked inside the chamber and released the breechblock, which sliced forward with a comforting click. He tucked the pistol beneath the mohair blanket on his lap, leaving both arms free to maneuver the wheelchair about-face to the terrace.

Uncertain how many would come this time, he waited with the confidence of a trained killer, retired—one who had extinguished many lives, but always, he insisted, in the line of duty. Now frail, he still possessed supreme confidence against any foe. A year ago, when they had tried to kill him—an attempted robbery, he told Croatian police—they had shot him in the thigh and shattered his femur. Alice, however, had been fatally wounded.

He blamed his own efforts to prevent war in former Yugoslavia for her death. He wished he'd never set eyes on the place. Nothing was worth losing Alice for, not even an entire nation. He wouldn't rest until he had found the bastard responsible for her death, directly or indirectly. The only problem was that he had no idea where to start—Bosnian Muslim, or Serb or Croat? They all had reasons for igniting the conflict in Bosnia, which had become a cesspool of political and religious vengeance and all-out war. They were all as bad as each other as far as he was concerned.

Boško, his friend and also his odd-job man, had reported that a stranger—Eastern European—had arrived on the Jadrolinija car ferry from Split that morning. The young man had been asking questions, offering bribes, and seeking information about the "retired British spy."

Fitzgerald looked out at the sea. He watched the sun dancing off the whitecaps and assessed his options: He, she, or they would probably come around the side of the house. He would have his back to them—so they wouldn't attack immediately. A few seconds was all he needed. Using the wheelchair—which he didn't actually need—as a foil would also help.

He took a salty breath and pulled the red tartan blanket up to his trim waist, then he downed the Teacher's. *My little beauty. Why pay more when it does the trick after two swigs?* With as much strength as he could muster, he threw the tumbler over the cliff in front of him and waited for the sound of breaking glass far below. *I'm just an old fart in a wheelchair, counting out my days in the sunshine …* he mused. At least, that would be his role on the call sheet today.

He squinted at the sea of diamonds and whistled "Land of Hope and Glory." A pair of dolphins skipped effortlessly across the waves like Olympic synchronized swimmers.

The gentle pounding of waves crashing on the rocks below took him back to his clandestine arrival on the island in 1945. The elite Special Operations Executive—SOE—had given Tito's Partisans an incorrect password resulting in a frenzy of automatic fire. Hoarse from shouting and soaked from bullets pounding the water all around them, they had eventually, and miraculously, negotiated safe passage onto the island. For Tito's Partisans, it was as though Churchill himself had arrived that day. Fitzgerald had fallen in love with the island, the country, and its people, and he would lay down his life for them if necessary. The problem now was that they were all trying to kill each other—Muslims, Serbs, and Croats alike. It broke his heart.

The drone of a car engine brought him back to the present. An island taxi, VW Passat or Opel Kadett, he suspected, hurtled down the single-track road to his villa. The car pulled up and a door slammed. The taxi departed. From the veranda, Fitzgerald heard a knock at the front door on the other side of the house, followed by some fist pounding. He remained still, enticing the visitor around to the side of the house.

The dolphins made one last dive and did not resurface.

He heard footsteps behind him. "You are the owner?" asked someone with a thick Eastern European accent. Fitzgerald couldn't quite pinpoint the country of origin.

The man's polite tone was amusing. Fitzgerald spun his wheelchair with one hand and took aim with the other beneath the blanket. "Good afternoon. Yes, I am master of the house. How can I help?"

The blond was barrel-chested with high cheekbones and a pointed chin—a Slav of some description—Serb? Russian perhaps? "Tell me what you have told the British journalist, or I will kill you."

"I beg your pardon?" Fitzgerald feigned ignorance.

"We know you met him. We know he trusts you." He pulled out a Makarov PM semiautomatic pistol with a silencer from behind his back and pointed it at the old man.

Fitzgerald nodded, eyebrows raised, eyes bright. "Yes, yes, of course, young man, anything to oblige. We've been expecting you."

We? An inkling of doubt flashed over the stranger's face. Fitzgerald planted his index finger on the trigger.

Drawn to movement under the old man's blanket, the blond straightened his arm to fire, but stopped suddenly in his tracks.

Fitzgerald flailed one way then the other, like a fish with a hook in its mouth. He gripped his chest, unable to breath, an intense rasping from his throat. His eyes rolled upward, he clawed at his chest. "HELP ... ME ..." he said, extending his right arm to the would-be assassin.

Tables successfully turned. In his youth, he had demonstrated considerable talent for amateur dramatics.

The visitor stepped forward. Agony on the old man's face vanished as he fired—the single shot pierced the man's heart. Then, adjusting his aim upward one notch, he fired a second shot to the forehead.

Target stop. I haven't lost my touch, if I say so myself.

Blond staggered, crashing headfirst down the veranda steps toward the cliff.

It was over, less dramatic than expected. In fact, Alice, the love of his life, made pulling the trigger easy. His eyes dampened. He had failed to protect the person he loved most in the world. He would never forgive them. Any of the buggers, whoever was responsible.

Boško appeared a few moments later. "Sorry, Sir Lawrence, I came as soon as possible." He spoke English with a thick Croatian accent.

"Thank you, Boško. I am indebted, my friend."

"Nema problema, gospodine." *No problem, sir.* They conversed in short bursts of English and Croatian (or Bosnian or

Serbian, pretty much the same language, depending on which part of the former Yugoslavia you were from). Boško grinned, revealing a set of gold-capped teeth. "Our people owe you many lives, Sir."

He was referring to the dozens of secret missions Fitzgerald had personally masterminded against the Nazis over the war years.

"You're too kind, Boško ..."

Fitzgerald peered at the young intruder's face awash with blood. "I hate it when they're young, don't care who sent 'em." He sighed. "Let's have him overboard ..."

Boško trotted down the veranda steps and crouched next to the corpse. He checked the man's pockets and grimaced. "Empty, gospodine." He dragged the body a few feet to the cliff and flicked it over with the toe of his leather loafer. Seconds later, they heard a heavy thud followed by seagulls squawking and taking flight from their feeding ground on the rocks below.

Fitzgerald nodded. "High tide. Give it a day or two. If our friend is washed ashore, he'll keep authorities guessing. He might even make it to Montenegro."

Croatian and Montenegrin police, he knew, were too swamped with arms and drug smuggling, not to mention the war, to waste time on an unidentified corpse.

Fitzgerald returned to the mantelpiece and replaced the Makarov into the secret compartment.

"Now, Boško," he said. "I fancy a trip to London. And switch the kettle on, please, there's a good fellow."

"Naravno, gospodine." *Right away, sir.* Boško completed his task with enthusiasm. "One year since the first attack, gospodine. When will they leave us in peace?"

"An excellent question, my friend. Unfortunately, I don't have an answer for you." He nodded slowly. "But I know someone who might."

PART I

CHAPTER ONE

Hyde Park Barracks, Knightsbridge, London SW7

Sunlight streamed through naked winter trees and melted the blanket of frost covering the largest royal park in central London. Over three-hundred-and-fifty acres and home to four-thousand trees, Hyde Park was once King Henry VIII's hunting ground. Steele's room in the officers' mess at Hyde Park Barracks overlooked most of it.

Once again, Captain Jack Steele had landed on his feet with this posting from British Army of the Rhine (BAOR)—to the most sought-after "jolly" the British Army had to offer: Household Cavalry Mounted Regiment in the heart of Knightsbridge, London. Household Cavalrymen were the only soldiers in the British Army who went to Harrods for their groceries.

At 6:02 am, he got up and dressed for physical training—PT—pulling on a red T-shirt army issue, olive-green lightweights, and Nike trainers. Steele made a couple of lackadaisical stretches in preparation for the three-mile run around the boating lake in Hyde Park with his troop—eleven men, one officer. The PT instructor noncommissioned officer (NCO) wasn't looking to break any records. As long as the troop passed the monthly battle fitness test (BFT), he didn't even care if the men broke a sweat. *After all, we're Household Cavalrymen. Why walk when you can ride, gentlemen?*

Steele finished with an impressive sprint but took a couple of minutes to catch his breath. For the umpteenth time, he made a mental note to self to get "really in shape." At Sandhurst, the NCOs had labeled him a *fat knacker,* and the epithet had stuck. In fact, he wasn't fat at all—not even thickset—but tall and, some would say, slender. Nevertheless, in fitness terms, he was certainly no gazelle, and unlike most of his fellow subalterns who had joined the regiment with him, there was definitely room for improvement.

Today, Steele was on Queen's Life Guard. His main duty was to mount the new guard at Horse Guards, otherwise known correctly as the ceremony of Changing The Queen's Life Guard (he always bristled when tourists called it Changing *of* The Queen's Life Guard). He returned to the officers' mess for a full English breakfast—another habit to break.

He grabbed the mandatory jacket/blazer to be worn over PT kit at breakfast—officers' mess dress code—and entered the dining room overlooking Hyde Park. He ordered two Cumberland pork sausages, two fried eggs, two rashers of crispy bacon, and two pieces of toast. Outside the large window was a view of the park that reminded him of a Lowry painting—pedestrians, cyclists, dog walkers, and equestrians, all resembling "Matchstalk Men and Matchstalk Cats and Dogs," the popular Lowry tribute song from the 1970s. He also relished the fact that even Knightsbridge millionaires could not breakfast with a view like this.

Glancing at a senior squadron leader who sat across the table reading *The Times,* Steele read the headline upside-down and immediately lost his appetite: Bosnian Serb Leader Rejects Sarajevo Cease-Fire—AGAIN! The carnage was spreading. His brother, Peter Steele, a freelance journalist, had been covering the war for several months. He would be in more danger now than ever before. Not that Peter would care what Jack thought. They hadn't spoken for five years, almost to the day. If, God forbid, a Sarajevo sniper or mortar round killed Peter, Jack would never forgive himself. But he just couldn't seem to bury the hatchet and forgive while his brother was alive.

"You're better off out of that bag of bollocks," said Henry, the squadron leader, munching on whole-wheat toast slathered with mounds of butter and marmalade. "Let 'em get on with it, that's what I say."

Twat head. Steele kept the thought to himself.

Henry spoke with an air of authority. "If you ask me, seal the borders, let 'em pummel each other to bits and have done with it."

"I think it's a touch more complicated, Henry." Junior officers called senior officers by their Christian names in the Household Cavalry.

"*Please*, Jack," Henry replied, sounding almost constipated.

Steele had no time to parry before the mess orderly approached with a silver tray carrying a folded note.

"For you, sir."

"Thanks, Corporal Crawley."

Steele took the note and read it:

Call Peter. Urgent

Steele did a double take. *What the bloody hell?* It crossed his mind that this was some kind of prank from a fellow officer, one who knew about his sticky relationship with Peter. But he dismissed the idea when he turned over the note and confirmed Peter's mobile number was correct. No one else knew it. Steele had seen Peter on television at a press conference gaggle at the Holiday Inn in downtown Sarajevo just a few days before. *Why back in London so soon?* he wondered.

Steele stood up. "Keep us all posted, Henry."

On the way back to his bunk, Steele decided he didn't have the remotest intention of returning Peter's call. He had to admit he was curious though. Not a word in five years, and now this. *Hate* was too strong a word, but it wasn't far off. The Steele twins—not identical but a very close resemblance—had fallen out big time, and Jack wasn't close to being ready to forgive Peter's turning his back on their arthritic, aging mother for the past five years.

8:15 am Savoy Hotel, Charing Cross

The Strand glistened after a short downpour. A stream of black cabs and an occasional red double-decker bus swished through giant puddles. Bright sunshine broke through a thick cloud, shattering Sonja Radovanović's image of Conan Doyle's London. She had read the Sherlock Holmes series twice. The first time was to practice her English, and the second round was for pleasure. But on this visit, disappointingly, she had yet to experience London fog.

Joking aside, she was grateful to be in London—a brief respite from Bosnia hell. Luckily, she had the resources and connections to leave Pale—pronounced *Pah*-lay, not Pail—the Bosnian Serb stronghold just outside Sarajevo. After a six-hour road trip to Belgrade and a short flight to London via Budapest, she was now ready to accept Sir Lawrence Fitzgerald's invitation. Sonja represented her father, Dr. Kosta Radovanović, leader of the Bosnian Serbs. For his part, Sir Lawrence Fitzgerald, apparently, was a representative of the British government.

Sonja had recently given an interview to Peter Steele, a freelance reporter, and the two had hit it off. It was after this interview that Sir Lawrence Fitzgerald, a personal friend of the great Tito himself and probably a former British spy, had invited her to London for "talks." If the man was to be believed, or more importantly, trusted, Fitzgerald had the authority to negotiate on behalf of the British government, which was why she had felt compelled to make the journey. Even now, she felt guilty for leaving her people during the bloody conflict.

Sonja tipped the cabbie with a couple of the small, weighty one-pound coins—the British authorities had given her one hundred pounds to cover expenses, a key to a flat in Holborn, and a map of the tube. Elegantly tall, with long black hair, narrow eyes, and slightly crooked teeth, she smiled at the Savoy doorman dressed in gray garb piped with gold braid, and he smiled back. It felt good to be in a place where strangers smiled at each other without worrying if they would take out a gun and shoot you because of your ethnic background.

She pushed the smoothly calibrated revolving door of the Savoy's grand entrance and entered the lobby. Striding past reception, she reached the breakfast lounge and heard a cacophony of foreign accents and languages—French, German, Arabic, Japanese, and, of course, American. *Americans are everywhere.* She wondered how long it might be before they deployed US troops on the ground in Bosnia—against *her* people.

Sonja looked around. One person fit the description. The elderly gentleman sitting away from the crowd in the far corner had white hair and wore a navy blazer with a "Brigade of Guards tie," he had explained earlier—"navy and burgundy stripe."

She approached. He stood up and smiled warmly.

"A pleasure, Ms. Radovanović." He extended a large dry hand. For reasons she could never quite fathom, she trusted people more when their palms were dry.

"How are you today, Sir Lawrence?" She gave a slight bow. His calm demeanor and air of confidence gave Sonja the impression this man might indeed possess the kind of influence and power needed to bring peace to her country. She had grown up with great respect for the British and their traditions of honor and fair play in everything, above and beyond cricket.

"Thank you, my dear, no need to stand on ceremony. Please have a seat."

She smiled wearily. "Thank you." She had no idea what these "talks" might bring, but now that she was sitting with a British knight in one of London's finest hotels, she felt the blood pulsing through her veins and was filled with a sense of optimism. Her father and his friends running the military campaign in Bosnia were stubborn and fanatical. Her greatest fear was that unless someone of her generation took responsibility, the war might go on for many years and many more thousands would die.

Sonja sat forward, perching on the edge of a wide Louis XIV armchair.

"Tea or coffee?" he asked. "The Lapsang souchong is the finest in London."

She nodded. "I would like to try it, thank you."

The waiter hovered. Fitzgerald ordered the tea and some scones with a conjuror's wave.

He uncrossed his legs and leaned toward Sonja. "Yesterday, I spoke to the commander of UN forces in Sarajevo."

"General Brown?"

Fitzgerald nodded. "You've met him. The security situation is grave." He paused. "You did a courageous thing, talking to our British journalist friend. Your father can't have been pleased. I think I am on the mark when I say that you have your peoples' best interests at heart—"

"I want peace in my country more than anything."

"Indeed."

"Like when we had Winter Olympics in Sarajevo. This was happy times for my people." Sonja shrugged.

"You have beautiful eyes, my dear. You remind me of my favorite animal, a tiger. I once came face-to-face with one in Africa."

"Thank you. I will take this as compliment. I think."

"Please do." He smiled warmly.

The waiter returned, set down a tray of tea, and poured two cups.

"Say when ..." Fitzgerald picked up the jug of milk and poured.

"Thank you."

"I will do everything in my power to bring peace to your country. As I mentioned, I have lived on the island of Korčula for many years. I love your country—truth be told I consider it *my* country too—and your people more than I can say. Tragically, my wife was murdered last year. If I had acted sooner, perhaps she might still be alive."

Sonja frowned. "I am very sorry for this. Who did this?"

"That remains somewhat of a mystery, but thank you for asking. I still think about her every minute of every day, of course, but that is not why you are here."

He leaned back and clasped his hands. "Half a century ago, I worked very hard for many years with and for my great friend Josip Broz, to ensure Yugoslavia and her future generations would live in peace despite rising ethnic tensions at the time."

"Tito?" Sonja's eyes widened. "This man was enigma. He was hero for my country."

"Indeed, he was. I am fortunate to consider him one of my closest friends. Alas, Josip Broz would turn in his grave if he knew what was happening now. Our efforts in those days have been dashed by ignoramuses whose inability to read the signs and signals and practice the noble art of diplomacy pains me more than you will ever know."

Sonja nodded and took a sip of tea. "I grew up in Tito's Yugoslavia. It was never Serbia or Croatia or Bosnia."

"Precisely. That is partly why we came to you."

"I don't understand."

"I would be lying, my dear, if I told you that your father is not the main reason we chose you. But it's not the sole reason. We think you are a patriotic young woman who is willing to make sacrifices for your country."

"*Sacrifices?*"

"There are many people like me who care deeply about former Yugoslavia. We have the strongest desire to change direction and pull your peoples back from the brink of a catastrophe, so to speak. And when I say peoples, I mean Bosnian Serbs, Bosnian Croats, and Bosnian Muslims."

"I'm interested in what you are telling me."

"Islamic extremism in the heart of Europe is a new threat for everyone. But your father and General Ratko Zukić have gone too far. Do you understand what they have done? They have far exceeded their powers and responsibilities to your people."

"I don't understand—"

Fitzgerald continued, "They have committed grave crimes against humanity—genocide, no less. Mass genocide."

Sonja froze; her eyes narrowed, her stomach churned. She felt sick. Sonja's worst fears washed through her. She had heard rumors, overheard conversations, but had refused to believe them. "You have no proof," she said, desperate not to hear the answer but sensing she was about to hear it anyway.

"I'm afraid … we do. My government has satellite photographs, radio intercepts, eyewitness accounts from those fortunate enough to survive."

Sonja shifted uneasily in her seat. She took a sip of the Lapsang souchong, which had somehow lost its charmed smoky taste. "What do you want from me?" The sudden rise in volume and panic in her voice made a few heads turn among those sitting close by. Sonja caught herself. "I am here for my people," she continued in a much lower voice.

Then Sonja took a deep breath and prepared to listen to what the white-haired British gentleman had to say, even though she wanted to get up and run all the way back to Sarajevo.

Fitzgerald cleared his throat. "We—the international community—will arrest your father and your godfather, Gen. Zukić. They're finished. They'll stand trial in The Hague for the most serious war crimes since World War Two." Fitzgerald's fatherly eyes stared right at her. "All we want you to do is help us arrest them."

Sonja swallowed hard. *Are these foreigners crazy? How dare they invite me here and expect betrayal?*

Fitzgerald continued, "My friend, Tito, was afraid of this … ethnic conflict destroying the foundation of Yugoslavia."

Sonja said, "We Serbs fought with you against the Ustaša in Second World War. And now you abandon us and offer sovereignty to Croatia and Slovenia."

Fitzgerald grimaced. "You are entirely correct, my dear. There are grave political inconsistences. But we cannot be seen to discriminate against the Muslim world. I call it oil-and-ter-rorist economics. The two don't mix but are inextricably linked. And I agree with you, the recognition of Croatia is premature."

"What do you want from me, Sir Lawrence?"

He smiled. "It's true we took our eye off the ball. The West is allowing Yugoslavia to disintegrate before she is ready—Slo-venia, Croatia, and now Bosnia. But you can help us stop the bloodshed in Bosnia." He paused. "Sonja, will you help us?"

"Why do you think I can help you?"

"Peter told me about your disappointment, your distrust of your father and his generals? Your godfather? If you want peace in your country, you must help us."

"Peter had no right—"

"He's trying to help … Tito was an extraordinary man. I believe he would want you to help."

"The British helped us against Nazis. Why do they desert us now?"

"In those days, our mission was simple: We found out who was killing the most Nazis and did everything in our power to help them kill more."

"And now?"

"Tito is no more. A new generation is upon us. *You* are the next generation."

Sonja leaned forward and poured herself more tea. "What exactly do you want me to do?"

"There's only one thing you can do, my dear. Listen carefully …"

CHAPTER TWO

Officers' Mess, Hyde Park Barracks, Knightsbridge

C apt. Jack Steele wrestled into his buckskin breeches and scarlet tunic. His orderly placed the whitened buff leather cartouche belt over Steele's head and shoulders, tucking it under the gold braided epaulet. Cuirass securely fastened, jackboots highly polished and stiff with beeswax, Steele hobbled down to the parade square. There, one of his troopers stood next to the mounting block holding the reins of Steele's cavalry black, born and bred in Ireland and whose name began with a letter corresponding to its year of birth. In this case, it was a horse called Norman.

At 9:15 am, Steele hoisted himself onto the horse's back and sank down into the white goatskin saddlecloth known as the *shabraque* that was de rigueur for all Household Cavalry officers. He hated the rigmarole of wearing ceremonial clobber on Queen's Life Guard. The novelty of riding around London in fancy dress had worn off quickly, but on balance, the embuggerance factor was worth it for all the fun parties and beautiful girls it attracted. *Nothing like a man in uniform*—the old adage was true. It all looked spectacular, but "tin-soldier" life, as combat soldiers referred to ceremonial duties in London, wasn't for anyone who needed daily job satisfaction and taxing of brain matter. As much as he had looked forward to serving at the Household Cavalry Mounted Regiment, the job itself was tedious and unexciting.

At precisely ten o'clock, the regimental corporal major, or RCM (there were no sergeant majors in the Household Cavalry, Steele often had to remind people)—began the inspection. The RCM's attention to detail was infamously meticulous: glass shine on jackboots; helmets, swords, and cuirasses highly polished; hoof oil uniformly applied; buckskin breeches correctly whitened with Blanco. And there was good reason.

The Life Guards, formed by the exiled King Charles II in 1660, was the senior regiment in the British Army. Together with The Blues and Royals—an amalgamation of the Royal Horse Guards (The Blues) and the 1st Royal Dragoons (The Royals)—they formed The Household Cavalry Regiment. As well as active service duties and postings around the globe, the Household Cavalry (Mounted) Regiment carried out ceremonial duties in London—Changing the Guard, Trooping the Colour, and Sovereign's Escorts for the Royals, foreign dignitaries, and heads of state, among the most prestigious.

At 10:30 am, the Hyde Park Barracks clock chimed half past the hour and the state trumpeter sounded the call. The Life Guards detachment—Steele in command at the rear—set off on the thirty-minute ride across central London to Horse Guards, Whitehall, a stone's throw from Trafalgar Square.

As they exited the barracks, the ceremonial detachment saluted the sentry by "carrying swords"—tipping the swords forward to the vertical. Steele's mount, Norman, was skittish. He squeezed his inside leg and flicked his right spur into the horse's abdomen. "Walk on," Steele said sharply, clucking his cheek twice in quick succession, "walk on, boy." He tugged at the reins, gave another dig with his spurs, and willed Norman to trot on a few paces—sitting trot, military style. Norman caught up and took his place at the rear of the detachment.

"EYES FRONT!" Steele bellowed the command, trying as best he could to imitate the RCM's raspy tone and volume. The men snapped head and eyes to the front. "SLOPE SWORDS!"

The noise of cars and motorbikes on South Carriageway

Drive next to Hyde Park gave way to the random clattering of hooves. Tourists pointed cameras to take pictures and video. This was the bit where he could relax. Riding out into tourist London on a horse in full ceremonial garb was a unique experience. The horses seem to know the way by heart, and, on a good day, it was a chance to sit back and let your mind wander for the thirty-minute ride to Horse Guards.

Steele's face was flushed and a little sweaty already. Riding through central London traffic in seventeenth-century military regalia was harder than it looked. Not least of the discomforts was the trick of balancing the point of the heavy steel helmet on your nose without it slipping forward over your face. At least it wasn't summer, when the heat might cause the head to swell so the helmet painfully squeezed the sides of your head. You might be in the saddle for eight hours for Trooping the Colour. One of his favorite NCO mantras from Sandhurst instructors came to mind. *No one said it was going to be easy, sirs.*

Today he also thought about Peter and wished for a sense of purpose in his life like his brother had. Peter was working in Bosnia, risking his life every day to bring truth and clarity to the world. He envied Peter, and the only reason it didn't consume him completely was because they never spoke. Peter was saving lives. Jack was a tourist attraction.

The police motorcycle outrider held traffic for the mounted detachment's right turn under Wellington Arch next to Apsley House, historic residence of the Iron Duke. As the procession wheeled, a black cab backfired and spooked Norman. Sword in one hand, Steele tugged his rein with the other. The horse clattered sideways up onto the pavement.

Then he saw him.

His brother, Peter Steele, was standing in Hyde Park just thirty yards away.

What the hell is Peter doing here?

But Steele wasn't sure who he was more shocked to see— his brother or Sonja Radovanović, daughter of the Bosnian war criminal, standing next to him. He eyed Peter and, even at a distance, immediately recognized Sonja from newspapers and television. Peter and Sonja were standing under a tree near an ice cream vendor's cart. *What the fuck!? No way on God's earth is this a coincidence, especially after this morning's message from my brother.*

Peter had recently interviewed the daughter of the renegade Bosnian Serb leader, and it made sense that the two knew each other. *But why are they standing next to each other in the middle of London?* Jack had read the article—he read all of Peter's writings—which he did to stay connected without staying connected. The article included a quarter-page photo of Sonja. She was attractive, almost beautiful, but not in the conventional way. She had long, dark hair and full lips, and something about her eyes had caught his attention. He had even found himself wondering if she had a boyfriend in war-torn Bosnia and whether, perhaps, Peter had flirted with her during the interview.

Steele lost his brother from view as the ceremonial procession continued across Hyde Park Corner.

★　　★　　★

Peter Steele knew that Jack would be at the rear of the ceremonial unit—the duty officer. The officers' mess staff had informed him that Capt. Steele was unavailable because he was on Queen's Life Guard, which was why Peter was standing in Hyde Park at this moment. Peter wanted to try and make sure Jack would return his call as soon as his brother got to Horse Guards. In all likelihood, however, Jack would ignore his message.

Peter had arranged to meet Sonja in Hyde Park immediately after her meeting with Sir Lawrence Fitzgerald, and he was planning to introduce Sonja to his brother later that day if at all possible.

Peter turned to Sonja. "That's his job. Beats working for a living."

"The horses are beautiful, but I hate military," Sonja replied.

The clanking of hooves and military tackle faded away from them in the distance across Hyde Park Corner.

Peter smiled knowingly. "So, what did you tell Fitzgerald?"

"I told him he is a crazy man. No deal," she said, her English accented with Americanisms.

"Seriously?"

"You think I can betray my father? And my godfather, Gen. Zukić?"

"Why not? They're insane. Both of them. Have you any idea what they've—?"

"I know this. But if I betray them, I betray my people. I cannot allow my country to die before it is born again. I don't agree with everything they have done."

"I should bloody well hope not."

"I am not responsible for them and soldiers they command."

"Maybe they didn't pull the trigger, but they're responsible for eight thousand deaths in Srebrenica. We are talking mass genocide. It's very, very bad news for you and your family. Can't you see that?"

"We don't know what happened in Srebrenica."

"You deny it?"

"I don't know anything anymore." Sonja looked away toward Park Lane. "Fitzgerald told me I have half-brother—in Goražde." Goražde was the one-hundred-and-sixty-square-mile Bosnian Muslim enclave surrounded by Bosnian Serb forces, similar to the enclave in Sarajevo. The hell hole, forty miles south-east of Sarajevo with one river, one hospital, and one bridge, was just sixty miles from Sonja's home and the Bosnian Serb military headquarters in Pale. It measured one mile end to end. Everyone knew everyone else's business, especially in wartime, and especially in this enclave cut off from the outside world.

"You never knew about him?"

"He is Muslim. His name is Dražen Rakić. I heard rumor when I was a child, but I never believed it."

"Fitzgerald has good sources. He's been around for a very long time, and I trust him. He told me Rakić' s father is one of the few men in Bosnia who can broker a peace deal for Muslims. He's a true independent from the hornet's nest in Sarajevo."

"If this man is related to me, I never want to meet him."

Peter understood her frustration. If there was one thing he'd learned in Bosnia, it was that you couldn't and shouldn't trust what anyone said, did, or promised. Politicians and leaders constantly lied-to-order and were never held accountable. Corruption was the norm, an understandable legacy left over from decades of Communist rule. "You could stay here with me," he continued, but failed to deliver the second half of his thought: *I'm falling in love with you. Damn it, this isn't the time or place.* "Work from here, help your people from London. I can help you contact Rakić. He probably wants peace as much as you do."

"Even if this man is my half-brother, I can't trust him. He's Muslim. My people will never trust him. We can make no 'deals' with Muslims."

Peter Steele shook his head. "You're missing the point. I can help you get in touch with him in Goražde—use my UN press credentials and my contacts. You can make him listen. See for yourself. At least try."

"Does he have family?"

"Dražen's father, Luka, is the mayor of Goražde. It shouldn't be difficult to find him."

"He is suffering like my people in Sarajevo," said Sonja. "We shell them every day." She stroked the mole on her right cheek and appeared to be lost in thought.

"Interesting you say *my people* when you talk about Sarajevo. You're shelling them too." Sarajevo had essentially become another Bosnian Muslim enclave cut off from the outside world. The only way in or out was by UN flight into Sarajevo Airport or across Bosnian Serb territory. There was also a rumor of a tunnel, but Peter had never been able to establish if this was fact or fiction.

"Of course," Sonja continued. "Before this war, we all live together in Sarajevo. Muslims are still my people."

"Precisely my point."

"But they are also my enemy now." Sonja grimaced and said, "My father never told me about this Rakić family."

"That's why you need to meet him. He's hugely influential. People trust him and will listen to him."

"Only Muslims will trust and listen to him."

"That's a start."

Sonja lowered her head and smiled. "I cannot stay here with you." Then she held his face with both hands and leaned forward to kiss him firmly on the lips. The kiss was so passionate Peter felt the blood pulsating through his veins. He quivered momentarily and then came back to earth, and back to the children standing in the queue at the ice cream cart who were giggling at what they had just witnessed.

Sonja said, "I have to go home to my people. I love you, and I want you to come with me."

Peter replied, "OK, I'll come with you."

Automobile, taxi, and lorry drivers waited patiently, accustomed to delays caused by pomp and ceremony in the heart of London. Capt. Jack Steele bit into his chinstrap and tasted metal and leather. There was nothing he could do about his brother for the time being. *I'm officer commanding Queen's Life Guard in the middle of Hyde Park Corner for God's sake.*

He squeezed his legs against the horse's abdomen, reined to the right, and flicked his spurs for Norman to trot on. Hooves scrapped and clip-clopped on the tarmac road. "Steady ... easy now," Steele countered.

The mounted Met policeman released traffic.

Steele reined to the left and caught up with his men. The detachment passed the famous Wellington Arch and crossed Hyde Park Corner to the top of Constitution Hill.

Between a Mercedes and a BMW, Steele noticed a cycle dispatch rider. The young man had sandy hair and a round face, and wore a green sweatshirt. The rider was watching the procession and adjusted the heavy load in the black delivery bag strung across his chest.

Steele made eye contact with the biker. He raised his voice over the tumbling of hooves and the idling car engines. "Biker … come here … quickly."

The biker glanced behind him.

"*Please … quickly,*" Steele hissed.

Seeing no one else within earshot, the cyclist freewheeled into Hyde Park Corner. He drew level with Steele at the back of the column but maintained his distance. "What is it, mate?"

It was forbidden to talk to the general public on Queen's Life Guard, but Steele was determined. *I need this biker.*

"See the couple behind us in the park?" he hissed again, "fifty yards behind the arch, under the tree near the ice cream cart?"

The biker turned, scanned, and nodded. "Yeah, see 'em. Woman with long black hair?"

"Yes. Follow them. I want to know everything. Call MOD London district and ask for the duty officer at Horse Guards. This evening. Captain Steele, got it?"

"How much, mate?" Given that London bicycle messengers had one of the highest fatality rates in the world for the lowest pay, no surprise that money would be the prime motivation.

"Name your price. Fifty?"

"Make it a ton?"

One hundred pounds? Like I have a choice … "Deal." Steele puffed his cheeks and exhaled sharply.

The biker gave a surreptitious thumbs-up. His front wheel wobbled as he stood on his pedals, made a quick U-turn, and sped away into the park. A hundred pounds was probably more than he earned in a day, perhaps two? *Anything to find out what Peter is up to.*

Traffic flowed once more around Hyde Park Corner as Queen's Life Guard processed down Constitution Hill toward Buckingham Palace and The Mall. Tourists continued to snap photos and shoot video oblivious to Steele's unfolding saga.

CHAPTER THREE

Horse Guards, Whitehall

After the Changing the Guard ceremony at eleven o'clock that morning, Steele had spent the day trying to watch TV news, read the newspapers, and be patient. At 3:55 pm, he was pacing back and forth in the officers' bunk. He felt sick and had lost his appetite. *Peter is swanning around London with Sonja Radovanović. What the bejesus is Peter playing at?*

Of all days for this to happen ... He'd decided to abort tonight's date—an unusually attractive young woman with broad hips and lovely breasts he'd met at a party in Hampstead. Shame. He'd been planning it for weeks, and, amazingly, she'd finally accepted his invitation. She had perfectly formed full lips, and he knew exactly where he wanted them to end up. The invitation to drinks in his private room at Horse Guards— with scarlet uniform and sword hanging up in the corner—had worked. It had been weeks since he'd had sex, and tonight had been a dead cert. *Damn Peter ...*

A few minutes before the four o'clock dismounted inspection at Horse Guards, there was still no word from the cyclist. He waited nervously for a call, which he knew might not come at all. Where was Peter?

Outside his window, tourists of all nationalities flocked to gawp, point, touch, and have their photos taken next to mounted Household Cavalrymen in their sentry boxes on Whitehall. A pretty Asian girl scribbled something on a piece of paper and slipped it into the jackboot of one of the sentries. Her telephone number, Steele suspected—the men often gathered "intel" on duty.

At 3:57 pm, there was still no word from the biker. Any messages would have to wait. It was time to inspect the guard.

At 3:58 pm, the dismounted Guardsmen marched out into the Horse Guards courtyard and formed up next to each other one by one. Steele pulled on his white cotton gloves, the finishing touch to an officer's uniform that since Victorian times had been known as Frock Coat Order of Undress. It consisted of a long black frock coat garment adorned with embroidered piping, black leather Wellington boots, sword, scabbard, and a white waist belt. He drew the sword from its scabbard, resting the blade on his sleeve to check for smears.

Glancing in the full-length mirror bolted to the wall near the stables, he adjusted his forage cap—not so far down he couldn't see under the peak, not so far back he looked like a bus conductor. It was true that all Household Cavalry junior officers might be mistaken for generals from a distance thanks to the peak with its abundance of gold lace decoration. The uniform even made Steele look handsome, and, as shallow and narcissistic as it sounded, it was partly why he had joined this particular regiment—tanks, horses, uniforms … you couldn't really go wrong, he had thought, when he signed on the dotted line for his Regular Commission into the British Army at the University of Exeter.

Steele hovered under the stone archway, surrounded by centuries of history, waiting for the clock to strike four. The familiar smell of horse manure was strangely comforting.

The door to the duty NCO's office flew open.

The Lance Corporal of Horse hurried out and stood to attention. "Sir … Commanding Officer wants to speak to you. Sounds very urgent, sir."

Steele walked down the corridor, his sword clanking on the stone slabs. He entered the guardroom and picked up the receiver lying on the desk. "Colonel …?"

"Write down this address," the plummy voice replied.

"I don't understand—"

"No time for questions. Just do as I say."

Steele picked up a Biro and scribbled down an address in Chelsea.

"What's this about?"

"I've just spoken to an Inspector Heath from the Met. You are to report to that address immediately. Drop everything. That's an order."

"My inspection?"

"Corporal of Horse can take over."

"Colonel—"

"Get changed and take a cab. We'll talk later."

The line went dead.

Steele hurried to his bunk and unbuttoned the frock coat. In the distance, at the bottom of Whitehall, the chimes of Big Ben struck four o'clock, closely followed seconds later by the Horse Guards' clock.

"Guard ... Guard, SHUUUN!" shouted the NCO guard commander.

Steele ignored his cue. At this point he was supposed to march into the courtyard, take the salute, and inspect the men. Instead, he tore off his uniform and changed into civvies in less than a minute.

The guard commander barked: "RIGHT DRESS!" Soldiers whipped head and eyes to the right, shuffling forward in penguin steps. "CARRY SWORDS!" The guard commander turned to the right and marched in a small circle to join the formed rank and wait for the orderly officer.

Wearing blazer, tattersall check shirt, and beige cords, Steele left the building and walked past the guard and out into Whitehall. The guard commander's jaw dropped three inches.

You'll work it out, Corporal of Horse. Initiative ...

Steele stepped off the deep Whitehall curb and hailed a cab from the sea of black taxis heading north toward Trafalgar Square.

"Beaufort Street, Chelsea."

"Right you are, sir." The cabbie flicked on his meter.

Steele climbed into the back seat and gripped the handrail. He rubbed the back of his neck and wondered if he was going out of his mind. *This doesn't happen … The police want me to go to Chelsea in the middle of Queen's Life Guard? On the same day as Sonja Radovanović and Peter turn up in London out of the blue? This is bloody insane.*

Now, of course, he wished he'd called Peter back immediately. The nasty feeling in the pit of his stomach ached. *The cyclist? Has the cyclist discovered something terrible?*

The cab driver made a quick U-turn, accelerated down Whitehall, across Parliament Square, and shot west along Millbank and the Thames Embankment toward Chelsea. Steele was familiar with Beaufort Street—the sister of a friend in the regiment had thrown a dinner party there the month before.

He climbed out of the cab, paid, and tipped the driver, who nodded begrudgingly at the pound coin Steele left. It was all he had.

As he crossed the street, Steele eyed a woman with shoulder-length brown hair coming out of number twenty-nine—his destination. She was wearing a white shirt, brown leather jacket, and red jeans. Momentarily distracted, he narrowly avoided being hit by a passing white van. Steele jumped clear, and the van's horn faded toward Battersea Bridge. *Bloody white-van man.*

He approached two police cars and a single ambulance parked outside the house. It didn't look good. A small crowd of onlookers had begun to gather across the street. As he walked past the police car, he saw a man wearing a green top who resembled the cyclist sitting in the back.

Now Steele's heart was thumping. *Why is he here?*

Steele walked up the steps and grimaced at the police constable standing sentry.

"I'm Captain Steele. I was asked—"

"Yes, sir. They're upstairs. Second floor."

He entered an elegant vestibule with a soft-under-foot bur-gundy carpet and a mahogany table against the wall adorned with a marble-based lamp. Several piles of post had been neatly arranged on the highly polished table.

He climbed four short flights of stairs and paused when he reached the second floor. The door to 2A was ajar. His heart was pounding harder now. He tapped gently on the door and walked in. "Hello?"

A man in plain clothes was walking down the snug corridor toward him. "Captain Jack Steele?"

"Yes."

"I'm Detective Inspector Heath. Thank you for coming at short notice." He paused. Then he said, "I'm afraid I have some bad news."

CHAPTER FOUR

Chelsea, London

The Beaufort Street flat had cream walls and wooden floors. Amateurish landscape pastels hung, frameless, on the walls of the pokey corridor that led to the sitting room, which Jack Steele entered first.

"What's this about?" he asked.

"When was the last time you saw your brother?" asked Heath.

Steele hesitated. *Trick question? What did the police want with his brother?* Steele said hesitantly, "I saw him this morning. But we didn't speak."

"I don't understand."

"I was on Queen's Life Guard. I saw him in Hyde Park." Steele checked himself—he stopped short of mentioning Sonja Radovanović. *Best not to complicate matters for now. Who knows what kind of trouble Peter might be in ...*

The inspector walked across the room and gestured to the area behind the sofa. Steele got the feeling he was supposed to follow. The inspector asked, "Is this your brother?" He pointed to a corpse.

Steele would always remember the sounds he heard at that moment—a double-decker London bus trundling past outside that made the wine glasses on the sink drainer ping against one another. And the smells—fried onions with spices from the kitchen and a trace of musty, dank laundry from the washing machine in the alcove next to the kitchen. Then he realized that the other, unfamiliar metallic odor was the smell of blood from Peter's lethal head wound.

A soft bundle of fur brushed his ankle. Startled, he lashed out with his foot before he realized it was a cat, apparently as startled as he was. The creature darted behind the sofa and exited the sitting room.

"Yes," he said, slowly. He swallowed hard and fought back tears, but it was no good. His insides told him he was about to throw up. The carpet was soaked with his brother's blood. Laying on his side, Peter had been shot in the face at close range. Steele noticed that the small entry wound through Peter's eye had caused the back of his skull to be blown open—matted bloody hair, broken bits of skull, and brains spilled onto the carpet. He took two steps back and tried to process his thoughts, which were now on rapid fire. The last thing he had expected to find here was his brother shot execution-style. *Why? Who the hell would do this? This is central London, not bloody Bosnia.*

"Did you see the girl in red jeans?" Steele asked. "What was *she* doing here?"

"She's an American journalist. We spoke to her and checked her credentials. Her story makes sense. She informed us that she worked with your brother in Bosnia. She was the one who called us."

"And the man outside in the police car?"

"He found the body."

Steele held his breath for a few seconds. "Who the hell did this?"

"I'd ask you the same thing, sir."

Steele glared at the inspector. "How would I know?"

"The woman found the young man inside the flat. He said *you* sent him?"

Steele snapped back at the inspector. "Yes, I asked him to *follow* my brother."

"Why?"

"Can we get away from here?"

"Of course. My apologies."

They moved back toward the door, and Steele made a dash for the bathroom. He couldn't help it. It wasn't so much the blood and gore from the head wound per se that made him wretch, but the fact that the blood and gore belonged to *his* brother, his family. He threw up into the lavatory. When he was finished, he rinsed off his hands and face and looked up at the inspector who was now observing him from the bathroom doorway.

"You were saying?" said the inspector, unmoved.

"What was I saying?"

"You were having your brother followed?"

"No, I didn't mean—"

"You said you were—"

"It was one time. Today. That's all. He showed up out of the blue." Steele rubbed his face with both hands and exhaled. "We hadn't spoken for ages. I received a message from him this morning asking me to call him. That's all I know."

"And the cyclist? He says he's never met your brother?"

"That's right. I hired him to follow Peter when I saw him in the park this morning."

"Was your brother *with* anyone this morning?" A new voice came from behind—a man had entered the flat and joined the conversation as though he had been there all along.

Steele, now puzzled, turned from Heath to the new man.

Heath said, "This is Colonel Edward Boyle. He's from your lot. Military intelligence." Heath smiled faintly, but Boyle did not return the gesture.

"Thank you, Inspector," said Boyle. He extended a clammy hand to Steele, who shook it cautiously.

"Am I under suspicion?" asked Steele looking at both men. His head was pounding. Nothing made sense.

"No," said Boyle. "Police just need to tick all the boxes."

Steele nodded. "I understand."

Boyle continued, "Why weren't you and your brother speaking?"

"Family rift, that's all. We had an argument about five years ago, and it was never resolved."

"Is that right?" The inspector scratched his ear.

"Yes, it is," replied Steele.

"Need a lift back to Horse Guards?" said Boyle. "We can talk in the car. My condolences." He glanced at the inspector. "The police will do everything they can, I'm sure." Boyle gave an insipid smile.

"Do you have any idea at all what happened here?" Steele asked the inspector as he turned to leave.

"The American journalist said it was probably connected with Bosnia. Peter was working on a 'hot' story, she said."

"What?" Steele grimaced.

"She wouldn't say what it was. Confidential and all …"

Steele said, "I suppose that's possible. Peter's been over there for several months."

"If that's all, Inspector, you have my card." Boyle gestured for Steele to leave.

"Again, we're sorry about your brother, Captain Steele," Heath added. "We'll keep you posted. If there's anything—"

"Thank you."

Boyle escorted Steele down to the street, keeping a close distance almost as if he was worried Steele might run away. He waved to a nondescript black car double-parked across the road. The car pulled up, and they climbed in.

"Horse Guards," Boyle said to the driver sporting a military-style crew cut.

"Roger that, sir."

Steele eyed Boyle. He doubted this man was military intelligence, but right now he was glad to have been plucked from police scrutiny. Then it hit him: His twin was dead. The nightmare had only just begun, and his life would never be the same again.

Primrose Hill, London

Mrs. April Steele was a young sixty-two. At least, that's what people said of her. *Young of mind, though sadly not so much of body,* she thought. Her brown hair as neat as possible—she mostly did her own color—she sat alone in her one-bed flat with a bow window that overlooked Primrose Hill Park on Regent's Park Road. She stared out of the window at the green lawns stretching across the park toward Lord Snowdon's bird aviary inside London Zoo. April thought about her sons, Jack and Peter. She loved both of them, and it broke her heart that her boys had fallen out for so long and, so it appeared, indefinitely.

But at least they came to visit occasionally, though never together. In fact, Jack had no idea that Peter even saw his mother. Perversely, this was one of the reasons Jack had refused to make contact with Peter. But Peter had made April swear to keep his visits a secret. She thought about telling Jack anyway, but she was afraid she might lose both of them.

Five years ago, the brothers had had a blazing row when Jack had announced his intention to join the army. This was another reason for their feuding. Peter hated the military institution with a passion and threatened to cut Jack out of his life if he went through with it, which, in turn, made Jack even more determined to join up. The boys—twins—had always been fiercely competitive, and their fight turned out to be a kind of final throwing down of the gauntlet after years of antagonism, goading, and conflict. They hadn't spoken since.

April shook her head, gave her Bengal cat a friendly pat, retrieved the envelope from the mantelpiece, and held it in both hands. It was addressed to "Jack from Peter," and she had the horrible sinking feeling that she might have to hand it over to Jack sooner than expected. No reason in particular; it was just a feeling.

Last week, Peter had made her promise that if anything

happened to *him*, she was to give the letter to Jack. Why, he hadn't said. *What is Peter up to that's so dangerous? What's inside this blooming letter?* She raised one eyebrow and petted the cat once again. "*You* are one of life's greatest pleasures," April said to one of her greatest friends.

Peter had not come to visit her this week. It was the first time ever he had told her he was coming and hadn't shown up. April was optimistic by nature—she had to be, to cope with the painful arthritis that had plagued her for years. She rubbed her knee joints that were now so stiff and painful she rarely went out these days. The medicine never worked. She sat down and placed the letter on her lap. She felt her body begin to tremble uncontrollably, and she used the permanently palmed tissue to dab a tear. *I'm never going to see Peter again.*

Thames Embankment, London

"Let me share our plans," Boyle began.

Steele threw him a look. "Is this a joke?"

"I wish it was."

"Do you know who killed my brother?"

"We have an idea. Peter was working for *us* on a very important story in Bosnia."

"*Us?*" Steele raised an eyebrow. He had no idea what was going on, but he sensed Boyle was no journalist, and Peter only ever worked for the media. Or so he thought. "I find that hard to believe."

Boyle said nothing.

The car sped along the Thames embankment toward Whitehall. "Where are we going?" asked Steele. "Horse Guards?"

"Your CO wants you back on duty tonight. Best to keep things simple for now. No need for tongues to start wagging just yet."

"I'd rather find out who killed my brother."

"Of course."

Jack thought about his mother. How should he break the news? Losing a child was one of the worst things that could happen to anyone, let alone his frail, arthritic mother. Again, he wished he could take back the rift with Peter and start over. *Wishful thinking. Hindsight is golden.*

"I don't believe Peter was working for the government," said Steele as the car rounded Parliament Square.

"I don't care what you *believe*," replied Boyle. "Peter was a highly valued asset. He was working hard to get us close to the Bosnian Serb first family."

That much, Steele admitted to himself, made sense. Sonja Radovanović had been standing right next to Peter. *Shall I tell this goon about Sonja? Does he know anyway? But I also need to protect Peter's reputation.*

Boyle continued, "We need your help to find out who killed your brother."

"What story was he working on?"

"It's better you don't know. For the time being." Boyle glanced at Steele and made a sucking noise with his cheeks. "The details might be what got him killed. Believe me, Jack, we're looking out for you."

"What do you want me to do?"

Boyle paused then turned to Steele. "We want you to take your brother's place."

Steele suddenly felt his heart pounding against his ribcage, and the breath was sucked out of him. "Go to Bosnia? You can't be serious?"

"If you're willing. And if you're not, we'll insist you go anyway. After all, you are a soldier, remember. You're in the army. And you speak the lingo, don't you?" Boyle delivered a smug grin to finish his thought. "Remember what they used to say at Sandhurst. If you haven't got a sense of humor, sirs, you shouldn't have joined."

Steele knew this to be true. But he also knew that Boyle's

Bosnia bombshell was delivered in earnest. A tour in Bosnia was an option for any serving soldier. He just hadn't expected it to come so soon and certainly not on the same day his brother had been murdered.

CHAPTER FIVE

Hyde Park Barracks, Knightsbridge

N ext morning, The Queen's Lifeguard detachment left Horse Guards at 11:30 am and arrived at Hyde Park Barracks close to noon. Steele dismissed his troop and dismounted. He was free for the rest of the day to pack his kit for Bosnia and attend to personal admin—army speak for administrative details like laundry, shopping, banking, packing, paying bills, and other details. He had one day to sort out his life and prepare for Bosnia, to pick up where Peter had left off …? That was how Boyle had explained the proposition. Steele had no idea what he was supposed to do for them, but Boyle had assured him that all the details would be taken care of, and that he would enjoy the full support and backing from the powers that be, including of course, his regiment. "Keep an open mind," Boyle had said.

Steele was, after all, a Sandhurst graduate, a commissioned officer in the British Army. He'd trained for this kind of "fast-ball" stuff. But he had not trained for the guilt he now felt for ignoring his brother for the past five years. It was this guilt that had made him say yes to Boyle immediately. He would even have to miss the funeral. The image of Peter's bloody corpse in the Chelsea flat was something he would see every day for the rest of his life. That much he knew already. He also knew that life would never be the same again … *Life is not a dress rehearsal, gentlemen. Anything could happen in the next twenty-four hours, and it probably will.* He had never fully appreciated the meaning of this Sandhurst mantra until now. *Everything* had certainly happened in the last twenty-four hours.

But before he did anything, he needed to visit his mother and deliver the news. Boyle had at least agreed to this one final task before Steele boarded his flight to Split, Croatia.

Steele went to his room in the mess, changed into civvies, and signed out of the barracks at the guardroom. As he walked across Knightsbridge, he glanced around to see if anyone was following him. He couldn't see anyone, but the events of the past twenty-four hours had made him acutely suspicious.

He flicked his blazer over his shoulder and jumped on the number seventy-four bus at the top of Sloane Street. He could have taken a taxi, but he always found it somewhat therapeutic and easier to think on the top of a London bus, especially during a weekday when it wasn't too crowded. Thirty minutes later, he passed the muted copper dome of Regent's Park Mosque that reminded him of the hundreds of smaller mosques, many of them destroyed, he had seen on the television news in reports from Bosnia.

Three stops later, he left the top deck, came downstairs, and picked his way through a cluster of strollers to exit the bus at London Zoo. He reached the canal bridge that led to Primrose Hill Park and slackened his pace. *How am I going to tell my mother? Where do I start?* She hadn't seen Peter for years, but that certainly wouldn't make things any easier.

He reached his mother's flat on Regent's Park Road, rang the bell, then let himself in the front door and then the flat door with his own set of keys. It was a week since he'd seen his mother, and as soon as he set eyes on her, he knew things would never be the same. It was just the two of them now. The bags under her eyes and drooping skin around the neck and upper arms made his heart skip a beat. *My mother won't live forever either.* April smiled, and he immediately saw that one of her teeth had fallen out.

"Hi," he said, giving her a hug and planting a kiss on her

bony cheek. "How are you, Mum? What happened to your tooth for goodness sakes?"

"Blessed nuisance … I've booked an appointment. My dentist said he can glue it back in."

"Really? That doesn't sound too hopeful."

"I'll be fine."

April had not been to the hairdresser for several weeks. The gray roots added ten years.

"Does it hurt?" he asked trying to avoid the main task before him. "Your tooth?"

April nodded. "I'm all right, thank you. Put the kettle on, darling."

Steele smiled.

As he filled the electric kettle, he still didn't know how he would tell her about Peter. Other random thoughts bombarded him. *If Mum dies now, I'll be completely alone.* He had never known his father properly, although they had met briefly on two occasions in a Hampstead pub five years ago. Steele had tracked him down, but the first meeting had been a disappointment, especially when his father had tried to cast doubt over Jack's claim to be his son in the first place—he denied the affair with April a quarter century before. The second meeting had gone smoother when Jack finally convinced his father-in-name-only that he wasn't "after money or out to make trouble," but just wanted closure concerning his father's identity.

Steele returned to the sitting room and reached for the TV remote to turn the volume down. Hard of hearing, April always watched her shows at twice the volume.

"I wish you two had been friends," April began. "It breaks my heart …"

"I know, Mum. Same here," Steele replied. He sat down. "I'm sorry, but I've got terrible news."

April looked him straight in the eye, and he immediately knew she already knew. He swallowed hard and said it anyway: "Peter's been—"

"I know." April nodded as if to confirm her earlier premonition. "I know."

"Peter's—"

"You don't need to say it."

"How did you know?"

"Peter came to visit me every week. He didn't come this week."

Steele frowned. "What?"

April continued, "You just didn't know."

"I thought—"

"He wasn't as bad as you think. He just couldn't bring himself to forgive you."

"Forgive me?"

"Yes."

"He told me he'd cut you off. That's why I—"

"He made me swear not to tell. I would never see him again if I told you he still came to visit."

"I don't understand. That makes no sense."

April's eyes glistened. "I never understood it either."

"It's okay, Mum. It doesn't matter now. I'm so sorry." He gave her another hug.

"You two never saw eye to eye. He was chalk, you were cheese."

Steele said, "Mum, Peter was murdered."

"I know."

"How?"

"A very dark feeling. My instincts are finely tuned these days." She smiled sadly. "Peter was supposed to visit yesterday. Last week he gave me this letter to give to you if anything happened, and I was worried." She handed him the envelope.

Steele eyes widened, and he took the note. So, his brother wasn't such a bastard after all. He just wanted Jack to *think* he was a bastard—knowing that one day Jack would discover the truth. All of which made Steele feel even worse. *I should have taken the high road.* Steele read the envelope:

Jack Steele (for your eyes only, brother.)

"Why would someone want to murder my son?" she asked.

Jack folded the envelope and tucked it away into the inside pocket of his jacket.

"I don't know, Mum. I promise to find out. They're sending me to Bosnia tomorrow. Peter was working on some kind of undercover story, and they want me to take over."

April leaned forward and gripped his forearm so hard he could feel her nails through his sleeve. She said, "If something happens to you, I'd be—"

"I know, Mum. But I have to find out why he died. They think it's connected." He took her warm, dry hand and cupped it with his. "I need to clear my head. I'm going for a walk. Maybe this'll give us a clue." He patted his breast pocket. "I'll be back to check on you. Cod and chips? You must eat something."

April shook her head.

"You sure? It's your favorite."

"No, thank you. I've lost my appetite."

Steele stood up, picked up the remote to turn up the volume on the television, and let himself out.

Ten minutes later, he reached the top of Primrose Hill and lost himself for a moment in the panoramic view of London—the City of London including St. Paul's Cathedral on the left spreading all the way over to Knightsbridge and West London to the right. He could even make out Hyde Park Barracks.

The chimes of St. Mark's Church on the other side of the park struck the half hour. He glanced at his watch and sat down on a bench, thinking back to the gruesome scene inside the Chelsea flat. *How in God's name is this happening? Why murder Peter? What the hell had he been up to?*

He opened Peter's letter. As he read, he took a deep breath, exhaled, and nodded to himself as things became clearer. Peter made no mention of working for the British government but explained that he was working on a story that might change the course of the Bosnia war—"for the better," it said. He talked about Sonja Radovanović and what a "special" woman she was, and how he was falling in love with her. Sonja had come to London to work on a peace plan for Bosnia with the British government that might end the war:

> *Sorry for my behavior, Jack—but promise me this: If anything happens to me, you must help Sonja. She's a sweetheart, and things were going well between us ... You'll love her. I tried to persuade her to leave her maniac father and his cronies in Bosnia, and work with me in London. But she refused and is probably back in Bosnia hell by the time you read this. And by the way, I have no idea who killed me ... So many players in this crazy war. But if you're reading this, my instincts were right. I had a bad feeling it might end this way. There are lots of people who don't want the peace plan to work—Germans, Russians, Brits, Americans, Serbs, Croats, and Muslims—everyone has their beef. It's screwed up big time. But I believe in Sonja, I think she can make a difference. Do whatever it takes. For me ... And sorry I messed up ...*
>
> *Your crazy brother, Peter x*
> *p.s. I'll be keeping an eye on you.*

Talk about a message from the grave. Steele exhaled again, trying to control the grief that had crept up on him. Peter had left one hell of a letter ... *I'm such an idiot.*

He read the note one more time and glanced up at the London skyline. He wiped his eyes dry and took a deep breath. This was here. This was now. Deal with it, damn it. For Peter, at least. His brother was dead, and not just dead—*murdered.* Now Jack was mixed up in the Bosnia war, which he knew very little about except for what he had gleaned from newspapers and television. He would be there within twenty-four hours. He acknowledged how mad this was, but he would do whatever it took for Peter's sake. He had led a frivolous life and concluded it was time to make a change.

Steele heard footsteps behind him.

"Mind if I join you?"

Steele turned, and the elderly man—a gentleman one might say, well-dressed, white hair, highly polished brogues—extended his hand. "Sir Lawrence Fitzgerald. Very sorry about your brother, Jack."

They shook hands as one of the many dog walkers on Primrose Hill allowed their Old English Sheep dog too far off the lead. It sniffed at Steele's heels. He patted the dog, and his life flashed before him as he recalled how his neighbor, a famous London fashion photographer, had once asked the eleven-year-old Steele boys to dog sit his Old English Sheepdog, Barnaby. He had even given them a signed black-and-white 8x10 photograph of the dog, which had sparked Peter Steele's interest in photography and cameras, and ultimately in journalism. *The butterfly effect ...*

"Good boy," said Steele, patting the dog, then turning to Fitzgerald. "We've never met?" he asked hesitantly. The dog trotted away.

"No. I knew your brother. He was helping us."

"You, too? Journalist or spy?"

The sarcasm was lost on the old man, or at least he didn't react.

"It was me who made Peter's initial introduction to Sonja Radovanović in Bosnia. She's currently in London for private talks."

"With you?"

"Yes."

The contents of Peter's letter was still racing through his mind. He wanted the truth. Perhaps this old man might have answers? "Peter was helping *you*? I don't believe it—"

Fitzgerald cut in, "You're trying to work out why Peter got involved with the daughter of the most wanted man on the planet."

Steele smiled. "You could say that."

"It's quite simple. I work for the British government, as does Edward Boyle, whom you've met. Odd fellow, I know. We are all trying to work out the quickest way to end the war in Bosnia. Can't do it by brute force alone, I'm afraid."

"And Sonja?"

"Allow me to buy you a drink?" Fitzgerald got up and motioned for them to start walking down the hill. "One of my old haunts is minutes away."

Steele rose, and they set off.

Fitzgerald continued, "I have lived in Yugoslavia—former Yugoslavia—for many years. I love the country and its people, and I know a great many of them. It came to my attention that Sonja has a Muslim half-brother, Dražen Rakić. His father is a prominent journalist and now the Mayor of Goražde. Because she's young and possibly not quite as fanatical as her father, we thought she might be interested in peace negotiations. I fed the intel to your brother, who, like any good journalist, made his own inquiries."

"You set him up?"

"Not at all. The information was genuine."

"Why Peter?"

"He's an excellent journalist. *Was.* I'm sorry."

Steele took a moment and eyed Fitzgerald. "Why Sonja?"

"We want *her* to help *us* sort out the mess."

"Negotiate with Muslims?"

"Correct."

"Aren't you doing that already?"

"Officially, yes. UN, EU, Foreign Office, a plethora of liaison officers, and Civil Affairs people galore ..."

"But you're not getting anywhere?"

"Right again. I told Peter that he might secure a great story if he helps us bring both sides together."

"What makes you think Dražen's father has enough clout to negotiate?"

"I was skeptical at first. There's a power vacuum in Bosnia, and a prominent journalist is just as likely to take power as a Communist party crony who's long in the tooth."

"Who killed my brother?"

"Your brother was helping to get Sonja closer to Dražen and his father, Luka. To facilitate the peace process."

"That's why he was killed?"

"Perhaps?"

"It can't be that simple." Jack suddenly felt himself flush with anger. "Peter was trying to help these bastards?"

"Ethnic tensions are overflowing. Unfortunately, nothing surprises me anymore. Bosnians are desperate. The country is on the brink of disaster."

"I need that drink."

"The Queen's. At the bottom of the hill." Fitzgerald waved his stick accordingly.

"I know it well."

"I'll brief you on the next few days."

"I can't wait."

CHAPTER SIX

Same day ~ High ground above Goražde, Eastern Bosnia

General Ratko Zukić, the Bosnian Serb military commander, stood at the edge of a hillside forest overlooking the town. His daughter, Svetlana, had committed suicide three weeks earlier, and, for the first time in his life, he had wept. Now he wanted revenge. Short, powerfully set and ruddy faced, he was a formidable figure both to the enemy and his own people, and, even before his daughter's suicide, his explosive temper was infamous. But he had never felt such rage as he did now. Gen Zukić blamed the Muslims for her death, even though she had explicitly threatened to kill herself if he didn't stop killing Muslims.

Now he wanted no part in any kind of negotiated settlement between Serbs, Croats, and/or Muslims. For him, it was all or nothing; victory, or death for the Serbs. He despised the international "peace" negotiators. Gen. Zukić wanted to annihilate all Muslims on Bosnian Serb territory and to hell with anyone who tried to stop him. It was simply none of their business.

The Muslim enclave beneath him was an official UN safe haven—except that it wasn't "safe" by any stretch of the imagination. *He'd* made certain of that. Locals were under siege and cut off. It was true that NATO had begun to flex its muscles with aggressive patrolling in the skies, a feeble attempt to intimidate his forces. He dared them to strike his people. If necessary, he would take on the world. It would take more than a couple of NATO fighter aircraft to deny his people victory.

He'd given orders that any foreigners found on Bosnian Serb territory must be arrested—almost no exceptions. There were a handful of United Nations Military Observers—UNMOs— who had permission to live and work there. He was deeply suspicious of any foreign delegations or efforts to negotiate. He believed Muslims had brought this war on themselves by holding a referendum on the future of Bosnia, knowing that Bosnian Serbs—the minority—would never agree to a Muslim-led parliament in Sarajevo.

A small detachment of Danish United Nations Protection Force (UNPROFOR) peacekeepers was deployed inside Goražde, but they had neither political mandate nor military firepower to defend *themselves* from Serb shelling or sniper and tank fire, much less the locals they were supposed to protect. The Danes spent their time securing their unit base, carrying out routine military administration—patrols, latrine duties, eating, and physical exercise—and apart from the occasional casualty evacuation, had little interaction with Muslims. Their presence was, in short, laughable.

All of which suited Gen. Zukić.

He scanned the high ground, nodding confidently. An obsequious grin crept across his face. The T72 tank unit redeployed from Sarajevo the day before had taken up fire positions around the hills to his left and right flanks.

Ruddy faced from *slivovica,* the Bosnian equivalent of Russian vodka, Gen. Zukić looked through his binoculars, scanning the town. His armored beasts were perfectly positioned for an offensive at any moment. He saw no sign of Muslim defenses or any capability to counterattack. *Worthless scum. The Turks—all Muslims are Turks—can hardly be described as worthy opponents.* They were equipped only with small arms and a handful of antitank weapons to defend themselves. Perhaps a hand grenade or three. They even had to use mules to smuggle weapons, ammunition, and supplies into the enclave by night.

Gen. Zukić positioned his tanks far enough away from the

front line to avoid Serb casualties. Not one Serb life, he vowed, would be lost in vain. This war would end one day, and his people would hold him accountable. But no one would lose sleep over dead Turks. Slowly but surely, he would squeeze the life out of them like pus from a boil.

Gen. Zukić turned to his chief of staff. "Može, može ... Hajdemo." *Yes, yes ... Let's do it.* "Ispali par rundi da im otvoriš apetit." *Fire a couple of rounds to whet their appetite.* He raised his arm then sliced it down like a Grand Prix marshal.

The first tank round shattered the silence. A dozen Serb conscripts cheered from the command post behind Gen. Zukić. An electric charge throbbed throughout his veins. He relished the *thwack-thump* of a tank round—a piercing, ripping explosion that annihilated anything and everything in its path.

The tank rounds hammered down.

Serb military intelligence estimated there were still approximately five thousand Muslims in Goražde: men, women, and children. At night, their reinforcements came and went, precariously picking their way across the confrontation line in the dark, the entire length of which could not be secured by Serbs. Conveniently, though somewhat perversely, the majority of Muslims had been ordered to remain *inside* Goražde, not by Serbs but by Muslim authorities. Defenseless civilians proved a highly effective propaganda tool for the Sarajevo Muslim government. They were able to coax sympathy and support from the international community, and to some extent just as important, the international media, during the to-date fruitless peace negotiations.

Another tank round exploded in the distance. Gen. Zukić imagined the screams of terror and pain. He turned to the troops behind him, who were grinning and slapping each other with excitement.

"Bravo! Bravo!" Gen. Zukić cheered with his subordinates as he watched the destruction unfold. A minute later he said, "OK, enough. Let the mice wait for their cheese."

By *cheese*, he was referring to the nightly airdrops of UN food aid. To his delight, the huge pallets plunging from the night sky dispatched by UN transporter aircraft had already crushed at least a dozen locals—including women and children.

The general walked a short distance up the hill and clambered onto a tank. He addressed the crew inside: "Your Serb brothers and sisters are proud of you, comrades."

The crew acknowledged their commander's praise by slapping each other on the back.

Gen. Zukić continued, "I am honored to serve with you, the great warriors of Republika Srpska."

The soldiers chanted: "RATKO! RATKO! RATKO!" Gen Zukić was their hero. He saluted, jumped down from the tank, and returned to his command post.

Primrose Hill, London

At 2:25 pm, Jack Steele and Sir Lawrence Fitzgerald entered The Queen's pub at the corner of Regent's Park Road and St. George's Terrace. The door groaned and then slammed behind them. They crossed to an L-shaped bar with shiny brass beer pumps. The lunchtime crowd had evaporated. Breaking TV news from Bosnia caught their attention: "Bosnian Muslims shelled by Bosnian Serb forces."

"What's new?" said Steele.

"Tragic," replied Fitzgerald.

"What'll you have? My treat." Steele was starting to warm to his new acquaintance.

Steele ordered a pint of London Pride and a half for Fitzgerald.

He pointed Fitzgerald toward a rickety table next to a large plate-glass window. "I'll bring them over."

At the bar, he monitored the television screen. Military commentators on Sky News were discussing the latest footage shot through a long telephoto lens showing the aftermath of shelling in Goražde. Gen. Ratko Zukić was to blame, apparently. But the true horror of the attack was lost on the remaining handful of lunchtime stragglers in The Queen's Pub, Primrose Hill.

Steele grimaced, shaking his head. *Jesus*, he thought. *How many more deaths? Had Peter fallen in love with the daughter and goddaughter of the men responsible? Were the Bosnian war lords using Peter to play politics? Or perhaps, according to Boyle, it was the other way 'round?*

The barman placed drinks on the beer towel, and Steele said, "And some black olives, please ..."

The handsome young Australian barman nodded. "No worries, mate."

Steele picked up the glasses and crossed to Fitzgerald, who, Steele had to admit, had a face you wanted to trust. Steele had been telling himself not to trust anyone. *Take one minute, then one day at a time, and I might somehow get through this.*

"Didn't spill a drop ... I was watching," Fitzgerald said.

"Years of practice." Steele sat down. "Cheers," he gestured, taking a sip. "I don't understand why you don't send your own people in. You really think I can take Peter's place?"

"You look alike for a start. You'll wear uniform as you move up country. UNMO Captain Steele. But you can change into civvies if it helps to get to Sonja and avoid suspicion."

Steele looked skeptical. "You want me to pretend to be Peter?"

"Just try and get close to Sonja and her people. Use your connection with Peter and Sonja as you see fit. Gauge her mood, find out if Sonja had anything to do with Peter's death. Where did she go after you saw her in Hyde Park?"

"You mean if she looks at me as though I'm a ghost, then she's guilty?"

"You get the idea."

Fitzgerald glanced up at the television and pointed. "And her father is committing genocide as we speak. We need to get you into the lion's den in Pale."

Steele sipped his beer. "You make it sound easy."

"General Brown will help us. And we have Boyle on the ground too."

"Why don't you or Boyle go? You both know Sonja."

"Sonja hasn't met Boyle, and I'm too old. I'm probably past that kind of thing. People know me, and Boyle works for the security services."

"With or for?"

"I'd rather not say. Anyhow, that's why your brother was so useful. He was *clean*."

"How does Luka Rakić and his son fit into this?"

"We want Sonja to meet with him. Muslims need to compromise on land swaps. It's not all about the big bad Bosnian Serbs. And the fact that Luka is in Goražde means that hardcore Muslims can't get to him. So, there might be room to negotiate."

Steele took a few gulps of tepid bitter and sighed. "You really think we can make peace over there?"

"Chances are slim to none," Fitzgerald said. "But we have to try. If nothing else, we want to arrest Gen. Zukić and Dr. Radovanović for war crimes."

Steele gave a sardonic frown. "Sonja will love that."

"That's where you come in."

"How?"

Behind the scenes, all sides were forcing things to a head—trying to break up the communist Yugoslav Federation as they knew and hated it. But the moderates want peace. People like Sonja."

"You expect her to betray her father *and* godfather."

"Time will tell. Peter thought she might, and he knew Sonja better than any of us."

Steele thought back to the letter. Could Peter really have grown so close to Sonja? Steele shifted on the velvet upholstered seat and angled himself directly at Fitzgerald. "What now?"

"You leave tomorrow from RAF Northolt. We'll brief you in Split. Boyle will catch up with you later."

"Why are you doing this?"

Fitzgerald drained his half pint and chuckled. "The British had dozens of spies in Yugoslavia during World War Two." He popped an olive into his mouth and paused for a moment to savor it. "Now my endeavors are for my wife, and for Tito, who was a great friend. I'm doing it for them."

"Makes sense."

"And I like to keep busy in my old age."

Steele nodded and glanced out at the long winter shadows sprawling across Primrose Hill Park. A young couple sat mischievously and flirtatiously on the first park bench inside the park sipping from champagne flutes and giggling. *Lucky sods*, he thought. *Where did I go wrong?*

CHAPTER SEVEN

Divulje Barracks, Split, Croatia

Steele entered the Ops Room at 12:22 pm and reported to the duty officer, a Welsh Guards captain with red hair and ruddy cheeks. Steele was expected. It turned out the two knew each other from Sandhurst, and they spent a few moments exchanging pleasantries and a couple of war stories from Camberley, Berkshire.

The captain said, "And there's a message for you … from"—he rummaged through scraps of paper strewn across his desk—"Sir Lawrence Fitzgerald. Ring a bell?"

He handed Steele the yellow slip.

"Yes. Thanks, Jeremy. Good to see you again."

"General Brown's driver is on his way down from Sarajevo. He'll pick you up in Split for the ride back up country. Big fellow. You'll know him when you see him."

"All the way?"

"You're top priority. Yes, all the way. It's about five hours to Sarajevo if you don't get stuck behind a convoy."

"Sounds good."

"I can't believe General Brown sent his own driver for an ugly donkey walloper like you" *Donkey wallopers* was an army nickname for members of the Household Cavalry. "Whatever it is you're up to, I'm impressed."

Steele smiled and nodded. "Thanks, again, Jeremy."

There was just enough time for lunch with the old man—the old friend of Marshal Tito himself, who he'd had a pint with in

49

his local pub two days before. Fitzgerald had returned to theater sooner than expected. This adventure was already more gripping than a le Carré thriller. Steele read the note:

Meet you at the café-bar with the turquoise awning and orange chairs on the harbor at one o'clock. Welcome to theatre. L. F.

Steele walked down a side road bedecked with palm trees to the officers' mess. He noticed the long jetty stretching out into the water and wished he had time to sit at the end and take in the sparkling turquoise Adriatic and ponder his "actions on" once he reached the war zone. He remembered one of Peter's friends telling him how much Peter had enjoyed taking a few days R&R on the islands off Split. It was easy to understand why. The Dalmatian Coast was truly stunning.

He entered the building, one of the many that had been vacated by the Croatian army—in return for astronomical rent the UN was forced to pay because it had no alternative to house its peacekeeping machine. He wasn't surprised to find the place, effectively a transit accommodation, deserted. Desperate for a quick shower, he found an empty bunk and got undressed. He had heard stories of water rationing in Sarajevo and knew it might be days or even weeks before he found piping hot water again.

Steele pulled out a fresh change of clothes and threw them on the bed. Then he wrapped his green army towel around his waist and headed to the showers.

He angled his face into the hard spray spitting down like needles. His breathing quickened; his body tingled. He lathered his hair with shampoo he'd found in the shower stall, inhaling the sickly melon scent as the steam enveloped him. His mind started racing about what might lie ahead—shelling, sniper fire, landmines, abduction, being arrested for spying? Anything was possible in war. But at least he was starting to feel something he'd never felt before. A sense of purpose. He was doing something important, doing his bit to end a war. In some small way, he also felt as though he was honoring Peter's memory and making amends for their petty, pointless sibling feud.

How could life be turned upside down like this in such a short space of time? He thought about the father he had never known properly and concluded that this fact alone was probably the reason he had joined the army in the first place. He had something to prove to himself; that he was a man, a complete person ... a warrior? And all because he hadn't grown up with both parents? It wasn't an uncommon situation. He had met several young men at Sandhurst and in the regiment who had come from similar backgrounds—brought up by a single parent, usually the mother. Absent fathers had a lot to answer for.

His own father had been sent to prison for being a conscientious objector—or "coward," as several of his Sandhurst colleagues had jibed after Steele had made the mistake of telling them his story. His father had refused to fight for his country, and Steele was making up for it? Perhaps. Peter, on the other hand, had always had a clear path to his future. He'd become a journalist and done something useful. Now he, Jack, would pick up where his brother left off. The only problem he could foresee was whether *he* was up to the task.

Back in his room, he changed into civvies—jeans, navy polo shirt, and brown leather Docksiders—then packed up his kit. His mouth watered at the prospect of lunch—grilled calamari and a glass of chilled white wine from one of the islands, perhaps? It might be weeks before he ate a decent meal again.

Sgt. Thomas, one of the unit drivers, was waiting for him outside the accommodation, and they drove along the Salonitanska Coast Road to Split town center. They passed dozens of Croatian conscripts wearing camouflage uniforms mixed with

Western sports gear—Adidas and Nike shoes—rifles slung across them like a fashion accessory. "Poor bastards," said Sgt. Thomas. "Dropping like flies in Mostar. Most of these poor sods are heading there."

"Cannon fodder."

"Right, sir. Life's a bitch, and then you die."

Twenty minutes later, they pulled up at the ancient stone gateway of the Diocletian's Palace in the heart of old town Split, known as *Stari Grad*.

"Looks like a great tourist spot," said Steele. "But where is everyone?"

"Fighting or dead, sir." Sgt. Thomas shrugged. "Don't forget, Yomper will meet you here in two hours." Sgt. Thomas pointed to a UN bus stop. "I'll drop your kit with him. Easier for you."

"Yomper?"

"General Brown's personal driver and bodyguard. He's a bit of a legend out here. Tough guy. You want him on your side."

"Thanks, Sergeant Thomas." Steele paused. "You've been here for a bit … any advice on how to survive?"

"Yes, sir. Unless you see it or hear it with your own eyes and ears, don't believe a word."

Steele nodded. "Got it."

"Watch yer back, sir. No one else will. Catch up with you in Sarajevo." Sgt. Thomas glanced in his wing mirror and pulled away.

Steele meandered through ancient passageways paved with smooth cobblestones worn down over centuries. Apart from a wizened old man sitting on a step and a stray cat wandering aimlessly, the place was deserted. Most locals who couldn't afford to live there without the tourist trade had left.

Five minutes later, he reached the other side of the walled city. Confined passageways gave way to a panoramic view of the port and glistening Adriatic Sea. To the left and dwarfing nearby vessels, an empty Jadrolinija passenger ferry stood idle. To his right, Steele saw the turquoise awning and orange chairs, his appointed meeting place for lunch. It appeared to be the only café-bar restaurant open for business along the recently renamed Obala hrvatskoga narodnog preporoda—*Promenade of the Croatian Peoples' Renaissance.*

Steele sat down and picked up a stack of Zagreb beer mats. He placed them at the edge of his table, then flicked them from underneath to see how many he could catch in one go. Two, three, four, five ... eight was his record. The waitress appeared, unimpressed with his tricks, and he stared at her. She might have been a Miss Croatia finalist. Stunning. But then Croatia was known for beautiful women.

"Am I the only customer?" he asked in Croatian. He had studied Russian and Serbo-Croatian, or Bosnian, at Exeter University and later at the Defense School of Languages in Beaconsfield just outside London. To date he hadn't done much with his somewhat obscure languages, mainly because the Ministry of Defense data base hadn't caught up with him.

"So far?" she said, her voice raising at the end in a question. "What can I get you?"

"I'm waiting for a friend

"He called already. He's on his way—said to order."

"How do you know it was for me—the call?"

"Do you see anyone else?"

Steele ordered grilled calamari and a glass of white wine.

The Dalmatian delicacy arrived several minutes later, but there was still no sign of Fitzgerald. I hate to eat alone, he thought. As Steele took a bite, the juice from the calamari spattered his T-shirt. "*Shit.*" He dunked a napkin into his water and scrubbed at the grease stain but was distracted by the arrival of a man on a moped pulling up across the road.

The man was unshaven with shiny black hair. He wore a dark shirt, jeans, and a denim jacket. Local change-dollar hood perhaps? The man got off his moped, squatted, and began to tinker with the engine.

Odd.

But then it dawned on him. The man was after the waitress—who wouldn't be? She was gorgeous ... playing hard to get no doubt. The guy probably had a date with her, lucky bastard. But Steele knew he would be wise to put romance, or sex, or both, well out of the proverbial mind's eye for the time being. He was on an important mission in a war zone.

Steele finished his main course and ordered an espresso. Still no Fitzgerald.

The man occasionally glanced up toward Steele but did not make eye contact.

The waitress returned a minute later.

"Here you are," she said, placing the coffee on the table. "Anything else?"

"No, thanks." Steele nodded toward the man, smiling. "Friend of yours?"

"I never saw him before." Seeing the man, she hurried back inside.

When Steele looked up again, the man's dark silhouette was heading straight for him. Steele raised his hand to block the sun and get a better view. The man was holding something close to his side. A weapon? A knife?

Neither. The man was holding a twelve-inch bayonet and there was no mistaking the murderous look in his eye.

GO! NOW!

His instincts screamed loud and clear. He'd guessed wrong—the man breaking into a jog had nothing to do with foreign currency—*everything* to do with him.

Steele jumped up. With both hands, he flipped the table so hard it bounced twice.

Glasses, plates and cups smashed onto the concrete. The man continued toward him, eyes glued to his British target.

CHAPTER EIGHT

Steele sprinted inside the café-bar. He'd been trained to kill with an SA80 assault rifle, a Browning 9 mm, even a 120 mm Challenger tank—but now the enemy was brandishing a bayonet and Steele was unarmed. The sound of crunching glass trailed him. The man strode across tables and chairs as though they were made of matchsticks. Thirty feet away at most ...

Inside it was dingy—wartime power cuts dictated that generators were used sparingly, so electricity was sporadic. A shrill female voice belted out a Croatian war ballad on the radio powered by the large 9V battery beside it. Steele stretched out his arms in front, his eyes growing accustomed to the dark.

"Hello?" he shouted in Croatian. "Anyone there?"

No answer. No help. The waitress had disappeared.

Steele plowed through the dining area toward the WC at the rear. Get inside and lock the door? Dive out the window? What if there was no window? Anything to create time and space between him and the attacker.

Halfway down the corridor, he slipped on a patch of water, clipping his head on the side of a washbasin as he went down. No way out. Steele was trapped, furious with himself that he had allowed himself to be cornered like a ferret.

He scrambled off the floor and threw himself through the swing doors of the WC—a hole in the ground with bars across a tiny window only a small child could wriggle through. The green-slatted doors to the WC wouldn't stop a fly, much less a psychopath with a bayonet.

Steele did a one-eighty and retreated from the restroom, turned right and continued, footsteps now close behind. At the end of the corridor, he swung right and entered the kitchen. Above two large pots on the stove, huge cooking knives clung to a magnetic strip. He lunged and grabbed the nearest one.

Questions flooded his mind but no answers. *Why me? Where's Fitzgerald? Did the waitress know this hood was coming?* The kitchen had one exit—the way he'd come in.

Footsteps outside. *Breathe …*

He tightened the grip on his knife, then—

The attacker kicked the door open. His expression was calm, his chestnut eyes focused. Fifteen feet separated them.

"What do you want?" asked Steele in Croatian.

His chest throbbed as the adrenaline surged through his body. If he could just get the man to speak, then perhaps he could reason with him? Then again, pigs might fly. With two hands, Steele grabbed the nearest large vessel of boiling water and hurled it at the attacker.

"Catch!"

Refusing to buckle, the man punched the air but failed to deflect the pot. He howled as hot water scalded his face and arms. The man bent double—a split second for Steele to pass by. He felt the cold handle of the kitchen knife in his right hand. *Use it*, said an inner voice. *You're a killer… a trained killer. That's what they taught you in the army for God's sake!*

But he wouldn't—couldn't—do it. He couldn't bring himself to stab his attacker even though his life was clearly threatened.

Steele hurled himself across the kitchen, snatched a fistful of the man's hair and slammed his head down on the metal grate with sufficient force to break the man's front teeth. He heard the crunch, then followed up with a blow to the back of his neck. He heard the bayonet clanging to the floor.

Pulsing with adrenaline, Steele bolted from the café-bar. His head was pounding, and his lungs were burning. *Clear the threat. Clear the threat.* He darted right at the first turn, breathing hard.

★   ★   ★

The area around the Diocletian's Palace was a maze of narrow medieval streets and passageways. Steele rounded the first, second, now third bend, losing his footing momentarily. He tripped, stumbled, but somehow kept going.

He cleared the next corner, and the next. He listened intently. Had he lost the maniac? *Take no chances … keep running.* He was gasping for air now, his lungs burning with every stride. The narrow streets became his ally. Steele prayed he could keep his advantage.

Up ahead, a small boy maneuvered his bicycle from a secreted courtyard. Both feet planted on the ground, facing Steele, the boy rocked his bike back and forth like a junior Evel Knievel about to make a jump. The boy grinned as Steele drew level. Too late—

Something hard clipped Steele's shin. It was the boy's front wheel. Steele crashed to the ground, scraping the side of his head on a slab of smooth paving stone.

The boy giggled, turned and rode off victoriously.

As he lay wheezing on the medieval cobblestones, a familiar sound—the slap-slap-slap of sneakers. *Damn it!*

Up and running.

High-pitched screams met him as he turned the next corner and saw three women in black across his path. The women huddled clutching one another. Bayonet man hurtled toward Steele, brandishing his weapon. He had somehow foreseen Steele's trajectory and now came at him from the front. The women scattered as the man ran at them, clipping and knocking one woman to the ground.

Steele took off in the opposite direction. His lungs burned, his heart was on fire and pounding against his rib cage. As the narrow streets twisted and turned, so did Steele with them.

Up ahead, a passageway curved right and led to a narrow side street only wide enough for a delivery cart. At the far end he saw a triangle of sparkling sea. He'd run full circle. He was breathless and exhausted. Even the adrenaline, it seemed, was fading.

Steele kept going.

Pounding ... pounding ... pounding. A white UN Jeep pulled up at the end of the street. He squinted, wiping the sweat from his eyes. Please God, help?

"Captain Steele?" A voice from inside the Jeep. The accent was British and markedly upper crust. "Come on, man, get in."

The rear door flipped open. Steele collapsed onto the back seat.

Safe ...

It took a few moments to catch his breath and stop wheezing. He turned round and peered through the rear window for the attacker who had now vanished.

"Sorry, I'm late," said Fitzgerald. "Spot of bother, I see?"

"*What?*"

Fitzgerald extended a large dry hand. "Good to see you again. Allow me to introduce my trusted friend, Boško."

Boško nodded and smiled. "Pleased to meet you, *Kapetan.*"

"Who *was* that?" asked Steele, looking through the rear window.

"I think we lose him," said Boško, scanning side streets as they moved off.

Fitzgerald eyed Steele's sweat-soaked T-shirt. "We'll soon have you back on your feet. Let's get you to the checkpoint and out of harm's way. Yomper will be waiting."

"How did you—?"

"We saw the mess at the restaurant. Didn't take long to find you. We heard the screaming."

"He tried to kill me."

"Or scare you?"

"*Kill* me."

"Unlikely. Almost certainly scare tactics."

"Well, he succeeded."

Steele swallowed and replayed the whole episode in his mind. He knew what he'd seen. The murderous look in the killer's eyes was unmistakable.

"What did he want?" asked Steele.

Fitzgerald raised an eyebrow. "Very simple. He didn't want *us* to meet."

CHAPTER NINE

UN Checkpoint, Coast Road, Split

As they drew up alongside the vehicle Steele recognized Yomper from the description that Jeremy, the Welsh Guards captain, had provided. Formal introductions were made, and Fitzgerald promised to be in touch when Steele got to Sarajevo.

Corporal Chris Jordan, known as Yomper, had broad shoulders and was built like a brick shithouse, Steele thought, but with a face that could only be described as angelic. Steele couldn't quite see how the man was as dangerous as he probably needed to be. But looks were often deceiving—that much he had already learned out here.

Steele opened the rear door and dumped his backpack on the seat. Then he opened the passenger door and climbed in.

A few minutes into the journey, Yomper said, "They're trying to locate Sonja Radovanović, sir. Better not fuck it up when they do. Boyle hates fuck ups."

"You know him?"

"Yes, sir. Wouldn't mess with him if I was you." Yomper spoke with a thick London accent.

"Where does he fit into all this?"

"Not sure, sir. I just follow orders. But he's the main man if Sonja Rad's involved."

"You're General Brown's driver? Bodyguard?"

"Both. When I'm available. I keep a watchful eye on him. He and I go way back to Hereford. He was my Selection OC."

Steele listened with interest as Yomper gave him a potted personal history: At twenty, Chris "Yomper" Jordan had joined the elite Special Air Service—SAS—known as The Regiment in army circles. While based in Hereford, UK, he had passed their infamous "selection" course with the highest score that year. At the time, Captain Rupert Brown—now Gen. Brown, UNPROFOR commander—had been OC SAS selection in Hereford. He had been wildly impressed with the speed and endurance of Yomper's forced march, or *yomping*, across the Brecon Beacon Mountains in Wales, and nicknamed him "Yomper." The name had stuck.

"You work for both of them?" asked Steele.

"If I told you, I'd have to kill you, sir."

Steele smiled. "Harsh but fair enough."

"Touché, sir. Touché …"

The UN Cherokee Jeep ascended the winding narrow roads away from Split. Not long afterward they crossed the arid Livno Valley. Ragged cliffs separated them from the coast as they traversed a Wild West plateau that joined Croatia to Bosnia-Herzegovina. *Route Diamond* was the military name for this mountainous road/route to the Bosnian capital.

"Where am I meeting General Brown?"

"Boss's residence, downtown Sarajevo."

Steele nodded. By *residence*, he knew Yomper meant Gen. Brown's command post and accommodation all in one.

"Word is that Radovanović is refusing to even meet or talk to General Brown," continued Yomper. "That's where you come in. You talk to Sonja, and fingers crossed, we're in."

"Can't wait." Steele understood that the mysterious Col. Boyle and Fitzgerald were using Sonja as bait to get to her father. *And* had used Steele's now-dead brother to get to Sonja. By sending Jack Steele to Pale, Boyle risked nothing. If anything happened to him, Boyle would plead ignorance and probably switch to some kind of "Plan C."

Steele took in the scenery below them stretching away from the precarious mountain road—an emerald-green lagoon with a backdrop of mountain ranges along the valley floor.

"Hungry, sir?" One hand on the wheel, Yomper reached back and retrieved two brown paper bags. "Lunch is on me. Compliments of the NAFFI."

"Thanks." Steele plucked out a packet of cheese and onion crisps and munched away.

"I'd get your head down, sir. You're a busy man once we get there."

"Roger that."

"Serbs won't rest until they demolish Sarajevo and Goražde. That's my take."

"I hope you're wrong." Steele licked the cheese and onion salt from his fingers and pulled out his ham and mustard on white. "I'll do my best. Just hope it's good enough."

★   ★   ★

Four hours later, they reached Sarajevo. Steele had dozed off a few times, but now he could feel the adrenaline pulsing through him as they drove down the infamous *Sniper Alley* in their soft-skinned Jeep. Sniper Alley was the "main drag" into Sarajevo where UN vehicles were routinely targeted by Serb—and occasionally Muslim—snipers. Yomper apologized for taking a risk of sniper fire in the soft skin vehicle. "Armored vehicles are hard to come by. Too heavy on fuel," he explained as he hit the accelerator. "Don't worry, sir. Keep everything crossed and we'll make it."

They hit 70 mph along the runway-like boulevard. The good news was there was little or no traffic. The bad news was no one repaired the roads anymore, and they barely missed crater-sized holes by inches more than once.

Suddenly the ping of a bullet came out of nowhere.

"Fuck!" said Steele.

"We're good, sir. Chill. If they wanted to inflict damage, they'd have fired more than one."

"Right."

"They're just letting us know they're there."

"Right."

Yomper said, "Per square mile, it's a toss-up between Sarajevo and Goražde for the most dangerous place on the planet."

"Interesting." Steele frowned. Surrounded on all sides by high ground, every inch of the city was vulnerable to sniper fire and shelling from the hills and other vantage points on Serb territory. Yomper explained how international journalists and their local interpreters traveled around in battered, bullet-ridden cars in search of stories to pull at heartstrings and cajole the international community into some kind of political or military action or intervention. Casualty figures were horrific, but still nothing changed from the international perspective.

They finally arrived at Gen. Brown's UN HQ compound known as "The Residence" in downtown Sarajevo, a stone's throw from the Bosnian government building. Close by was the famous Sarajevo sports stadium that had been converted to a makeshift cemetery bedecked with at least 2,000 graves and wooden "headstones." Steele thanked Yomper for the ride from Split, grabbed his kit from the rear, and entered the officers' accommodation building inside the compound. He would trust no one—friend or foe, international or local, military or civilian.

He dumped his backpack in the accommodation wing. Steele was sharing with an Egyptian UN officer. Then he made his way to the dining hall close by, his boots skidding on the greasy surface of the floor. No daylight entered the room; thin neon tubes cast a desolate glow on pasty French Foreign Legionnaires eating dinner … *Very depressing*, Steele thought. He was already feeling claustrophobic. Sandbags packed the window spaces, and Steele wondered who had filled them all. He was glad he wasn't a private soldier. Most of the headquarters' staff never left the building. When the UN pen pushers and button tappers weren't sitting in front of computers and communications equipment, they slept or watched TV for their six-month tour of duty. There wasn't exactly anywhere to go for a night out.

Steele carried his tray across the dining hall. He sat down at one of the long, empty tables and stared at the miniscule portions of food, although *food* was technically a bit of a stretch. Contrary to his expectations, the French battalion catering was inedible: over-cooked, colorless vegetables dumped next to a sliver of braised liver as tough as leather.

Two mouthfuls later, an explosion rocked the building. A grenade? A shell? A tank round? had landed on the roof. Steele dropped his spoon and hit the floor, expecting everyone else to copy his "actions on." From his position halfway under the table, he looked up and flushed red with embarrassment. No one else in the dining room had moved an inch. They hadn't even paused conversations. It was as if absolutely nothing had happened. Apparently, they were used to this Sarajevo "music"—between one thousand and fifteen hundred shells a day were landing in downtown Sarajevo. How could anyone ever get used to this?

On the next table, a Danish UNMO captain with red hair and beard was staring at him, grinning. It was hard to see how old he was because of the beard. *"Boom! Boom!* Welcome to Sarajevo," he said in near-perfect English with a Scandinavian singsong lilt. "Captain Jensen. You are a new arrival?"

"Yes. I'm Jack Steele. What *was* that?"

"Shell. It's okay … it's normal," continued the Dane. "This building can withstand a nuclear bomb." He grinned. "The old Communists were sure to protect themselves."

"That's a relief." Steele slid back onto his chair and brushed himself off from a seated position.

"I'm based in Goražde. It's worse there. Things are very bad. But it's going to get much worse, trust me." The Dane wagged a knowing finger. "Germany is going to recognize Croatia today. It's a big mistake. Everyone wants their independence—Muslims,

Serbs, Croats. This party has just begun. You know?" The Dane grinned and got up to leave. "Be safe."

It was true, Steele thought. Germany's official recognition of Croatia did not bode well for peace in Bosnia. Even Steele's limited understanding of the politics told him that it was a mistake. Official recognition of Croatia, part of former Yugoslavia, would just piss off the Serbs even more. He pushed his main course to one side and tried the soup.

Gnat's piss.

He cleared his tray and went back to his room still hungry. In the stairwell, he kicked several chunks of thick glass to one side and peered through a small hole to see where the shell had landed. Then he was drawn to a loud chorus of jeering male voices a couple of floors down and decided to investigate. French Legionnaires were also based in this building. They were watching football or perhaps boxing on satellite TV? He might enjoy a nightcap. A beer?

Three floors down in the basement, Steele discovered a live boxing match no less, complete with mini raised boxing ring, scoreboard, and trainers with towels around their necks. The main attraction was two French Foreign Legionnaires beating each other to pulp. The Sarajevo streets were too dangerous for any kind of regular physical exercise, so, Steele supposed, this was how the men let off steam. *Rather them than me*, he mused, again thanking his lucky stars that Sandhurst had not required officer cadets to box each other on the grounds that boxing was unbecoming of a commissioned officer except if you were joining the Parachute Regiment.

He scanned the spectators—a crowd of sweaty muscle-bound warriors in French army uniforms. Scratch that. These were Legionnaires, and there was a difference; these were the toughest soldiers in the French army by reputation. Those outside the ring wore expressions way more ferocious than the two men inside, who both looked as though they had stepped foot inside a boxing ring for the very first time. The men watching had worked themselves into a frenzy of testosterone. Blood streamed from the nose of the larger combatant. Undeterred, the second man skated on blood as he delivered piston punches. The crowd jeered and cheered for their man. The noise was deafening. Steele turned and retreated.

A Legionnaire standing near the door said, "Mon Capitaine ..." He beckoned Steele into the foray, hammering his fist in mock victory as the fight got louder.

Steele glanced at the man's rank and replied, "Non, merci, mon Caporal. C'est gentil ... Ça va." *No thanks, Corporal. It's kind of you, but I'm fine.*

He moved off slowly, not wishing to seem impolite. Manners were important when mingling with UN allies, namely the French.

On the way back to his room, Steele wasn't sure which was more disturbing—the soldiers' indifference to the shell at dinner or the Legionnaires delight as they watched the bloody and barbaric boxing match. This really was a war zone, a far cry from the ceremonial duties on Horse Guards Parade.

He climbed back up the stairs to the third floor and entered the officers' accommodation wing. Other ranks were one floor below, and all female ranks the floor above. The Egyptian army major he was sharing with was probably asleep. There wasn't much else to do in a war zone after a sixteen-hour shift in the Ops Room.

"Switch the light on, if you want," said a voice from the cocoon of a sleeping bag.

"Thanks."

Steele was hoping to get his head down without polite conversation. The room was warm, stuffy, and reeked of stale sweat. The smell alone made him feel nauseous and even claustrophobic. He looked around in the dark and saw a faint outline of sand bags piled high against the window. There was a six-inch gap at the top allowing a glimpse of the inky night sky. He collapsed on top of his sleeping bag. It was too hot to get inside it, and he hated that dank pong of army *gonk bags,* as they were known. How many previous owners did this one have? Had the quartermaster forgotten to wash it?

A little while later, he was jolted from his twilight sleep by a piercing crackle of machine-gun fire clattering in the near distance. One round thudded into the bulletproof glass behind the sandbags.

"*Stup,*" said the Egyptian, referring to the name of the bridge a few blocks away. "Same thing every night. They shoot at shit. They shoot at Muslims. They shoot at us. There is no difference to them."

"Muslim or Serb?"

"There is Muslim and Serb on both sides. I don't understand these people. I don't understand this war."

"Bullets sound close."

"Yes, it's close. The front line is three hundred meters from here."

"You sleep through this?"

"Sure, like a baby. You get used to it."

And sure enough, the Egyptian was snoring a few minutes later. Steele decided he preferred the sound of bullets half a mile away to snoring a few feet away.

Already Steele was looking forward to Pale. Anything was better than this hell- hole—an entire city without running water, electricity, or food taking sniper fire and fifteen hundred shells a day. It didn't bear thinking about.

The small-arms skirmishes kept him awake for a couple of hours. Etched on his mind was the red paint graffiti splashed on the remnants of a demolished house along the airport road. It read, Welcome to Sarajevo!

At least someone still had a sense of humor, even though the people of Sarajevo had little choice in the matter. Laugh and survive, or cry and die.

CHAPTER TEN

UN HQ, Sarajevo, "The Residence"

At 9:06 am, Steele walked outside and looked up at the apartment buildings towering above UNPROFOR headquarters in downtown Sarajevo. Every surface and facade was pitted and charred with black patches, bullet marks, demolished brickwork, and large holes where tank rounds and shrapnel had struck. Most of the destruction was courtesy of Bosnian Serb tank and artillery rounds. Some was self-defense, and some of it was so-called blue-on-blue "friendly" fire—Bosnian Muslims firing at their own side by mistake.

The sun beat down on a patch of manicured grass below the UNPROFOR HQ Ops Room. Steele took a few moments in the sunshine. So far, it was a quiet day by Sarajevo standards—no shelling or small-arms fire since dawn. Local cafés and restaurants across the street were open for business—with luck, they might enjoy an hour or two before the shelling began and they would have to close. The reason for the early morning respite was simple: Serb soldiers drank *slivovica* every night and were sleeping off hangovers.

The resolve of Sarajevo residents was legendary and extraordinary. To raise awareness and money for the war effort, local entrepreneurs had manufactured T-shirts and postcards with "Made in Sarajevo under wartime conditions" printed on them. Steele's favorite was a postcard of Superman with *Sarajevo* as the Superman logo on the hero's chest. He would use his postcard as a bookmark.

Ten minutes to go before his briefing with Gen. Brown. Steele was looking forward to meeting one of the most respected generals in the British Army. Gen. Brown was a no-nonsense, ex-SAS hero, who was out to "knock these buggers heads together" as he was fond of telling the international press corps. Steele wondered how much Gen. Brown knew of the information Boyle had shared with Steele. Boyle's plan for Steele to infiltrate the Bosnian Serbs seemed contradictory, or at least incongruous, to the UN peacekeeping mission.

Steele scanned his surroundings—hundreds of communist-built matchbox dwellings with balconies onto which people now walked and risked their lives just to hang up some washing. The high-rises were an easy target for Serb infantry and armor hidden well within range around the Skenderija hills overlooking the southeast of the city. It was a sharpshooter sideshow—every apartment was a sitting target. Only fate would decide, Steele thought, which one was the next to be targeted and/or obliterated—the neighbor to your right or left, above or below, or *you*?

Major Brian Small, UNPROFOR Chief Ops officer, exited the building and walked up to Steele. A short, thickset Royal Engineer with mouse brown hair and a mustache, Maj. Small had volunteered to stay in Sarajevo for yet another tour of duty—his fourth. Apparently, he had no close family to return home to. A confirmed bachelor, some said, while others suggested the only reason he had stayed was to find and marry a local girl half his age to take home to his village of Ross-on-Wye near Gloucester.

Steele shook hands with Maj. Small and gestured to the balconies in civilian apartment buildings. "Why don't they go underground? Live in basements?" Steele asked.

"They're exhausted—mentally and physically. All they have left is their pride and self-respect. They'd rather play Russian roulette in the comfort of their own homes than live like rats in the dark."

"Makes sense." Steele followed Small across the grass.

"Ready for your excursion to Pale?" Small asked. "We've been expecting you. Sorry about your brother. Good man. I met him a few times."

"Thanks." Steele changed the subject. "How's General Brown performing in this nightmare?"

"He's a shrewd operator, but he's still finding his feet. This isn't the Falklands. Things aren't black and white. Serbs are messing with us big time. Playing us in many cases. That's why we sent for you when your brother ..." Maj. Small paused. "A personal connection." He made no attempt to conceal his skepticism. "Don't let it go to your head. We thought the family connection would also make things easier to get back in with the Serbs. You even look alike."

"Makes sense."

Steele pondered the major's response for a moment, then said, "Why not bomb them into submission? The Serbs. A taste of their own medicine." He pointed to the hundreds of burned-out apartment buildings all around the city.

"NATO would be the one to do it. We're peacekeepers, remember?"

"Yes," replied Steele.

"It might come to that. But the UN has a conscience."

"If you say so."

"Others don't, of course." He smiled. "Let's go."

They stepped over heavy-duty electric cables running from the main generator at the rear of the building and entered UNPROFOR HQ. As they reached the second floor, a much louder *clump* than usual—meaning the explosion was close by—shook the building. Impact probably less than a mile, Steele thought.

"Another day, another shell ..." said Steele, careful not to overreact by diving to the ground this time.

"Quite." Maj. Small frowned and disappeared into the Ops Room full of military staff. Steele followed, watching Small as he got an instant read of the situation. "It's bad, gentlemen," Small said out loud. "It's *really* bad."

British, French and Belgian staff officers and NCOs were glued to television screens. Everyone froze for a few seconds trying to process the attack, but they all knew it was too late to do anything about it. They were watching the Bosnian TV BiH local news feed as well as CNN, which was broadcasting the same images. Ironic, Steele thought, that when disaster struck, it was the journalists and cameramen who were often first on the scene to serve as eyes and ears of the UN military peace-keepers. Perhaps he should have become a journalist like his brother.

A British Army staff sergeant shouted, "Let's go people— they want everyone down there ASAP."

"What happened?" Steele's eyes followed the sergeant running to the stairs.

"They hit the marketplace. Thirty or forty dead," the sergeant replied. "At least." The man shot down the stairs.

Steele trembled involuntarily. He couldn't begin to fathom what that kind of carnage would be like. Unlike the censored images that reached living rooms around the world, local Bosnian TV BiH showed live feed, raw, *uncensored* footage. Locals were numb to the horror and preferred to see the reality. Many used the long, uncut scenes of death and destruction on their television screens to identify friends and family—it was quicker than waiting for notification from the authorities.

The UNPROFOR Ops Room staff watched the incident— what would later become known as the Market Massacre— unfold in disbelief. The scene resembled the sickest *Slasher* movie—a shaky camera revealed dismembered body parts, pools of blood and hysterical cries from victims and rescuers. Mass carnage amid fruit, vegetables, tins of Coca-Cola and market stalls.

The images made Steele sick to his stomach. He took several gulps from some bottled water he found sitting on a desk. The dismembered limbs made him light-headed, and he was about to sit down when Small shouted, "Let's go. You speak the lingo, don't you?"

"Yes."

"They need us to observe."

Steele followed.

"I wouldn't normally risk my life for these bastards," Small continued, "but General Brown wants us all there."

Bloody hell, thought Steele. *Literally.* They ran downstairs and jumped into a Jeep at the UN transport pool.

Five minutes later, the Jeep pulled up in a side street as near as they could get to the atrocity. People caked in blood and dust walked and stumbled from the marketplace, shouting, screaming, shaking, crying, and holding their heads. Steele and Maj. Small turned the corner and saw the mangled wreckage of the market stalls—twisted metal frames, torn awnings, pools of blood, and charred wooden tables. Survivors tended the very seriously injured and ushered the walking wounded to a stream of private cars doubling as ambulances already flowing in and out of ground zero. They all knew another shell could land at any moment, but the rescuers toiled to save friend and neighbor in spite of the danger.

Steele watched a man carried away on a stretcher, screaming—half of his right leg was missing. Loose sinew and strands of skin were indistinguishable from the material of the man's camo trousers, all of which flapped and bounced with the motion of the stretcher.

The *whizz-bang* sound of another shell came from nowhere. Everyone knew another shell was possible, even likely, but it was still a terrifying shock.

Steele's world went mute for a few seconds before his hearing returned, but his sight was unimpaired.

Stretchers were dropped, bodies rolled across the ground like pieces of meat. People scattered, then rallied yet again a few moments later, once it registered that they were still alive and untouched by Serb masters in the surrounding hills.

More hysterical human wailing topped the air raid siren. Even the piercing siren could not drown out the sound of human suffering.

Maj. Small looked at Steele. "The medics are here. We prioritize casualties, but our task is to observe and report back. That's how we help these poor bastards, okay?"

Steele frowned. Then he said, "How about we lob a couple of shells back at the Serbs? Is that too much to ask?"

"More than our job's worth. Not without UN authority and half a dozen UN resolutions."

"When will we find out who's responsible?"

"UNMOs are on it. They can work out the point of origin from the trajectory of the round. If the launch site is too close to the confrontation line, we may never know."

"The Bosnian Muslims would shell their own people?"

"Unlikely, but anything goes in war—"

"Wait—" Steele crouched down beside a young woman gasping for breath. Her face and hair were plastered with blood, tiny pieces of glass and metal stuck in her head. But she was alive. Together, they sat her against a wall. Steele was afraid she would choke on her own blood. Two locals ran over to pick up the casualty and carry her to a waiting car.

Maj. Small gave a quick sitrep, a situation report, into his Motorola handheld radio and turned to Steele. "If you ask me, NATO's the only thing that's going to knock some sense into these fuckers. UN's got no balls. The Serbs are watching our reaction right now. They'll do it again unless we hit back."

"Can General Brown do anything?"

Maj. Small looked over Steele's shoulder. "Here he comes. You can ask him yourself."

Amid sirens and car alarms set off by the explosions, another UN Jeep had pulled up. Gen. Brown got out and returned Steele's salute. The UN commander led the group to a protected spot inside a shop front with no windows.

"Captain Steele?" Gen. Brown extended a hand.

"Please to meet you, General."

"Life Guards?"

"Yes, sir."

"Welcome to hell. But you knew that already."

"Whatever I can do—"

"You know why you're here?"

"I have an idea."

"Dr. Kosta Radovanović, leader—or president, as he likes to call himself—of his self-declared Srpska Republika, has asked to speak to your brother in person. Apparently, Peter knew his daughter?"

Steele hesitated. He said, "Yes, the plan is for me to pick up where Peter left off. Apparently, he was working on something important with Sonja." This was the story Boyle had told Steele to adopt. *You met her in London through your brother, and now he's dead. You're all we've got.*

"Excellent. Anything to bring the warring factions together." Gen. Brown spoke quickly. "We're not sure what Dr. Radovanović wants, except that Peter's name was mentioned. We *must* keep lines of communication open. That's where you come in. He obviously trusted Peter, and we hope you can make the connection with Sonja. My understanding is that you'll use Peter's UN press credentials to get to Sonja, and then it's up to you."

Not much of a connection, Steele thought. *I've never even met her.* "When do I leave?"

"Immediately. I'm sure you'll be relieved to get out of here. Not much you can do anyway." Gen. Brown waved to a second

UN vehicle behind his. "You've met Sgt. Thomas. He'll drive you to the Pale checkpoint. You're on your own from there."

Maj. Small added, "You can get changed and grab your kit on the way. You have Peter's ID?"

"Yes."

Maj. Small turned away to answer a call on his radio.

Gen. Brown said, "Radovanović is sending an escort for Peter Steele. See what he wants, Jack. Remember, we need to keep them talking. Check in at the UNMO house in Pale when you can. You can sleep there. They're expecting you."

Steele saluted. "I'll do my best, sir." *What on earth have I got mixed up with here?*

Maj. Small snapped his radio back to his belt and pointed to the chaos. "General Zukić is blaming Muslims for this. He says the Bosnian government shelled their own people."

Gen. Brown said, "I doubt it." He turned to Steele. "Find out anything you can as soon as possible. We have to stop this madness."

Steele saluted and climbed into his waiting transport. "How are you, Sgt. Thomas?"

"Nice to see you're still in one piece, sir. Welcome to hell."

"Thanks."

"You're welcome, sir."

Sgt. Thomas selected first gear and left hell.

CHAPTER ELEVEN

The Sarajevo Markale Massacre, as it became known, would turn out to be one of the war's worst atrocities. Sixty-eight deaths and one hundred and forty-four injured in a few moments from a single 120 mm mortar round. Limbs and heads were torn from bodies in the confined space of the Sarajevo Markale, or marketplace. Although the Serbs were the obvious culprit, the origin of the mortar round was never proven definitively. But for now, Steele was driving to meet—technically speaking—the man responsible.

He was nervous, and for the first time since he had seen Peter lying dead, Steele contemplated his own mortality again. Oddly enough, he had not been afraid of death during the Market Massacre catastrophe. Probably the adrenaline pumping through his veins.

Now his emotions heightened—one moment fear, the next a surprising sense of optimism, then back to fear. Besides heading into the unknown, he sensed an opportunity to make a difference to the outcome of this war. For Peter's sake and for the poor souls who just perished, he would do his best to help.

They returned briefly to the UN HQ. Steele changed into civilian clothes but packed his uniform. He hung Peter's press credentials around his neck. His plan was to revert to his own identity as soon as possible. But Peter's ID would help get him through the various checkpoints.

The UN Jeep skirted the airport road, its perimeter serving as the de facto confrontation line. The suburb of Dobrinja was an exposed and isolated neighborhood to the west of Stup

Bridge, close to where Steele had spent his first night in Sarajevo listening to the undisciplined *rat-tat-tat* of small-arms fire.
They passed row upon row of pockmarked, abandoned housing
estates, many reduced to rubble. Wanton destruction was harder
to stomach, Steele decided, when the sun was shining against a
cloudless blue sky.

Mockingly, Steele saluted as they passed a disabled JNA T34
tank stuck in a ditch north of the airport. The tank had become
a landmark and photo opportunity for new arrivals. Only the
foolhardy, however, stopped at the tank, which was in direct
line of Serb sniper fire. A Norwegian photojournalist had been
shot dead trying to pose in front of the tank on his first day in
Sarajevo.

Steele asked, "Airport open today?"

"Not with the situation in Goražde," said Sgt. Thomas, shaking his head. "No one's taking any chances. You can't just sit
on your flak jacket during the landing and hope for the best
anymore," he added. "Not like the good old days when it was
just the odd round they sent our way. Serbs use automatic fire
on UN aircraft now. They're bloody desperate and insane if you
ask me."

"I'll be sure to drive back to Split."

"Wise move."

"Did you ever have any close calls?" asked Steele.

Sgt. Thomas said, "During my very first landing in Sarajevo,
the C130 dropped so suddenly, I vommed over the poor sod
next to me. But I sat on my flak jacket. Best way to stop one up
the arse, sir. That was my most eventful landing." Sgt. Thomas
smiled.

They passed through the first checkpoint with a cursory
ID check and nonchalant wave from the Serb conscript. Then
they began the ascent along the twisting mountain road; a light
covering of snow made Sarajevo look even more desolate down
below.

"No wonder there's so much damage," Steele continued,

looking down at the birds-eye view. "It's a turkey shoot. They can hit anything in the city from here."

"And they do ... frequently, sir," said Sgt. Thomas. "That's the point. No fucker's safe, including us doughnuts working down there."

"So, basically, the Serbs are winning?"

"Bloody right, sir—complete stranglehold on the city. Dr. Radovanović's mob controls seventy percent of BiH territory. But no one knows how long they can hold out, and how long before NATO bombs the shit out of them."

As they climbed higher and drove through a forest, Sgt. Thomas asked, "Want to see the front line, sir?"

"Are we that close?"

"Around the next bend—cuts across close to the road." He pointed left. "I know some of the Serb boys. They'll give us a quick tour if they're awake. They're bored shitless most of the time."

"Let's do it." Steele had been curious to see the front line, or "confrontation line" he'd heard so much about on the news for months—two sides dug in fifty meters apart, ready to murder each other. Bizarre. Barbaric. It reminded Steele of an old black-and-white WWII movie he'd watched as a boy where British and German soldiers had climbed out of their trenches on Christmas Day to mingle and toast each other, only to return to their prospective trenches moments later and resume battle.

They entered a corridor of snow-laden fir trees. Sgt. Thomas pulled over at the side of the deserted road. They climbed out of the vehicle and walked to a small log cabin next to a formation of trenches tucked behind a clump of trees near the road.

A Bosnian Serb soldier emerged from the cabin with two crossbelts of 7.62 mm ammunition draped across his chest. Unshaven, with a large black mustache dominating his upper lip, he welcomed them. He said in Bosnian, "Ahhhh ... Dje si, bolan, sergeant?" *How are you, my mate the sergeant?* He stressed the second syllable in sergeant. The soldier continued in staccato pidgin English. "How is my friend, Queen Elizabeth?"

Steele had to smile.

"She's good, Rajko. She sends her regards," replied Sgt. Thomas. Then to Steele, "He thinks I'm the dogs' bollocks because I'm allowed to drive back and forth across the confrontation line." *Dogs' bollocks* (as in *testacles*) was army speak for something great or spectacular.

They all shook hands. Steele retreated a few inches to avoid Rajko's stale breath—a predicable mix of *rakija*, cigarettes, and halitosis. Not much of a surprise considering toothpaste and toothbrushes must be in short supply up here, Steele reasoned.

"Meet my friend, Captain Steele," said Sgt. Thomas. "He's a friend of Sonja Radovanović."

Rajko smiled, revealing teeth with more metal than enamel. He eyed Steele suspiciously for a few moments then said, "Yes, yes. I hear about you. Journalist?" He turned, beckoning for them to follow. "Come, you have visitor."

Steele didn't understand who might be waiting but followed Rajko down some steps through a low doorway into the hut. On the other side of a muddy trench another set of wooden crates made into steps led back outside—the escape route.

Rajko peered through a slit in the log wall looking downhill toward the front line. "Muslimani," he said. "Pedeset meter. Danas. Boom! Boom!" *Muslims. Fifty meters. Today. Boom! Boom!* He pounded a fist into the opposite palm.

"Heavy fighting and skirmishes today, I think he means," Sgt. Thomas said.

"Tri Muslimani." *Three Muslims.* Rajko held up three fingers and sliced his thumb across his throat, nodding enthusiastically, and apparently waiting for Steele and Sgt. Thomas to get as excited as he was about the death of three Muslim soldiers. "Tri Muslimani! Bam, Bam!" he repeated, as he gestured with an imaginary rifle.

Steele faked a smile. Turning to Sgt. Thomas, he said, "Nice friend."

"Don't worry, sir. He's harmless. Besides, we have other business."

"We do?"

Rajko stooped to avoid the wooden supports holding up the trench. "Please, sit down. Drink coffee? *Rakija?*" He waved his hand, thumb and little finger protruding, pointing to his mouth with excited eyes. Even in the trenches, alcohol was, apparently, available.

"Thanks," said Steele. "Coffee's great." He couldn't imagine what kind of coffee would be served in this filthy hovel. On the other hand, it was bloody freezing outside, and he wouldn't say no to hot liquid of any kind.

Steele looked around. Wooden ammunition boxes were strewn about. Some lay on their sides, empty, and some stood full of 7.62 mm ammunition link. Rations were sparse, but ammunition was plentiful, it seemed. None of the eating utensils had been washed. *If it'd been summer, Steele thought, there would be ants crawling all over the encrusted meat and potato leftovers on the army tin plates.*

Rajko opened the stove's metal grate and stoked up the glowing logs. He picked up a tin and scooped some ground coffee into a small vessel, then added hot water from a kettle and began to stir. Moments later he poured the thick, syrupy potion into a triangular metal jug with a long handle and placed it on the stove's red-hot surface.

"Real coffee," said Steele, rubbing his hands together.

"Yes, yes. You like?"

Several bullets popped less than fifty meters away.

Steele and Sgt. Thomas ducked.

"It's okay … it's okay…" Rajko assured them in English, listening carefully, pausing, and holding up his index finger. "Ma nije nishta … Samo se igrayu s'nami." *It's nothing. They're just playing with us.*

Steele frowned. "Fun."

Rajko continued, "We used to be friends with d'em. Brothers. Cousins. We lived together in Sarajevo. Winter Olympics, you know?"

Another burst of small-arms fire rattled around in the forest. Rajko sucked in his cheeks and wagged a finger left and right as if to dismiss the danger. He handed Steele the cup of coffee and grabbed a bottle of clear liquid—*probably rakija?*—from behind an ammo box, pouring a generous amount into his own metal cup. "You like?"

Steele relented. "Why not?" This was how business was done out here, he thought. It was the only way to alleviate the routine: endless boredom interspersed with brief moments of terror. Steele felt as though he was sitting in the WWII movie trench he had thought about earlier.

"One day they're fighting hand to hand," continued a familiar voice, "the next day they're shouting back and forth swapping news of family and friends. Crazy bastards."

Col. Edward Boyle emerged from a dark corner section of the trench. "The Bosnian army has a strong criminal element. The government can't control them, which makes things more complicated for us—"

"Colonel Boyle?" Steele looked at Sgt. Thomas for an explanation.

None followed.

Trebević Mountain, Pale, Sarajevo

Boyle grimaced and inhaled sharply as he sipped piping hot coffee from Rajko's metal cup, burning his lips in the process. "We deliver humanitarian aid to the locals in Sarajevo, but most of it gets siphoned off to the BiH army."

"What are you doing here?" asked Steele.

"Terrible business this morning. Gotta stay focused, though. I'm here to brief you on the next phase. Can't trust anyone at headquarters, I'm afraid. Never know who's listening among our little UN pool of international brotherhood and unity."

Steele frowned. "Interpreters?"

"Spies, Jack. They're everywhere. We have an arrangement with our friend, Rajko, here. Many a successful cease-fire has been negotiated in this very trench." He smiled, nodding at Sgt. Thomas, who took his leave and waited outside.

Boyle continued, "General Brown doesn't know everything about our plan." He sipped his coffee. "Jack, we've left you in the dark for your own protection. We want you *inside* the Radovanović inner circle. Without that, what I am about to ask of you would be impossible."

Steele's stomach flipped. Boyle was certainly full of surprises, mostly unpleasant ones.

"The truth is, Jack," continued Boyle, "Dr. Radovanović didn't request to see you. We got word to *him* that you, Peter Steele, have urgent news about a new peace deal. Our own peace recipe so to speak. Sonja is supposed to back up your story, if Sir Lawrence has done his job."

"Sounds complicated."

Boyle held up his hand. "Let me explain. We need you close, or should I say, in close proximity to Sonja's family." Boyle crossed his fingers. "We want to arrest Dr. Radovanović and Gen. Zukić for war crimes. And we're going to need your help."

Steele frowned and shook his head. "You're joking." The notion that he had now become some kind of conduit 007 operative was utterly absurd. "You're insane."

Boyle gave Steele a half smile. "Can we count on you, Jack?"

"No. Why? That's not why I'm here."

Boyle sighed. "Why *are* you here?"

"My brother's dead. I want to find out who killed him and why. And maybe help these poor bastards somehow. I didn't come to arrest Bosnian Serb war criminals."

"Your brother was helping us, Jack. That's why you're here.

Correct me if I misunderstood—you're here for *him?*" Boyle's eyes narrowed.

"Right. Yes, that's right. But—"

"We think Peter might have been …"—he paused, as though assessing if Steele had any inkling of his next thought—"romantically involved with Sonja. There was talk of a wedding."

Maybe Boyle doesn't know everything after all? Steele wondered. "I don't think so." His instinct was to keep the contents of Peter's letter to himself for now.

Boyle stared back at Steele. Then he said, "Think about it, Jack—big picture and all. Peter was good at his job. He was making a difference, and you can too. We need to get these bastards. You saw for yourself what happened today. War crimes tribunal in The Hague is gunning for them. We'll contact you via UNMO Pale or the American."

"The American?"

"The journalist. Her name is Staci Ryan. The one you saw outside your brother's flat in Chelsea. I promised her a story."

"What story?"

"Let's just say we have an arrangement."

Steele nodded, unconvinced. Now more than ever, he didn't know who or what to trust or believe.

CHAPTER TWELVE

The Pale mountain road was cloaked in fir trees laden with snow that formed a cocoon, a tunnel, as though protecting those who passed beneath. It might have been any ski resort mountain road in Europe, but the front line was a hundred meters to the left, and Steele wasn't thinking about skiing.

"What's going to happen, Sgt. Thomas?"

"You mean the war, sir?"

"Yes."

"NATO is champing at the bit to bomb the Serbs. General Brown wants to broker an agreement—"

"What kind of agreement?"

"Serbs have agreed to deliver all heavy weapons to UN collection points. Problem is that UN peacekeepers are unarmed—which means the Serbs can take *back* the weapons and ammo whenever they feel like it."

"Defeats the whole purpose."

"That's right, sir. And who knows how many weapons they've kept for themselves? They're playing games."

"All's fair in love and war …"

"Except this isn't a war, it's a peacekeeping operation."

Steele exhaled sharply. "Any sign of Serbs pulling back from Goražde?"

"They dropped off artillery pieces yesterday at the UN collection points. But then the Market Massacre …? Nice double bluff, perhaps? SAS observers have reported tanks moving toward Goražde. Doesn't look good."

"SAS?"

"They're everywhere. They call themselves JCOs—Joint Commission Observers. General Brown's idea. They're supposed to monitor the front lines."

"Gather intel?"

"That's right."

"And Goražde's next for the slaughter?"

"If they haven't started already."

Sgt. Thomas shifted down a gear as they began the steep climb up Trebević Mountain. Pale checkpoint was at the top.

They pulled up to the wooden barrier at a fork in the road. The left fork, Sgt. Thomas explained, led to Pale town proper, while the right fork would take them to the ski lifts. Sgt. Thomas gave a friendly grin to the guard, then handed the young soldier a packet of Marlboro Lights. "That should do the trick, sir," he said under his breath. Even though Steele was expected at the Pale checkpoint, Sgt. Thomas was prepared for trouble. Lines of communication were often blurred in these parts.

The barrier went up, and the soldier in blue camo overalls waved them through.

As they pulled away from the checkpoint, three gunshots double-tapped behind them. It seemed more like warning shots than an act of aggression.

Steele checked the rearview mirror. "They're waving at us. They want us to stop."

Sgt. Thomas braked. "Your call, sir. I can gun it if you want."

Steele shook his head. "Reverse up."

They backed up to the checkpoint.

The larger of the two Serb soldiers waved his handheld radio and said in broken English, "We have new order. You go up Jahorina." His AK-47 half slung, finger on the trigger, he gestured toward the steep right fork gradient behind him. "Make right turn, go for one mile. It's okay?"

"It's okay. Understood." Steele guessed the Jahorina mountain road was otherwise off limits to UNPROFOR. Many of the smaller roads and tracks led to artillery positions and were almost always mined. If he proceeded, the Serbs could set up an ambush and accuse him of spying. But that was a chance he had to take.

"It's good," the guard replied. "You go now." The guard, unshaven with sunken, black-ringed eyes, was firm.

"Let's go," said Steele, giving Sgt. Thomas a nudge.

They drove up a winding road that turned into a dirt track. When they reached the other side of a forest, they found themselves on high ground with a stunning view into the valley behind them. A ski slope came into view. Steele and Sgt. Thomas looked at each other. They both smiled. It was an odd sight: At least fifty soldiers in uniform were on the slope—but none of them were skiing. Instead, they were riding up and down on the chair lifts without skis … *Joy riding.* The only people skiing—about ten of them—were women and children in civilian ski gear.

Passing a small hotel on the left, Steele noticed that every window had been blacked out. Half a dozen military vehicles were parked outside. *A command post of sorts? Why had the Serbs allowed them up here?* It didn't make sense.

A handful of soldiers watched them drive past but did not try to stop them. "Cam net left, thirty meters," said Sgt. Thomas without turning his head. The canon of a Serb artillery piece was sticking out of the camouflage netting.

"Fifty-five millimeter …" said Steele.

"That boy can hit Sarajevo. We're within range." Sgt. Thomas frowned. "This whole thing, sir, it's well fucked up."

"I agree."

The track petered out, and Sgt. Thomas stopped in the car park next to the ski lift. A young dark-haired man in a blue camo police uniform shuffled over to them on crutches. The lower half of his right leg was missing.

"That's Darko, Pale police chief," said Sgt. Thomas. He cut the engine. "Poor fucker's lost half his leg since I last saw him. We went skiing together once."

"Skiing?"

"He was out of fuel, so I offered to give him a ride, and he offered to lend me a pair of skis. Win-win. But that was a year ago, in the good old days when they weren't blowing each other to pieces and slitting each other's throats, *and* they still had an ounce of respect for the UN."

Darko stood and waited for Steele and Sgt. Thomas to reach him. "Captain Steele, you wanna ski?" He pointed to his leg. "Look at me. I only need one ski."

Steele laughed. He couldn't help respecting a man who could make light of such a tragedy. The poor guy had lost half his leg *and* he was the local police chief. At the same time, he couldn't help wondering how many people Darko might have shot or killed in this war, or at least given the order to kill.

Darko shrugged. "Landmine," he continued, "Evo, nash rat ..." *Welcome to our war...*

"Please," said Darko, pointing at the ski lift that wound continuously up and down the mountain. "Your driver can leave now. You have meeting at the top of mountain."

"I'll wait, sir," said Sgt. Thomas.

Steele walked over to the wooden ramp at the foot of the chairlift and waved good-bye. "You can go. I'll be fine." He decided a certain amount of bravado was necessary. The more courage he could muster, the more he thought he might make it through this first test. "Thank you."

"Roger that, sir." Sgt. Thomas hesitated and then returned to the SUV.

About one quarter of the ski-lift chairs were occupied—some soldiers were sitting alone, others in pairs. They all seemed relaxed—making the most of their well-earned twenty-four-hour leave pass from the front line, Steele concluded.

"Why aren't they skiing?" Steele asked Darko.

"They're afraid. They don't want to break any bones. They cannot fight Muslims with broken leg."

Steele nodded. "Good point."

"Please," said Darko, gesturing to the chairlift.

Steele slid onto a moving chair. He pulled down the guard-rail and allowed the lift to sweep him off his feet and ascend. He looked behind to see his UN Jeep snaking back down the track, a tiny white matchbox far below.

Steele was alone.

The wind picked up and whipped his face. The cloudless sky and bright winter sun gave no warmth. He looked around again. The suffering in Sarajevo had not reached this idyllic spot.

It took five minutes to reach the top. Edging forward, Steele prepared to jump off the chairlift. The soldiers ahead of him made the descent from the chairlift look easy without skis and poles. Others did not even attempt to dismount and simply rode straight back down the mountain. Dozens of soldiers smoked and chatted at the top as they took in the view.

Steele jumped to the right but misjudged the depth of the snow. He missed his footing and tumbled a short way down the slope.

Nothing serious. He got up, brushed himself off, and trudged back up the slope, digging his toecaps into the icy layer of snow. He reached the top and squinted at the silhouette of a figure wearing a thick green overcoat and military fur hat with ear flaps. Behind the figure, two soldiers, rifles slung, stood next to each other.

"Zdravo!" said a woman's voice. *Hi!* The woman extended both arms. "I am very pleased to see you, my darling."

CHAPTER THIRTEEN

Jahorina Ski Resort, Pale

Stunned, Steele stood upright and brushed the snow off his jacket and trousers. In front of him stood Sonja Radovanović casting a long shadow across his face. A mass of dark hair cascaded from beneath her hat. Her face was wide, but Steele had to concede that she was more attractive than he had suspected from the brief glimpse in Hyde Park from afar. Not beautiful, he thought, but much more attractive close up than in the photographs I've seen in newspapers. And under the drab-green greatcoat, she wore the unmistakable garb of the Bosnian Serb army. Even though the uniform looked too big for her, it suited her athletic frame.

"You came back."

"Yes," Steele said hesitantly.

She moved closer. "I always knew you are a good spy." Then she kissed him firmly on the lips. "Peter, I am so happy—" Sonja stopped midsentence and starred at Jack, the surprise across her face unmistakable.

That didn't last long, he thought.

She knew almost at once. There was no point in pretending to be Peter, as Boyle had suggested. Boyle had been watching too many spy movies. Pretending to be Peter was absurd.

"You are Jack," she said slowly.

"I can explain," Steele began, shielding his eyes against the bright snow. "Peter's not here."

"Where is he?"

"Sonja. Peter's dead. I'm sorry. He was murdered."

Sonja studied him closely for what seemed like half a minute but was really just a few seconds. Then she said slowly, "I was afraid for this. I warned him. There are many people with bad interests in this war." She shook her head slowly, eyes welling and on the verge of overflowing. "We have many problems in my country. Your brother was different. He wanted to talk with us and help us. He wanted to tell the truth, write about our side of the story. He has seen for himself that we are not bad people." She paused. "I was in love with your brother."

"I know he liked you a lot." Steele decided it wasn't the right time to share the precise contents of Peter's letter. Peter had not mentioned *love* per se, but he suspected Peter had indeed fallen for Sonja. However, he still preferred to keep his cards close to his chest and wasn't convinced Sonja was telling the truth. *Trust no one.*

"What did he say?" Sonja asked. "Did he talk about me?"

"He told me you love your people." Steele took a deep breath and smiled. "He was my brother. Of course, he told me about you."

"But you were fighting."

"Family rift," Steele said. "Probably wouldn't have lasted forever." He wondered if she could tell he was lying.

"My people are suffering. They need help."

Steele wanted to scoff. *That's not what the rest of the world is thinking.* Probably not the right time for his next thought, but he said it anyway: "Why are your people pounding Sarajevo? I was there today. Dozens of people were slaughtered. Your snipers are killing innocent women and children fetching water."

"They leave us no choice. This is war. Muslim snipers provoke us when TV cameras are gone, when no one is looking. They are sneaky like a fox. Your media sits and judges, but they do not come and talk to us in person. CNN and BBC journalists report only from Muslim territory. No one comes to Serb territory to make reportage."

It is true, Steele thought. Fitzgerald had explained to him that most journalists stayed in the Bosnian government territory within the logistically more practical and accessible confines of Sarajevo. They were unable to cross confrontation lines to present both sides of the argument. But foreign journalist logistics, of course, was hardly an excuse for mass murder by one of the sides.

He said, "Does it matter where journalists are standing? Which territory? They can see how many people are dying."

"You are naïve. If a journalist is standing on one side, talking to our people, they will see things from our side. They experience a different truth. These journalists must tell the truth from all sides."

"Your men have killed thousands of innocent people who can't defend themselves … Sarajevo, Mostar, Tuzla."

"Do not believe everything Muslims tell you. They exaggerate. It is in their best interests to lie and exaggerate everything."

"The Market Massacre today?" Steele blurted out. "I was there. I saw it. That was no exaggeration." He felt sick just thinking about it.

Sonja shook her head. "I swear to you on my life—Bosnian Serb army is not responsible for this massacre."

Steele was silent. *How could she know for sure?* He wanted to believe her, but the truth was he didn't know who or what to believe, and this was only day three in theater.

Sonja continued, "One day I will prove this to you. Muslims shell their own people." She pointed toward downtown Sarajevo in the far distance. "But we have other business."

Even though he was wearing a winter jacket, Steele wrestled with the cold, trying to shake off mild shivers. They were his body's reaction to adrenaline and nerves now fading; fear and cold remained. *Other business? What did that mean?*

Sonja cupped her hands and rubbed her face. "I know your people want to kill me."

His next thought made him feel awkward, even disloyal. *I don't even know her, but I am extremely attracted to this woman.*

"Who?" he asked.

"Peter told me this. He told me many things about your people, your government."

"I don't think—"

"Listen to me—"

"No one wants to kill you, Sonja," Steele continued. "I came to help. Peter was here to help. No one wants World War Three in the heart of Europe. People are on edge. Leaders are concerned."

Sonja was unmoved. "My country needs more than your concerns."

"I came to offer you a chance for peace before NATO bombs your troops." Boyle had instructed Steele to start here. "Your father *must* return to the peace table." Steele was mindful of his task: *Orchestrate the arrest of Sonja's father, Dr. Kosta Radovanović, and his sidekick, General Ratko Zukić.*

Sonja was unimpressed with the offer. "If NATO or UN attack us, they know my father will slaughter Muslims. We also know that NATO does not want blame for starting World War Three."

He said, "You need to stop the slaughter and stop the siege of Sarajevo. Those people are dying like rats in a cage for God's sake."

Sonja began to move away from him, her footsteps crunching in the snow. "We did not ask for this war."

"Who did?" Steele followed Sonja to the ski lift.

"Muslims held referendum for sovereignty of Bosnia-Herzegovina, and we refuse to take part. Understand? We boycott. The referendum was unfair because my people were minority. No matter what, we lose. Of course, Muslim wins referendum, so now Muslim is ruler of Bosnia-Herzegovina."

Steele stared intently. So far, he had to admit she was making sense. He really could see both sides. *Welcome to the conundrums of international politics.*

Sonja concluded: "This is not justice, we cannot accept this."

"It's a mess, I agree. But the killing—"

"International community meddles in our affairs, some countries more than others."

"Germany?" Fitzgerald had explained to him how Germany's premature recognition of Croatia had completely, in his words, "buggered things up." Even after living together for half a century in socialist harmony, Germany's alignment with the fascist Ustaša during World War Two meant that the Serbs were their natural enemy.

Sonja nodded. "They recognize Croatia, and they hate us."

Steele glanced at Sonja's two bodyguards watching him closely. He wondered if her father was far away and how much power Sonja had over him. *Perhaps this woman has more power than most people think?*

"Peter was coming back to marry me. He promised me."

Steele smiled nervously.

"He didn't mention that." That certainly *wasn't* in the letter.

"I told him this would help us. My father thinks outside world will look upon us more positively if I marry Englishman. He thinks it can help us politically."

"I don't understand. Were you in love with each other?"

"There are more important things than love. But yes, I loved Peter."

Steele nodded. "My brother is full of surprises. Living and dead."

Sonja rested her hand on Jack's forearm. "Peter said he would do this for me."

Boyle's words from the night of the murder echoed inside Steele's head. *It's better you don't know everything for the time being.* Had the mysterious Boyle known about this wedding idea all along?

Sonja said, "You will take his place?"

Steele had not been expecting this. A bolt from the blue. Something he would need to wrap his head around in a split second and make a quick decision. The idea was ridiculous. He hadn't foreseen a wedding, but he *was* here to take Peter's place, whatever that might entail.

It struck him that all good "spies" needed to be good actors. He hadn't signed the Official Secrets Act or anything so dramatic and permanent. No one had made him sign on any dotted line, but how else could he describe his current job title?

Steele smiled. "Of course," he said, the absurdity all but slapping him. "Anything for Peter. When were you planning to get married?"

"Wednesday," Sonja replied, her expression deadpan.

"*This* Wednesday?"

"Correct."

"That's in two days?"

"Correct. I will tell my father about Peter. He will be very grateful that you have agreed to help. Thank you, Jack."

So much for pretending to be Peter, Steele thought.

CHAPTER FOURTEEN

6ème Arrondissement, Paris

At 9:06 am the next morning, two highly polished black Mercedes Benz S500 sedans—flanked by three French police cars—waited outside Casino Supermarché on rue de Buci. A small group of men and one woman huddled in the middle of the street opposite Bar du Marché. They wore expensive suits and sunglasses despite the typically gray Parisian sky.

The police had temporarily cordoned off the market street for the VIPs, but pedestrians were allowed access to the busy market stalls. One couple, recognizing Klaus and Katya Reithoffer, the German foreign minister and his wife, paused their conversation and bowed in sympathy. They, too, had heard the tragic news.

It was Valentine's Day, but these flowers symbolized the opposite of life, love, and romance. The old woman approached Reithoffer, thrust a small posy toward him, and offered her condolences: "Monsieur … Je suis désolée …" *I am so sorry, sir …* His face ashen, Reithoffer accepted the flowers and mouthed a silent thank you. A policeman ushered the woman away.

Kerstin Reithoffer had been studying art history at the Sorbonne. Now, staring at the precise location where his only daughter had been struck by a car less than twenty-four hours before, Reithoffer sensed that his love affair with Dalmatia was over, and even partly to blame for his daughter's death. He did not share this with Katya, much less another thought that told him her death was connected to his hatred of the Serbs.

Klaus Reithoffer was one of the highest-ranking politicians in the German CDU—Christian Democratic Party—whose conservative values had dominated Germany for many years. Before his move into politics, which had seen him fast-tracked to the top of the German political circuit, he had been a career diplomat for almost three decades. He and his wife, Katya—short for Ekaterina—had enjoyed more than a dozen diplomatic postings around the world. Their fondest memories, however, were of Croatia, Katya's homeland, many years before its breakaway from the Yugoslav Federation. Based in Zagreb, they had spent unforgettable weekends—their Deutschmark worth ten times more in Yugoslavia than elsewhere in Europe—traveling up and down the Dalmatian Coast, island hopping to their heart's content.

Mrs. Reithoffer wept behind her sunglasses, and every now and then she lifted them to dab a tear. Reithoffer squeezed her hand, more for show than genuine affection, and certainly not for Valentine's Day love. Outwardly, they were together, but inside they were worlds apart.

"Herr Reithoffer—" A German aide interrupted Reithoffer's dark thoughts, approaching with yet another bright bouquet tied with black ribbon. Reithoffer gestured to the mounting pile of floral tributes that was turning the pain in his heart to anger. "Over there ..." he said in German after he read the card that read:

PRÉFECTURE DE POLICE DE PARIS COMMISSIONER

The commissioner had personally assured him that their investigation would uncover any foul play and that justice would prevail. But what kind of justice? Certainly not Klaus Reithoffer justice. That much he knew.

Once the aide had retreated, Reithoffer returned to Katya and patted her arm. "It's okay," he said. "I promise to find out what happened." His shattered heart could not muster anything more comforting.

Another senior French police inspector introduced himself, offering a list of theories about what had happened. The man talked, and Reithoffer nodded but wasn't listening. Inwardly, he was seething. Almost twenty-four hours since the tragedy, and neither the red Citroen nor its driver at the center of the hit-and-run had been traced.

"I am sorry for your loss," the inspector concluded.

"Thank you." They shook hands.

Useless French pigs. Reithoffer had little faith in their ability to solve this one. He was certain that the Serbs were responsible for this atrocity. But he couldn't exactly reveal details that would expose his part in the Bosnia debacle. The man who had murdered Kerstin—yes, he was sure it was murder—was probably knocking back *slivovica* in a Serb enclave in Eastern Bosnia by now, boasting of his conquest.

Reithoffer couldn't bear it any longer. He took Katya's hand—*maintain a unified front*, he thought—and walked across to Bar du Marché. "I know who did this," he said. "I'll make them pay."

"Empty words and a promise I doubt you can honor," she replied. Katya's voice dripped with contempt.

"They made threats," Reithoffer continued. "Those bastards threatened to kill her."

Katya froze.

"What are you saying?" Her words came slowly. "Kerstin was in danger? You didn't tell me—"

"Threats, propaganda … *kwatsch* …"—nonsense.

"But now you have proof?" she asked, mindful of his hatred for Serbs. Even though she was Croatian and knew the history of her country better than any foreigner, Klaus Reithoffer had lectured his wife many times about Croatia's right to sovereignty and self-determination; why Croatia deserved to be rid of their dominating Serb masters in Belgrade. She said, "Please, Klaus, we must bury our daughter in peace and with dignity."

He could tell she was afraid of what he might do. "I'll take care of this. I swear there will be no more violence," he lied. At the same time, he made a promise to himself that he would do whatever it took to avenge his daughter's death.

Katya lowered her sunglasses and said, "I need coffee."

"Wait for me in the car," Reithoffer replied. "I'll fetch it."

For months he'd been sickened and outraged over Serb ethnic cleansing in Bosnia. He'd voiced his opinions publicly and often. Now that they had killed his daughter, he would exploit his political influence to support the Croatian government—overtly and covertly—against their enemies. By killing Kerstin, the Serb pigs had sealed their fate.

He eyed the media crush at both ends of the street. TV crews and reporters were arriving, poised like runners on a starting line. The eyes of the world were watching, hungry for their story. Despite the pain, he would hold it together. "*Verdammt doch mal,*" he muttered. Damn it. *In less than one week, I will be president of the European Union.*

As Katya walked away, Reithoffer's gaze lingered on the dark red stains of blood in the street, and he fought to erase the horrific images in his mind of his daughter's final moments.

Sarajevo Airport, Bosnia

The RAF Hercules C130 rattled and shook as it made its final descent into Sarajevo Airport, which today happened to be "open" because the threat level of shelling and sniper fire was low. As advised by journalist colleagues, Staci Ryan sat on her flak jacket to ward off stray bullets from snipers on the ground. Other less-experienced passengers followed her lead.

Bosnian Serb snipers were reportedly taking random potshots at UN aircraft landing in Sarajevo, but the threat was not acute enough for the RAF pilot officer to abort his flight mission today. He would take the risk. Humanitarian aid supplies were desperately needed in Sarajevo. The final decision to land was always left to the pilot. Staci knew she had been lucky to catch a plane ride on a first-come-first-serve basis from Split and was also happy to take her chances with stray bullets.

"Prepare cargo for landing ..." the RAF copilot announced over the Tannoy. Crew members checked and tightened cargo stowage, and UN, civilian, and journalist passengers clung onto the straps behind them for extra support, wedging their feet against the cargo in the belly of the aircraft.

Staci's stomach flipped as the C130 aircraft dropped steeply and unexpectedly.

The sudden dive to earth was the best way to avoid sniper fire. Many of the passengers appeared to be regulars, sitting on their flak jackets, nonchalantly reading a newspaper or battered paperback. They might just as well have been sitting on an NJT—New Jersey Transit—train commuting from the suburbs to the city, Staci thought. *This trip better be worth it!*

UN CIVPOL—civilian police—aid workers and international journalists seemed unruffled by the potential danger. On the contrary, most were visibly excited, enjoying the thrill. War junkies were addicts like any other, she thought. Instead of alcohol, sex, or gambling, these guys got their fix from war zones where they were forced to live on the edge, knowing that although the chances were generally slim, a bullet or a shell might end it all at any time. Narrow escapes from mortar rounds, sniper fire, and land mines were a daily occurrence in Sarajevo.

She turned to the Pakistani major sitting next to her. "Here we go," she said, smiling and holding up crossed fingers.

"Don't worry," the major shouted in a clipped accent above the engines. "Serbs are sleeping off their hangovers. It's too early for them. They haven't eaten breakfast yet."

Staci smiled, then felt nauseous. She gripped the brown paper sick bag with both hands as though her life depended on it. She closed her eyes, waiting for the giant rubber tires to screech on the tarmac. This trip *would* be worth it, she told herself. This story would change her life—and her bank balance—forever. This much, Boyle had promised.

Thirty minutes later, Staci arrived at the Hotel Holiday Inn courtesy of the UN shuttle bus. She entered the lobby and began to mingle, searching for her contact. Her eyes flashed from one ID card to the next. She had never seen so many international aid workers, military, and journalists in one place—UNPROFOR, UNHCR, MSF, NATO, BBC, CNN, AP, IRC, EC Task Force, and many more. Then she saw him—the man who would lead her to Jack Steele. His name was Colonel Edward Boyle.

CHAPTER FIFTEEN

Pale

Ten miles east of Sarajevo, Steele had been ordered not to leave town by Pale authorities for his own safety. Sonja had told him he was under a kind of "town arrest." He took a spare room at the UNMO house one field away from the Dr. Radovanović headquarters and residence, and awaited further instructions from Sonja or the Bosnian Serb authorities.

One day until the "wedding."

He was permitted to walk around the town but was shadowed by an armed militiaman, for his own "security and peace of mind" they had said. *We don't want anything to happen to you.*

After introducing himself and overnighting with the UNMOs, he'd concocted a cover story about why he was there in the first place, a story that would be backed up by Maj. Small in Sarajevo. The next day, Steele changed into civvies and walked into town. The militiaman followed at a discreet distance, avoiding eye contact. Steele wasn't exactly a prisoner, but he wasn't free to hitch a ride back to Sarajevo either. Not that he wanted to; this place was heaven compared with the hell of the besieged Bosnian capital.

Reaching Pale town center, he was struck by the calm. This was the closest Serb town to Sarajevo outside of artillery range, but looking at the wooden stalls and tables stacked with fruit and vegetables in the marketplace, it was hard to believe they were less than ten miles from the fighting and shelling.

Middle-aged and elderly women in brightly patterned floral headscarves scoured the market tables for the best deals, bartering from stall to stall, their shopping bags bursting with tired-looking but edible produce.

Young military conscripts and new recruits lined up outside the police station, ready to enlist and fight for their cause; unshaven old men wearing heavy wool, army-green overcoats, squatted in groups on the pavements smoking the last flakes of tobacco from withered cigarette butts and hand-carved pipes.

In the far distance, Steele heard the soft *boom-boom* of artillery and mortar shells. Sporadic units of military trucks and tanks—the only traffic around—headed toward Rogatica and the infamous Bosnian Muslim enclave of Goražde. A blue police transporter van, the occupants' AK47s visible, cruised past Steele. The combatants eyed Steele suspiciously; every foreigner was a potential enemy or spy.

When it began to drizzle, Steele ducked into the only café in town. He stood in line to order coffee, Turkish-style—thick and syrupy.

"Ja bi kava, molim vas," he said in Bosnian. *Coffee please.*

The waitress had jet-black hair and bright red lipstick. She looked as though she had never smiled her entire life. But who could blame her? It was anyone's guess how many of her family or friends might have died in this war already. She scooped ground coffee into a small copper vessel, added hot water, and slid the vessel onto a sizzling hot plate. Seconds later, the lava-like liquid began to erupt and was placed on a brass tray with an empty cup. The aroma made his mouth water.

A voice behind him said, "That looks delicious. Don't mind if I do."

An American accent, one he did not recognize. He turned to see a woman, clearly not a local, sitting in the corner by the window. Visually, he now recognized her from the brief encounter outside Peter's flat on the day of his brother's murder in Chelsea.

Steele did not show his surprise, but part of him was pleased to see Staci Ryan in the flesh. *Perhaps the American has some answers?*

He said to the waitress in Bosnian, "And one more for my friend."

"I'll bring it to you," she replied.

Steele walked over to Staci.

She said, "Happy Valentine's Day."

"I'd forgotten what day it is. Same to you." He smiled hesitantly.

"Staci Ryan. Have a seat." She extended her hand, and they greeted each other officially for the first time.

"Nice to meet you, Staci."

Steele grabbed a spare wooden chair from another table and sat down.

"Did Boyle tell you about me? I saw you at the flat. I'm very sorry about your brother."

Steele eyed Staci and nodded slowly. "What were you doing there? How did you—"

"I didn't. I had no idea he was dead until I got there. Boyle sent me to connect with Peter."

The waitress set down another brass tray with Staci's coffee. Steele waited for her to leave.

"What are you actually doing here?" He leaned toward her, elbows resting on the table. "Boyle told me to expect you, but *why* are you here?"

"I need to get to Goražde?" said Staci. "Can you help me?"

"I'm not sure …"

"You have connections here."

"I've only just got here."

Staci took a sip of coffee from the miniature porcelain cup and said, "Look, Jack. Every journalist in the world wants to go to Goražde."

Steele frowned and said, "I'm staying put. I have business

here. I'm not allowed to leave." He wasn't willing to share the whole marriage story. At least, not yet.

"You don't get it, Jack. There's going to be a friggin' shit show in Goražde. Gen. Zukić has positioned his forces along the confrontation line. They've completely surrounded the place … with tanks."

"I get it. General Brown has threatened NATO air strikes if they don't pull back—"

Staci scoffed. "Don't be naïve. The Serbs are gonna take Goražde no matter what."

"Not necessarily. Brown told Zukić that the Bosnian Serbs have three days to withdraw heavy weapons from Goražde. That was yesterday. Deadline expires in forty-eight hours."

"They'll attack and *cleanse* before the deadline. You know what that means. *Ethnic cleansing?*"

"And you want a ringside seat?" Steele stirred his coffee.

"I'm a reporter. That's what I do."

Steele took a sip. "I can't help you."

"Really? Nothing you can do? I have to say I'm disappointed. Your brother had more balls." She raised an eyebrow. It was as though she was waiting for his reaction to her throwing down a gauntlet.

"Thanks. And we've only just met."

Staci said, "See, Jack. You can't help them make peace if you stay in Pale. That's why you're here, isn't it? Like the rest of us? War and peace? Sorry if I misunderstood. I thought you wanted to make a difference like Peter was going to." She stood up and headed for the door. "No worries, I'll figure it out by myself."

"Wait …" Steele followed and they left the café-bar.

Avoiding a horse and cart pulling a full load of firewood, they crossed the road into the marketplace. Most of the rickety tables were empty now. A handful of old men and women stood behind them, as though on guard, hoping to sell every last vegetable. Seeing the empty market stalls, Steele felt a shiver run down his spine as he recalled what had happened at the marketplace in Sarajevo—sixty-eight innocent people killed instantly and many more maimed for life. He knew the Bosnian (Muslim) government couldn't reach Pale with their artillery, but just being in a marketplace now in this part of the world made him nervous.

"How did you convince Boyle to help you?" asked Steele.

"I smiled sweetly and promised to take him to dinner when we're both back in London. He delegated Sgt. Thomas to give me a ride."

"Sgt. Thomas gets around."

"I couldn't have got here without him."

Steele glanced behind them and checked his escort, who was still tailing him. A Serbian folk song crackled from the small exterior speakers dotted around the market square. All good. The escort could not hear his conversation with Staci. He probably couldn't speak English anyway, but Steele wanted to make sure they could not be overheard.

Steele paused, then said, "I need to ask you something."

"Sure."

"Have you heard of the Sarajevo Protocol?"

She said, "Sure. You know about that too? Who told you?"

"I've been briefed. Who told *you*?"

"Luka Rakić. He was a prominent Bosnian journalist before the war. Now he's the mayor of Goražde."

"How did you find Luka?"

"I was working on a story. Luka found *me*—"

"Then what?"

"He said Peter knew Sonja, and that she might confide in him."

"About the—?"

"Yes, the Protocol. But Peter and Sonja had already left Bosnia. I followed them all the way back to London. That's why I was trying to meet Peter in Chelsea."

"How did you get his address?"

"Your people."

Steele frowned, more confused than ever. "I don't have people."

"Boyle," she said.

"Boyle gave you Peter's address?"

"Yes."

On one level, her story made some sense, but for the moment, he wouldn't allow himself to completely trust Staci Ryan. He needed more information.

They reached the far side of the market square and walked up the now-deserted road toward the UNMO house and the Hotel Panorama. "Why did Luka Rakić choose you?"

"I've no idea. He liked my face? He read one of my articles? Anything can happen at the Sarajevo Holiday Inn. The whole world is there. I came here looking for a story a few weeks ago and the story found me."

Steele asked, "Did he show you this Protocol?"

"He said he needed my help and would show me the original next time we met. That was the last I heard."

"What's in the Protocol?"

"I don't know exactly. But it might bring peace to this goddamn hell hole."

"A *peace* Protocol?"

"I guess."

Steele lengthened his stride. Listening to Staci's story had reminded him about Sonja. He wanted this war in Bosnia to end, and he also wanted to help Sonja. Peter would have wanted that too. He was doing this for Peter—a chance to do right by him.

Steele said, "What else do you know about the Protocol?"

"Apparently, Tito himself declared that if ethnic conflict ever threatened to break up Yugoslavia, the Serbs had the right to take over. The entire country would become a Serbian Sovereign state."

"But Tito was half-Croat, half-Slovene."

"I know. I don't get it either."

"How would the Serbs ever be granted full sovereignty?"

"By doing what they're doing now—use the mighty Yugoslav Peoples' Army to annihilate and crush the opposition anywhere in former Yugoslavia. They started in Croatia and now Bosnia."

Steele frowned. "It doesn't make any sense."

Just then Steele heard a familiar sound—a low squeaking, grinding, and rumbling that shook the ground.

"Tanks," he said. "More than one."

They turned into the UNMO house driveway and waited.

Staci said, "They're getting ready to flatten Goražde. If the Russians get involved, things will spiral out of control very quickly."

"I'm starting to see how this might end," he said.

"Badly." Staci nodded in agreement.

"Right. This war is one big mess."

"You can say that again."

Steele said, "I want to help you. But ..."

"But?"

He stopped and turned toward Staci. "I'm getting married tomorrow."

"What did you say?" Staci stifled a snigger. "Who to?"

"I'm marrying Sonya Radovanović ... tomorrow."

"That's funny."

"No, I'm serious."

"What? Why?"

"Apparently, that was Peter's plan. At least, he agreed to it. And then I agreed to stand in for him."

"Whoa ... Now I'm the one who's confused."

"Me too. But you've got nothing to worry about." Steele shrugged.

"Why's that?"

"Boyle told me to keep you informed."

"Okay, I'll be there."

"No, you're not invited."

"Why?"

"You're not on the guest list."

"What?"

"Sonja hasn't fully explained. But she told me it was a private affair. A few friends and family to make it look good."

"No problem, understood. But it sounds weird."

"I don't disagree."

"Just be careful. I have to work on the Goražde story anyway."

"Maybe I can get Sonja to help you?"

"That would be great. They won't talk to me, I already tried." Then she said, "Seriously, be careful, okay?"

"Thanks."

In the distance, Steele caught sight of the tanks rumbling out of the town toward Goražde. Steele walked up to the UNMO house, and as Staci continued toward the Hotel Panorama, he turned and said, "I know where to find you."

Staci gave him a casual salute and said in a British accent, "Cheers!"

PART II

CHAPTER SIXTEEN

Saint-Germain-des-Prés, Saint-Sulpice, Paris

The next morning, Wednesday, February 15, Klaus Reithoffer sat with his wife, Katya, on the terrace of Hotel Lutetia at 9:05 am. The five-star hotel was on Boulevard Raspail a few blocks from where their daughter had perished. The Reithoffers weren't planning to stay for long in Paris.

Their German-French security detail kept a discreet distance. The couple spoke in hushed tones and could not be overheard. A screen of potted fir trees and a black fence hid them from passersby. Outdoor gas heaters kept them warm.

Klaus Reithoffer ordered a continental breakfast with a side of Provence herb salami, but when it arrived, he'd already lost his appetite. He gulped his espresso and sipped at his freshly squeezed orange juice. Then he told his wife about his conversation with the Croatian president, Stjepan Tudjman, and that he had offered to "help" the president.

"Serbs are savages," Reithoffer said. "They are pigs, and they will pay for our daughter's life."

"Please, Klaus. You don't know—"

"Radovanović will pay."

"You don't think I'm hurting too. It's bad—"

"I will crush the Serbs."

Katya glanced at the security detail. "We must bury our daughter," she said, lowering her voice. "There is nothing more we can do here. Let's go home, please Klaus."

"In my heart, I know who did this—"

Katya leaned in across the table, seething. "You need proof."

"Proof would be useful, but not essential. I promise you that Serbs will pay for the life of our daughter."

Pale, Sarajevo

People say it is the happiest day of your life. But this wedding, deep in the heart of Bosnian Serb territory, had nothing to do with love and devotion. It was more about Queen and country—at least for now. Capt. Jack Steele was about to marry one Sonja Radovanović, only daughter of Dr. Kosta Radovanović, self-styled president and leader of the infamous Bosnian Serbs, and goddaughter of Gen. Ratko Zukić, leader of the Bosnian Serb army. It was a marriage of interests. Jack Steele was helping out British security services.

This was business—British military intelligence business. MI6, or perhaps even CIA? He couldn't be sure. *It certainly wasn't for pleasure*, Steele thought as he stood at the altar, sweating profusely. He felt like the proverbial bomb disposal expert—it could all explode in his face at any moment.

This marriage and his relationship with Sonja were a calculated move intended to bring about the arrest and capture of the Bosnian Serb leadership, taking him one step closer to that goal he had chosen for his brother's sake. At least, this was how Boyle had spun the situation and Steele's part in it during their conversation the night before that took place in UNMO Pale's satellite telephone-equipped office.

Steele waited patiently inside the faded gray-and-white Serbian Orthodox *crkva*, or church, in the Bosnian Serb capital, Pale. Apart from the three UNMOs stationed on Bosnian Serb territory and Staci, he was the only foreigner in town. He had successfully penetrated the heart of their war machine. He was marrying its daughter, for Christ's sake. It felt good. Sonja and Peter had made a plan, and Jack was willing to pick up where Peter had left off.

But Steele, probably more than anyone else, was fully aware that he was no clandestine operative, and these fragile nerves were not those of an expectant bridegroom. He had been thrown in at the deep end and was perilously close to being exposed. He could be imprisoned and possibly worse for spying if Sonja and her Bosnian Serb brethren decided to turn against him. As citizens of a former communist state in the midst of bloody conflict, these were paranoid people ready to slaughter innocents and probably Western spies too. He had promised himself to trust no one, yet here he was putting his life in Sonja's hands. She could turn on him in a second and have him thrown in jail. There was no emotional connection between them. At least, not yet. It was, after all, Peter who had fallen for Sonja. In any war zone, every situation was extremely volatile, but now here he was thinking about affairs of the heart. *Enough.*

Wearing a jacket and tie he had borrowed from Danny, the owner of the UNMO house, Steele clasped his hands together and bit the inside of his cheek until he tasted blood. *Perhaps I'm more nervous than I realize.* He rocked slowly back and forth, waiting for Sonja, his clammy hands stuck together. He was deceiving her people, and he could feel at least thirty pairs of eyes—Sonja's family, friends, and local dignitaries—drilling into the back of his neck. Staci, thankfully, had stayed away. But his personal mission was to find out who killed his brother *and* complete Boyle's mission by any and all means necessary. That much he had also promised Fitzgerald in Split.

The crkva, thick with candle smoke, was bathed in a warm orange glow. Incense irritated the back of his throat, and he swallowed frequently to stop himself coughing. Through the haze, he saw a young boy with blond hair smiling at him from the choir as he sung. *Foreigners were somehow special in these parts.* It was odd and a little sad, he thought, the unmerited respect Eastern Europeans lavished upon Westerners. They elevated Western democracy to be-all-and-end-all status, the answer to future happiness and prosperity. But the reality was, of course, a different story.

The choir sang unaccompanied, eight-part liturgical harmony. The vocal tone was exquisite, even to Steele's untrained ear. Behind the altar, a sea of icons dripped with ancient, jaded gold leaf. Hissing candles cast a dim, sulfurous glow on the ceremony. As surreal as this was, it was no outer body experience: *Infiltrate the Bosnian Serb leadership by any and all means necessary. But if anything goes wrong, you're on your own.* Despite Boyle's ominous warning, Steele had, surely, surpassed the man's wildest dreams? Steele was about to *marry* Sonja Radovanović, *to love and to cherish, to have and to hold, for richer for poorer, in sickness and in health* ... If this wasn't infiltration, he was damned if he knew what was. The more he thought about it, the more the adrenaline began to flow. His mind flipped back and forth—one minute it felt as though he was dreaming, the next it was back to the here-and-now reality.

He glanced over his shoulder. Sonja was walking down the aisle, clutching the arm attached to a hulking bearlike frame of a man: her father. His unruly mass of gray hair flopped disobediently over one eye. Dr. Radovanović looked more like a scruffy teenager in a suit than the leader of Republika Srpska. What right did he have to lob fifteen hundred shells a day onto innocent people trapped in besieged Sarajevo?

Bosnian Serbs had refused to take part and vote in the Bosnia-Herzegovina independence referendum, maintaining their allegiance to Serbia proper. So far, Republika Srpska did not enjoy any semblance of international recognition—diplomatic or political—but militarily, they continued to defeat Bosnian government forces, gaining territory, and ethnically cleansing the enemy to order. If marrying Sonja Radovanović could help stop this, Steele was ready and willing. *More useful than riding around on a horse playing ceremonial "tin soldiers" in London,* he thought.

Sonja glanced up as she approached the altar. Shadows danced across her face behind a cream lace veil. She reached

Steele and placed her hand on his forearm. Steele thought it was amazing how some women had a touch that could send a sensual shiver down your spine. They were few and far between—but Sonja was definitely one of them. He had known immediately after their first kiss at the top of the ski lift.

"Ready?" Steele said, smiling, the corners of his eyes crinkling.

"Yes, ready."

As Steele began to discover all he needed to know about the Bosnian Serb first family, he was beginning to find Sonja more and more attractive. He wished he hadn't promised to report back every morsel of info to his masters in Sarajevo. For now, the marriage meant nothing to him, but he started to think it might. The more he thought about how his brother had fallen in love with Sonja, the more he felt he might be heading for the same fate. But this marriage would have no legal standing. It was a show, and that was all … at least for the time being.

Facing the altar, he stared at the man-sized gold iconostasis in front of him.

Our Holy Father Peter of Galateia stared back. But this was war—albeit someone else's—and lives depended on his performance. Muslims, Serbs, and Croats weren't the only lives at stake. The international community—Britain, France, the Netherlands, Belgium, Egypt, Pakistan, Russia, Malaya, and others had sent blue helmet or blue beret UN troops for peacekeeping duties in a country few of their soldiers had even heard of. The whole world was in Sarajevo, but few, it seemed, had any clue how to stop the war.

It was a complex scenario. No one was stopping the shelling, raping, and ethnic cleansing to give history lessons. Sonja had given her explanation on the way to Pale one day earlier: "Sarajevo is capital of Bosnia-Herzegovina," she explained, "with mainly Muslim population. Bosnian Serbs are mostly peasants and farmers who live in the countryside. But Bosnian Serbs and Croats also live in Sarajevo—many of these stayed when this conflict broke out. They never believe that armed skirmishes would lead to full-blown war."

Steele had agreed it was a mess and had seen the reality for himself. While locals in Sarajevo crisscrossed neighborhood streets searching for bread and water, they were surrounded, bombarded, and shot at by their Bosnian Serb cousins in the hills overlooking the city. Incestuous enemies, he concluded. Former Olympic rifle team men and women on both sides put sharpshooting talent to murderous use. Civilian targets—male and female, no age discrimination—were fair game. Primitive battles were fought around exposed residential neighborhoods amid an ever-shifting confrontation line. The traumatized civilians of Sarajevo were ensnared in a vicious war fueled by decades, even centuries, of hatred and intolerance. Josip Broz Tito, legendary leader of the Socialist Federal Republic of Yugoslavia, had kept a lid on ethnic tensions. But he had died in 1980, and the legacy of his iron fist had finally melted. Steele was starting to fully appreciate the complicated web of history he was now trapped in.

The choir stopped singing.

The Serbian priest chanted an Orthodox prayer and made the sign of the cross. His monotone voice was soporific. Steele recalled his brother's first day in Sarajevo—unusually, Peter had written to Jack about driving a wounded soldier with his lower leg hanging off to the main trauma center, Koševo Hospital. The young soldier was carried into the hospital on a stretcher, the bloody stump and sinews of his lower leg flapping freely—umpteenth landmine victim that day. "Could have been me," Peter had written. "I felt sick. But even the wounded soldier was no preparation for my first visit to the city mortuary—the lingering stench of rotting corpses, children among them, mixed with the unforgettable smell of disinfectant and the stink of death." Now Peter had joined them.

Surrounded by those responsible for so many deaths, the priest continued: "Kapetane Jack Steele, uzimate li za ženu ovde prisutnu Sonju Radovanović?" *Do you, Jack Steele, take here present Sonja Radovanović for your lawful wedded wife?*

"Da." *Yes.* A shiver slithered down his back. He suddenly felt guilty. Was this war really any of his business? Why did the West always think they could crash in and solve other people's messes?

Black robes kissing the stone floor, the priest's dark brown eyes focused intensely on Sonja, as though performing a satanic ritual rather than a marriage ceremony. He asked the same of Sonja.

"Da, uzimam," she replied. *Yes, I do.*

A minute later, the priest made the sign of the cross and declared in Bosnian, "You are now husband and wife. Please kiss your bride. God bless you and protect you in these troubled times."

CHAPTER SEVENTEEN

Steele gingerly raised Sonja's veil. He leaned toward her and kissed her on the lips. They gazed at each other with wide eyes. She wasn't classically beautiful; her face possessed almost a hint of masculinity. But for him, Sonja's eyes possessed compassion and depth he found alluring. Yes, it was her eyes he loved. Sonja stroked his cheek for an instant.

He mentally pinched himself. He had a job to do, but he wondered how far the job would continue into his wedding night. *Perhaps this insane mission has unforeseen advantages after all?*

Glancing around at the largely female congregation, he smiled. Middle and old-aged women looked haggard and lined beyond their years. They had gathered to mark this occasion—"celebration" was a word rarely used nowadays. Their husbands were either dead or on the front line.

Steele's stomach was churning. *Can I really pull off this blasphemous fraud?* he thought wryly. Luckily, in the candlelit church, no one could see the redness in his cheeks or the lie in his heart. He had often wondered what it would be like to stand at the altar, especially since his own mother had never been married. He had never seen a picture of her in the proverbial wedding dress. He had never felt complete, not knowing his father, and he hoped one day that his own marriage might fix that. He wondered if Peter had felt the same way. But now the job came first. His wedding—the real thing—would have to wait.

He took Sonja's hand. "Zdravo ..." *Hello.* He was nervous. If Gen. Zukić, Sonja's godfather, discovered their secret—he'd probably kill him or at least lock him up. Or, he might be tossed into a mass grave near Zvornik or Srebrenica like hundreds of Muslims, possibly thousands according to latest CIA intelligence reports.

Steele said, "You look gorgeous—"

"You too," she replied. "Beautiful boy."

He smiled. "Hardly ... but thanks."

Steele was awaiting further instructions from his military intelligence controllers. Today was the first step: he was an official member of the Bosnian Serb first family. The next step was to get even closer to Sonja and her family and find out as much as he could about their operations: logistics, locations, intentions, and most important of all the date and time when Dr. Radovanović and Gen. Zukić would be in the same location so that British Special Forces—probably the SAS—could swoop down and snatch them.

"Idemo," he said. *Let's go.*

Sonja looked radiant. Her cheeks were the perfect shade of pink. She had the wide eyes of an angel and the skin of a child. They kissed again. Sonja tasted sweet. He could pretend for now.

They processed down the aisle and, reaching the exit, were met by a biting cold wind that originated from Jahorina mountain. Sonja's parents, Dr. Radovanović and his wife, Slavica, followed behind, and they gathered on the steps of the church with family and friends dressed in ill-fitting—many had lost a lot of weight during the war—but prized wedding attire.

For the Bosnian Serbs, Steele thought, this union with Sonja was a symbolic glimmer of hope, a wartime love story—"British reporter weds president's daughter," the local headline would read. Many locals would consider the marriage a PR coup, recognition no less, and perhaps a measure of political support from Robert Grange, the British prime minister, himself. Any kind of recognition would be crucial now that the Bosnian Serbs had categorically rejected the Bosnian Muslim government as their political, military, and religious masters.

With the exception of a UN vehicle, Samarni Brijeg, Pale's main thoroughfare, was deserted. A white 4x4 Toyota 4Runner with large black UN lettering on the sides and roof was waiting outside the church, engine running.

After Steele ushered Sonja down the steps toward the waiting car, he turned and glanced up at the church's gray slate dome and admired the delicate dentil molding and brickwork arches that made Serb Orthodox crkvas so enchanting. Through a gap in the faded apartment buildings opposite, he caught a glimpse of the snowcapped mountains. Their scenic beauty clashed with his images of Sarajevo wartime carnage. The confrontation line, it seemed, separated two planets.

In the cold air, Steele's breath was visible; Sonja's too. The muffled *clump-thump* of artillery shells reverberated like a clay pigeon shoot in the distance. Wedding guests appeared numb to the shelling just as Dr. Radovanović and Slavica seemed oblivious to the escalating devastation caused by their stranglehold on besieged Sarajevo.

Sgt. Thomas got out of the vehicle. "Wait up, sir," he said, jogging around the front of the 4Runner and saluting. "Let me open the door for the happy couple." Sgt. Thomas had been assigned to be Steele's official driver for the day.

Steele saluted. "Thanks for coming, Sgt. Thomas, we're lucky they could spare you."

"Fast ball, sir. No *wucking furries.*"

Sgt. Thomas reached the rear passenger door and held it open for the bride and groom. "Wouldn't have missed it for the world, sir," he said, raising an eyebrow and flashing a cheeky smile at Sonja. "Where to?"

Sonja smiled back. "My father's residence. You are also invited." She turned to Steele, squeezing his hand. "I love you," she said loud enough for everyone to hear.

Playing her part well, Steele thought.

A small cheer erupted behind them followed by some grinning and nods of approval.

"I ja tebe volim," he replied. *And I love you.* That much she had rehearsed with him on the ski slope the day before.

The choirboys threw confetti at them. Tiny scraps of old newspaper fluttered down on the group. Sonja waved her hand to clear the confetti. "Idemo!" *Let's go!* They climbed into the Jeep.

Dr. Radovanović stepped forward and shook Steele's hand through the rear window of the 4x4. He said, "I congratulate both of you. I am very happy for my British son-in-law and my beautiful daughter. Your love means great things for Serb people." The politician in him was unable to resist the crowd, and he turned to include them, wagging his large index finger as though delivering a speech. "We will defeat Turkish aggressor. Mr. Steele will enjoy our beloved country, and your children will live here in peace one day."

A huge explosion rocked the ground.

What the bloody hell!!!! Everyone closed their eyes and waited for the worst. Steele could hear a ringing in his ears as it took him a few moments to grasp if he was alive or dead, and wait for the dust, stone, and glass from the church's windows to settle.

Members of the congregation, the young ones at least, ran for cover. Others were flung to the ground by the blast. At least two perished instantly. Steele's hearing slowly returned, as though resurfacing from under water. A combat fighter jet roared away into the distance high above them, its payload dispatched with deadly precision.

Men, women, and children screamed hysterically. As if in cinematic slow motion, flurries of white plaster, debris, and dust lingered in the air and slowly descended onto the dead and wounded.

Steele's ears were ringing. This could not be happening. *None of the warring factions have warplanes ... This is NATO airspace, damn it!* No one had given warning of an attack, much less one so deadly.

Steele clenched his fists and strained to listen for the aircraft's return. He wound down the shattered windows to prevent them falling in, then slammed the 4Runner's rear doors.

The church was all but demolished. Women and children stumbled around helplessly—blind, arms outstretched, searching for someone or something to touch, feel, or grasp. Blood streamed down faces caked with dirt. Most of the women wore black, but he could see dark patches of blood on their dresses. Local police and soldiers were already on the scene administering help and first aid.

Sonja said, "Drive! Go!"

Steele glanced behind the church where the missile had landed. Old women lay motionless in the rubble—at least three or four dead, maybe more. Slaughter was the only word. This was a direct hit on the church.

Sweet Jesus. Who had sanctioned this massacre?

CHAPTER EIGHTEEN

"In God's name, what happened?" Sonja said, disorientated. Her accent, usually mixed with a trace of American, was thick Bosnian again.

Steele spotted Dr. Radovanović being manhandled into the back of his Mercedes limousine by a scrum of bodyguards. Sonja's father was alive.

"Sonja ..." He gestured to her father.

Sonja saw her father and crossed herself. "But my mother? Where is my mother?"

Steele shook his head and placed his hand on her back to comfort and calm her. With his other hand he reached for hers and held it firmly. "She's probably in the car with your father. I'm sure she's fine."

"I am worried. She can't survive this. You don't know her. She is mentally weak."

Steele scanned the scene. "I don't see her. She must be in the car already."

One ... two ... now three old women were sprawled in the rubble; more were possibly trapped underneath it. Then he saw the boy chorister stumble into the street. His face was ashen, and he was bleeding heavily, his white cassock soaked with blood. The boy collapsed to his knees.

"Wait!" said Steele.

Sgt. Thomas said, "We have to clear the area, sir."

What if that was my boy? Steele thought. "Just wait," he ordered. "I'll be back in a second."

Sgt. Thomas obeyed and slipped the gear lever back into neutral.

Steele jumped out and ran to the boy. *This is my fault.* He had the sinking feeling that his own physical presence at the church was somehow connected to this brutal attack. *But why?* He tore off the boy's jacket and placed it firmly on his chest to stem the flow of blood, maintaining pressure as he secured the sleeves around the boy's skinny torso.

A green VW Golf pulled up beside them, and a man in his late fifties with gray hair jumped out. "Dobro je … Sad je dobro." *It's okay … it's okay now.* The man seemed to be saying that he would take over and presumably take the boy to hospital.

Steele nodded and sprinted back to the Jeep. As he scrambled inside, he heard the man shouting, "Hvala, gospodine." *Thank you, sir.*

Steele made a chopping motion. *"GO! GO! GO!"*

Sgt. Thomas obeyed. He selected first gear, gripped the wheel, and slammed his foot on the accelerator. The UN 4x4 ignited. Steele steadied himself, one hand on the handrail above the window, the other pulling Sonja closer to him. He scanned the sky—no aircraft in sight. In their dark purple and blue camo jumpsuits, Bosnian Serb *policija* swarmed onto the bombsite, arms gesticulating—they were shouting into handheld radios, tending the lucky ones still moving or groaning, ignoring the dead. Rarely exposed to such carnage, the Pale policija zigzagged between the fallen, prioritizing the wounded and searching for signs of life in the injured. Until now, this Serb stronghold had escaped shelling and airstrikes.

Sgt. Thomas sped away. Steele regretted leaving the boy, but at the same time he was confident the boy was in safe hands.

On the edge of town, sirens pierced the air, wailing, screaming. But Steele's mission echoed loud and clear inside his head: *We're counting on you, Jack,* Boyle had said with a firm handshake. *For Queen and country, make us proud, Jack,* he had repeated with a pat on the back. *We need to get those bastards if we want to stop this war.* In retrospect, Steele would later express doubts as to whether the arrest of the Bosnian Serb leadership would do anything at all to bring peace. But for now, he was caught up in the carnage he had witnessed and experienced firsthand.

A second later, another explosion rocked the ground, more deafening than the first.

The aftershock of the impact somewhere near the crkva shook their 4x4 chassis. Sgt. Thomas grappled with the steering wheel to keep control and managed to keep going straight. The unidentified aircraft roared overhead, again pulling away too fast and steep for Steele to identify it.

"Lucky we left when we did," said Steele.

Sgt. Thomas leaned forward over the steering wheel looking at the sky. "It's one of ours, sir."

"Damn it." Steele shook his head in disbelief. *Why would NATO attack the wedding?*

"F-16, looks like. American …"

"Can't they bloody see us?" Steele was spitting with rage. "Can't they see a big fuck-off white Jeep with big fuck-off UN letters on the side?"

"Big time screw up, sir." Sgt. Thomas frowned, the sweat running down his face. "Ops Room knew it was your wedding, sir. They were the ones who sent me here."

Steele nodded. "Of course they knew it. It makes no sense."

Sgt. Thomas was right. If this *was* NATO, someone had made a cataclysmic error. Steele reeled through the possibilities in his mind: Bosnian government? Bosnian Serbs? JNA—Yugoslav People's Army? HVO—The Croatian Defense Council? There was a no-fly zone. *It* had *to be NATO. And that makes even less sense.*

Sgt. Thomas pointed to the black dot in the sky. "He buzzed us, sir, when you were inside the church. Honestly, I thought he'd come to wish you luck."

"Get us out of here."

"Where to, sir?"

"Sarajevo, via Pale checkpoint."

"Roger that, sir. And Miss Sonja?"

Steele looked at Sonja. "I think she should come with us."

"I can't," she said. "I have to get back to my father."

"Let's find out what the hell is going on first."

Halfway down the mountain road to Sarajevo, the Pale check-point consisted of a wooden pole rested across two plastic chairs in the middle of the road next to a small hut.

"Don't stop for anyone," Steele said.

"Yes, sir."

Steele turned to Sonja. "I'm sorry. It'll be okay, I promise. There must be an explanation."

Sonja looked at him. He suspected that she had read his expression perfectly: *I have no clue on God's earth what just happened.*

"Okay, you're right," Steele said. "This makes no sense."

"My father will kill those responsible ..." Her eyes teared, but she spoke defiantly. "This is crazy. I don't understand ... this is my fault. I should not have married you. I should not have listened to Fitzgerald."

"It's not your fault, Sonja. Trust me."

He gave her a hug, but wondered if she would ever trust him again.

Steele glanced left and right out of the windows and got his bearings from the twisted metal skeleton that was once the Sarajevo Winter Olympics bobsleigh run. A galaxy of bullet holes peppered the layers of terracotta rust. The skeletal bobsleigh was a reminder of the good old days—a former Yugoslavia when

Serbs, Croats, and Muslims celebrated, not desecrated, their multicultural roots and Tito, their leader. The derelict structure snaked next to the road for a few seconds before disappearing into snow-laden fir trees.

Usually, five or six soldiers, AK47s at the high port, hovered at the checkpoint. Now it was deserted.

Sgt. Thomas said, "Let's hope they didn't leave any surprises."

Steele knew he meant landmines, which were often scattered across roads and tracks in disputed territory to keep the enemy at bay and disrupt UN freedom of movement. They were more reliable than hungry Serb conscripts. Landmines didn't wander off in search of food, cigarettes, and *rakija*.

Steele leaned forward, scanning the checkpoint, and searching for hazards. "Steady … Slow down."

Sonja let go of his arm. "Our country is more important to my father than me."

Steele frowned. "Not true."

"My father … He did not try to save me. You saw this. He left without me."

She was right. Immediately after the first explosion, the unscathed Dr. Radovanović had not even looked or called out for his daughter. "Your father's men were doing their job," Steele said. "There was nothing he could do."

"Thank you," she said. "But we both know that's not true."

Sgt. Thomas saw a vehicle blocking the road and tapped the brakes. Two British soldiers were standing next to a British Army Land Rover, the preferred transport of the British SAS, known here on the ground as Joint Commission Observers—JCOs.

"Thank God," said Steele. "Our knights in shining armor."

Sgt. Thomas nodded. "Right, sir. It's one of ours."

"You know them?"

"Big bastard on the right … hangs out at UNPROFOR HQ. His name's Yomper. Cocky bastard, they say, bit of a maverick."

Steele said, "I know him. He's a good man."

"What does he want?" Sonja asked.

"I've no idea," Steele replied.

Sgt. Thomas eased off the accelerator and the vehicle rolled to a stop.

Both SAS troopers raised their weapons and took aim at the 4Runner. Steele was surprised. He'd expected a friendly welcome, especially after the devastation in Pale. At least they weren't Bosnian Serb paramilitaries who might detain them for hours. The SAS had probably been sent to escort them safely back to Sarajevo. *Who dares wins:* The SAS motto sprang to mind. *You can count on the boys from Hereford,* he thought. *At least I hope so.*

Sgt. Thomas switched off the engine. They opened the doors to get out—

"Stay put, sir," Yomper shouted. "Hands where we can see 'em."

"What's going on? It's me, Captain Steele." Steele was wearing civies, but surely Yomper recognized him even if he was inside a vehicle.

Yomper made no acknowledgment that he knew Steele.

Sgt. Thomas said quietly, "Do as he says, sir. They're jumpy fuckers—trigger-happy."

Steele put his hands up and nodded for Sonja to do likewise.

"Keep your hands on the wheel," the second SAS trooper said slowly.

Sgt. Thomas obeyed.

Steele looked at Sonja. "Don't worry, everything's going to be okay."

"You said that already, and things just got much worse."

Sonja was right. Steele was way out of his comfort zone. *Nothing makes sense.*

Yomper spoke softly into a Clansman radio strapped to his chest.

Then the unmistakable *chuck-chuck-chuck* of an RAF Chinook twin-engine helicopter grew louder until it hovered a hundred feet above them. Fresh snow and ice swirled and billowed around them, torpedoed from the trees by the Chinook's twin rotor blades.

Yomper cautiously approached the 4Runner, jamming his SA80 rifle into his shoulder with one arm. With the other arm, he opened the door, leaned in, and pulled Sonja—albeit gently—from the vehicle. "Come with me, Miss," he said politely.

"What the hell's going on?" Steele turned—

"Do yourself a favor, sir. Shut the fuck up," said the second SAS trooper.

"SAS or no—" began Steele.

Yomper said, "Best to wind your neck in, sir."

Message understood—end of protest, for now.

There was no mistake here and no confusion. British Special Forces, the SAS no less, were abducting Sonja from under his nose, and he was helpless. The frustration made his stomach churn.

He watched as the Chinook's rescue harness was lowered. Yomper stood behind Sonja and slipped the harness over her head and arms. She looked at Steele, and from her expression, he could tell she blamed *him* for everything.

Sonja did not resist.

Yomper looked up high above them and gave the thumbs-up to the helicopter crewman whose legs dangled in the open doorway of the Chinook. The crewman acknowledged Yomper, and Sonja rose into the air like a pantomime fairy on a theatrical wire. She reached the aircraft and was pulled inside.

The Chinook banked away with its precious cargo as quickly as it had arrived. Yomper and his colleague climbed into their Rover. "Wait five, sir, then you can go. And don't take it personal. This came from the top."

"Where are you taking her?" asked Steele.

"Somewhere safe, sir."

Steele watched the Chinook disappear into the distance. The SAS Land Rover executed a tricky five-point turn on the ice and slithered its way down the narrow mountain pass toward Sarajevo.

Steele climbed into the front passenger seat. "Give it a minute, then back to the Residency."

"Roger that, sir," Sgt. Thomas replied. "Bloody hell, sir. What the fuck was that all about?"

"No bloody clue."

"Me neither, sir."

CHAPTER NINETEEN

UNPROFOR HQ, Sarajevo

Steele took two paces forward, pulled his feet in, and saluted—British style—long way up, short way down. "What's going on, Colonel?"

It was less than two hours since the Pale air strike, and no one had said anything as he entered the UN HQ. Nothing on the radio about the attack on the way in either. It was as though it had never happened.

Col. Edward Boyle sat behind his desk, his gray hair slicked back. He looked up with sunken eyes and forced a smile.

"Come in, Jack. Good to see you." He slid a tray across his desk toward Steele. "Tea? Coffee? Powdered milk, I'm afraid. Don't want to upset the natives." He gestured toward a metal-framed chair opposite. "Have a pew."

Behind him, a British Army clerk shut the door, rattling the battered windows crisscrossed with brown tape—a half-hearted attempt to make them blast proof. For more than thirty months, Bosnian Serb artillery had pounded the city with up to fifteen hundred shells a day. UNPROFOR HQ had often been targeted, sometimes for no other reason than the Bosnian Serbs felt their demands to the UN were being ignored. But even the Bosnian government, it was rumored, had ordered the shelling of UN headquarters for publicity and to draw attention to the UN's unsuccessful attempts to deliver fuel and food aid into their besieged city. The civilians had been squeezed beyond breaking point … again … and again … and again. It was official—Sarajevo really was hell on earth.

At the start of the mission two days earlier, Boyle had slapped Steele on the back and wished him well. Steele didn't know Boyle's precise rank or position, and knew better than to ask outright. Rather than military intelligence as the police inspector in London had said, Steele suspected SIS—Secret Intelligence Service—otherwise known as MI6. The man's crumpled uniform, the length of his hair, and his lackadaisical army salute suggested he *was* a civilian. Every time Steele saw him in person, he liked Boyle less and less—clandestine meetings, seemingly impossible tasks, and a certain rogue nature all led Steele to think he would end up in a very bad place. But then he thought: *Peter... I'm doing this for Peter.*

Steele sat down. "Coffee, please. NATO standard …" *NATO standard* was British Army speak for milk and two sugars.

Steele waited patiently for an explanation. The smell of freshly brewed NAAFI—Navy, Army, and Air Force Institutes—coffee blended with the unpleasant stench of a nearby urinal wafting down the corridor. Anyone who'd spent time in Sarajevo was used to the smell. Sewage and human waste had to be manually flushed with buckets of water collected by hand from UN-manned bowsers and standpipes dotted around the city. Even UNPROFOR was subject to water rationing.

Steele scraped back the short strands of black hair plastered across his forehead. He had been sweating profusely during and after the Pale attack. It was the first time Steele had seen the mysterious Boyle sitting behind a desk in an actual office. So, he *was* part of the operational establishment after all? But which part?

A small desk lamp with a black metal shade cast its shadow across the senior officer's bony face. Boyle had a long neck and torso, and an unusually large Adam's apple, which Steele found himself staring at. Boyle stirred both cups longer than necessary while staring back at Steele.

Finally, Boyle said, "Congratulations, you're still in one piece."

"Not much to celebrate."

"You're alive, aren't you?"

Steele didn't respond, even though Boyle had a good point. He *was* lucky to be alive. The Pale crkva had taken a direct hit. Thirty seconds earlier and the entire wedding party would have perished, including himself. "Did they deliberately miss the target?" Steele asked. "Or did they screw up?"

Boyle sipped his coffee. "Only five deaths, thank goodness."

"What happened?"

Boyle shook his head. "Most unfortunate. I understand your frustration. Collateral damage, I'm afraid."

"I'd love an explanation."

"Sorry, Jack. It's classified."

Steele paused. Boyle was deadly serious. *Supercilious bastard.*

"Where's Sonja?" he asked.

"Also classified. Not to worry. She's fine."

"Colonel—"

"I'm sorry, Jack."

"Where she is?"

Boyle stared at Steele for a few seconds. Then, almost snorting with amusement as the lightbulb went off, he said, "Don't tell me you've fallen for her? The wedding was pretend, remember?"

"Of course."

"Could get *very* complicated if you've fallen for her, Jack. What is it with the Steele boys?"

It had been many years since someone referred to them as *the Steele boys.*

"We thrive on complications. I think you'll agree my mission is pretty complicated."

"*Was* ..." Boyle paused. "We have a situation, Jack. Change of plan and government policy, you might say. No one knows how this war is going to play out. It's not looking good."

Steele still wanted an explanation. "A warning would have been helpful."

"I understand."

"It might have saved my life."

"Driver was supposed to warn you. Prize cock-up. Like I said, all very unfortunate."

"You gave me this mission. I deserve an explanation."

Boyle frowned and leaned forward. "It's not a Q-and-A session, Jack." His voice dripped with sarcasm. "You are paid to do your duty, which includes obeying orders. No one owes you an explanation. Let's leave it at that, shall we?" He forced another plastic smile.

Steele's cheeks reddened. He wasn't finished. "NATO bombs us, innocent civilians are taken out, the SAS abducts Sonja, and you want me to *leave it at that*?"

Boyle frowned. "I'd keep those observations to yourself if I were you. Or you may find yourself—"

"You're threatening me now?"

"You decide."

"Screw this." Steele surprised himself. Swearing at a senior officer was a court-martial offense; he needed to rein it in. But Steele didn't believe this man was an army officer, and he was furious to have been used as cannon fodder for whatever nefarious reasons.

"Are you in love with her?" asked Boyle.

"Of course not," Steele lied. He wasn't sure how he felt ... it wasn't out of the question that he was falling for Sonja.

"Then why all the fuss?"

"They *bombed* us—"

"We've been sucked into a bloody civil war in case you hadn't noticed. Sarajevo is one of the longest sieges in modern warfare. We don't have time to concern ourselves with your emotions. No one gives a shit about the Radovanović family. Do you understand? We just need to round them up and have done with it."

"Where's Sonja?"

Boyle formed his fingertips into a steeple and bounced his fingers gently against his lips. "She's in good hands."

"I promised her father—"

"Radovanović is playing a dangerous game. The international community is gunning for him. He's the last man on earth I would make promises to."

"That's why you sent me to Pale, remember? To get close to them?" Steele exhaled with frustration. "Okay, what's the latest on General Zukić?"

"Radovanović and Zukić are murdering, raping thugs. General Zukić is on a mission to exterminate 'marauding Turks'— his words for Muslims. General Zukić stands by while his men slit the throats of children."

"You believe that?"

"I'm afraid so. We have witnesses. The village of Potočari two days ago."

"*Shit.*"

"Precisely. We have to take these buggers out once and for all. This is Europe, not bloody Afghanistan. We can't allow this to go on."

"I was getting close to them."

"You have every reason to be pissed off. It was worth a try. But the future of the European Union and peace in Europe is at stake. NATO, UN, EU and the United States all have their interests. It's not easy to keep everyone happy. This is an extremely fluid and dangerous situation."

A loud rumble shook the sky. It wasn't thunder.

Boyle looked at his watch. "They've started ... bless their little 50 millimeter mortar rounds. Right on time."

As evening beckoned, the grind of mortars and artillery shells, and the crackle of small-arms fire punctuated their conversation. Serbs pounded Muslim positions yet again, and Muslims returned with small-arms fire, which was about as effective as shooting paintballs.

Steele continued, "What am I supposed to do? Pretend this never happened?"

"Yes—"

"I married the girl. I'm concerned."

"The wedding was a sham. You did well to get as far as you did."

"We got married—"

"Which is why you're being RTUed. You fly back home tomorrow. I've briefed your commanding officer. He's looking forward to your return. The Queen's in residence and the cavalry blacks miss you."

"Very funny." Steele shook his head. *There's no way I'm being "returned to unit."*

His mouth tightened. Ceremonial mounted duties in the heart of tourist London were the last thing he needed after the past twenty-four hours. Or perhaps he was wrong? Perhaps it was *exactly* what he needed? Then he thought about Peter. *I can't let Peter down.*

"Take my advice, Jack, put it all behind you," continued Boyle. "Enjoy London. Go to the pub. Play some polo. That's what you donkey wallopers are good at, isn't it?"

"I don't play polo."

"Croquet then?"

"I don't believe this." Steele stood up.

Boyle said, "General Brown's order. It's final. And yes, you can go now."

Gen. Brown was known to be a no-nonsense, ex-Special Forces commander who, the men liked to say, "didn't fuck about." His decision was *always* final.

"Nothing personal. I'm just the messenger."

Steele didn't believe him, but there was nothing else he could do.

Boyle leaned back in his chair, signaling that their meeting was over. "Sergeant Thomas will drive you to Split at zero-six-hundred hours tomorrow. Report to the adjutant at Divulje Barracks. He'll get you on the next flight back to Blighty."

"Colonel—"

"Thank you for your contribution. I'm sure General Brown will write you a glowing report."

"He hardly knows me."

Again, the fake smile. "Trust me. He knows all he needs to know."

Steele took a step backward and clicked his heels—a cavalry tradition—even though his uniform was still in his backpack, which had been returned to him by UNMO Pale. "Permission-to-carry-on, Colonel, please?" he said begrudgingly.

Boyle nodded.

Steele felt sick as he closed the door. He was gutted. *This can't be happening ...*

Outside, he crossed the gravel path to the transit accommodation—two gray Portacabins perched on cinder blocks. He entered, took a deep breath, and regretted it. Again, the acrid smell of urine lingered. Sanitation was abominable. "Time to get out of this shit hole," he muttered. *But* not *to London ...*

The only good news—and it wasn't much—was that on Wednesdays, the French infantry battalion handed out quarter bottles of red *vin de table* with the evening meal. Steele would be first in line.

CHAPTER TWENTY

Ivančevo Village, Central Bosnia

The village of Ivančevo perches on a mountain hairpin bend halfway between Sarajevo and Tuzla. Yomper and his 2IC—second-in-command—Corporal Jim Dawes, made use of the rustic seclusion for interrogations. Less than two hours from Sarajevo, it was their preferred safe house, far enough from the international media circus for them to work undisturbed.

There were only ten single-story homes in the village of Ivančevo. Most of them had been boarded up and secured by the owners. Bosnian Muslims had fled from attacking Bosnian Croats, and several weeks later when the confrontation line had shifted again, Bosnian Croats had returned to eject Bosnian Muslims. Yomper couldn't keep up with *the twat-head politics* and *bullshite*, as he called it. Whatever your ethnic roots in this war—Muslim, Croat, Serb or bloody Eskimo—you were screwed. But he wouldn't lose any sleep over the victims. This wasn't *his* war, and he had a mortgage to pay, as well as his aged mother's exorbitant nursing home fees.

Boyle had approached Yomper in a Camden Town pub in London a few months earlier and made him an offer he couldn't refuse—especially since Yomper's identity had been compromised due to a Ministry of Defense clerical error. He was unable to work undercover in warzones for the SAS. Boyle invited Yomper to join an elite private security firm known as Black Cobra. But this was not its real name. Yomper had no idea who he was working for exactly but was assured that the British Army would not interfere with the arrangement. He shook hands with Boyle and was handed an envelope with a fist full of notes amounting to an obscene amount of money for a private solider.

He had received *two* monthly salaries ever since, Black Cobra's compensation far outweighing his army salary.

Another UN convoy—third one today, fourteen trucks—thundered through Ivančevo village bound for Tuzla. Trucks passing just inches from the buildings splattered mud and dirt onto the walls and windows of the houses. These single-track roads were not made for UN humanitarian aid convoys. A piece of glass from the kitchen window smashed onto the floor as the convoy shook the safe house. The noise of the trucks was deafening. Yomper waited for the convoy to clear.

"That's it," he said. "Let's do it."

Standing in the cramped kitchen, he took out a manila folder from his Bergen backpack. A passport-sized photograph of Sonja Radovanović was stapled to the top right-hand corner. Flipping through the file, Yomper gestured toward the front door. "Make sure it's locked," he said.

"No fucker stops here anyway," said Dawes, briefly picking his nose as he walked over to check the door.

"We don't take chances, remember?"

Dawes nodded and rattled the front door. "What's she in for, boss?"

"Same as always, she's got something they want."

"What?"

"I don't know exactly. It's something worth snatching her from a British UNMO captain. And, by the way, she's Radovanović's daughter."

"Fuck me sideways. Sweet." Dawes wiped his sweaty hands on his combat trousers. He opened the door to the basement.

Yomper closed the file. "Go easy. Don't damage the merchandise."

"Short and sharp," said Dawes. "Just how we like it. Let's see what she knows."

UNPROFOR HQ, Sarajevo

Miles away at UNPROFOR headquarters in downtown Sarajevo, Boyle knocked on Gen. Brown's door. Boyle considered himself exempt from reporting to anyone outside his masters in London. Although his rank and uniform were sheer pretense, he was supposed to pay lip service to Gen. Brown's UN command and keep him in the loop on operational matters. But in reality, as far as Boyle was concerned, this meant keeping Gen. Brown in the dark as much as possible. Boyle, working for the private security firm known as Black Cobra, was fully aware that no one else in this small theater of war knew the truth—it was Boyle who was in charge of a small top-secret operation known only to the prime minister and a security services inner circle. Juggling all the various governmental and national players was tricky to say the least.

Boyle entered and made a half-hearted attempt to salute, but was taken aback when he saw that Sir Lawrence Fitzgerald was also in the room.

Gen. Brown looked up. "Where's Steele?"

"I've sent him packing. RTUed him," said Boyle. He turned to Fitzgerald. "I thought we agreed your sphere of operations is Split?"

"You thought wrong."

"Better watch that ticker of yours, Sir Lawrence, coming this far up country."

"Nonsense, my dear Boyle. When people start to take me for a fool, I'll go anywhere to prove them wrong."

Gen. Brown looked at Boyle and said, "What's your plan?"

"We've taken Sonja. We want to see how much she's willing to bend—for the love of her people. Now that she knows we mean business."

Fitzgerald unzipped his Barbour jacket and said, "You've done what?" His voice was staccato in disbelief. "That was not part—"

"Calm down, Sir Lawrence. Before you have a heart attack."

Gen. Brown shook his head. "I don't like this, Boyle, or whatever your real name is." He pressed an intercom button and said, "Brian, step in for a moment."

The door opened and Maj. Brian Small, Gen. Brown's aide, scuttled into the office.

Gen. Brown said, "My understanding is that Captain Steele is under *my* command."

"That's right," said Maj. Small.

Gen. Brown turned to Boyle and looked him in the eye. "Steele speaks Bosnian and is now officially married to Sonja Radovanović, which is the scenario I thought we were aiming for?"

Boyle nodded. For now, he would play along and give away as little as possible. "Correct."

Fitzgerald said, "Forgive me, but what the hell are you really doing here? I've spent fifty years living in this country, and I know the people. What you asked me to do in London I did for *them*. What you asked of me in Split, ditto. But you forgot to mention NATO air assaults on the people whose hearts and minds we were in the process of winning over."

Fitzgerald then did something that surprised everyone given his age. He reached out and caught Boyle by the scruff of the neck. "You need to tell us what the bloody hell is going on?"

"That's enough," Gen. Brown said.

Fitzgerald released his grip on Boyle, and for the first time since Boyle could remember, he needed a few seconds to recover his composure.

Gen. Brown continued, flaring his nostrils. "I thought we sent Steele to Pale for a reason: We are trying to round up the Bosnian Serb leadership. That's what I thought this was about. War crimes? The next thing I know"—Gen. Brown glared at

Boyle—"you've all but started World War Three on a church in Pale. How am I supposed to stop these buggers fighting and make peace?"

Boyle said calmly, "We were using him as bait, General. Like his brother, Steele is young and keen, and perfect for the task. And that suits us. Or rather, *suited* us."

Gen. Brown stood up. "Damn it, get to the point. Bosnian Serbs are digging their heels in. NATO is on my back and about to start a war. Tell me what you're up to before I have you escorted on the next flight out of Sarajevo."

Boyle smiled. *Bless him*, he thought. *So loyal ... so earnest and full of integrity. Time to feed Brown a tidbit to keep him on side.* "First off, Steele is entirely expendable. Secondly, we need him to really want this. That's why I've sent him packing. If he truly wants to help, if he wants to make a sacrifice, he needs to do it for *him*."

Fitzgerald said, "I don't follow."

"He needs to get 'involved' with Sonja for real. Not because we ordered him to. The only way I can see that happening is to let him go it alone. Let him go native. Then we can monitor him, but his 'performance' will be genuine and hopefully work in our favor."

Gen. Brown said, "But that's precisely what he was doing."

Fitzgerald raised his bony hand, nodding slowly, and gave an ironic smile. "Now I understand," he said slowly. "Your goal is to *assassinate* them. Not arrest them. Both Gen. Zukić *and* the Bosnian Serb president ... That's what this is all about."

Boyle ignored the hypothesis. "Gentlemen, you might have heard about the Sarajevo Protocol. Our understanding is that if the Protocol is found and our information is correct, the Bosnian Serbs will *never* make peace. Bosnia's neighbors, Turkey and Greece, will inevitably be sucked into the conflict with catastrophic consequences. And the Russians would almost certainly take sides with the Bosnian Serbs ... It would be World War Three in the heart of Europe."

Gen. Brown asked, "What's in this damn Protocol, for God's sake?"

"It's a document. But it's complicated and classified."

"Don't patronize me, Boyle. When your people need help, you're the first to come running. I'm not asking for the crown jewels. I just want to be kept in the loop."

Boyle exhaled. "I'll share what I can."

Gen. Brown asked, "How do you know it's even authentic, this Sarajevo Protocol?"

Fitzgerald remained silent.

Boyle said, "We're confident the document is genuine. If it's made public, the Bosnian Serbs will never give up their fight for sovereignty in Bosnia-Herzegovina. The war will go on for a decade."

Gen. Brown said, "I've told Gen. Zukić that he has two days to withdraw heavy weapons from Sarajevo and Goražde. I don't want to use NATO, but I might have to. Where's the Protocol?"

"We don't know. That's the problem. But right now, I believe Steele might be our best hope of finding it. He's close to the Radovanović family, and they want it too. He thinks he's heading home tomorrow."

"Why send him home?" asked Fitzgerald, trying make sense of Boyle's reasoning.

"If he returns to Split, then he's not the man for the job. If he heads back to Pale to take matters into his own hands, we can make real progress."

Gen. Brown drew a deep breath and exhaled. "You have two days. NATO's chomping at the bit to level Serb fire positions. It's a great opportunity for them to show their firepower. They're out for blood. I hope your plan works."

Boyle said, "I understand, General. Right now, Steele thinks Sonja's in danger. I suspect he will try to find her."

Gen. Brown said, "Why so sure?"

"Why wouldn't he? He's young and inexperienced. And fortunately for us, he's already emotionally involved. If he had any doubts about her being in danger, dropping the NATO bomb on Pale convinced him."

Gen. Brown shook his head. "That's obscene." He paused and said quietly, "I don't approve of anyone using my officers as bait."

"If or when we need to go public with progress on the peace process, the media will trust a British Army officer. It'll work in our favor."

Brown sucked his cheeks in as though he had a toothache. "Are you sure about this Protocol thing? What if you're wrong?"

"London says the consequences are too unthinkable to ignore."

There was a knock on the door. "Sir!"

"Enter," said Maj. Small.

"Urgent signal, sir," said the army clerk. She stepped smartly into the room, brought her feet in and saluted. She handed Maj. Small a signal, saluted again and exited.

Maj. Small studied the signal. "Oh, Christ," he said. "We have less time than we thought."

Gen. Brown frowned. "Now what?"

"The Germans are pushing for a vote on Bosnia," said Maj. Small. "Today."

"In Strasbourg?"

"Looks like it. They want sovereignty."

Gen. Brown said, "Sovereignty? First they recognize Croatia. And now Bosnia? Are they insane? Recognition of Bosnia-Herzegovina would be a catastrophe."

Maj. Small nodded. "No question. Probably no coincidence that Klaus Reithoffer just became president of the European Union. Germans hold all the cards now."

Boyle said, "General Brown, we must find the Protocol. I also agree that it's too early for Bosnia's recognition." The satellite phone he carried at all times vibrated. He unclipped the small carrycase and noted the caller ID. "It's London."

Gen. Brown said, "Tell them we don't have a magic wand,

and we don't like what we're hearing from Strasbourg." He gave Boyle an icy glare. "Where *is* Sonja?"

"With Yomper at the safe house in Ivančevo."

"Say no more. I'll have her returned to her father tomorrow."

Boyle nodded. "Makes sense. Let's hope Steele takes the bait."

Gen. Brown said, "I'll make sure of it."

Boyle added, "You might want to stay in Sarajevo, General. Let your boys do the transfer."

"Thank you, Boyle. And you might want to shut the fuck up."

CHAPTER TWENTY-ONE

9:15 am Hotel Panorama, Pale

Earlier that morning, Steele had changed into British Army combats, his UN blue beret complete with an officer's embroidered UN badge. He had hitched a ride with UNMO Pale from Sarajevo back to Pale. To hell with Sgt. Thomas and the ride to Split. To hell with the courts-martial as he officially went AWOL for disobeying Boyle's order. Sarajevo Airport was closed again, so it would have meant enduring the six-hour bumpy ride back to Split, then an equally uncomfortable Hercules C130 flight to London and back to meaningless oblivion, which is how he now saw life there. It was true, once you had experienced an active war zone, ordinary life seemed less important and verging on banal. When people were willing to shoot their neighbor and success was measured in swatches of land lost or gained, life took on a sharper dimension.

Steele scrutinized the tank convoy from his table at the window in the Hotel Panorama restaurant. He and Staci had a clear view of the road and were stunned into near silence as they watched the cavalry arrive—literally. They could hear the squeak and grind of heavy metal tank tracks churning across the snow, gravel, and potholes on the road to Goražde. The column of T74s came into view—this was a blatant and unapologetic violation of Gen. Brown's ban on heavy weapons and armor inside the Sarajevo demilitarized zone. But still worse, these tanks were heading toward the small, near-defenseless Bosnian enclave of Goražde.

The UNMOs had told Steele that lone tanks in Pale were commonplace. But in these numbers—there were two tank squadrons at least—the signs were ominous. Then it dawned on him. Either Bosnian Serbs forces were going to surrender their armor to UN collection points—chances slim to none with pigs on top—or they were on the offensive as Staci had suggested two days before when they had first met at the café.

"Oh my God," said Steele, "they're heading East to Goražde."

Staci nodded. "Looks that way."

They watched for several minutes as the tanks—a seemingly endless armored juggernaut—rolled by. The column moved nontactically—hatches open, commanders' heads poking out for fresh air before they went tactical again near Goražde. Steele sipped at his espresso but had no appetite for the side of eggs he had just ordered.

Staci said, "I'm glad you came back."

"I was in two minds, trust me."

"I can't believe they took Sonja."

"We'll get her back somehow. She's one of the reasons I'm here."

Staci sipped her coffee. "If the Serbs attack Goražde, Muslims will be slaughtered."

"That's the second reason."

"And NATO—can they or will they do anything?"

"NATO will crush the Bosnian Serbs." Steele shook his head. "I don't get it. Why would the Serbs risk that?"

"I need to talk to Luka Rakić."

"Impossible. All telephone lines are down."

"I have to warn him. He has family—two children."

"You don't think he knows? He's the mayor, for Christ's sake."

"Why should he?"

"Maybe the UNMO's are doing their job and reporting the illegal movements of Bosnian Serb heavy armor."

"What about Sonja? Do you think she will contact Luka if *you* ask her?"

"Boyle told me they were keeping her safe. I've no idea where she is."

Staci took a deep breath and exhaled. "Will you come with me?"

Steele did not answer. He stared out the window at the tanks lining up at the bottom of the driveway on the main road. "Well, it's either ride horses in London or do something useful and make sure you don't get yourself killed."

"Yes! Now you sound more like Peter." She gave a nonchalant double tap on the table.

Steele leaned back and interlaced his fingers behind his head. "We need to find this Protocol before the Serbs do, and we need Luka and Sonja to talk to each other. As there's no sign of Sonja and I can't go back to Sarajevo, I suppose we head east."

Staci smiled. Then she said, "There's only one problem."

"I know. How do we get to Goražde?"

"Precisely."

"Let me think about it."

"And I need to call Sarajevo if we are going to do this. I have to let my editor know."

"No problem. We can go to the UNMO office."

"Thanks."

"Thank me when we get to Goražde."

"Roger that, sir," she said with a British accent.

Goražde, Eastern Bosnia

After more than an hour of relentless pounding, the Serb shelling finally subsided. The morning onslaught was over. Dražen Rakić, a rangy fifteen-year-old Muslim boy with a shaggy black mop and the beginnings of facial hair, opened the pantry door in the kitchen of the two-bedroom apartment. He didn't know it yet, but Dražen would play a pivotal role in the outcome—good or bad depended on which side you were on—of the Bosnia war.

The boy peered through the gaps in the tape that covered the kitchen window. Shielding his eyes from daylight, he said, "It's okay … it's okay. Chetniks missed us today."

To Muslims, all Serbs were *Chetniks*, a pejorative slur and reference to Serbian-nationalist and royalist paramilitary organizations, which had operated in the Balkans during both World Wars.

The windowless pantry wasn't an underground shelter, of course. But it was the safest place in an apartment under mortar and artillery fire. No one dared use municipal shelters once shelling began—safer to stay home and off the streets.

Dražen, Amira, his mother, and Selma, his sister, had been sitting in the dark for nearly three hours. As soon as the sirens began to wail, the power had been cut. Every half hour Dražen had lit one of their rationed candles for a few minutes for a break from the dark. Luka, his father, had taught him to be responsible and to take charge in Luka's absence.

Today's barrage had been more intense than ever before. When would it end? For now, at least, Dražen was ignorant of recent death and destruction in the streets. Dražen's father, Luka Rakić, had been a prominent Sarajevo journalist and was now mayor of Goražde. He would be home soon.

"Come on, you guys, it's okay," said Dražen, coaxing his family out of their shelter.

Plastic sheeting, courtesy of the United Nations High Commission for Refugees—UNHCR—covered the kitchen windows but let sunlight stream through. Dražen opened a small cupboard in the kitchen and took out a cylindrical metal biscuit tin with Lady Diana wearing her royal-blue engagement outfit on the side. It was time for their treat, and Dražen was in charge of the biscuit tin and its contents.

Dražen and Selma each took a piece of shortbread. As he stuffed the bag back into the tin, he paused to glance at the tattered envelope wedged at the bottom with initials scribbled on the outside.

S. P.

As always, he was tempted to look inside the envelope. As always, he hesitated and did not. His father had given strict instructions to open the envelope only in the event of Luka's death. This was their secret. Dražen replaced the bag and slid the tin back onto the top shelf behind some empty cereal boxes.

From a lower shelf, he took a plastic bag sealed with a metal clasp. Inside was a hunk of stale bread. The family had rationed it, eating only tiny portions every day. He took out four plates, broke the bread, and put a piece on each plate. He set the fourth plate aside for his father.

Dražen scurried around the kitchen preparing lunch. The shelling had stopped, and his father would be home any minute. He struck a match and lit a candle. Then he placed a large metal cup of water atop a small wire frame made from a coat hanger over the candle flame. The water would eventually boil, and he would use it to make mint tea, his father's favorite hot drink. Dražen carefully stirred the leaves to infuse as much flavor as possible without the leaves disintegrating. Until the next UN or nongovernmental organization (NGO) aid convoy penetrated Serb checkpoints, their breakfast, lunch, and dinner would be stale bread and mint tea.

"I hate this food," said Selma.

"Be grateful," snapped Dražen. "It's more than our soldiers on the front line get. Most of our people have nothing—"

The front door opened.

Luka Rakić entered, his brow heavily furrowed. His long, wavy gray hair that complimented his beard was scraped back over his head. He looked at his family and sat down at the rickety kitchen table. After a few moments, he seemed to relax a little and managed a smile. As long as his papa was smiling, Dražen had hope and a small flicker of cheer.

Luka reached into his jacket pocket and carefully unwrapped a wad of paper tissues. Inside were two squares of dark chocolate. Brother and sister each took a piece.

"Hvala, tata. Baš ti hvala," said Dražen. *Thanks, papa. Thanks so much.*

Luka finished a mouthful of bread and said, "Terrible news today."

Casualty figures, Dražen thought. It had been another day of indiscriminate shelling. "Why does the world allow this? When will they help us, tata?"

Luka shook his head. "Seventy-nine today."

"How many dead?" asked Dražen. He had assumed seventy-nine wounded.

"Seventy-nine dead—one third of them young ones. One hundred eighty-nine wounded. The hospital is at breaking point." Luka took a sip of his tea then pushed his plate away without finishing the bread. "Thank you, my boy. Tata's not hungry today."

★   ★   ★

Dražen always watched his father leave for work and longed for the day when he could go with him. Through a slit in the plastic sheeting, he watched his father close the gate and walk down the street.

When the first shell landed, Dražen was stunned for a few seconds. Then he was terrified. His father had disappeared from view moments before. Dražen did not dive to the floor, nor run with his mother and sister back to the shelter. He stood at the window, ripped open the plastic to see outside. His father came into view.

"Tata, pazi!" *Dad, watch out!*

Luka did not hear his son. He was looking for safe passage back to the protection of the apartment building.

A second shell landed nearby. The explosion was close enough to make Dražen turn for the pantry. But he stopped. Their building was still unscathed. Dražen was transfixed, almost as if he could sense the tragedy about to unfold.

"Tata!—" Luka glanced up toward his son in the window, a determined look on his face. "Ne!" *No!* shouted Dražen.

At that moment, a third shell landed in front of the house, and his father went down. Debris tore through the apartments left and right, above, and below. His mother shouted, "Draženne! Dođi ovamo! Molim te!" *Come here, Dražen! Please!*

Even before the smoke, dust, and shrapnel had settled, Dražen knew his father was dead. Everything slows down when tragedy strikes. But for Dražen, it was the opposite—the last ten seconds became one—the incoming shell, the explosion, his father running, falling, and dying all seemed to unfold in a split second.

Staring at the corpse, it was as though Dražen himself had died. In truth, he wished he had been killed instead of his father. Dražen turned and walked to his mother. As soon as she saw his face, she began to wail. His expression told Amira everything she needed to know—her cries filled the air and pierced the depths of his heart. She sank to the floor, crying, sobbing, rocking slowly back and forth. Selma crouched next to her mother and hugged her.

Dražen wasn't sure which parent to tend to first—the living or the dead. There was nothing he could do for his father now. Or was there? Shall I go outside and touch him, stroke his face, tell him one last time that I love him?

A fourth shell landed, and there were muffled screams from apartments close by. Dražen believed that when you died, your soul went to heaven, to a better place. But now he wondered if his father's soul, struck down so brutally, could even reach that special place? He felt his legs go from under him. He lay on his mother's lap, curled into a ball and sobbed.

A minute later, Dražen, breathing more calmly now, thought about the secret envelope inside the Lady Diana tin—and he felt guilty.

CHAPTER TWENTY-TWO

2:45 pm Goražde, Eastern Bosnia

Less than a mile from the Rakić family apartment, Gen. Zukić surveyed the scene. He stood near a JNA T-55 tank on the high ground above the town. In one hand, he held a pair of US army binoculars, confiscated from a UN peacekeeper at a Sarajevo checkpoint. With the other hand, he slapped his cell phone shut and nodded enthusiastically to the young captain next to him. Then, slicing his hand in front of his chest, he signaled for the attack to cease.

"Dosta!" ordered his aide-de-camp into a handheld Motorola radio. *Enough!* "Sve jedinicama! Prekid vatre!" *All call signs cease fire!* He repeated the command.

"You see, Captain, the more NATO squeezes us, the more we squeeze these Turks." He stood for a few moments with his fists resting on his hips. He was calm and confident. "Remember, God is with us ..."

"Yes, Comrade General." The captain stepped back and lit a cigarette. Looking down at the town he said, "General, you think we will find the Protocol down there?"

Before the captain could insert the cigarette between his lips, Gen. Zukić slapped it from the man's fingers and stamped it into the ground.

"Understand, Comrade Captain, there are things we do not speak about. Those who have permission to talk openly know who they are. *You* are not one of them."

"Yes, Comrade General. I understand. Please excuse me."

Gen. Zukić glanced down into the valley. "I like you. You are a loyal officer. Don't worry, we will find the Protocol and win this war." He gave the captain a squeeze on the shoulder. "Let them think we are devils. They know nothing of our plans here."

3:06 pm Eastern Bosnia

As promised during the meeting with Boyle and Fitzgerald the day before, Gen. Brown drove toward Ivančevo village to meet Yomper, and to personally take charge of Sonja's safe return to Pale. Halfway between Sarajevo and Ivančevo, Yomper left Dawes and climbed into the UN 4Runner driver's seat with Sonja in the back and Gen. Brown switching to the front passenger seat.

They headed south on mountain roads toward Pale via the outskirts of Sarajevo.

"I am very sorry for the attack," said Gen. Brown. "It's not why we are here. We are going to get you back home safe and sound. It won't happen again."

Sonja remained silent and refused to make eye contact. She had trusted these foreigners once already, and genuinely thought she might be able to work with them for peace. Her father had encouraged this, or so she thought. *Perhaps I misunderstood his intentions?*

"And I apologize too, Miss Radovanović," said Yomper. "I was following orders."

"I don't care," said Sonja. "I trusted your Fitzgerald. And look what happened."

Neither Gen. Brown nor Yomper could argue with her reasoning.

Gen. Brown said, "Sir Lawrence asked me to give you a message." He turned to face Sonja. "He said he still believes you want peace. He wants you to meet with Luka Rakić if possible. You shouldn't tell anyone in your family or the military."

Sonja said, "I promise you nothing. You should leave us to sort out our own problems."

Nothing more was said during the one hour-plus journey to their destination at the Pale checkpoint. "Please tell your father, I am ready to talk to him whenever he is ready."

Sonja said, "It will not happen. Perhaps you should talk to your friends at NATO first."

Sonja climbed out of the 4Runner and walked to the Serb Jeep on the other side of the unremarkable checkpoint.

Darko, the Pale police chief, was waiting for Sonja. He escorted her back to the house otherwise known colloquially in the international community as the *Republika Srpska presidential residence.*

Grinzing, Vienna, Austria

Nearly twenty years before, almost to the date, Klaus Reithoffer had met his wife, Ekaterina, on a blind date at a *Heuriger*—a winery-tavern—in Grinzing, Vienna. A friend from Cologne University had played matchmaker. *Altes Presshaus* still had a reputation for the best local cuisine in the Austrian capital, serving wine from the establishment's own vineyard. Reithoffer had suggested this same venue for the secret meeting with the Croatian president, Stjepan Tudjman.

The Reithoffers sat in the back of their chauffeur-driven Mercedes sedan as the driver made a right turn onto Cobenzlgasse in the picturesque northern suburb. Traffic clogged as tourists alighted from a steady stream of luxury coaches arriving from all points in Europe to visit the hostelries.

The Reithoffers dodged their way through hungry, thirsty tourists sporting day sacks and bum bags, all heading into the pumpkin-colored Heuriger. Once inside, Reithoffer made himself known to the manager, who showed them toward the rear of the tavern.

No one recognized the VIP guests. The white-shirted staff

with black aprons waited long medieval-style outdoor tables, ferrying liters of white wine, bottles of mineral water, halves of roast chickens, and sides of pork back and forth. Even if they had been aware of the VIPs in their midst, they would not have been distracted from their work. Such was the work ethic of the Viennese waiter.

"This is foolish," said Katya in German. "Someone will see us."

Reithoffer cleared his throat and adjusted his tie. "As long as no one can *hear* us … that is the important thing, Katya."

"Why are we here?" she said, as they crossed the cobblestone *innenhof,* or courtyard.

"You'll find out shortly. Listen to the conversation."

The manager led them to the secluded section reserved for private parties. "Your guest has arrived, Herr Reithoffer," he said, raising one eyebrow.

The Reithoffers entered.

The room was gloomy apart from one corner where the sun was streaking through wooden shutters not completely closed. The table was covered with white linen, immaculately laid and decorated with flowers and carafes of red and white wine. The Croatian president sat patiently with his entourage. Tudjman wore a mediterranean-blue short-sleeve cotton shirt. He was holding a glass mug of white wine *Gespritzte*—a mix of wine and sparkling mineral water—which he gulped down like lemonade.

"How are you, Mr. President?" Reithoffer began in English, the easiest way to converse. "Thank you for coming." They shook hands. "Allow me to introduce my wife, Ekaterina."

"It is an honor to meet you, Mrs. Reithoffer. Congratulations to both of you on your husband's new appointment as president of European Union." Then he strode across the room to the wooden shutters and pushed them open a few inches. "This is better. I like to see my food." He chuckled. "Let us study the menu, yes?"

Tudjman gestured to his two bodyguards standing behind him. They took their cue to leave the room. When everyone was seated, Tudjman raised his glass. "Your health." He took more gulps. "My country is indebted to you, Herr Reithoffer."

"Thank you." Reithoffer raised his glass. "I recommend the *halbes*," he said, referring to the most popular item on the menu—a half roast chicken. "It's served with the finest potato salad."

The manager stood near the door, snapping his fingers and directing his staff in and out as efficiently and unobtrusively as possible.

Within minutes, the food had arrived, the doors were closed, and Klaus Reithoffer began to set out his master plan. "You have told me, Mr. President, that we can rely on your support over the war in Bosnia."

"Nema problema." *No problem.* "Of course, I keep my word. We are soon to be a sovereign nation. And this we owe to your country."

"I wish to share my proposal with you, but first—" Reithoffer picked up the jug of white wine and topped up all the glasses around the table with a crisp Rhine Riesling. "Another toast ..."

Goražde

No one in the family had mentioned it earlier, and, in truth, he had forgotten about it himself. But today was Dražen Rakić's sixteenth birthday, one he would never forget. His mother had said she wanted to identify his father's body alone. But the tall, gangling Dražen insisted on accompanying his mother to the mortuary located at the local school. Selma, his sister, stayed home. His father's body had been whisked away by the local municipal cleanup crews now accustomed to disposing of bodies as though clearing refuse.

A stray dog was yapping incessantly, but the fighting had ceased for the time being. Arm in arm, mother and son ventured onto the street for the short ten-minute walk. Dražen could smell the stench of death in the air one block away from the school. Or perhaps it was his imagination?

Once inside the building, an old man with a five o'clock shadow led them down a corridor to a room opposite the main hall with a No Entry sign on the door. Dražen swallowed hard. In peacetime, the school hall had doubled as a gymnasium, like in many other schools. Now, even the corpses fought for valuable storage space there until they could be tagged, identified, and buried.

They entered the room and approached the table—three planks of wood precariously balanced on columns of empty plastic beer crates. Dražen prepared himself. He took a deep breath and held it. Then he took shallow breaths through his mouth. Out of respect for his father, he didn't want to retch. He felt almost faint at the thought of seeing his father's corpse. *Keep breathing,* he told himself.

Clutching his mother's arm, he felt Amira's body tense before it gave way to a steady tremble. The old man pulled back the UNHCR plastic sheeting to Luka's shoulders. Thankfully, his face was intact, wearing a peaceful expression as though fast asleep. A second was all they needed to see the body.

It was his father, but it wasn't really. Dražen was thankful for the large UNHCR lettering on the plastic that covered the rest of what he had been told was a mangled body.

It was done. Body identified. Dražen took a deep breath. The smell was unbearable. He mustered every drop of self-control to stop himself retching. His mother, however, began coughing and sobbing uncontrollably as they exited the school. Outside the main door, her knees finally buckled. Dražen tried to support her, but she collapsed to the ground.

A Danish UNMO captain with red hair and beard pulled up in his UN vehicle, got out, and approached the mother and son.

"Do you need help?" he asked. "My name is Captain Jens."

"We are fine." Dražen thanked him and insisted they could manage. The UNMO continued into the building, then turned. "We are making plans for an evacuation—women and children. You want to sign up?"

Dražen shook his head. His government would probably not allow anyone to leave the town, and Dražen would stay here until the last moment. His father would want that.

A minute later, Amira had recovered her composure, and Dražen escorted her from the school. Two days earlier, his father had read out names of three hundred and sixty-five people who had perished that week. Now Dražen would add his own father's name to the list. Now *he* would be the one to read out names on local radio.

The distant *boom-boom* of Serb artillery made him stop for a moment to gauge the intensity of the shells, whether or not another attack might be imminent.

Amira said, "Maybe we should go with UNPROFOR—the evacuation? We should have stayed in Sarajevo. It is safer there."

"No, Mama. Tata wanted us to be together. He wanted us to stay here." Dražen smiled. "He is counting on me."

Amira sobbed. "Why did we come here? I hate this place. We should—"

"Mama. This is our home now. Let's go."

CHAPTER TWENTY-THREE

Grinzing, Vienna

Reithoffer wiped his greasy fingers with a linen napkin. As always, the *halbes*—half roast chicken—was delicious but messy. He was full and a touch light-headed, but ready to do business. Nothing would stop his plan now that he was in the same room as President Tudjman.

He took one more gulp of his white wine *gespritzter*. Then he said, "Croatians have suffered heavy losses against Bosnian Muslim government forces."

"Yes. First Vukovar, now Mostar. We have lost thousands. Split has lost half its male population," Tudjman continued in his broken English, then grimaced. "And the old bridge in Mostar was a catastrophe—I concede this was our big mistake."

The world-famous medieval bridge completed in 1566 spanned the Neretva River in Mostar and had separated Bosnian Croat from Bosnian Muslim forces. An HVO tank—Croatian Defense Council—had destroyed the bridge during heavy fighting.

President Tudjman ripped off a chicken leg on his platter. He wiped his mouth before each bite. "You must understand, Klaus," he said between mouthfuls, "we can never live with Muslims. Too much blood has been spilt. Croatian people are very proud. We cannot go backward."

Reithoffer was prepared for this. "Europe will modernize—with or without you, Mr. President. We are not blind. We see the progress your country has made, and we believe Croatia will be an asset to the European Union." He leaned forward, elbows resting on the table. "But we *must* find a solution. This war threatens the peace and stability of Europe."

Tudjman smacked his lips, savoring his succulent chicken. Finally, he said, "I agree. Tell me how we must proceed."

"The Serbs must pay a price. They have killed and slaughtered thousands, including my own daughter in Paris."

"I am sorry for your loss. God rest her soul. You are sure Bosnian Serbs are responsible?"

"Yes."

"Why?"

"They do not like my politics. I know this. But Kerstin did not die in vain ... She has helped me see the way forward—"

"This isn't the way forward," said Katya, addressing both men. Then to her husband, "This is not how we honor our daughter."

"*Please*, Katya." His glare was enough to silence her. He turned to the Croatian president. "I believe we have mutual interests."

Tudjman smiled. "What of NATO and the United States?"

"They are not willing to sacrifice their own until their interests are threatened. The American people will rebel one day. Democracy is never certain in any country, even America."

"We have made territorial gains against Muslims in West of Bosnia."

"I congratulate you, but it is time to concentrate on the Serbs. You *must* join with Muslims against Serbs in Bosnia. This is the only way."

Tudjman shifted uneasily. "And the arms embargo? The British and French will never lift this. Without lifting it, the Muslims have nothing to fight with."

"I will take care of this." Reithoffer smiled. "And the Americans, if necessary. Let's just say, they will be our new best friends."

"You are an ambitious man."

"I am a pragmatist. I hate Serbs, and I want my revenge. I will be doing a great service for the countries of Europe."

"The UN safe area—Goražde—will be crushed if we attack Serbs. Gen. Zukić will obliterate them."

"Sometimes victory is bittersweet," Reithoffer said. The safe areas are an obstruction to peace. Everyone knows Goražde must eventually fall. It is not practical to keep it under Muslim control."

"And Sarajevo?" Tudjman took a gulp of wine.

"Once the Serbs lift the siege, you can make your arrangements with Muslims for postwar Sarajevo."

"And this pleasant lunch will remain our secret?"

"We will not meet again in person. Not until we celebrate Serb defeat in Bosnia."

The Croatian president stood up and stretched his hand across the table. "As Americans say: you got yourself a deal."

Tudjman dabbed his mouth with his napkin and signaled to his group that it was time to leave. The president and his entourage gathered their possessions and left the private section of the Altes Presshaus.

Reithoffer pictured him climbing into his bulletproof Mercedes, driving through the outskirts of Vienna toward the Austro-Slovene border, then to Croatia and reaching Zagreb by dusk. It was an unofficial visit. No one would ever even know he had left Croatia.

Reithoffer looked at his wife once the room was empty. "Also?" he said in German. *Well?*

"This is madness."

"Kerstin has not died in vain."

"And what if Serb terrorists kill us too? What will you achieve?"

"No one will touch us."

"I pray to God." Katya closed her eyes and shook her head.

"Can you live with blood on your hands, Klaus? Thousands of Muslims will die in Goražde if you let them fight. The Serbs will crush them."

"The Serbs will never rule Yugoslavia. We will squeeze the life from Dr. Radovanović and his daughter."

"None of this will bring *our* daughter back, Klaus. You will *never* bring her back."

"Of course, I know this."

Reithoffer got up and walked to the window overlooking the courtyard packed with wine-and-beer-sloshing tourists enjoying the bright winter sunshine. An Austrian brass band, men and women with red faces wearing white shirts, green tunics, and lederhosen, blasted their instruments to the delight of the crowd.

Reithoffer nodded slowly. "Either you are with me, or you are not. Can I count on your discretion, Katya?"

"I am not a politician," she hissed. "I am your wife. You have always listened to me. You trusted my opinions. This will end in disaster—for both of us."

"Answer my question." He waited.

"On our wedding day, I promised to love, honor, and obey, until death us do part. I will keep this promise."

"Thank you, my dear."

Bosnian Serb HQ, Pale

Dr. Radovanović stood at the French windows in the dining room of his headquarters. He had a clear view of the main road leading out of Pale to Goražde. The UNMO house and driveway were in full view from his vantage point. His staff monitored all UNMO movements and patrols, as well as their own military movements.

A column of Serb tanks came into view. "Our units are on the move." It was an affirmation, not a question.

Darko, his chief of police and military liaison officer, confirmed with a nod, then said, "Yes, Excellency." Darko put on his peaked cap and picked up his briefcase. His movements were sharp, aggressive, and full of unnecessary effort, as though he was determined not to let his disability—his amputated leg—stop him functioning like he used to.

Dr. Radovanović, a psychologist in his former, prewar life, could not help analyzing all those around him. As far as Darko was concerned, regretfully, it was only a matter of time before he would have to be replaced. He needed men who could mentally *and* physically react at a moment's notice to a volatile wartime situation. Darko was a cripple. He would have to go.

"NATO will never dictate to Bosnian Serb people," said Dr. Radovanović. "Do you understand?"

"Yes, Excellency."

"They took my daughter, but they will never take my country."

"They did not harm Sonja, thankfully. I am happy she is back with her family where she belongs."

Dr. Radovanović jabbed his finger at Darko, lecturing him. "Soon we will take Goražde. We will show the west what it means to meddle with Republika Srpska."

"Yes, Excellency. We will certainly be victorious against Turks. What about UN spies in Goražde—UNPROFOR? What should we do with them?"

"General Zukić will decide. They should not be there in the first place."

"I agree."

"Let us monitor Steele. He has a visitor. An American. Perhaps she has some new information?"

"The Protocol?"

"Yes. The British and Americans want to find it as much as we do. Steele can still help us, I think. But I don't trust him like

I trusted his brother. I think Jack Steele might be responsible for the attack on us."

"But he was nearly killed also," Darko said. "It makes no sense."

"I understand. But remember this is war. Things are not supposed to make sense."

Dr. Radovanović called through the open door to his secretary. "Svetlana? Bring coffee, Svetlana?"

She replied obediently. "Immediately, sir."

Dr. Radovanović turned toward his police chief. "Very good, Darko. I await your news from Goražde. Allow Captain Steele to do our work for us. Monitor him from a distance. NATO will not attack us. I am sure of it. We have Mother Russia on our side."

Darko saluted. "It will take more than NATO warplanes to destroy the Serbian soul." He reached the door, turned and saluted again. "I will bring any news immediately."

"Allow the woman to move freely."

"The American?"

"Yes."

"I understand."

"And Sonja must stay here at home. I forbid her to leave."

"Understood."

"Thank you, Darko. *Only unity saves the Serbs!*" Radovanović grinned and held a fist in the air.

Darko exited and closed the door behind him.

Radovanović picked up the telephone and dialed his wife's extension one floor above. "Slavica? How is our daughter?"

"She's good," Slavica replied. "And you, Kosta? Did you speak with General Brown?"

"No. It is too early. Don't worry, my dear. Everything is under control. Sonja is home safe and unharmed."

"But you must promise me, Kosta. You cannot allow our

daughter to be in harm's way in the future. Please, I am begging you. My nerves cannot take another shock like this."

"Trust me, Slavica. Do not worry. There is a reason I am leader of our country."

"I understand."

"Sonja is not allowed to leave Pale."

"I agree. It is for the best."

He hung up and switched on the television, tuning to CNN International, one of his most helpful tools and sources of information for his strategy against the international community.

CHAPTER TWENTY-FOUR

UNPROFOR HQ, Sarajevo

Boyle felt a wall of tension growing between himself and Gen. Brown. Not that he needed to be Brown's best friend—but he had to remain diplomatic.

Maj. Small left the room.

Boyle was treading a fine line. He knew he would now have to reveal a piece of the Black Cobra plan to placate Gen. Brown, who, after all, was the UN commander on the ground, and supposedly in charge of this ungodly peacekeeping mess. Officially, Gen. Brown was working for the United Nations, not the British government. Boyle would have to give Gen. Brown *something*, especially if Gen. Brown insisted on going to Pale again—and possibly Goražde. The general seemed intent on in-person negotiations with the Bosnian Serbs. He was desperately trying to coax them to the negotiating table.

Gen. Brown, bristling with indignation, folded his arms. "Your people, or group, or secret order, or whatever the bloody hell it is, tried to assassinate Dr. Radovanović. Are you out of your mind?"

"It was meant as a warning. It went wrong. I've explained already. We will only assassinate in extremis, and if all else fails," Boyle lied calmly.

"On whose authority?"

Boyle dodged the question. He was forbidden to use Black Cobra's name. "General, the NATO attack was meant as a deterrent. We have to hold off for as long as possible. NATO air strikes will not help us, you said so yourself."

"I'll make that decision when the time comes."

"Sir, if the British government doesn't get its hands on the Sarajevo Protocol, both of us will be out of a job, and we'll probably never find another."

"If the Serbs don't pull back, I have to order NATO to bomb."

"I understand, General. But the priority is the Protocol. I think Steele can do it—"

"Steele?"

"I think he'll find the Protocol with the right support."

"Steele has zero experience in Special Ops. What can he possibly achieve unless he's inside the Bosnian Serb circle of influence?"

"Remember, General, we didn't choose Jack Steele. Sonja Radovanović chose him and his brother—we never thought they'd become close. Peter Steele was emotionally involved. He fell for her. We couldn't have planned it better."

"You expect me to keep NATO fighters at bay so that one man can search for a needle in a haystack? I prefer to stick to my ultimatum."

"That needle will prevent Europe spewing its guts and save decades of suffering."

Gen. Brown paused before Boyle said, "Orders are orders, General Brown." Boyle allowed himself a self-satisfied smirk. He knew he had the upper hand. He knew the British government was on *his* side, although not "officially." Looking at Brown, he sensed they would be on the same page before long. "And besides, Steele has some help now."

"What kind of help?"

"Staci Ryan—an American journalist with impressive credentials. It will help us win the propaganda war domestically and internationally."

"You mean the PR war?"

"Yes, Staci has contacts on all sides of this war, and when we get what we're looking for, she will sell whatever message we need to sell."

"But if the Protocol is authentic—?"

"Staci can confirm it's a fake if and when we need her to."

"How?"

"She'll write an article. And the British government will confirm this too after 'careful examination' of the document. As long as we are in physical possession."

Gen. Brown took off his beret and scratched his forehead. "An American journalist is your hired help?"

"She works for us, yes."

"An American journalist? Is that supposed to instill me with confidence?"

Boyle ignored the sarcasm.

Gen. Brown said, "Don't go anywhere, Edward. You are to remain at headquarters. If you leave, I'll have you arrested."

Pale

"You're right," Steele said to Staci as they walked up the UNMO liaison office driveway away from yet another newly arrived troop of tanks. "If we do nothing, General Zukić will do what he does best—wage war. The demilitarized zone will never materialize because the UN won't allow NATO to strike—they have too many men, potential hostages, on the ground in Bosnia."

"You've lost me," said Staci. "I thought General Brown was prepared to use NATO?"

"I don't think he will. It's a threat. It will destroy his legacy if he bombs one of the sides. We have too many men on the ground."

"And if you're wrong?"

"Then we might regret destination Goražde."

"How much time do we have?"

"The deadline for withdrawal of heavy weapons is two days away. So far, the Serbs have ignored the order. Tanks are heading to Goražde. The UN hasn't got the balls to start bombing Serbs. Without Russia's blessing at the UN Security Council, it's not going to happen. The UN wouldn't risk it."

"What are you saying?"

"The Sarajevo Protocol is one thing. But someone has to stop the Serbs …"

"You mean physically stop them?"

"Yes."

"Isn't that what UNPROFOR is for?"

"No, UNPROFOR is here to make peace, not war."

"So, you think *we* have to stop them?"

"Have you got a better idea? No one else is going to do it."

"They didn't train me for that at journalism school. How do you plan on doing that?"

"Back to the original plan. If Sonja can't help us, we bring Luka to Sonja, or get them talking somehow."

"That's a long shot."

"You're the one who wanted to go to Goražde."

Staci smiled. "If we find him, you'll let me break the story?"

"I can't stop you." He looked toward the main road where tanks were idling and re-grouping into convoy order. "We'll talk to the UNMOs, see if they can help us with transport."

"I need to make that call, get a message to my editor," said Staci.

"I'll arrange it. Don't give your guy too much info. We don't want to screw it up before we start." Steele smiled nervously.

They reached the front door of the UNMO house and liaison office. Steele knocked on the door and entered without waiting for an answer.

Transport is one challenge, he thought. *But how on earth do we stop dozens of tanks destroying Goražde?*

★　　★　　★

2:58 pm

The UNMO office was empty. Danilo, the Bosnian Serb land-lord, entered from the family side of the house and informed Steele that the UNMO patrol had left thirty minutes before, but that he didn't think they'd be long. They rarely stayed out for more than an hour without telling him.

Steele thanked Danilo, who retreated to his living room. The family's quarters was also on the ground floor. Staci heard the sound of small children, apparently watching children's TV, in the next room. Steele turned to Staci and pointed to the SAT phone. "Help yourself. It's on us." Then he walked toward the entrance. "I'll be outside ... Tank spotting. Looks like they're leaving."

Steele left the house.

This was her chance.

She picked up the SAT phone and listened for a dial tone. She followed the instructions taped to the top of the SAT phone box to get a line of communication and then dialed the number for Col. Boyle at UNPROFOR.

It worked. The wonders of modern science. The phone lines were down across the front lines, but this technology pinged to a satellite and back so she could talk to Sarajevo just a few miles away.

"Boyle," a voice said.

"It's me," she said. "Can you talk?"

"I'm listening."

"He's going for it. We're going in together."

"Excellent."

"We'll find it." Staci glanced out the window to see Steele monitoring the tanks.

"He's as driven as you are, I think," Boyle said.

"Yes, I—"

"Which, remember, is why we have an arrangement."

"I hope you know what you're doing." She paused briefly.

"One more thing: I care about these people. Yes, I want my story, but not at the expense of innocent civilians."

"I understand, my dear."

Patronizing asshole, she thought. "Keep your side of the bargain, and I'll keep mine."

"We have a deal."

"OK."

"When you find it, Staci, guard it with your life. Even if you have to separate from our dashing UNMO."

Staci didn't answer. Boyle's disregard for human life was already plain as day. He had made this clear after the botched NATO attacked that killed five innocent Bosnian Serbs. She suspected that he had been involved indirectly if not directly. But she reminded herself of her priorities: career and financial reward. She said, "I won't disappoint you. I'm good at my job." Staci pressed the end-call button.

Of the hundreds of international journalists working in Bosnia, Boyle had chosen *her*. She knew she was one of the best; talented and intelligent. She knew she made heads turn. The trifecta was a potent combination in any war zone ... and anywhere else, for that matter.

She walked outside and said, "Thanks. I'm all set."

Steele said, "I'll call the UNMOs on the radio. They should be back soon."

"Great."

"I think I know the best way to Goražde."

"Really?"

"The only problem is that if we're caught, the Serbs might shoot us."

"I love your positivity."

"And if the Serbs don't shoot us, the Bosnian army might shoot us instead."

CHAPTER TWENTY-FIVE

Pale

D r. Radovanović lowered his binoculars, picked up his coffee, then sniffed the milk jug, and put his coffee down again. It was just after 3:00 pm. He called through the open door to his secretary, "Svetlana, bring fresh milk."

Again, he looked through the binoculars. "They're in the UNMO house. Steele with the American."

Darko said, "As we suspected all along, Excellency, they are working together."

There was a squeak of rubber-soled combat boots in the corridor followed by a knock at the door. Colonel Milan Kostić, chief of staff to Gen. Zukić, saluted and entered. He waved a piece of paper at them—it was a UN fax. "Comrades, our contact at UNPROFOR HQ just sent this—"

Darko took the fax and read aloud: "Reithoffer to visit Sarajevo today."

Dr. Radovanović slapped his hand so hard on his desk that the teaspoon bounced off the saucer and clattered to the floor. *"Sick-en-ing,"* he said slowly. "European Union has no business here. We are tired of this interference."

"What does this mean?" asked Darko.

The Bosnian Serb president paced nervously back and forth in front of the French windows, his face reddening with every step. "They throw sovereignty at Croatia for nothing. Now they kiss Muslim feet." Dr. Radovanović was spitting. "Their hypocrisy is endless."

"We cannot trust Reithoffer," said Col. Kostić

"If the German pigs had waited," Dr. Radovanović grimaced, "our country would be alive. Now we are dying. Just like they deceived us at the start of First World War. Germans are always to blame."

Dr. Radovanović believed, as did many Western offices, that the recent German-led push for Croatia's sovereignty was at best severely premature, and at worst a catastrophe, not only for Serbs but for the entire former Yugoslavia and Europe.

"Why must they tell us how to rule our country?" continued Darko. "The Turks will pay for this."

Dr. Radovanović said, "European Union caves in to Germany's influence over Croatia. They do not care about Serb people."

Col. Kostić asked, "What shall we do about Reithoffer?"

"Nothing for the time being. General Brown has given us two days to withdraw from Goražde and Sarajevo. But NATO will not bomb. Our brothers in Moscow have expressed support. They will not tolerate NATO aggression."

"Why is Reithoffer coming to Sarajevo?" asked Col. Kostić.

"To show support for the Turks, of course," replied Dr. Radovanović. He sat down and placed his fingertips together. "We will show them who rules Bosnia."

Col. Kostić said, "We will attack the Turks, Excellency?"

Dr. Radovanović said, "Once we find the Protocol, we will attack Goražde and cleanse the Turks."

Hatred in his eyes, Col. Kostić replied, "I will make necessary preparations with Gen. Zukić."

Dr. Radovanović said, "Inform our sympathizer at UNPRO-FOR he will be rewarded for his loyalty." He looked again at the UNMO house through his binoculars. "Their patrol has returned."

The UNMO patrol—one officer from Ireland and one from the Czech Republic—entered the house. "It's like a game of chess," Dr. Radovanović said, grinning, "and knowing who will win."

Col. Kostić chuckled. "It is an honor to serve with you, comrades." He and Darko saluted and left the room.

At 9:08 pm, Major Geraghty, the Irish UNMO Pale, dropped Steele and Staci at the side of the road three miles southeast of the town. Up ahead, a Serb tank, the last in a convoy that spread out over half a mile, idled at the side of the road.

"Sorry we couldn't help with the vehicle," said Maj. Geraghty in his Dublin lilt, "but you wouldn't make it through the next checkpoint in a UN Jeep. I think you're crazy, but this is the only way." He wished them luck and gave a salute that was more of a wave. Then he climbed into his Jeep, did a three-point turn, and departed.

They were on their own.

Steele peered ahead into the darkness. Did the convoy have any kind of rear protection? Unlikely, but he had to double-check. They approached the tank through the forest from the flank. No sentries at the rear of the convoy. He gave Staci a thumbs-up.

They crept closer to the tank. He signaled for her to wait for him in a ditch at the side of the road. The tank crew was nowhere to be seen or heard. He climbed onto the back deck, crawled up the side of the turret, and carefully leaned down to inspect inside the open hatch. The noise and exhaust of spewing tanks gave him all the cover he needed.

All clear. The tank was empty.

As he had hoped, the crew was probably at a briefing or resting up in the woods nearby—more comfortable than the hard metal engine covers of a tank.

He slipped from the turret forward and down into the driver's hatch and maneuvered himself into the seat. Once he had selected first gear, he poked his head out the hatch toward the ditch.

"Let's go ..." he hissed to Staci.

She approached and said, "You know how to drive this thing?"

"I'm a tank commander. It's my job."

"I'm impressed."

"Get in. We're going to Goražde to find your friend ..."

"And save the world?"

"Something like that."

Staci placed two hands on the side of the tank and climbed up onto the metal beast and down inside the turret. "Where do I sit?"

"Commander, loader, or gunner's seat. Take your pick."

She lowered herself through the turret hatch and into the main body of the tank.

Steele reached behind and tapped the metal footwell. "Put the headset on." Leaning back, Steele could just make eye contact.

Staci pulled the helmet on and placed the boom mic toward her mouth. "So we're going to drive down the main road into Goražde in a tank?" She sounded skeptical.

"Troops on the ground are always the last to know what's going on. No one's going to know any better. Maj. Geraghty mentioned at least four checkpoints—so unless you want to walk thirty miles through mined forests ...?"

"You're nuts."

"I know. But this is our best bet. We don't have much choice."

Staci adjusted the headset. "Stinks in here."

"Nasty smelly things, tanks," Steele said reassuringly. "Keep the headset on. It's going to get loud."

"You don't say," she replied, shouting already as Steele revved the engine.

Steele pulled a lever to lower the back of his seat, allowing himself to drop into a horizontal position. He closed the driver's hatch. Adjusting the periscope, he selected first gear, then depressed the elephant-sized accelerator pedal for a few seconds before shifting to second. He gently tugged at the steering levers on his right and left to maneuver his way past the other tanks on the side of the road. The beast moved slowly, its huge metal tracks squeaking like a mechanical monster. "Let's hope there's enough fuel."

"Copy that," she said.

Slowly … easy does it. Through his periscope, he saw the silhouette of a Serb soldier standing in front of him. At first he thought he would have to run him down, but the man jumped clear and waved, as if apologizing for getting in the way.

One hour later, the lone tank reached a clearing on the edge of Goražde. Peering through the periscope, Steele could see other tanks up ahead—perhaps a kind of forming-up point for a possible attack?

Just then, Steele saw a blinding flash of white, then red and orange light, through the periscope, immediately followed by a huge, deafening explosion. The column of tanks to his front lit up like a firework display.

He pressed his foot to the ground.

"Hold on. Brace yourself." He didn't wait for Staci to reply.

Over the groaning engines and the static on his headset, Steele heard the thunderous boom of a fighter jet wash overhead.

"Sweet bloody Jesus," he shouted. "Geraghty was right. He said NATO would attack, or send a warning. I didn't believe him."

"What are we going to do?"

"We keep going. That's what tanks are for. We have to warn the Muslims—" Steele grappled with the steering levers, narrowly missing men and tanks in his path. "The Serbs will have to retaliate."

"What about UNPROFOR?" asked Staci. "Can't they protect the town?"

"Peacekeepers aren't allowed to attack warring factions."

Just then, their tank clipped another tank, which had taken a direct hit and was immobilized. As they passed, it was on fire. Steele pulled sharply to the left, but hitting an inanimate object—a boulder or rock, perhaps?—was forced to stop dead.

He slammed the gear lever into reverse.

Adrenaline surged through him. "Radovanović is playing UNPROFOR like a violin. They think giving the Serbs a bloody nose will change things. They forget the Serbs have Russians for a safety net."

Silence. No reply from Staci.

The tank kept moving. He leaned back to see Staci, or at least her legs. The gunner and commander's seats were empty.

Staci had disappeared.

CHAPTER TWENTY-SIX

UNPROFOR HQ, Sarajevo

"Y ou cannot fight a war from white-painted vehicles," said Gen. Brown for the second time in a week; the first time had been to a BBC journalist during a recent press conference. "That's our problem right now."

"Thank you for meeting with me, General," replied Klaus Reithoffer, the newly appointed EU president. "I apologize for the short notice. And thank you for accommodating us."

Gen. Brown had delayed his recce to Pale to stay in Sarajevo and meet with Reithoffer, who had unexpectedly and inconveniently arrived unannounced. Well-meaning Euro VIPs swanning into theater causing all kinds of security and logistical problems bugged the shit out of him. But after nearly thirty years in the British Army, Gen. Brown had learned to kowtow if and when necessary.

Gen. Brown spent several minutes explaining the sensitivity of the security situation to Reithoffer—executing his peacekeeping mandate in war-ravaged Bosnia would be impossible if NATO bombed the Serbs to the negotiating table *without* consulting UNPROFOR—especially, he was at pains to point out, when he himself was trying to achieve the same goal *without* punitive measures on the Serbs. NATO had denied bombing the Radovanović wedding the day before, but this evening's strike on Serb tanks would be much harder, if not impossible, to conceal. The Russians were also running out of patience. "I don't think it will be long," concluded Gen. Brown, "before Moscow wades into this ethnic quagmire with some heavy-handedness of its own."

Gen. Brown paused for breath, but sensed Reithoffer's reluctance to listen to his message. "Bottom line—I need Serb armor and heavy weapons under UN control. I can't do that if you're pressuring NATO to attack before the end of my ultimatum."

"I understand, General. We want the same thing. But you cannot trust the Serbs."

"Sir ... Mr. Reithoffer—"

"*Bitte*, you can call me Klaus—"

"What is the purpose of your visit, Klaus?"

Reithoffer said, "We must defeat Serb aggressors, butchers of innocent people. How many died in the Markale Marketplace Massacre?"

Maj. Small said, "Sixty-nine dead, two hundred injured. Radovanović denies any part of it."

"Thank you, Maj. Small. That was helpful." Gen. Brown frowned.

"You trust Radovanović?" asked Reithoffer.

Gen. Brown smiled calmly. "As you say, I don't trust anyone."

"You think the Bosnian government did this?" Reithoffer scoffed.

Brown said, "I don't rule anything out. The Belgian UNMOs are examining the trajectory of the Markale mortars. We're awaiting confirmation."

Reithoffer's nostrils flared. "Radovanović cuts off fuel, food, and humanitarian assistance to this city, and you think the Bosnian army shells its own people? *Spinnen Sie?*" He took a breath and repeated in English. "Are you insane?"

"The Market Massacre was abhorrent and the most obscene act of this war to date. But I repeat that bombing the Serbs into submission won't work either. I came here with an open mind and an open heart. I came here to keep the peace and stop the war. I did not come here to start World War Three."

"You exaggerate, General." Reithoffer loosened his tie and undid the top button of his pale-yellow shirt.

Gen. Brown shot Maj. Small a look that said, *I am about to punch this man in the face.* Then he said, "If the UN *or* NATO—to most Bosnians they're the same thing—continue bombing, we become nothing less than a Bosnian government air force. We will set a precedent that will change the course of UN peacekeeping indefinitely."

Reithoffer said, "General Brown—"

"I refuse to take sides, and I will not be part of a solution that kills Serbs one minute and expects to negotiate over breakfast the next. *Five* Bosnian Serbs were killed at the church in Pale!"

"General Zukić is killing Muslims while he plays chess with his commanders on the hills above Goražde. I saw a photograph in a Belgrade newspaper," said Reithoffer.

"Yes, they are playing a dangerous game," said Gen Brown. "But we need to play their game and win."

"What do you suggest?"

"I have already suggested," Gen. Brown said slowly, "that we get the Russians on board with the international community; that we demand all heavy weapons are withdrawn from Sarajevo, Goražde, and Srebrenica, within forty-eight hours; and we demand an immediate cessation of hostilities. Ultimately, we have NATO firepower, but I am reluctant to use it until absolutely necessary."

"Do you have the situation under control, General Brown?"

"It's under control, Klaus … Mr. President."

Reithoffer nodded. "You have twenty-four hours. After this, I will demand NATO bombing raids continue."

"Thank you. I'll take it."

Gen. Brown stood up, barely able to conceal his frustration. "Major Small will take care of your needs. How long do you plan to stay?"

"Once I am satisfied we are on the same page, I will return to Strasbourg."

Eastern Bosnia

"Where the hell did she go?" Steele said out loud as he drove the tank around the next bend. His aim was to clear the immediate danger from NATO fighters, as well as Serb commanders once they realized a tank had been stolen. He pulled the right steering lever, braked, and came to a stop under some trees at the side of the road.

Still no sign of Staci. *Where the hell is Staci?*

Steele heard a voice outside shouting in Bosnian. Someone was climbing onto the tank, about to look inside.

A Serb NCO was in the press-up position leaning down inside the tank. "Everyone okay?" he asked in Bosnian.

His head partially hidden from view, Steele leaned back slightly and shouted in his best Bosnian, "Yes, thank you, comrade!" He prayed the noise of the engine would disguise his accent sufficiently. "No problem here, they'll be back in a minute," he said, referring to his nonexistent crew.

The NCO flashed a thumbs-up. "Get going as soon as possible. Screw NATO! We have Muslim ass to kick."

"Fuck, yes!" Steele used his best Bosnian expletive.

His response seemed to satisfy the soldier, who jumped down from the tank and ran back down the road to warn the next call sign.

Steele couldn't risk another soldier climbing on his tank. Looking around, he moved off slowly, pulling back on the left stick to maneuver round a stalled tank in his path. He desperately wanted to stop and search for Staci. But now the column of tanks behind him was on the move, coming up fast.

"Jack?" The voice came from nowhere. It was Staci, and she was somehow behind him.

"Where are you?" He heaved a sigh of relief.

"What's up?" She stuck her hand through into the driver's compartment. Then he understood. Staci had slid across the main armament to the loader's side of the tank and hidden under the tarpaulin used to cover the ammunition.

"Didn't want anyone finding a female stowaway. I hid after the first explosion. Then I heard someone climbing onto the tank," she said. "Who was that?"

"A junior commander checking up on us. You can relax, he's gone."

"NATO took action sooner than we thought?"

"They could have destroyed the entire convoy. It was just a warning this time."

"Doesn't seem to have done much good. The entire convoy is moving toward Goražde. God help Luka."

He squeezed her hand. "It'll take about twenty minutes to get there."

"Maybe I was wrong."

"About what?"

Staci said, "You have got balls after all."

10:47 pm

Riding a main battle tank along country roads was like sitting on a conveyor belt with square rollers. Suspension was virtually nonexistent in this metal box on tracks. Steele's head was pounding. Even with the driver's hatch open, he felt nauseated.

Fifteen minutes later, the lone tank stopped.

"I might throw up," said Staci.

"Me too."

Steele peered at the murky outline of the road. He saw nothing but the matte black of night. He climbed out of the driver's seat and helped Staci out of the main turret compartment. "You don't have to do this, you know," he said. "Last chance to pull out."

"It's fine," she said. "For the first time in my life, I feel like I'm doing something useful."

They clambered down from the tank.

"Fair enough," he said. "Same here." Steele smiled and picked up the backpack provided by the Irish UNMO he had stowed in one of the side bins. Inside the backpack were provisions, including a flask of coffee, sandwiches, chocolate bars, and a map of the area. He studied the map for a few moments to get his bearings. "We're close to the front line. We'll go on foot now. We need to lose these guys."

"You're the boss."

"Woods and high ground are best. Bosnian forces don't have enough men to cover the entire area. They have small mobile units on patrol, playing cat and mouse with the Serbs. Let's hope they're not trigger-happy."

"What if we run into the Serbs?"

"Let's pray we don't run into either."

"Amen, Captain."

They headed into thick forest next to the road. Steele glanced back at their tank, engine left running like a growling, smoking monster.

Steele and Staci broke into a jog for several minutes. They negotiated predatory tree roots and branches at head height that seemed hell-bent on gouging their eyes out.

Staci was the first to stop. Panting, she begged, "Wait. I can't—

"Gotta keep going. When they find the tank, they'll follow our trail."

"Don't they have more important things to worry about?" Staci set off again to catch up. "Will they attack Goražde tonight?"

"I'd rather not guess. Let's just get there."

"That sounds bad."

"It's a lose-lose situation. NATO has made up its mind to flex its muscle. It needs to show it can do something, make a difference in this conflict. Serbs are the bullies, and NATO can act with or without big brother America pulling all the strings."

"I don't know. Washington has to be in on this?"

Steele held out his hand so Staci could keep up with him. "You're right. It's a love fest between Washington and Zagreb. Croatia becomes a US ally behind the former Iron Curtain—it's perfect. The US is building a space-age embassy in Zagreb as we speak, the biggest listening post in Europe since World War Two."

Staci cursed as another branch slapped her neck. "Which leaves the Bosnian Serbs exposed, and de facto devils?"

"And masters of ethnic cleansing. They're not helping themselves."

"So, Washington and London decide the outcome of this war?"

"Possibly. Either way, Radovanović is playing into their hands. The Serbs don't get it. Their hate for Muslims is the perfect distraction for others to exploit them."

Steele slowed, thinking about the efforts that London—and Boyle—were going to in order to locate the Sarajevo Protocol. But for now, there was no need to share his true opinion about Boyle.

As they moved past black shapes and shadows over rough terrain, Steele was taking mental note of the overall landscape to see if there were any tree groupings, distinct contours, or streams. This would all be very helpful if it became necessary for them to retrace their steps. They climbed, descended, slid forward, backward, and sideways, got their feet soaked, and became scratched, scraped, and bruised all over.

Forty-five minutes later, he reckoned they were close.

Out of nowhere came a loud *CRACK!* "Get down," he hissed, pulling both of them to the ground.

"Was that for us?"

"I'd put money on it."

"Are you sure?"

"Who else?"

Silence.

Steele got up, crouching, moving slowly, searching and probing for safe passage across an invisible front line into Goražde.

CRACK! Another bullet. No mistake this time—someone was firing at *them*.

"What now?" she asked, as they lay glued to sodden leaves and dirt.

"It would help to know who's shooting."

Steele lay still, breathing heavily through his nostrils. "I'm going to talk to them ..." He took a deep breath and exhaled. "Zdra-vo!" he yelled in two long syllables. *Zdravo* was typically a Serb greeting. He'd used the word on purpose, believing Serbs posed a greater threat than Muslims if they were caught.

Silence. *Maybe I guessed wrong?*

He tried again in Bosnian. "YOU SPEAK ENGLISH?"

Another shot rang out.

He changed his mind. The shooters were probably *inside* the safe area, therefore Muslim. "Please," he continued, "I'm Captain Steele—UNMO. I'm with an American journalist. We want to talk to the people of Goražde. We want to help."

He listened carefully and thought he heard voices.

Finally, a man's voice said in broken English, "How we know you? How we trust?"

"We'll stand up," said Steele. "We're unarmed. Look, no weapons."

Gesturing for Staci to stay down, he stood up slowly.

"How gallant," she said quietly. "I hope you know what you're doing."

Standing tall, hands in the air, he saw human shapes about thirty feet away. He picked his way forward a few steps toward them and was blinded by a flashlight, ruining his night vision.

"Come ..." said the voice. "Hands up. How many you are?"

"Two. There are two of us." He nodded to Staci. It was safe to show herself.

She stood and raised both arms and said quietly, "I'm scared, Jack. Correction—I'm terrified."

"It's okay," he replied. "Believe me, this is good news."

"It is?"

Just then there was another explosion—much smaller than the earlier attacks on the tanks. This was more like a grenade. A small area of terrain lit up around them. The men approaching immediately turned and ran for cover.

A counterattack.

A barrage of small-arms fire broke out to and from Steele's left and right.

Serbs? Muslims? An ambush? God knows.

For twenty to thirty seconds, a dozen blinding flashes in all directions made him realize they might not survive; and if they did, it would be a small miracle.

Steele lost eye contact with Staci. He shouted in vain. The noise was ear splitting. As he scrambled for cover, he got caught in thorny barbs of bramble bush. He broke free and was forced to run, covering his ears as he did so. He looked back, but saw no sign of Staci. Either she'd escaped in the opposite direction, or she'd been shot and was bleeding to death.

He stopped, preparing to go back and find her as the explosions subsided. He felt responsible for her. Steele promised she'd be safe. Immediately he began to backtrack. He fought the brambles and made for the clearing where he'd last seen Staci.

Then Steele tripped. Lying on his back, he was again blinded and deafened by grenades, small-arms fire and flares ripping across him in every direction. He couldn't decide which way to run—forward, backward, sideways? He rolled onto his stomach.

It was a lie. Goražde, a United Nations safe area, was a very dangerous place.

Now on his front, he felt a ring of cold steel resting on the back of his neck—a rifle barrel. It sent a tingle down his spine. He raised both hands.

"Chetnik spy," said the man standing above him. "Come with us."

Whoever had found him was Muslim. Steele no longer knew if that was good or bad news.

CHAPTER TWENTY-SEVEN

UNPROFOR HQ, *Sarajevo*

At 7:13 am the next day, Boyle paced back and forth, head hung low, thinking fast. He had wanted this telephone conversation with Robert Grange, the British prime minister, to be positive. But all he had was bad news. No, worse— this was disastrous news.

"I'm sorry, Prime Minister," said Boyle, "things have not been quite as clear-cut as we'd planned."

"Not good enough, damn it." Grange was on the verge of shouting. "I have Washington breathing down my neck like a spaniel with bad breath, and NATO pleading with me to allow the strikes to continue and give the Serbs a bloody nose. I need the Sarajevo Protocol. Then we can bargain."

"One more day, sir. We need one more day."

"You have twelve hours. NATO wants to make its mark. They've destroyed a few tanks. But that was a warning. You *must* give me something concrete by end of today."

Boyle said, "I have every confidence—" He had no such thing, and he knew it.

"I was assured Black Cobra is the best, and I need your best work—*now*."

"Twelve hours, Prime Minister," said Boyle. As he spoke, he looked at Gen. Brown, who had been patiently waiting to speak to the PM. "I'll need General Brown's full support." He looked at Gen. Brown with a sour expression and handed him the receiver.

Gen. Brown frowned. He didn't like surprises, and Boyle was full of them. "Prime Minister, we are engaged in a peace-keeping operation—"

"You're our best man, Rupert, but there's no discussion here. Give Boyle everything he needs. Do we understand each other?"

"Prime Minister—"

"No discussion, Rupert. Sorry, I'm in the middle of a cabinet reshuffle and all kinds of Euro bullshite here. Gotta go." Grange hung up, and Gen. Brown glared at Boyle.

Maj. Small entered, waving a fax in Gen. Brown's direction.

"Now what?" snapped Gen. Brown.

Maj. Small said, "Sir, the tanks we were monitoring have advanced—current position five kilometers outside Goražde." He handed the signal to Brown. "Our intel says they appear to be preparing for a final assault."

"*Fuck it!*" spluttered Boyle, looking around the room for support where there was none. "If they attack, it's World War Three. Russia's bound to retaliate."

"I agree," said Gen. Brown. "We have to stop them. If you had told me what was happening in the first place, I might have been able to do something."

"The British government wants the Protocol. We're ninety-five percent certain where it is—and who's got it. Let me do my job."

Gen. Brown said, "I don't trust you, Boyle."

"We have our orders, General—you and me both. Steele and the American journalist are close. She had been working a contact, a Bosnian journalist called Luka Rakić. We think he knows where it is."

Maj. Small frowned and shook his head. "Rakić the journalist?"

"Yes."

Maj. Small said slowly, "He's dead."

"What?" The color drained from Boyle's face. "When? How?"

"One of our local interpreters heard the news on Goražde radio—killed by a mortar round in front of his teenage son. War stinks."

Boyle sat on the edge of the desk, visibly deflated. He rubbed his cheeks, trying to think clearly. "Okay, we'll find the boy. Maybe he knows something."

Gen. Brown shouted, "Yomper!"

Yomper pulled his feet in at the doorway and saluted.

"I've had enough of this bullshite," Gen. Brown continued. "Here's what's going to happen." He looked at Boyle. "*You* are going to stay here." Brown looked at Yomper. "*We* are going to Goražde."

Boyle said, "But the prime minister—"

"That's a direct order, Boyle. Maj. Small will have the MP arrest you if you leave the compound." Gen. Brown nodded at the major. "You can entertain Klaus Reithoffer if you get bored. You've both gone rogue if you want my honest opinion."

Gen. Brown picked up his revolver and holster lying on his desk. "Ready, Yomper?"

"Yes, sir."

"First stop, Pale."

Boyle said, "What am I supposed to do with Reithoffer?"

Gen. Brown did not answer, but as they exited, Yomper said to Boyle, "Try some takeout Ćevapčići, sir. Treat yourself." Ćevapčići was the local meat delicacy Sarajevo was known for. Even during the bloody conflict.

Goražde, Eastern Bosnia

Steele squinted as they took off his blindfold. There were two figures—skinny teenage boys at first glance—standing on each side of him. Despite their size, they had the look of a wounded dog about them. They pushed him from a dark green VW Golf caked with mud and snow. He looked around.

From the outside, the house was pitted and pockmarked

with bullet holes and shrapnel damage. *No wonder*, he thought. They were less than fifty meters from the front line—he could see the end of the houses marking the river just one block away. Its isolation, with rubble, bricks, and debris everywhere—no doubt about their location on the confrontation line.

He was escorted into what appeared to be some kind of command post. The Serbs were probably close by. If they were watching through binoculars, they would be able to identify him and lob a shell in their direction. *Not good.*

Once inside, he looked around. The walls looked as though they were about to collapse. The air was damp and heavy. The doorways were mostly without doors. Instead, some had loose material or plastic nailed to the doorframe hanging down. Steele smelled trappings of frontline warfare—rotting refuse, urine, and burned coffee.

The Bosnian Muslim soldier wore jeans and sneakers with a military camouflage combat jacket, a Bosnian government ID tag around his neck, and an AK47 assault rifle slung across his chest. Steele was shoved through a doorway and fell onto floorboards of a bare room. "You are lucky, mister," the teenager said in broken English. "If not for this woman, we would shoot you."

"Jack. Thank God." Staci was sitting on the floor holding a mug of hot tea, steam rising.

"What happened?" he said, glancing at his escort, who left the room and stood guard outside.

"I kept asking about you. They think we're spies. JCOs." *Joint Commission Observers*, otherwise known to be British SAS, were Gen. Brown's eyes and ears along the confrontation lines. It made sense that any foreigners found in the confrontation line zone might be mistaken for JCOs.

"They have a point. They found us right on the confrontation line."

"They think we called in the last attack. Four of their men died, Jack."

"They think we're working with the Serbs?"

Staci nodded.

Steele asked, "Who's in charge?"

"No one's talking."

"Your friend, Luka? Did you ask for him?" Steele crouched down to rest with his back against the wall.

"Dražen Rakić is on his way."

"Dražen?"

"Luka's son? Apparently Luka left him in charge."

"How old is he?"

"He's a teenager."

"Where's Luka? We need him."

"I don't know."

The curtain to their room flicked open, and a young soldier flanked by two more armed teenagers said, "Enough. No more talking."

Steele noticed the safety catches on their rifles were off. Teenage fingers on triggers made him nervous. He said, "I'm sorry about your men."

"They would die anyway," said the second teenager. "If it is God's will, we shall die. Chetniks are preparing final assault. But you know this. You are Chetnik spies."

"No, we're not," said Steele calmly. "I am a British UNMO, and we've come to help you and your people."

The second teenager said, "We are lucky if we die. Understand me? If Chetniks take us, this is worse than death."

The first teenager cocked his rifle and pointed it at Staci. "Shall we save her from pain and suffering, Chetnik spy?"

Steele raised both hands to calm everyone. "Please … listen. We need to speak to Luka Rakić, not his son. It's very important we talk to him."

The first soldier pointed his rifle at Steele's head. "The only way you can talk to Luka is when I shoot you."

"I don't understand."

"Luka Rakić is dead. You are a bad spy."

Steele froze. Then he slowly shook his head, confused. Then he looked at Staci, trying to work out his next move. "I'm sorry. I don't understand."

"What you don't understand? This is war."

"How did he die? When?"

"No more questions. Dražen Rakić will arrive shortly. You can ask him yourself."

A few minutes later, the door opened and Dražen Rakić entered. The exchanges of small-arms fire outside started again. Steele sensed that the tension was building on both sides of the confrontation line. Inexperienced in war though he was, he too was starting to get a sixth sense of the escalating sights and sounds of battle that inevitably led to more bloodshed. There were definitely safer places to be arrested and held at gunpoint. He wouldn't be surprised if a shell ripped through their building at any moment. He thought of Peter and what Peter might do in this situation. Then he looked at Staci and was propelled back to the present.

"Why you want to see my father?" asked Dražen in English.

Staci broke in. "Dražen … We are very sorry about your father. I knew him, and he was a great man."

"How you know him?"

"We were working on a story. Dražen, the safety and security of your people depends on *you* now. I know it seems like there's no way out. But we want to help."

"My people need me. We will show the Chetniks what means freedom."

Steele eyed Staci, who smiled sympathetically at the boy. "Please, Dražen, listen … Luka told me about a secret document, the Sarajevo Protocol? The Protocol can stop this war before more blood is spilled."

"Nothing can stop this war. It is our destiny. But we will

fight and die for our people here and for our Muslim brothers in Sarajevo."

"Your father asked me to help—"

Steele guessed she was lying.

Dražen scoffed sarcastically. "British and Americans—you said you would help us. But you lie. We are like stray dogs ... sick, bloody. You kick us when we are down. We dig through piles of trash for food. No one cares about us. No food convoys for weeks."

"Staci and I—we care," said Steele. "We risked our lives to come here, right? Your father knew about the Protocol, that it would change your country's future. Did he ever mention it, Dražen?"

"No. You are lying. You have done nothing for us."

Steele said, "If you know where it is, you can help save your people, *all* of them. The Serbs want it. It's their excuse to destroy your town. They won't stop until they find it."

Steele stood up and took a step toward Dražen. In one seamless movement, both soldiers cocked their weapons and pointed them at Steele. Suddenly the skinny teenagers performed actions like characters from *The Terminator*.

"Dražen," Steele said, "let me explain."

The soldiers glanced at Dražen, who gestured for them to lower their weapons.

"If you decide to hide that document," Steele continued, "know that you are killing your own people and perhaps all of us in this room. There will be no end to this war."

"My father told me what to do. It is none of your business. It is between us and Chetniks. But I hate Chetniks. I will never talk with them."

Staci said, "But your father didn't know the whole story. The situation has changed, Dražen."

"*Nothing has changed.* Chetniks move closer—killing us, squeezing us to death ... Shelling, shelling, shelling. This is all my people know. Chetniks will never be content until every Muslim is dead."

"You need to show us where it is," said Steele. "The document."

Dražen frowned, gnawing at one of his fingernails and appeared to be weighing his options. "I do not understand this document—yes, my father called it *SP—Sarajevo Protocol.* He told me if international community does not save us, I must use document to make peace. But he did not say how. He told me it might cost many lives, so I did not tell anyone about it."

"I understand," said Steele. "But given its importance, we must share it with the world at the right time." He pointed to Staci. "Staci is an American journalist. She has contacts every-where. People will listen to her." Steele had no intention of sharing the Sarajevo Protocol to the world, but right now the end justified the means. "But we think you should talk to Sonja Radovanović. My brother … he was a journalist … he was try-ing to get your father to talk with Sonja."

"I don't care about Sonja. She is Chetnik. Her father, Rado-vanović, Serbs and Croats … they want to kill Muslims. Even British and Americans are afraid of our customs, our culture. They want to wipe us from Europe. We are dirt, we are scum." Dražen's eyes dampened, not from sadness but from anger.

Steele said, "That's not true, Dražen. Many are supporting your government. More killing will not bring peace. One day Gen. Zukić will be brought to justice. This is your country as much as theirs. Everyone knows that. Yugoslavia was the envy of Eastern Europe—Serbs and Croats were your neighbors, your husbands and wives. You must help us, before it's too late. Where is the Sarajevo Protocol?"

"You are lying." Dražen raised his voice over the small-arms fire becoming louder by the minute. "You are Chetnik spy, and I have my duty. My father told me what to do. I will obey him." Dražen turned to the guards and said, "Take them."

The guards pointed their weapons at the two foreigners. Steele glanced at Staci and said, "It's okay, do as they say." He bit nervously at the inside of his cheek and eyed both teenage guards, who both rested their index fingers on the AK47 triggers.

"My father told me you would come. But I do not trust anyone. First I need to find out the truth for myself. We will see if UN helps us now."

Steele and Staci were ordered to turn around so they could be blindfolded. Steele's heart sank. *We were so close.* For him, there was no doubt now that the Sarajevo Protocol existed, but how much did Dražen Rakić really know? How much *could* he know? *He's just a teenager,* Steele thought. Had Dražen's father entrusted him with the location of the Sarajevo Protocol? Steele doubted it. But at least now he finally understood why the British government wanted this secret document so badly, and why they were prepared to sacrifice anyone—*including me*—to get it. They were probably convinced its existence would ignite conflict in Europe for the next decade. And if the Brits wanted it that badly, it made sense that others would go to any lengths to get it too—like the Serbs, not to mention the Russians, who had a finger in every intelligence pie.

It also explained why Steele had had several close calls with death starting the day he had seen Peter and Sonja in Hyde Park. London, Split, Sarajevo, Pale, and Goražde. Everywhere he went, death and destruction followed. There were certainly others who probably suspected he was a British spy searching for the Sarajevo Protocol. *Damn it, I am basically a British spy for God's sake.* In their place, he would probably have issued the same order—*kill Jack Steele if necessary. Find the Protocol.*

Blindfolded, he felt a vice-like grip clamp his arm. He could feel Staci tripping and stumbling behind him. They were escorted from the house and bundled into a car. The doors were slammed shut and locked from the outside.

Steele and Staci were left alone with near distant sounds of battle.

CHAPTER TWENTY-EIGHT

8:51 am Somewhere between Pale and Goražde

With checkpoint clearances hastily arranged, Yomper drove the white UN armored Range Rover through Pale en route to the beleaguered Goražde enclave.

As they drove through the countryside, Gen. Brown realized how hard it was to appreciate the beauty of the Bosnian countryside when war rages all around. Now, with a few moments to spare, he wondered at the enchanting snow-covered landscape. Even after all these years since he'd read the book, it reminded him of C. S. Lewis's Narnia—*The Lion, The Witch and the Wardrobe*. The locals proudly described the 1984 Sarajevo Winter Olympics as paradise. Gen. Brown himself had been a member of the British Army bobsleigh team that had tried but failed to qualify for the Olympics. *That* was the only time he had imagined years earlier that he would ever have reason to spend time in Sarajevo.

Gen. Brown switched on the local radio station at 9:00 am. He and Yomper listened intently to Dražen's radio broadcast from the Goražde enclave.

"Hang on a minute, sir." Yomper adjusted the dial for better reception. Dražen was reading the latest casualty figures over the airwaves, pleading for help from anyone who was listening, demanding military and humanitarian intervention from the international community. It was a remarkable mix of infomercial, political speech and an impassioned Mayday distress signal.

"The boy's articulate," said Gen. Brown. "So many of the locals speak excellent English."

"Better than my Bosnian, sir. That's gospel."

"I sympathize with Dražen. Serbs are about to obliterate Goražde. I can't allow that. The UN would never recover from mass murder in the heart of Europe on our watch. The Markale massacre was already the last straw. Damn it, I promised we would protect these people."

"I'm ready, boss. Whatever you need." Yomper tugged down on the steering wheel to avoid yet another pothole.

Gen. Brown jabbed at the radio. "He's begging for our help. He says we've abandoned them ... And he's right."

Yomper nodded in agreement. "Time for NATO?"

"No, absolutely not. If NATO destroys one more Serb target, the people of Goražde are scuppered."

The satellite telephone mounted in their command vehicle began beeping.

Gen. Brown snatched the receiver and put it on speaker. "Brown."

"General Brown, this is Klaus Reithoffer. You must return to Sarajevo." Reithoffer's voice pitched two tones higher than normal. He seemed irritated.

"Damn it, man, *I'm* in command here. Who in God's name do you think you are?"

"Bosnian Serbs will pay for their crimes. You must return to Sarajevo."

"You gave me twenty-four hours."

"Change of plan. My sources tell me General Zukić is about to attack Goražde. There is nothing you can do."

"Thanks for the update." Brown shook his head in disbelief. "Have you been talking to the Americans, Mr. Reithoffer? Your wife wouldn't approve."

"*Nicht verstehen.* I don't understand."

"Ekaterina agrees with me."

"What kind of games are these?"

"Your wife called me. I am sorry about your daughter. Please accept my condolences. I didn't know—"

"You have no business with my wife. She has nothing to do with this—"

"She insisted our conversation was off the record. But, interestingly, she did mention your … and I quote: 'personal vendetta against the Serbs.' I'm sure your new friends at the EU would be fascinated to hear about that. I had the foresight to record the conversation."

"This is madness. You are well beyond your station, General. I could terminate your position with one telephone call."

"I don't think so. I was sent here by the UN, not the EU." Gen. Brown glanced over at Yomper as the vehicle hit another bump. "I wish you luck with that, Mr. Reithoffer. But let me ask you something: Do you have any proof that the Serbs are implicated in your daughter's death? After my conversation with your wife, it seems you too might be well beyond *your* station."

"No one gave you permission to talk to my wife. My wife has nothing important to tell you."

"I don't need permission. She called *me*. I also find it interesting how remarkably enthusiastic and quick off the mark your country was to recognize Croatia's sovereignty. And now Bosnia?"

"She is just my wife. She plays no role in these matters of state."

"You underestimate her, Mr. Reithoffer. *Klaus*. She told me about your telephone call with the Croatian president in Paris and your subsequent meeting in Vienna. You're a busy man, Klaus—"

"I am warning you, General Brown—"

"She also said she would be willing to pass on the details to any journalist I should care to choose."

Silence.

"Let me remind you," said Reithoffer slowly, "that I am president of the European Union, and I will contact Robert Grange immediately. If you do not return to Sarajevo, I cannot be held responsible for your safety."

"Is that a threat?"

"NATO is ready. Do you think US, UN, and EU will allow this war to ignite? We cannot allow this to continue."

"Correct, Mr. Reithoffer. But according to the agreement I personally brokered with all parties, we have ten hours to find a solution. You also gave me your personal assurances. I don't understand what has changed."

"You think you can trust these people?"

"I have to try. Meanwhile, you'll forgive me if I continue my mission given to me by the secretary-general of the United Nations." He paused for effect. "And I suggest you talk to your wife before you make any hasty decisions or telephone calls to London."

Gen. Brown hung up.

"Nice one, boss."

"Food for thought, I think."

"Bloody cheeky, Kraut."

"You have a way with words, Yomper."

"Thanks, boss. But that one needs a good punching."

"I agree. Put it at the top of our to-do list."

Goražde

Steele and Staci were left tied up, blindfolded, and gagged in the VW Golf for several minutes. Then the car rocked gently as someone climbed in, started the engine, and drove off with them in the back.

Steele tried to orientate himself and managed to wind down the window an inch even though his hands were tied in front of him. He listened carefully to try and work out the direction they were traveling, staying alert for any cues that might give them a chance to escape at an opportune moment. No one had tied their legs together, so, theoretically, they could run and help untie each other later.

The lull in shelling and small-arms fire signaled, he sensed, that a heavier bout of artillery and tank bombardment was imminent.

Steele turned his head left and right, and his bound hands found Staci's for a few moments. He squeezed her hand and said quietly, "It's okay. We're going to get out of this." Although he couldn't be sure, he sensed they were heading toward the front line, or at least parallel to it. In this small town, the enemy was never far away.

Then he heard the brief whistle of an incoming round the second before impact. The back blast from the shell caused them to veer off course for a moment, then zigzag, before the unknown driver regained control and continued. The car rattled violently as the driver pressed the accelerator hard to clear the threat.

Steele said, "Shit! What was that?"

"Not even close," said a voice Steele recognized. "Welcome to Goražde."

Steele answered, "Dražen?"

"No one drives in daytime. It is very dangerous. This is why we waited. Sorry for the inconvenience. I will untie you soon."

"What are you doing, Dražen?" asked Staci.

"Every day they shell us. Every day my Muslim brother, my sister, or my neighbor can die."

Steele said, "Where are we going?"

"We go to my house. I have something for you."

A minute later, the VW Golf pulled over.

Dražen leaned into the back seat, pulled off their blindfolds, and clipped their bindings with the hunting knife on his belt. "Quickly," he said. "We will be safe inside. Serb positions are on the other side of that hill. But no direct fire."

They climbed out of the car. Steele eyed the nondescript house with white stucco walls bearing the pockmarks of mortar round damage that nearly every house sported like a badge of honor.

"Thank God," said Staci. "This trip hasn't been as much fun as I thought."

Dražen said, "Everyone abandons us—General Brown abandons us—but I hope you will help us."

"We'll do our best," said Steele. "Why the change of heart, Dražen?"

"Let me say, this is war, and I trust no one. But it is better for you, that my men think I am against you. I can't trust any of them one hundred percent."

Dražen ushered them inside. It was dark and dingy. But for now, at least, it was sound cover.

9:51 am

One mile from Dražen's safe house and high above the town, Gen. Zukić scrutinized the battleground in front of him for the final onslaught. He sat on a folding chair slung with gray canvas. The chairs were positioned on each side of a wooden chessboard. Gen. Zukić slid his queen three squares diagonally toward his opponent's bishop. "Šah-mat," he said, eyes glinting mischievously at Col. Kostić, his chief of staff. *Checkmate.*

Expecting Col. Kostić to concede, he stood up and walked to the vantage point atop the hillside. In fact, he had left a way out of the checkmate for his staff officer, but he enjoyed testing Col. Kostić to see if he would dare challenge him.

"Pobijedili ste, generale. Odlična igra." *You win, General. An excellent game.* Gen. Zukić got up and joined his commander. They looked at the town. Even from this distance, the physical devastation was clearly visible.

"And the rats scurry around," said Gen. Zukić. "You concede too easily, my loyal friend—like the vermin below. You had a way out"—He pointed at the chessboard—"Your knight."

Col. Kostić found his mistake and nodded. "Unlike the wretches down there!" He chuckled obsequiously.

They both knew Gen. Zukić wanted and needed to win today, both on the chessboard and on the ground. Events were coming to a head. There would be winners and there would be losers in the next twenty-four hours.

Gen. Zukić dabbed his face with a red cotton handkerchief. He thought about his daughter who had committed suicide two weeks before. His eyes reddened. What had he done? How had his life come to this? The whole world hated him; his men pretended to love him, but he doubted their sincerity. His daughter had said as much weeks before she took her own life. He had, she told him, put his country before family, and she hated him for it. Now he had nothing to lose. He had to destroy the enemy.

"Someone will pay," he said to Col. Kostić but really more to himself as he emerged from his morose reverie.

"Yes, General."

"I will show them. The world interferes with our freedom, our rights, our interests, and I will show them how we fight for survival. Americans and British will learn from *us.* They want us to defeat the Turks for their own interests. I understand how they think. They want to blame us for everything."

Gen. Zukić was certain about what was best for his self-proclaimed "Republika Srpska." His eyes scanned the contours of land; he wanted all of it under his control. He pinpointed his tank positions, which were expertly camouflaged in a tactical arc. His tank crews were well disciplined, unlike his infantry conscripts. To date, his tank crews had carried out his orders to the letter.

A Bosnian Serb army Jeep pulled up yards away on the dirt road. A staff officer came out of the tented command post, approached the driver of the Jeep, and took possession of the messenger's signal. He jogged over to Col. Kostić, gave him the signal, and Col. Kostić scanned the paper. "General, we have important news."

Gen. Zukić was gloating, staring at the chessboard, thinking of future victories.

"General Brown has given his word," said Col. Kostić. "He guarantees no further NATO attacks if we withdraw heavy weapons, as agreed."

"Brown is not a politician," Gen. Zukić replied. Then he chuckled. "He follows orders. They are worried that Russia will intervene. Now they are making deals. So predictable."

"I understand, General. But perhaps this is an opportunity for peace?" said Col. Kostić. "We have achieved our military goals. The Muslims are cut off. Let them think we will attack, and they will surrender. We are superior. Is it necessary to slaughter everyone in Goražde? If they survive our attacks, they will scurry away in the night like rats."

"You must look at the larger picture, comrade. We must have the Protocol in our possession. We must defeat the enemy."

"If it exists. What if this Protocol is propaganda?"

"I did not ask for your opinion, but I will tell you something. Sonja Radovanović told me the truth. I am her godfather. I am closer to her than my own daughter—God rest her soul. The Sarajevo Protocol says that Serb people have the right to rule Yugoslavia including Bosnia-Herzegovina. Do you understand?"

"We will be exposed, comrade General, the whole world against us. Just like the First World War. Again, they will blame us because of the Germans."

"Germans have much to answer for. Even the British government understands this … Our esteemed leader, Josip Broz Tito, wrote this Protocol with the British after World War Two. It is our right. British MI6 is working hard to find it also. British interests are at stake. But we will find it first. Sonja told me it is in Goražde. We will allow Captain Steele to find it for us. Let him extract it from Muslim rats."

"What do I tell them? General Brown? UNPROFOR? They're waiting for our reply."

"Tell them we accept the terms. We will pull back by 18:00 hours tonight."

"You agree to a cease-fire, General?"

"No, of course not. We are buying time. We continue the fight for Goražde."

"This is our last chance, General. NATO will attack …"

Gen. Zukić pulled his shoulders back, filled his lungs, and smiled. "We have time. Everything is under control." He glanced down at the chessboard, picked up the knight that could have won the game, and threw it in the air. He did not catch the knight but instead allowed it to fall, then ground it into the dirt with his boot.

Shortly, his tanks would be in position to destroy the town of Goražde once and for all.

Sarajevo would be next.

CHAPTER TWENTY-NINE

10:01 am

Dražen closed the front door and said, "This area has heaviest shelling. Now you will see how our people are living for three years." He looked at Staci, continuing in broken but respectable English. "You are journalist ... You will write about your experience with us?"

Staci nodded. "Sure."

Steele was suspicious. This didn't make sense. They had already offered to help him earlier. Why would Dražen suddenly trust them and put them in harm's way at the same time?

A soldier waiting inside the house locked the front door. No one, it seemed, was going anywhere.

Steele said, "Why the locks?"

Dražen did not answer.

Staci added, "We've come to help you, Dražen." Distracted, she looked around, overwhelmed by a new smell. "What's that smell?" she asked.

Dražen explained. "The smell is our second mortuary—four houses from here. There is a big cellar to store our rotting corpses. We have no choice. We have no refrigeration. It is too dangerous even to bury our dead or burn them." He beckoned them to follow him along an empty dank corridor and opened the door to a room at the end. "Please, you will get good sense of fighting in here."

Steele and Staci glanced at each other, puzzled. They entered the room.

The window was boarded up with planks of wood. There were no shutters or windows on the exterior. Steele stayed to one side of the room away from the windows and told Staci to do likewise. He had a good sense of direction. The window faced the arc of Serb firepower pointing at Goražde. Then he snatched a glimpse through a gap in the wood of a Serb tank repositioning in the distance.

Before Steele had registered what the tank was doing, he saw a puff of smoke exit the barrel and heard the muffled discharge of a tank round. Less than a second later the *whizz-bang* of a 100-mm round exploded close by. It sounded closer than it was due to the layout of the other buildings.

"That was close," said Steele.

"No, not even," replied Dražen.

Steele and Staci exchanged a glance.

"I will come back later," said Dražen. "I must make announcements. The fighting begins again."

Steele said, "The Sarajevo Protocol?"

"First you must learn to trust me."

The door to their room opened, and Dražen left. The door was secured by a guard from the other side.

"What the hell does that mean?" said Staci, wandering into the middle of the room.

"Keep away from the window."

"At least they let me keep my backpack." She moved back and placed the backpack on the floor.

Silence.

"So now we're human shields?" she said.

"Not exactly. No one knows we're here, which is probably worse. If the Serbs know this is a command post of some kind, we're screwed."

A minute later, the door opened again. "Here," said Dražen, throwing a mobile telephone in Steele's direction. "It's international. Tell your friends about your vacation and the conditions in Goražde. Perhaps you can persuade them to help us."

The door closed.

Steele examined the mobile telephone. "It works."

Staci said, "Breaking news?"

"CNN … BBC? You chose."

"They want to use us to send a message."

"I'd probably do the same time. Pretty sharp of Dražen, I'd say."

"Okay." Staci nodded slowly. "I guess you're right." She stared at him for a few moments, seeming to have trouble making up her mind. "Jack," she continued, "I want to tell you something." She leaned against the wall and sank to the floor.

"The suspense is killing me."

She forced a smile. "I'm sorry, Jack. I'm not exactly who you think I am."

UNPROFOR HQ, *Sarajevo*

Boyle and Reithoffer stood at the entrance of the UN HQ in downtown Sarajevo. Both were smoking in silence after a brief exchange of small talk. They surveyed the Sarajevo soccer stadium that was now a working cemetery.

"Makes you think, doesn't it?" said Boyle.

"*Jawohl*," replied Reithoffer. *Certainly does.*

Maj. Small approached the men from the Ops Room inside the building.

"It's not safe to leave, Mr. Reithoffer," said Maj. Small. "Airport is reporting sporadic small-arms fire. It's closed until further notice, I'm afraid."

As the newly appointed European Union president, Reithoffer was itching to get back to Strasbourg. He knew the airport closure could mean hours, days, or even a week before flights resumed. The only other option was to drive. But that meant the risk of being held up at the infamous Sierra One checkpoint to exit Sarajevo. If the Serbs felt like it, they might block them for hours.

"How long?" he asked. "I do not want to be here when NATO resumes operations."

"Impossible to say, sir," said Maj. Small. "But I have a suggestion ... Tomislav Haler, the Bosnian Croat leader, just had a meeting with the Bosnian government today. He has also been delayed and would like to meet you. He's in the building."

Reithoffer loosened his tie and gave a fake smile. "It would be my pleasure."

The last thing he actually wanted was to get involved in the concerns and gripes of the Bosnian Croats. Though aligned with Croatia and Tudjman, the Bosnian Croats had a list of priorities that did not necessarily mesh with Croatia's policy in Bosnia. Reithoffer was beginning to regret his impromptu visit to Sarajevo. *These people are so primitive,* he thought.

"You can use my office," said Boyle. "I'd like to meet Mr. Haler too. Knowledge is power and all that."

Reithoffer nodded uneasily. He knew he could not refuse the meeting with the Bosnian Croat leader because it would certainly be taken the wrong way. Or, he conceded to himself, precisely the right way. *The last thing I want is to be lectured on Bosnia war and peace.* He should have listened to Katya—this wasn't the way to spend the first week of his EU presidency. But he had wanted to be certain, in person, that *his* plan for Bosnia would succeed, and that Gen. Brown did not jeopardize or spoil his plan in any way. "You didn't answer my question, Major Small. How long before we can leave?"

Boyle said, "This is a bloody war. Do you understand what that means, Mr. Reithoffer?"

Reithoffer shot back. "You people have five thousand UN peacekeepers here, and you cannot guarantee airport security."

Boyle said, "You people have a ten-billion-dollar budget and you can't make these imbeciles talk to each other? Germany mishandled Croatia's sovereignty from the start. It's a prize cock-up. That's why people like me have to come out here and risk our lives to mop up your ludicrous policies."

Maj. Small said, "Herr Reithoffer, if you'd like to follow me."

Reithoffer stamped out his cigarette. "Recognition would have happened sooner or later."

Boyle said, "But 'later' might have saved a few thousand lives. Get my point?"

Reithoffer ignored this last barb and turned to Maj. Small: "I am ready to meet Haler. Let's get it over with."

Minutes later, a gaggle of sweaty, tousled, middle-aged men in ill-fitting suits and loose neckties arrived in the hallway outside Boyle's UNPROFOR office: The Bosnian Croat delegation had been smuggled into Sarajevo through a tunnel that ran beneath the airport. At President Tudjman's insistence, they had been holding secret talks with the Bosnian government to broker a power sharing agreement after the conflict. They planned to leave Sarajevo in a more civilized manner than the way they had arrived. By helicopter. But their intentions had been thwarted because the airport had been forced to close.

"Please, gentlemen," said Maj. Small. "Come in and make yourselves comfortable. Refreshments are on the way. We'll keep you informed of the security situation at the airport, of course. Thank you for your patience."

Reithoffer and Tomislav Haler shook hands. Boyle remained a silent observer.

Haler began, "I would like to thank you for your efforts. You have an excellent grasp of this war." He spoke awkwardly, as though he had trouble breathing after ascending a flight of stairs, which he hadn't.

"It is a pleasure to meet members of the Bosnian Croat Federation." Reithoffer had no intention of mentioning this chance meeting to anyone. The last thing he wanted was to be seen to have switched allegiances from the Bosnian government to the Bosnian Croat Federation.

Haler took off his jacket and sat on the edge of the desk. "I am delighted we had this opportunity to meet. I have sensitive information which I thought should be given in person."

Reithoffer said, "I am listening, Mr. Haler."

"Our meeting with the Bosnian government was disappointing. Understand, it is important for us to separate from Muslims within the framework of a future Bosnian Federation. We will only work with Serbs."

Reithoffer felt sick to his stomach. Such intentions would ruin his plan for revenge. "This is premature, Mr. Haler," he said calmly.

"We witnessed terrible slaughter in Croatia. International community knows what happened in Vukovar. A bloodbath. We do not want this to happen in Bosnia-Herzegovina."

"I agree." Reithoffer was lying.

Haler continued, "We need Bosnian Serbs in order to make things work in our country. We lived side by side with them for many years. We can make things work with them."

"What are you saying?" Reithoffer smiled blandly, attempting to keep an air of calm.

"We will *never* live and work with Bosnian Muslims as our neighbors. This possibility died with the destruction of our sacred Mostar Bridge."

"The Croatian Defense Force destroyed the bridge," Reithoffer reminded Haler.

"We were provoked."

Reithoffer took a deep breath. "*We*—the people of the European Union—are running out of patience," he said. "Your people have also committed atrocities and war crimes. We will bring the Serbs under control, as you ask, but ultimately, there must be a united Bosnia—Croats and Muslims."

Haler stood up. "You and your people—all of you—are guests in *our* country. This is not Croatia. This is Bosnia-Herzegovina. Bosnian Croats also have interests. And I am telling you—politely, but firmly—we will not work, live, or breath with the Muslims after this war. We demand any peace agreement include provision for an independent Bosnian Croat Federation."

Boyle frowned but did not speak. Reithoffer noticed the concern written across his face.

Reithoffer looked directly at Haler and said, "You understand this will derail the peace process?"

"You understand peace is worthless if we lose our identity."

"You people and your ethnic identity," Boyle said *sotto voce*, but loud enough so that everyone could hear.

Haler said, "We are proud people. We have much to offer the world. We can't accept Turks' influence on our children and our future."

Reithoffer wanted to spit. The audacity was more than he could bear—this former tin pot communist state dictating to *his* European Union. *Damn it*, he thought, *I'm tempted to recommend that NATO immediately hold the Bosnian Croats accountable for cease-fire violations and noncompliance.* He had a deal with Tudjman, and now this Bosnian Croat clown was moving the goal posts. The situation was unacceptable.

Reithoffer continued, "I understand your situation, Mr. Haler. We have many problems with the Bosnian government. They play games and change the rules to suit their interests. Give me some time to think about your concerns. If you will excuse me." For now it was best not to be drawn into a debate.

Tomislav Haler stood up, and the two leaders bid each other farewell. "Thank you, Mr. Reithoffer, for your understanding."

"Good luck, Mr. Haler. And thank you. I will be sure to pass on your concerns."

Haler left the room with his entourage.

"So, you see, Colonel Boyle," said Reithoffer. "We need NATO's assistance, and we need it now."

CHAPTER THIRTY

Kiselyak, near Sarajevo

Tomislav Haler wasn't sure which was worse—braving cavernous potholes in the back of a UN military ambulance or risking arrest and the embuggerance factor at the infamous Bosnian Serb Sierra One checkpoint. This time, however, they crossed the Serb checkpoint on the outskirts of Sarajevo unimpeded and reached UNPROFOR BiH command headquarters in Kiselyak in good time. This hulk of a building had been a hotel in peacetime, an ugly mass of sprawling concrete that looked as though a spaceship had landed in the middle of the Bosnian countryside.

Haler climbed out of the ambulance used to smuggle him out of Sarajevo. He was relieved to see his luxury Mercedes E-class waiting opposite the UN gatehouse as arranged. Only UN vehicles were allowed inside the compound. He prayed he would need never step foot inside a military ambulance again, but was grateful for the cover it had afforded him.

From Kiselyak, it would be a short drive back to Vitez in central Bosnia where he would overnight at the British battalion known as *Britbat*. Tomorrow he would head south to Mostar for an important meeting with a retired British Royal Marine general who was now the head of the European Community Monitoring Mission—ECMM—to discuss prisoner exchanges with the Bosnian army.

Haler started across the road with a friendly nod to Davor,

his driver, who was waiting in the Mercedes. The driver got out to take Haler's overnight bag from him.

Haler said, "Wait for me here. I need cigarettes." Certain Bosnian VIPs and their staff were permitted to use the British NAAFI shop inside BiH Command with a special ration card. Haler was one of them.

Then Haler changed his mind. He decided Davor might enjoy the opportunity to buy cut-price cigarettes without having to pay a small fortune on the black market. Haler gave Davor a $100 bill and his UNPROFOR ration card. Then he scribbled a short list.

"Hurry," he ordered. "Buy your wife some perfume."

"Thank you, gospodine. I'll be quick. No problem."

Haler had refused an UNPROFOR military escort to Vitez. He felt the threat level from Bosnian Muslims did not merit another bothersome request and the red tape that accompanied it. As he saw it, there was at least a respectable level of security and mutual respect between Bosnian Muslims and Croats. No UN escort necessary.

It would turn out to be the biggest mistake of his life. Had he accepted the offer, a two-armored vehicle escort might have afforded the protection to save him. He would have been able to take cover and scramble inside one of the UN vehicles.

Davor showed his ID to the UN guard and disappeared inside the former Hotel Kiselyak.

Five seconds later, a deafening explosion shook the ground and Haler was catapulted ten feet into the air. He landed on a large boulder at the side of the road.

A siren wailed.

The commands and shouts of French and Danish UN officers and NCOs echoed across the parking lot of the Hotel Kiselyak HQ. Pandemonium ensued inside. The headquarters had never come under direct attack. Skirmishes between Bosnian Muslims and Bosnian Croats were sporadic in these parts—the Muslim-Croat demarcation line ran right through the middle of BiH Command. UN observers were able to monitor the fighting without leaving the hotel. Until now, both sides had respected the sanctity of this UN base.

A twenty-year-old Bosnian Muslim translator working inside the BiH Command UN Ops Room rose from his desk and made his way along the corridor through a fire door and to a stairwell overlooking the car park. He surveyed the scene of the explosion and homed in on the Mercedes Benz. He noted that the automobile had been badly damaged, but that Haler had not been inside during the explosion. The Bosnian Croat leader was lying on a boulder at the side of the road near the car. He was still moving.

The translator took out a cell phone with a prepaid card and made a local call to his masters in Sarajevo.

Barely a minute later, a second shell landed, this time twenty feet from what was left of the Mercedes, destroying the large boulder and Tomislav Haler along with it."

Sarajevo, two minutes later ...

Maj. Small rushed into Boyle's office. "Two shells at BiH Command, Kiselyak."

Boyle and Reithoffer looked up. "*Shit,*" said Boyle. "Never a dull moment ..."

Maj. Small continued. "Haler's dead."

"Who's responsible?" Boyle asked.

"No word yet. UNMOs are checking trajectories."

Boyle turned to Reithoffer. "Who did you call when Haler left the building? I saw you calling someone."

Reithoffer smiled. "Assassinating the Bosnian Croat leader does not help me in any way. We need Muslims and Croats to work together against the Serbs."

"Serbs have no reason to attack the Bosnian Croats."

"Alija Izetbegovic is a very angry man. He's upset with everyone."

Izetbegovic, the Bosnian president, was known for his hard-line approach. But it didn't make sense that he would order an attack on the Bosnian Croats.

"It's a mess." Boyle sighed. Then, to Reithoffer, "That's the beauty of this little genocide-in-the-making. All we can do is put out fires. The pact between Croats and Muslims could blow up in our faces at any moment. I suggest we put all efforts on Steele and the American before Bosnia implodes."

"Haler's death changes everything. We need to come down hard on the Serbs before the Muslims and Croats start fighting. The more time we give Serbs, the more they will take advantage," continued Reithoffer. "Time's up. I am going to recommend NATO takes action immediately. No more waiting."

Boyle shook his head. "No. At least talk to General Brown in person. You've got to warn him. We have people in Goražde."

"I already spoke to him. It was foolish of me to entertain the notion that the CIA, or MI6, or whoever you are working for, could bring Serbs to the negotiating table," said Reithoffer. "I have no choice. Haler is dead. Bosnia is about to explode."

"Know that we will hold you responsible for any harm that comes to UN peacekeepers and especially General Brown," added Boyle. "Not to mention the fall out if your actions make this situation worse than it already is."

"I promise to keep you informed." Reithoffer left the room.

Boyle walked to the window. He peered through gaps in duct tape and surveyed the panoramic view of Sarajevo. His gaze wandered across the cityscape—scorched apartment buildings, Zetra soccer stadium surrounded by coffin-shaped wooden stakes for headstones, and huge, gaping holes in apartment buildings where people continued to live in their apartments if they had escaped a direct hit.

A few months earlier, it had seemed like a relatively straight-forward mission when all sides seemed willing to negotiate. Boyle recalled the fifty-strong Band of the Coldstream Guards marching in their scarlet uniforms and bearskins in the soccer stadium before a friendly football match. The band had been invited to Sarajevo to boost morale, show the world that Sara-jevo was fearless and back in business. Back then, it had seemed like a great opportunity to show off his influence with the pow-ers that be to Black Cobra, in return for which he would earn a small fortune.

"I'll show them. All of them," Boyle muttered to himself. "God damn it, I'll show these bastards."

6:25 pm Goražde

In virtual darkness, Steele continued his conversation with Staci. She had confessed that she was working for Boyle, or at least Boyle had been feeding her information about *him*. After the initial shock, Steele wasn't surprised that Boyle had approached Staci. It made perfect sense; she was a young, attractive, capable journalist as well as an outsider.

He moved to the window and looked through the boards nailed to the wooden frames to get a better look at the Serb tank on the hillside to the West. It changed positions every few minutes.

Outside, it was twilight. Glancing at the tank, he understood how the citizens of Sarajevo felt—never knowing when you, or your home, or your family, or your neighbor might be hit. Every moment might be your last. How many more civilians would be killed or maimed from orders given by Gen. Zukić? *Who* would be next? The psychological toll this war was taking on its citizens was simply impossible to fathom. Steele's own father had been a psychologist. It was also more than ironic, he thought, that Dr. Radovanović had been the Sarajevo football team's full-time psychologist, but the war meant that he was now fighting his former team players and shelling the men he used to care for.

Steele asked Staci, "Are you helping Boyle for the money?"

"He promised the story would be worth it—a thousand times over worth it. The BBC will beg me to work for them, he said. That's the dream, you see, Jack—little old me, an American from Pennsylvania, working for the BBC. We all gotta dream, right?"

Steele, incredulous, was smiling in the dark. Although he understood how Staci could have got to this point, he still had to ask, "You trusted Boyle? You realize that is madness, right?"

"The guy came up to me in North London—I was at Camden Lock market—and he said, 'How would you like to work for *us*?' I look at him like he's nuts."

"Boyle?"

"Yeah, I thought he was hitting on me. But he said, 'You'll continue your work, you'll be based in London, and you'll receive generous compensation on top of your current job.'"

"How much?"

"That was *my* first question. I mean, if you're going to work for a shady organization, you need to know how much, right?"

"I suppose ... "

"Let's just say it was an offer I couldn't afford to refuse."

"You call that journalism?"

"An 'opportunity' I told myself. Us Americans like opportunities. It's in our nature to seize them."

"What was the deal?"

"An exclusive on the scoop once Black Cobra has everything it needs."

"Black Cobra?"

"Boyle's people. Or should I say people behind his people."

Steele shook his head. "Complicated."

"Yes, it is."

"And they use you if they need media coverage?"

"You bet."

"What makes you think they won't hang you out to dry once your usefulness expires?"

"Fifty thousand pounds in my account, and the same again next month, so I'll take the chance. And if they do, it's not the end of the world. I can always run with the story on my own."

"Who's paying them? Who hired *them?*"

"I don't know … SIS? CIA?"

The heart-to-heart came to an abrupt halt as two shells exploded in quick succession close to the house.

Steele pulled them both to the ground. Straddled face down on the floor, Staci continued as if nothing had happened. "Look, this Sarajevo Protocol is big. I want to find it."

"Me too. But I'd rather not die in the process." He crawled over to the wall.

"Can we trust Dražen?"

"I don't think Dražen wants to kill us. I think he wants to teach us a lesson and make the best possible use of us at the same time. The international community let them down big time. We're an extension of them. So, he wants to use us or punish us. Put yourself in his shoes."

Staci shifted to her knees. "But we've got something they need."

"What?"

"Dražen's lost faith in the outside world, right?" She reached for her backpack and took out a mini tape recorder. "I have everything on this." She held up the recorder.

"What is it?"

"A conversation between Boyle and Luka before he died. It explains everything. Luka is threatening to hand over the Protocol to foreign journalists if the UN deserts the people of Goražde. If Dražen hears his father, he'll help us perhaps?"

"Where did you get that?"

"Boyle didn't send me in empty-handed. He thought I might need it."

"Why did you wait so long?"

"I was saving the best till last. And I would say we're in a pretty big hole right now. I had no intention of 'confessing' to you either. But things have changed."

"Being here is definitely a game changer." Steele pointed to the recorder. "And *that* is also a game changer."

He walked to the door and banged on it.

"Molim vas!" he shouted. *Please!* "Trebam razgovarati s Draženom!" *I need to speak to Dražen!*

The clatter of small-arms fire crackled in the middle distance.

Then silence.

CHAPTER THIRTY-ONE

Sarajevo Airport Road

The airport settlement and virtually every single now-uninhabited house on the airport road were so badly destroyed that it resembled an over-the-top war movie set on a Hollywood back lot. But the charred skeleton of a burned-out tank and a dead German shepherd told any observer that the scene was very real.

With a no man's land buffer zone stretching away on both sides, the road along this particular section marked the confrontation line proper. It was too dangerous to clear mines or repair shell craters here. It was a slalom course for all drivers. Neither side trusted the other enough even to arrange for corpses to be collected or to have the road repaired without attack or retribution.

Behind the tank, daubed on a plain brick wall, graffiti read:

Welcome
to
Sarajevo

Sarajevo's sense of humor despite their darkest hour.

The UN APC ambulance shifted gears along the airport road, and Reithoffer repeated today's mantra: he would never ever return to this wretched city, war or no war. *No one can help these people*, he thought. *They can't even help themselves*. And yes, he had meant what he'd said about NATO attacking the Serbs—it was only a matter of hours. He couldn't care less about any of them anymore, Serb, Croat, or Muslim. Each was as bad as the other, and this latest news with the Bosnian Croats was the final straw. None of them could be trusted. He truly believed the only path to peace was to bomb all sides to the peace table; and he would make sure the Serbs came out worst.

Before leaving UNPROFOR headquarters in Sarajevo, Reithoffer had spoken to the NATO Liaison Officer (NATO LO), who had informed him that NATO commanders in Naples were waiting on the weather. Bosnian Serb targets had been allocated, but there was a thick layer of cloud over Republika Srpska. The NATO LO explained that before air strikes could be executed, the thick cloud would have to clear. *So much for cutting-edge, twentieth-century warfare,* he thought.

"Attention all passengers," said the Egyptian vehicle commander, "unauthorized checkpoint ahead. You are to remain inside the vehicle until I give the all-clear."

"Thank you." Reithoffer nodded cooperatively.

The high-pitched whirring of the armored ambulance slowed to a steady hum. Reithoffer heard the word "landmines" over the headset.

"Problem?" asked Maj. Asim, a Pakistani UN officer sitting next to Reithoffer who had also hitched a ride and was hoping to get to Split for some R&R.

"No, sir," said the vehicle commander, "it's just that—"

A muffled *crack-thump* hit the front of the vehicle—

The ambulance came to an abrupt halt.

Reithoffer was no soldier, but it sounded like a high-velocity round had struck. The windows were made of bulletproof glass, but even this round had penetrated the windscreen. The Egyptian commander built like superman slumped to one side. Still alive, he was holding his shoulder where the bullet had entered. Blood oozed through his fingers, and a dark red patch began to seep through his uniform.

Reithoffer glared at Maj. Asim. "Do something! We're under attack!"

Maj. Asim scrambled forward, unfastened the commander's breast pocket and pulled out a field dressing. He handed it to Reithoffer and told him to hold it down firmly on the man's wound. Unusual for Reithoffer, he did as he was told.

Asim snatched the Clansman Pressel box next to the driver and squeezed. "Hello Zero-Alpha … Hello Zero-Alpha, this is Major Asim, over …"

Silence.

"Hello Zero-Alpha … Hello Zero-Alpha, this is Major Asim … No duff! No duff! Urgent message, over …" *No duff* meant that the message being transmitted over the radio net was authentic and under no circumstances should it be considered any type of drill or exercise.

Silence.

Reithoffer turned to the rear. Someone was opening the door of the ambulance.

"Hello Zero-Alpha, this is Major Asim, urgent message, over …"

Reithoffer gave up trying to stem the flow of blood from the commander's shoulder. He shunted down to the rear door to grab the inside handle and prevent the person on the other side from gaining access.

But he was too late. Whoever was on the other side was quicker and stronger.

The door opened, and daylight poured in.

A huddle of armed soldiers wearing a hodge-podge of camouflage attire stood outside.

"Quickly," said the one who appeared to be in command. A tall, thin man with gray hair and dark skin, his face deeply fissured, said, "I am the commander. We mean you no harm," he said calmly. He held a photograph in his right hand and was looking directly at Reithoffer.

Maj. Asim broke in, "My name is Major Asim. I must protest. I demand that you allow us to continue immediately." He pointed to the wounded man. "This man needs urgent medical attention. We have guaranteed freedom of movement."

"Unfortunately, sacrifices are sometimes necessary, Major," replied the local commander.

"Who are you?" snapped Reithoffer. "I demand you allow us safe passage. We have urgent business."

"Believe me, *gospodine,* no business is more urgent than the business we have with you."

Reithoffer blinked nervously, appearing confused. For the first time, he noticed the insignia on the man's arm—*a Bosnian government soldier.* He had assumed, incorrectly, they were farther into no man's land and had been stopped by Serbs. "What do you want?"

The commander took a step back as his men pulled Reithoffer from the ambulance. They manhandled him into a battered yellow Trabant waiting a few yards away, engine running.

"You are making a serious mistake, I am warning you."

The commander turned to the UN personnel inside the ambulance. "We wish to borrow the esteemed leader of the European Union. I am sorry for your commander. Please proceed, I hope he makes a full recovery."

These were the last words Reithoffer heard before the Trabant's door was slammed shut and a hood was placed over his head.

As the hood plunged him into darkness, he immediately thought of Ekaterina. *Will she even care?*

1:46 pm Goražde

The house was damp and dilapidated. Steele reckoned the entire structure would collapse if another shell landed close by, or worse, made a direct hit. And if there *was* a direct hit, the odds of surviving were slim to none. But worse than thoughts of death was the prospect of failing. Jack Steele did not want to *fail.* He wanted to find the Sarajevo Protocol. He wanted to help innocent victims of this catastrophe of war and prevent more suffering before it was too late. He had to stop the diplomatic, political, and military wheels turning before more NATO attacks spiraled the situation out of control—the Serbs would then retaliate against Muslims *and* UN personnel.

"It doesn't make sense," he said quietly.

"You don't say," Staci replied. "This whole war doesn't make any sense."

"I mean the Sarajevo Protocol doesn't make sense."

"Why?"

"Maybe we're both wrong."

"What?"

"You might be lying to me but not know you're lying." He placed his hands on her shoulders. "If there's one thing I've learned in Bosnia—never believe anything, unless or until you see it with your own eyes."

Staci took a moment. Then she said, "They hired me. They want that document. You think they gave me false info?"

"Maybe."

"Why would they set me up? They need me."

"I don't know. Smoke and mirrors? False trails? But I think we're being used—both of us—in something much bigger."

"What's bigger than this hellhole?"

An explosion rocked the house, causing the walls to shake violently.

From the force and sound of it and how violently the walls shook, Steele guessed a tank round had pierced the building immediately next door. It was close but it had missed them. The only problem was that where there was one tank round, another usually followed in quick succession.

When the dust settled—literally—Steele saw daylight peeking through a small hole in the wall on the far side of the room. He ran across the room and kicked the bricks several times until they began to crumble. He kicked again to make a hole large enough to crawl through.

They both ducked down and scrambled through the opening on hands and knees, then over the rubble and debris outside.

"If another round follows this grouping, we're dead," he said.

"I understand."

"Move."

The intensity of small-arms fire—no shells—increased over the next few minutes. They heard screams and cries for help in the near distance. *Another Serb attack? The final Serb attack?* Not surprisingly, the teenage boys guarding them had vanished. The small-arms fire was mainly outgoing—precious ammunition sprayed wastefully from Muslim trenches on this side of the river. *Save your ammo!* he wanted to scream. *You're going to need it!*

They crouched down behind a wall to the rear of the house. Steele looked around for better cover. "Boyle didn't know if I would follow his orders. That's why he sent *you*," he continued. "Just to make sure."

"I don't get it."

"We accomplish more together. He sent you to make me keep looking—the journalist and the soldier. I'm a naïve young officer. Why send the pros in when amateurs will get the job done. I'm expendable, and you're his one-woman media machine when the time comes …"

"Without the risk."

"Correct."

"Boyle set *me* up with Luka. That's why Luka 'chose' me." Staci shook her head, frustrated she hadn't seen the real scenario sooner. Then she said, "Now what?"

"Stay down and stay close."

They moved off crouching low, hugging what little cover there was across the wasteland rubble.

As they crept around the side of the house where the first tank round had struck, Steele spotted a car halfway down the block.

"Let's try the car ... it's our best option."

The tank was five hundred meters away on a ridge high above the town. He moved up to the side of the house and shot a glance around the corner toward the front line.

It didn't make sense. There was no way the tank on the hill could have hit the side of the house from its current position.

From Steele's right flank behind a tree-covered copse, the familiar roar of a tank's turbine engine made him turn. Another tank glided down the hill toward them, its barrel aiming directly at them.

Does the gunner already have us in his sights? he wondered.

"Can he see us?" asked Staci.

One moment later, another explosion ...

"There's your answer!"

A tank round slammed into the side of the house where they had been moments before.

"OK," said Steele. "I've officially lost my sense of humor. They can see us. We need to split up. *Now.*"

1:51 pm

"Do you see them?" asked Gen. Zukić, turning the focus ring on his Zeiss binoculars.

Gen. Zukić and Col. Kostić had a bird's eye view of Goražde. They had been monitoring the house where Steele was held. Gen. Zukić ordered the tanks to move to new fire positions.

"Destroy the house," he said, smiling.

Col. Kostić looked nervous. "General, you said keep them alive?"

"Correct. Look carefully, comrade ... they left." He handed his aide the binoculars. "The house was a command post. Destroy it. Do you see Steele?"

"Yes, I see him. He's clear of the target."

"And the girl?"

"Yes."

"The Turks locked them in the house. They don't trust foreigners either," he said with a sneer. "This is *our* war. These are *our* people, *our* land."

"General, confirm your fire order."

"Destroy the house: we will force them toward our unit on the left flank."

"Understood."

"I wish to speak with the British spy as soon as we capture him. We can't wait any longer for the document."

Col. Kostić held up his radio and issued the fire order.

CHAPTER THIRTY-TWO

Steele knew they were too close to the house. Another burst of small-arms fire from the tank's machine gun made confetti of the grass bank next to them.

But now they were under fire from another direction.

"*Shit.* There's a Bosnian fire position behind us!" he shouted to Staci. "*Get back to me!*"

Steele wasn't sure which army was actually firing at *them. Or are we just caught in the wrong place at the worst time?*

Staci obeyed, crawling along the ground toward him.

"Elbows, knees, and toes," Steele hissed.

"Coming ..." Staci gritted her teeth. She was more athletic than he'd imagined, hugging the ground like a Special Forces vet.

She reached him. "I thought you said split up?"

"Changed my mind. We're caught in the middle of a firefight, and neither side gives a shit about our peace plan."

"I get the picture."

They ducked at the sound of more bullets.

"The Muslims behind us think we're Serbs." He gestured toward the Serb tank.

"Got a white flag?"

"Too late for that. They'll cut us down in a second."

"I was kidding. We should have stayed in the house."

"The one they just flattened?" Steele nodded toward the house.

Staci looked back. "I missed that. These maniacs work fast."

They crawled again down the zigzag of a trench away from the fiercest wave of gun fire.

"Never mind, I'm—" The sound of a semiautomatic weapon being cocked inches behind his head made him stop.

Bang!

For a moment, Steele thought it was all over. There was a deafening explosion right next to his ear, but the instant ringing that followed made him realize he was still alive. After a few more seconds, the ringing subsided and he heard laughter.

He turned around and saw three gun barrels pointing at them. Steele could almost taste the cordite. One of them had just fired a shot that passed inches from his head. The shooter was smiling as if the entire scenario was some kind of huge joke.

Down on one knee holding an AK47 assault rifle, a Serb soldier waved toward the Muslim fire position and taunted the enemy. "We have your British and American spies. Thank you!"

Still crouching, but now pointing their weapons toward the Muslim trench and then back to Steele, two Serb soldiers escorted him back along the trench next to the road toward the second Serb tank's position.

The first soldier mocked, "How was your visit to Goražde? Did the Turks treat you well?"

Steele did not reply.

The second soldier said, "Did you pray in their mosque?"

"Before we shelled it?" added the first. He snorted and laughed at the same time. "You are lucky," he continued. "Our president has sent for you."

Steele recalled his Sandhurst instructor's mantra: "Anything could happen in the next twenty-four hours, gentlemen … and it probably will."

Thankful to be dragged to safety, but furious he had been so close to Dražen and perhaps the Sarajevo Protocol, Steele hated to admit he was further away than ever to finding it. So far, their venture into Goražde had achieved nothing.

Rogatica checkpoint, near Goražde

At 1:57 pm, the white armored BBC Landover was waiting at the Serb checkpoint a few miles outside Goražde.

"That's the last bloody thing we need," said Gen. Brown, who was generally a fan of the BBC, but like most senior officers, he didn't like being door-stepped. A press conference was one thing, a useful strategic tool at the right moment for the right set of circumstances. Media clout and journalists were important—a newspaper quote or headline was, if needed, the quickest way to get your message to the world's corridors of power—the White House, Downing Street, even the Kremlin. But here and now, Rogatica checkpoint was the last place he expected to see the BBC. It wasn't the time or place for a soundbite.

"Good morning, Matt," he said, opening his door, recognizing the BBC reporter. "Of all the gin joints in all the towns ... "

"Lucky you, eh, General Brown?" Matt Arlidge thrust the microphone at him. The fur cover acted as a windshield, but Gen. Brown always found it irritating to have the furry Muppet-like object thrust in his face. "General, regarding recent NATO air strikes—"

"Sorry, Matt. No comment."

But the camera was running. Arlidge would keep trying. This was a game of cat and mouse—sometimes the general needed the journalist, and sometimes it was the other way round. Today, it was Matt Arlidge who needed a sound bite, and both men knew it. Arlidge pushed the microphone a few inches closer, as if this might encourage Gen. Brown to speak.

"Sorry, Matt. No comment," he repeated and smiled. Gen. Brown managed to stop himself raising the flat of his palm toward the camera lens. Even a raised hand on the BBC's *Six O'Clock News* could be misconstrued and used against him to spin the story of the day. His best course of action was to give the journalist *something*. A news nugget. Finish the interview, negotiate his way through the checkpoint and be on their way. He knew the BBC would not get through the Rogatica checkpoint without a pile of permission slips, and even then it depended on the mood of the guard and local commanders on duty at the other end of the military hotline.

Arlidge's boyish face was a sharp contrast to the General's withered expression. "Can you comment on the abduction of Klaus Reithoffer this afternoon?"

What did he say? Gen. Brown allowed himself one blink of an eye and one glance at Yomper, whose expression mirrored his own thought: *First I've heard of it too, Boss,* it said. They had left Sarajevo less than an hour before and seen Reithoffer there in person. On the other hand, it was highly improbable that Arlidge would make up such an event.

Gen. Brown said, "If these unconfirmed reports are true—"

"Reuters have confirmed the report, General." Then, sensing Gen. Brown's surprise, Arlidge changed tack. "Are you saying this is the first time you've heard the news?"

"No, Matt, I'm not saying that." Gen. Brown paused, gathering his thoughts. This was an unexpected bombshell and complicated matters beyond belief. "As UNPROFOR commander in Bosnia-Herzegovina, I am responsible for the safety and security of all personnel including VIPs. We are doing everything we can to locate Mr. Reithoffer, and I am confident he will be returned safely. We believe there has been some kind of misunderstanding." Gen. Brown was going for the quick bluff.

Arlidge continued, "Has anyone claimed responsibility for the abduction? Do you know his precise whereabouts?"

Not wishing to complicate matters, Gen. Brown paused and glanced at Yomper, who was giving him the *time-to-wrap-up* look. Gen. Brown said, "Understand this: Those responsible are not helping the peace process. That is all I have for you now."

Arlidge wanted more. "As UN commander in Bosnia, General Brown, how do you respond to your critics, who charge that you have little to show for your first three months here?"

Gen. Brown replied calmly, "As I've told you before, we can't fight a war in white-painted vehicles. The history of former Yugoslavia is extremely complicated. A humanitarian mandate is one thing; stopping the fighting and killing is quite another. Unfortunately, we are operating under the first of those scenarios. The international community must take a stand and send a clear signal to all sides that we expect a peaceful solution. We can't do it alone."

"Do you agree that the Serbs should be 'bombed' to the peace table?"

"No, I hope that will not be necessary. As I said, a peaceful resolution would be the most desirable. As the deadline for the handover of heavy weapons approaches, I am confident that all sides will comply. We have our units waiting at UN collection points."

"How confident are you that the Serbs will comply?"

"Dr. Radovanović is aware of the consequences if they do not."

"Given the latest onslaught in Goražde as recently as this morning, do you believe the Serbs intend to comply?"

"I have received personal assurances from Dr. Radovanović that his forces will comply. Ditto the Bosnian government."

Arlidge glanced at his cameraman and raised a questioning eyebrow; a sign, Gen. Brown guessed, to see if enough tape was left, or enough battery power for the camera: *The next question must be important.*

The cameraman nodded and replied with closed thumb and index finger.

Arlidge continued, "Some may find your optimism unfounded. Bosnian Serb forces continue to kill and maim in Sarajevo, Goražde and Srebrenica, and there are renewed tensions between Bosnian government and Bosnian Croat HVO forces in Kiselyak, *and* we're getting unconfirmed reports that Tomislav Haler, the Bosnian Croat leader, was the casualty of a mortar attack in Kiselyak this morning." Arlidge paused for effect. "Would you agree that UNPROFOR is losing credibility and control, and failing its mandate?"

Gen. Brown shifted uneasily. He was used to the hard-hitting questions, but now, after the latest bombshell about Reithoffer, he didn't want to make things worse. He needed to find out what the hell happened to Reithoffer and Haler. And fast.

"Until we are certain of Mr. Reithoffer's and Mr. Haler's situation, it would, of course, be irresponsible to comment, or worse, speculate." Gen. Brown cursed himself for sounding like a politician.

Arlidge said, "Final question, General: Can you confirm reports about British Special Forces being forced to leave Goražde to allow a final onslaught against Bosnian government forces?"

"No comment."

Arlidge nodded. "And can you confirm or deny the existence of a secret document known as the Sarajevo Protocol, and that one of your men—Captain Jack Steele—has been sent to find it with an American journalist by the name of Staci Ryan?"

Gen. Brown gave the hint of a smile, a vague attempt to throw the journalist off his clearly defined trail. *Boyle?* he thought. *Surely not. Why would Boyle leak that?* "Captain Steele works for me ... I have heard no such reports. As for the American, I've no idea who that might be," he said very calmly. *How does the BBC know about Steele?*

They both knew he was lying. But for Arlidge, a denial was still useful. "Thank you for your time, General Brown."

"My pleasure, Matt." Gen. Brown walked back to his vehicle and nodded to Yomper to climb in.

He slammed shut the heavy armored door with a *clunk*, pointed to the sat phone on the middle console, and said, "Get Downing Street on the blower, *now*."

CHAPTER THIRTY-THREE

8:09 am Bosnian Serb HQ, Pale

Steele and Staci spent most of the night locked in a Jeep at gunpoint at the Serb command post in a forest near Goražde. At dawn, they were driven to Pale. The Jeep pulled up outside the Radovanović residency, the de facto Bosnian Serb "government" HQ. A soldier escorted them to the dining-cum-conference room. Coffee and juice awaited them on a side table.

"My mouth tastes like a sewer," said Steele.

"Me too," said Staci. "Why are they being so reasonable? I thought we were spies. It's making me nervous."

"Perhaps we're all they've got?"

"Give me a break. We're hostages?"

"No, this is PR, pure and simple. I hope."

Staci sipped her strong black coffee.

Steele said, "Apart from Russia, they don't have many friends."

"They're betting NATO won't bomb? It's a death wish."

"This room is probably wired."

"I doubt—"

The door opened. Two armed soldiers, or militiamen, in blue camo uniform stood either side of the double doors. A net curtain inside the room danced a jig as the through draft reached the only open window.

Dr. Radovanović and Gen. Zukić entered.

"No listening devices," said Dr. Radovanović with a grin. "But these walls have ears. They tell us everything that happens in our country."

Steele studied both men as they shook hands. This was the first time he'd seen Dr. Radovanović and Gen. Zukić standing side by side. Steele immediately felt the urge to wash his hands.

Dr. Radovanović was the larger of the two by far. He was, as people said, a bear of a man. But Gen. Zukić was just as imposing in a powerful, Sumo-wrestler kind of way. He was much shorter and stockier, and Steele thought he looked younger than he did on television. In most of the news footage Steele had watched, Gen. Zukić looked red-faced, angry, and almost buffoon-like. But now, in person, there was an unmistakable intelligence in his piercing blue eyes, as well as a calmness and the self-confidence of a supreme military commander with "everything under control," as Bosnians liked to say. *General Zukić,* thought Steele, *is even, one might concede, a strikingly handsome man.*

"I am delighted you are safe," continued Dr. Radovanović. "UN and Muslims have no regard for Serb people or foreigners. We have much to discuss. Please to be seated."

Gen. Zukić remained standing. Steele, Staci, and Dr. Radovanović sat down at the large, highly polished table.

Gen. Zukić glared at Steele. "Mladić," he said, "imaš samo jedan život." *Young man, you only have one life.*

The statement was loaded. Steele grimaced, trying to disguise the feeling of intimidation churning in his stomach.

Gen. Zukić surprised Steele by continuing in fluent English: "We are sick of UNPROFOR spies. We know why you are here." He took off his peaked cap, revealing sweaty strands of dark gray hair pasted across his scalp.

"We want to help," replied Steele. "I don't work for General Brown. I'm not with the SAS." Technically, Steele wasn't lying. But he also knew he was clutching at straws, trying to distance himself from Fitzgerald, Boyle, Gen. Brown and the powers that be that landed him here in the first place.

Dr. Radovanović took a less confrontational tone. "But why you let them take Sonja?"

"I had nothing to do with that. The attack. Sonja's abduction. The last time I saw her was in Pale. I'm sorry ..."

Silence.

"You can't hold us here," said Staci. "I have international press accreditation. Are we under arrest?"

"I will explain," said Dr. Radovanović, placing his large palms together in front of his chest. "We have a complicated situation—"

"This situation is an outrage," Gen. Zukić snapped.

Steele felt his skin tightening—goose bumps. He was talking to two of the most infamous war criminals in the world. *These guys are mass murderers. Why do they seem so civilized?*

"First let me remind you that you are both dispensable," Dr. Radovanović continued.

"Thanks," said Staci quietly. "That's comforting."

"Yes, even you, Miss Ryan. Americans must learn they are not invincible. Republika Srpska has an 'understanding' with the British and American governments. But this is not why we wanted you to visit us today."

"The Turks will invade Europe," Gen. Zukić added abruptly. "If it wasn't for Serb people, Muslims will rule Europe."

Steele saw the veins in Gen. Zukić's neck bulge and his face blush deep red. The Serb general was certainly passionate about his convictions. He meant what he said, and Steele was left with an overwhelming sense of dread as he realized he wasn't going to be changing any minds about the war with the men in this room.

Dr. Radovanović continued. "The CIA has warned us that Islamic terrorists intend to use our country as entry point to Europe. Muslim terrorists think we are weak and that we are not prepared for their sophisticated methods ... But they are wrong."

Steele broke in. "And this is why you slaughter Muslims in Sarajevo and Goražde? Not exactly the road to peace."

"Please do not insult us, *Jeck*. We are not how you think of us. We did not support Bosnia referendum, because we knew that we would lose. We did not want Muslim government, and we did not want this war."

Gen. Zukić continued, "Our people are farmers and peasants. But they are good people. They do not deserve to lose everything their parents and grandparents worked and died for. Don't forget we fought with British in World War Two."

Staci said, "Where does the CIA fit in?"

Dr. Radovanović raised an eyebrow and said, "We are pawns in this game. This is international politics—our country and this war are a sideshow. The CIA has failed its people for half a century—they have caused the deaths of thousands of American soldiers, foreign agents, and innocents. They are incompetent because they are ignorant of the people they say they are helping. They don't speak our language, but they dictate who will rule our people in former Yugoslavia. They don't know our culture, but they want to make peace for us. They don't ask what we want, they decide for us."

Steele nodded, feigning sympathy. "I think it might be more complicated, but I understand your argument." *Dr. Radovanović has some serious grievances, but his methods are objectionable.*

Gen. Zukić banged his fist on the table. "We will send Muslims screaming for mercy. We will not rest until every Turk, and every British and American spy is purged from our land. UN are spies," he shouted pointing at Steele.

Staci turned to Gen. Zukić. "I am sorry about your daughter. Was Ljudmila's suicide connected to this war?"

"Her name was Svetlana. My wife is Ljudmila."

"I apologize," she said.

Steele's heart sank. *This isn't the time for psycho-games. Is Staci trying to get us shot?*

According to news sources in Belgrade, Svetlana Zukić had committed suicide a month before. Apparently, father and daughter had not spoken since the start of the conflict in Bosnia, and it was widely rumored that Gen. Zukić's pivotal role in the conflict had caused a family rift and ultimately his daughter's suicide.

Gen. Zukić fell silent, staring intently at the American. He did not answer.

Dr. Radovanović smiled as if trying to calm the atmosphere. "The British and Americans have taken action to stop the terrorists. Don't forget that suicide bombers are preparing to knock on your door, *Jeck*—London, Manchester, Birmingham … Manchester United will not be happy." He grinned. Steele was becoming used to Dr. Radovanović—ever the psychologist—and his MO of making light of very serious matters to make his point.

Steele said, "Are you saying this war is about terrorist attacks on Western Europe?"

"Yes. Both your governments are running around—how do you say?—'scared like headless chickens.' They come to us, and we agree to help."

Staci said slowly, "Jack, that makes sense. Yugoslavia is the buffer zone, the gateway to Europe."

Steele saw her excitement—for Staci, this story might be the scoop of a lifetime. *If this war is ultimately about Islamic terrorism, and it can be connected to Western or European interference, it would certainly be a blockbuster story. For Staci, this is like being at the heart and soul of the story's conception.*

Steele turned to Dr. Radovanović. "But you've lived with Muslims and Croats for centuries."

"*Our* Muslims … New Muslims are not welcome here. Our great leader, Tito, knew this would happen one day."

"Is that what the Sarajevo Protocol says?" asked Staci.

Dr. Radovanović nodded. "Yes, we must find it."

Unable to disguise his confusion, Steele said, "You are working with British and American authorities?"

"They will never admit this, of course."

Steele was incredulous. He held up both hands. "Wait,

you want us to believe *our* governments have sanctioned your actions?"

"You are working for the British secret service. You already know the answer."

Steele shook his head and smiled. "If I did, I wouldn't be sitting here."

"No, Jeck, you misunderstand. You work for them, but you do not know precisely what you are doing for them. You are nice young man, but you are naïve."

The irony hit him. Steele had said the same thing to Staci hours before. *You might be lying to me but not know you are lying.*

Steele thought about Boyle's role as the omniscient commander. Pieces of the puzzle were coming together. Boyle had played him well, kept him in the dark from the moment his brother had been murdered in Chelsea. Boyle knew he would need Steele to take over where Peter's dealings had come to an abrupt stop. From the moment Steele had arrived in Bosnia, Boyle had allowed him to set his own trap and step in. They had allowed Steele to think *he* was making the decisions, but, in fact, Boyle had carefully orchestrated every move: the meeting with Sonja and her father, Staci's arrival, their venture into Goražde using information Staci—or Boyle?—had provided. It made Steele sick to his stomach to think that Dr. Radovanović might be telling the truth. It also made him question his entire existence and frame of reference as a British Army officer. It was one thing to help the good guys, but if the good guys were in fact not so good, what happens then?

"Interesting," Steele said. "Please, explain, Dr. Radovanović"

"They want you to find the Sarajevo Protocol and share it with the entire world. Then everyone can sympathize with Muslims because we are big, bad Serbs."

Steele took a deep breath, still not clear. "Suppose that's true, what do you want us to do?"

"You must return to Goražde. Rakić family knows where it is hidden."

Staci said, "Luka Rakić is dead."

"Convince the boy—he will trust you now that you have 'escaped' from Bosnian Serb army."

Steele understood at last. "And once we have the Protocol, you can destroy Goražde and use it to convince the world of evil Muslim intentions—a 'holy war' on the Muslim terrorists of former Yugoslavia?"

Dr. Radovanović nodded. "My daughter chose an intelligent young man to help us. That is why I allowed you to marry her. This was an excellent idea, do you agree?"

Everything was starting to make sense. So, it was Sonja's father who had planned the marriage charade. Steele had taken the bait just like his brother. It was very clever. Boyle, Sonja, and her father—they were all somehow involved. "Touché, Dr. Radovanović. Round one to you. I think I understand at last."

Steele felt exasperated and powerless. *And yet I still don't know exactly whom or what to believe anymore.* Was this an elaborate conspiracy by the West to thwart Islamic terrorism by igniting a civil war? Or was the Sarajevo Protocol an ingenious ruse by Bosnian Serbs to facilitate genocide of Muslims?

He continued, "You knew NATO would strike our wedding?"

"Not exactly. We know there are always risks in war. This attack was a miscommunication between our military officers, but we do not hold NATO responsible."

"Innocent people died. *Your* people."

"Captain Steele, open your eyes. Thousands have perished around us. We are used to death. You think a few old women and a chorister will change us?"

"The boy died?" asked Steele. His heart sank.

"It was unfortunate occurrence. Maybe this will convince *you*?" said Dr. Radovanović. "We are not the only ones you think are misguided."

Dr. Radovanović stood up and moved away from the table, scooping up various papers and files. "Bring me the Protocol, Captain Steele. It is a simple task. Believe me, neither of you will leave Republika Srpska alive unless you help us. And if you try to escape, we will find you."

Dr. Radovanović and Gen. Zukić left the room.

Steele sat for a few moments, trying to fit all the pieces together. He eyed Staci. "Okay, we go back to Goražde. We don't leave until we find it." He lowered his voice. "But not because he says so."

"I'm sorry?"

"I'll explain later."

PART III

CHAPTER THIRTY-FOUR

6ème Arrondissment, Paris

Katya Reithoffer wasn't the kind of woman to sit around waiting for things to work out. She preferred to take the initiative and ensure things worked out her way. Having taken an overnight train to Paris, she had planned to return to Strasbourg later that day to join her husband on his return from Bosnia. But now everything had changed.

It was 10:37 am. She walked up the steps of the Saint-Michel Metro. A shiver ran down her spine as she recalled the last time she had been in this *quartier*—neighborhood—the day after her daughter's death, or—according to her husband—murder. Now she was on the hunt for truth—for this was far more important than her husband's abduction in Sarajevo. He could take care of himself. Or at least, that's what he had spent their entire marriage telling her when she tried to help him either personally or politically. But now she was determined to find out if her suspicions were true. *What role did Klaus play in my daughter's death?*

One hour earlier she had received word that Klaus was "missing"—at first, they had avoided the word "abducted"—but her friend at the German embassy in Paris had confirmed it when she pressed him further. Local Bosnian militia had abducted her husband on the outskirts of Sarajevo, but no one could make any sense of it. Klaus was a champion of the Bosnian government. Local black market criminal gangs in Sarajevo were a possibility too, but no ransom had been demanded, and ultimately the gangs had ties to the government anyway, so that scenario didn't make sense either.

She cared little for her husband by now, and she could not deny their marriage was almost over. Now that Kerstin had died, she reflected, the bond between husband and wife, a mother and a father, was all but a title. But she still needed to know if her husband had lied to her: Was Kerstin's death a freak hit-and-run accident? Or was it murder as Klaus had suggested? And was Klaus involved?

The Paris sun bounced off the gleaming Citroens, Peugeots and Mercedes jostling for the quickest lane on Boulevard Saint-Germain. Katya could hear all kinds of street music coming from different directions—Peruvian pipes, French accordion, and even bagpipes. Her daughter would never enjoy this music again. Mother and daughter would never again go shopping in the rue St. Honoré, or have lunch sitting outside a Paris bistro in the Latin Quarter. They would never again visit the Louvres and discuss their favorite French impressionists—Monet, Cézanne, Pissarro.

She walked past a handful of market stalls on rue de Buci, and, briefly, caught the scent of freshly cut flowers standing in their red buckets on the tables. An old homeless man shoved a tattered paper cup at her. Instinctively, she ignored him. A few steps later, however, she retraced her steps and handed over a ten-euro note. For a moment, she felt better for her gesture, but she conceded a few seconds later that her offering had been more for *her* benefit than the beggar's.

Katya reached Bar du Marché and stopped on the pavement opposite. Observing the hustle and bustle on the street, it was impossible to believe that anyone—let alone her own daughter—had died here a few days before.

She crossed the road and sat down at a table under the red awning as her daughter had done many times. The aroma of fresh croissants from the boulangerie opposite and the freshly ground coffee inside the café was pure Paris.

The waiter arrived promptly.

"Espresso, s'il vous plait ..." she said. *Espresso, please.*

"Oui, Madame, tout de suite ..." *Coming right up, Madame.*

When the espresso arrived, she added brown sugar crystals, took a sip, and waited for the caffeine to kick in. She watched a delivery truck bringing more flowers to the market and observed an old lady buying a small bunch of orange roses on the stall opposite. Katya guessed it might be a daily ritual for the old lady because she seemed to know the flower seller well. Katya loved Paris, and it was nothing less than devastating that she would never again share the city with her daughter.

Still, Katya could not summon the courage—to find out the truth. She finished the shot of espresso and ordered a second.

Ten minutes later, she finally got up and walked into the café. If her suspicions were correct, it would be the end of her marriage and possibly her husband's political career. Yes, she might be about to shoot herself in the foot, but she didn't care. She had to know.

★   ★   ★

Once inside, Katya saw the barman she remembered from their last visit. She had hoped to find him working today. He was standing behind the counter next to the espresso machine, jet-black hair, unshaven, bags under the eyes, wearing a black T-shirt.

"Bonjour, Monsieur," she said, smiling confidently.

"Bonjour, Madame," he replied. "Take a seat, please. The waiter will be over in a minute."

"No, Monsieur. I came to talk to you." She removed her sunglasses.

The barman stopped drying the wine glasses. She detected recognition in his eyes—perhaps he remembered her from their official visit, or perhaps he had seen her on the news?

"Oui, Madame. S'il vous plaît?" he said. *Go ahead, please, Madame.* "You are Madame Reithoffer?"

Katya continued in French. "Yes, that's correct. My daughter was killed—"

"Of course, Madame, I remember very well. Please accept my condolences. Your daughter was a beautiful young woman. She often ate breakfast here with us."

"Thank you." Katya smiled again and waited a moment before asking, "I need your help. I saw my husband make a call from his mobile phone that day, when the police brought us here. He came in to buy an espresso."

"Yes, I remember. I was standing right here reading the newspaper." He pointed to the payphone attached to the wall at the end of the bar. "But he used the payphone, Madame, not his mobile."

Good, she thought. The barman had passed the first test. That day, she had not gone back to the car as her husband had suggested. She remained on the street and observed her husband inside making a call from the payphone.

"Can you remember what he said … the conversation, anything at all? It's very important for me to know."

"I don't remember, Madame. Many people, many conversations. I am too busy to listen to them." He smiled sympathetically and continued drying his wine glasses.

"Please. It's very important. Anything at all?"

The barman stood for a moment, massaging his chin, which sounded like sandpaper. He exhaled sharply, ballooning his cheeks, raising both shoulders as only the French can do. "Bosnia? It is possible he talked about Bosnia."

"Yes, that makes sense. Can you be more specific?"

He paused, frowning as he tried to remember. "He said something like … 'forget Serbs,' or, 'Serbs threatened my family.' Yes, I remember now. He talked a lot about Serbs."

"In English?"

"Yes."

"Anything else?"

"I don't remember …" He frowned, again massaging his chin. "Wait … I heard him talk about Croatia also. The future of Croatia?"

Ekaterina's eyes watered. She'd heard enough—enough to know that Klaus had lied to her. He had acted on his warped convictions that day in Paris. He had always planned to set Croats and Muslims against Serbs, as he had threatened many times. Serbs, and even Russians, had threatened *him* and told him to mind his own business or he would regret it. She had begged him to heed these warnings, but he had ignored her, and Kerstin, their daughter, had paid the ultimate price. Her murder was almost certainly an act of political revenge.

The barman leaned forward. "Are you all right, Madame? Would you like a glass of water? Something stronger?"

"Thank you, Monsieur. I will be fine." She walked to the door, wiping a tear from her cheek.

Wherever Klaus Reithoffer was, she hoped it was hell and that he would rot there. Andrea was dead, Klaus had lied, and she hated him.

The barman watched the German VIP cross the street and disappear into the crowd of market-goers. A blond man who had been sitting alone in the rear of the café got up and seemed to follow her.

"Merci, Monsieur. Bonne journée."

The blond said nothing. He left the café, and he too disappeared into the crowds on the rue de Buci.

Katya made the short walk to Metro Mabillon at the intersection of rue de Buci and Boulevard Saint-Germain. The flower stalls had lost their charm, and the stall owners seemed to look at her with pity. Or perhaps she was imagining things? She paused at the top of the Metro steps to listen to a young man wearing a beret playing a piano-accordion duet with a portable stereo at his feet.

She stood for a moment, lost in the music. A small boy went up to the man and dropped a fistful of coins into the accordion case. She dipped her hand into her pocket and also dropped some coins. Then she walked down the steps and waited on the Metro eastbound platform, direction Porte d'Auteuil. *Change at Sèvres Babylone and head north to the Place de la Concord for a nice long walk along the Seine to the Tuileries Gardens. Yes, that will help clear my head.*

Katya stared at the tracks, transfixed on the small dark shapes darting to and fro … She looked closer and realized they were mice. Their small furry shapes and movements made her shudder.

Headlights appeared from the left as the next train descended into the station. A cold wind almost knocked her off balance. She couldn't wait to get back to her cozy Strasbourg apartment even though a divorce storm was brewing.

Three seconds before the front of the train drew parallel with her, she felt a hand tapping her in the small of her back. Odd that someone had recognized her from behind. She turned, smiling politely to catch sight of an attractive, middle-aged blond man—but before she completed her turn, his hand became a piston and shoved her violently into the path of the approaching train headlights.

The last thing Ekaterina Reithoffer saw before she died were mice running from the train as her body fell toward them.

CHAPTER THIRTY-FIVE

Goražde

Col. Kostić ordered the driver to turn left. It was 11:15 am They were ten minutes from the Goražde frontline. Col. Kostić sat in the front passenger seat, and Steele and Staci were in the back of the battered military Jeep. No need for restraints or weapons, Col. Kostić had reassured his men. These foreigners were ignorant of their fate and would cooperate fully.

Col. Kostić was Gen. Zukić's closest military advisor. His unwritten job description included all manner of unsavory tasks Gen. Zukić himself did not wish to be associated with. No matter. He knew the British officer and the American wouldn't give him any trouble. Foreigners were easy to control on his territory when they had no idea what was about to hit them and were unarmed.

"Relax," he said. "We have a few minutes. We are taking the safest route." *Pathetic creatures*, Col. Kostić thought. His president had told the foreigners that they were on some kind of ridiculous treasure hunt—a secret document written by Tito was now in the possession of the Muslims. They had believed every word. In reality, he was escorting them to their deaths. Not in Serb hands, of course—the bullets would come from Muslim trenches. UNMOs would be tipped off and sent to the location afterward. They would discover the bodies and report to the entire world that Capt. Steele and Staci Ryan—Western spies—had been shot by Muslim snipers. This was the scenario he and his men were about to engineer.

Steele asked, "How will we find you again?"

Col. Kostić said, "We have people on both sides, Captain. Complete the task. Don't worry, we will find you."

11:19 am

The Jeep accelerated up a long, winding country road. Deserted meadows gave way to scenic mountain pastures on higher ground. Steele couldn't decide who he trusted least—Serbs or Muslims, Col. Kostić, Dr. Radovanović, Gen. Zukić … or even Staci? Col. Kostić could do anything to them now, and no one would ever know. They were completely cut off, they had zero backup, no radios, no UN vehicles, no weapons—this was a catastrophe waiting to happen.

On the other hand, even if Dr. Radovanović kept his word and they made it back to Goražde, there was no guarantee they would find the Protocol and no guarantee that Dražen and his men would release them unharmed. How would Steele explain their detention by Serbs? Dražen wouldn't believe the story about them escaping. He was bound to think the worst; that they really were Serb spies.

An aircraft flashed across the sky—left to right.

Steele said, "NATO?"

"Yes," replied Col. Kostić, surprisingly enthusiastic. "Our NATO brothers have turned against us. Nema problema,"—*No problem*—"this is just the beginning."

An explosion rocked the ground.

Through the open window to his right, Steele saw a bright orange flash and felt a wave of heat from the artillery position on a hill next to the road. Col. Kostić was right. NATO was bombing a Bosnian Serb artillery position. The aircraft vanished after one payload.

Col. Kostić said, "Keep going … faster." Then he turned to Steele. "See how they attack our defensive positions." Col. Kostić's voice was calm, as though resigned to the attacks. "We do not want to fight NATO. But we are afraid that Muslims will break out and attack us."

"Muslims are the aggressors?" Staci laughed. "You're kidding, right?"

Steele shot Staci a look to temper her outburst.

"Let me explain," Col. Kostić said. "We did not start this war. CIA had a crazy idea against Muslims, and we agreed to help." He shook his fist as he spoke. "And now we are the criminals. This is not justice."

Steele said, "Who *is* responsible?"

"We fight back when Muslims attack us."

"What about the Srebrenica atrocities? Are you denying that?" asked Staci.

"I have no idea what you are talking about. Thousands of refugees are there, and we try to help them."

Dr. Radovanović had not allowed international observers into Srebrenica. The IRC had been turned back many times. Steele knew Col. Kostić was lying.

Col. Kostić continued, "How will you find the author of this Sarajevo Protocol?"

Steele raised a finger and leaned forward. "Author?"

"The author is alive." Col. Kostić smiled.

Staci said, "I thought Tito wrote the Sarajevo Protocol?"

Silence.

Staci said slowly, "Now I get it … It's a hoax? The Sarajevo Protocol exists, but not as we thought?"

Col. Kostić nodded. "You are very intelligent for American. Almost as clever as British. You are using your brain."

Steele said, "Hide the secret you don't want anyone to find … in the hell hole you are trying to destroy?"

"Especially if that secret is a lie to begin with," added Staci. "But if the secret is a lie, and you don't want anyone to find it, why are we going back there?"

Steele was beginning to understand, or so he thought. But he didn't like his conclusions and would keep them to himself for the moment.

The Jeep slowed down; the driver pointed ahead. "Five hundred meters."

They continued until Col. Kostić said, "Pull over."

"Why do you need *us*?" Steele asked.

"Excellent question, Captain Steele," replied Kostić. "The truth is that we do not need you."

Steele and Staci exchanged glances.

"We will tell the world how British and Americans want to rewrite European history. But first, to give credence to our cause, we will return your bodies to the UN: *a tragic incident—Captain Steele and his American accomplice killed by Muslim snipers on the confrontation line in Goražde.* The world will understand that it is not only Serbs who have snipers and kill Westerners."

Steele's nostrils flared. In the mind of this madman, Col. Kostić, they'd become a simple commodity; human collateral. It was a terrifying thought.

"What would you gain?" Steele shifted uneasily. "By killing us?"

Col. Kostić's raised eyebrows signaled this was a stupid question. "We boost morale and adjust our standing in the eyes of the world. As you know, we are not popular. When you are shot dead by Muslims, people will see that we are not so bad."

"Your idea or General Zukić's?" asked Steele.

"This is General Zukić's order. You can understand, Captain. You are a soldier, and soldiers follow orders."

Steele knew no one would lose sleep over two Western deaths, especially if people thought the Muslims in Goražde were responsible. A tragic accident, they would say. Mistaken identity. *Captain Steele was a British soldier and Staci Ryan a war journalist—they both knew the risks. The confrontation line is a dangerous and unpredictable place.*

About five minutes, he reckoned, to find a way out. If he failed, their bullet-ridden corpses would be served on a plate to CNN before the end of the current news cycle.

11:23 am

What's in it for Colonel Kostić? Steele asked himself repeatedly. *What would make Colonel Kostić change his mind, even for a second? It had to be huge: something political? Financial? How do I persuade Kostić to disobey General Zukić's order and let us live?*

Col. Kostić turned to his driver. "Keep going ... a bit further."

The driver slowed to 20 mph. The confrontation line was close. Whatever Col. Kostić had planned was minutes away.

What Steele then saw ahead of them didn't make sense. A UN Russian BTR-80 APC hurtled toward them. UNPROFOR units did not operate this deep inside Bosnian Serb territory. Was this part of Col. Kostić's plan? If not, could the Russians somehow save them?

The Russian flag was clearly visible, flapping atop the APC's radio antenna. In these parts, the Russian flag—more than any other UN member nation—afforded more protection than any other UN armored vehicles with three-inch armor plating. Russians and Serbs were brothers, or at least cousins. *The Russian vehicle commander,* Steele thought, *is probably a twenty-year-old conscript on some black-market mission from the Muslim safe area.*

The whirring of the Russian APC grew louder. *This might be our only chance.*

There would be enough men and firepower inside the APC to save them. But how to stop their vehicle? And even if Steele managed to stop the APC too, there was no guarantee that the Russian crew inside would support a British Army officer and an American journalist over Col. Kostić. He prayed the BTR-80 would pull over and stop their vehicle for a routine security check. *Please God,* he said to himself. *Peter, I could use your help too.*

But an inner voice told Steele to take the initiative and save himself.

His next move might have killed all of them, but he did it anyway. There was no other way out. He looked at Staci and hissed, "Sorry. Hold tight."

As they drew level with the APC coming from the opposite direction, Steele threw himself forward, diving into the front seats. He grabbed the wheel, and before Col. Kostić or his driver could react, Steele steered the Jeep into the side of the APC.

The two vehicles collided with a deafening crunch of metal. Steele's vehicle bounced off the APC's huge wheels and spun full circle. Their windscreen shattered instantly and fell away. The Jeep rolled onto its side, then its roof, finally landing on its side again. The battered chassis's engine hissed as it came to rest. The APC, unscathed, slammed on its brakes and came to a halt.

Steele's world went black.

CHAPTER THIRTY-SIX

Moments later, Steele opened his eyes. A few inches from his head was a pistol in its holster on the Jeep driver's waist. Steele tried to move his arm, but nothing happened—only a dense, heavy feeling he couldn't quite place. Turning his head, he saw why—the full weight of the Serb driver was lying on his arm, now completely numb.

He pulled. Still nothing.

"You are a foolish man," said Col. Kostić slowly. The voice came from behind. "But you will not live to regret your heroics."

"Go to hell," said Steele. He was concussed, he knew this, but was recovering slowly. He tried to remember where he was. Who had been injured? Anyone killed?

Sonja? Where was Sonja? No … Sonja was in Pale?

Breathe.

He could feel cool air and looked around. He was lying half way out of the Jeep window. Now he remembered. The windscreen had shattered on the first roll. Someone from the outside was tugging at his arm and trying to pull him out.

A Russian voice said, "Eta xorosho. Tixo … tixo …" *It's okay. Easy now.*

Steele raised his left arm. "Please," he said in Russian, "the woman …?" The Russian soldier looked into the rear of the vehicle.

"Da … djevushka xorosho." *Yes … the girl is fine.* "Poyexali … Let's go." The Russian was insistent.

Steele nodded as he was pulled out of the vehicle and away

from the Jeep. "The woman's okay? Is the woman okay?" he repeated.

"Da, da ..." came the reply. *Yes, yes.*

Steele heard other voices, but he was too weak to sit up. Col. Kostić was talking to the Russians—no, he was arguing with them. Steele counted six UN Russian soldiers. Their commander was shouting back. Two of the Russian soldiers walked to the Jeep.

Steele tried to roll over, but it was too painful. Everything hurt. He couldn't move. His eyes were full of water or something. He blinked several times and saw red. Blood was running into his eyes from a gash on his forehead.

A shot rang out. Then another—it sounded like a pistol or an AK47 on single shot mode.

Then silence.

A dark silhouette covered the sky. Someone was standing directly over him. He squinted, trying to focus. He wiped his eyes and face with the back of his free hand. He could feel blood running down the back of his hands and wrists.

Then he saw clearly: Col. Kostić was looking down at him.

"Zdravo!" Col. Kostić pointed his pistol at Steele's face. *Hello!* "You have failed your mission, Mr. Peace Man. You will not destroy my country."

In his semidelirious stupor, Steele was transfixed on Col. Kostić's trigger finger, anticipating its tiniest movement or twitch. Scenes, events, people from his life reeled inside his head, electronic pulses firing in his brain: his Church of England primary school in London, his mother, his great aunt Flo, his best friend from high school whose father was a famous Welsh tenor, his French girlfriend from Monaco he'd met on a bus, Sandhurst, Russia, Iraq, and now Bosnia ... his entire life, just like people said, flashed before him.

Col. Kostić said, "Samo sloga srbina spasava." *Only a Serb can save your soul.*

Steele refused to close his eyes. If he was going to die, he wanted to watch to the very last moment just in case he could save himself—somehow, some way.

UNPROFOR HQ, Sarajevo

"I can't do it," said Maj. Small. "I don't have the authority." He flexed the polystyrene cup of coffee he'd been nursing, realized it was cold, and placed it on the table. "I don't know what I can tell them."

Boyle's voice grew louder. "Tell them General Brown demands NATO cease bombing raids," said Boyle. "The commander is in Goražde and in direct danger."

If anything happened to Gen. Brown, Boyle reflected, his masters at Black Cobra would hold him responsible. Killing the UNPROFOR commander was *not* part of his brief. But more importantly, he was still confident that Steele and Staci would find the Sarajevo Protocol.

It was imperative he stop the NATO attacks.

"I've been trying to reach General Brown all morning," said Maj. Small.

"Try again."

"He might be separated from his vehicle."

Maj. Small picked up the sat phone and redialed. "No reply."

Boyle shook his head. Things were not going according to plan. *I'm losing control of the situation.*

There was a squeak of rubber outside the door.

A tall young captain with a receding hairline and a square jaw entered the office in such a rush that he almost fell into the room. Holding a signal, he began to read: "Sitrep: Kiselyak eleven-fifteen hours. Croats and Muslims heavy fighting. Kiselyak has fallen to the Muslims."

Maj. Small twitched nervously. "What's wrong with these people? Serbs pounding Goražde, and Muslims and Croats slitting each other's throats in Kiselyak. Can it get any worse?"

"Yes," said Boyle. "It probably can. Much worse."

Goražde

Steele changed his mind and closed his eyes. He lay spread-eagled in his high school playground in North London, begging the class bully not to kick him in the head. The bully kicked him in the stomach instead. Determined never again to be a defenseless jelly, this was one of the reasons he had joined the army. He *really* hated bullies.

But now he wasn't begging, this wasn't high school, and he wasn't dreaming. He was praying his life would be spared, and Kostić would not—execution style—pull the trigger now inches from his face.

He listened to Kostić's breathing. *So calm,* he thought. *The bastard is about to shoot me, and he's so bloody calm … Think, damn it, think …*

A short burst of automatic fire exploded above them. Steele opened his eyes.

Col. Kostić staggered forward his full weight landing on Steele's abdomen and winding him. Adrenaline kicked in. Steele rolled one way then the other to untangle himself from Col. Kostić, who then managed to push himself up off the ground and stumble back to his Jeep.

Whoever had fired the shots did not intend to kill.

Steele tried to stand but was too weak. He felt light-headed and collapsed.

Staci shouted, "Jack, you okay?"

He looked up and back behind him to see Staci holding an AK-47 rifle. *She* had pulled the trigger.

The Russian UN peacekeepers from the APC froze.

Col. Kostić drove away, and Staci fired one more burst for good measure.

"Put the gun down," said Steele, barely audible. "I'm okay. Let's stop while we're still alive." He glanced in the other direction. There were enough Russian soldiers, he calculated, to protect them from stray Muslims who might appear now that Col.

Kostić was gone. But Serb reinforcements might arrive at any moment, especially after the bursts of small-arms fire.

A Russian sergeant stepped forward and took the AK-47 from Staci, the one she had taken from Kostić's driver. She looked shaken, and her body trembled as the Russian sergeant walked her back to his APC.

A second Russian NCO said in English, "My name is Staff Sergeant Sergei Tretyakov, Army of the Russian Federation. What you are doing here?"

Steele couldn't help smiling. He loved Russians. "Zdrastvyute ... Spaciba vam bolshoi." *Hello ... Thank you very much.* He waved feebly. He continued speaking in Russian, "It's complicated—"

"We must leave for Sarajevo," interrupted Sgt. Tretyakov. "It is not safe for us here. You will please explain on the way."

"No. You don't understand. That's the wrong direction. We have to get to Goražde."

"Impossible, Captain—"

"Please, listen," Steele continued. "If we leave them alone, the people of Goražde will perish. The only way to stop the carnage is to get to Goražde. All of us. I need you and your men to escort us."

Sgt. Tretyakov grimaced and said, "We have only one APC. General Zukić's men will attack if we cross the front line."

"You're Russian. You're flying the UN and the Russian flag. They won't attack their friends."

The Russian hesitated. Then finally, he said, "What is our mission?"

"If we can stop Serbs shelling Muslims, NATO will cease-fire on the Serbs. That was the short version—time's up. We gotta move now."

"We drive into town?"

Steele nodded. "Straight across the front line."

Sgt. Tretyakov glanced at his men and said, "You are a British captain. We are UNPROFOR soldiers. My men will obey your orders. It is our duty."

Steele let out a sigh of relief. "Thank you. Spaciba."

Sgt. Tretyakov clicked his heels and saluted. The two men shook hands.

Steele said. "Let's go."

"*Poyexali ...*" Sgt. Tretyakov repeated in Russian to his men who sprang into action and mounted the APC.

Steele smiled at Staci and made a prayer sign in gratitude. She had saved his life.

CHAPTER THIRTY-SEVEN

Ten minutes later, the Russian BTR-80 APC crossed the confrontation line unchallenged and drove into the center of Goražde. The best place to start, Steele decided, was the UNMO office. They might know Dražen's location—and the safest and quickest way to find him.

A UN flag marked the UNMO office located on Main Street, which ran from the River Drina through the center of town. They stopped outside the former bank building, which Steele was surprised to see standing tall after all the shelling. In fact, most of the buildings around them were surprisingly untouched.

Recent UNMO sitreps—situation reports—had reported many buildings demolished by artillery, tanks, and wire-guided missiles. The UNMOs had also reported that the main hospital and bank buildings were badly damaged. But now, in close proximity to both buildings, Steele saw no evidence of the destruction. *That's odd.*

Steele and Staci entered the building and followed the handwritten signs to the UNMO office located one flight down in the basement.

They found the office, and Steele introduced himself.

The UNMO had a red beard and wore a Danish military uniform with the rank of captain. He stood up and said, "It's about time someone took some interest." They shook hands. "Jensen."

Steele was struck by Jensen's aggressive tone and there was what could only be described as a wild look in his eye. He looked quite simply like a man who had 'gone native.'

Then Steele recognized him.

It was the Danish captain from the dining hall in Sarajevo he had encountered on his first night in Bosnia. "We met in the mess hall in Sarajevo."

Jensen nodded. "Hello again. What brings you to hell?"

"I'm looking—"

"It's terrible, you know," Jensen broke in, "the entire world has deserted us. The UN has left us for dead." He spoke as if he was talking to himself, his gaze not focused on Steele or Staci.

Steele noticed that Jensen was unusually unkempt for a soldier, albeit in the middle of war-torn Goražde. His hair was longer than Steele had noticed a few days ago. His red beard needed a serious trim.

"That's not true," Steele said, trying not to judge Jensen too harshly. The poor bastard had probably been posted in Goražde for weeks if not months.

"Really?"

"We're here to help. The Russians too." Steele turned to Staci. "This is Staci Ryan, an American journalist."

"You're too late. It's too late to help these poor bastards. We have destroyed the soul of these people. We did our best. We are powerless against the Serbs."

Steele shook his head. "We need to find Luka Rakić's boy, Dražen."

The Dane nodded. "No problem, I can help you," he said. The Rakić name seemed to strike a conciliatory chord in Jensen.

"That's great," said Steele. "You know him?"

"Of course, the boy is in charge here after his father died. People look to him for leadership. His father was a good man and a brave man."

Staci said, "Can you take us to him? Now?"

Jensen nodded, the corners of his mouth pulling downward. "This place is crazy, but I know where to find him. Let's go." He seemed eager to leave the dingy basement office and eager to help.

They left the building and climbed into the back of the Russian APC. Jensen gave the driver directions, and they set off.

Steele said, "Where's the damage you reported in your sitreps?"

The broad-shouldered Dane looked at Steele. "Listen, my friend, these people have suffered worse than hell. That's what matters. They need all the help they can get. Men, women, and children have survived living hell."

Steele smiled, feigning sympathy. "Why exaggerate the reports? What about facts?"

"Facts? The *fact* is that innocent people have been slaughtered on their streets by Serb snipers and shelling. Babies and children are dying in the hospital because this town is under siege and no one cares."

"You exaggerated your casualty figures."

"You would have done the same. Believe me."

Steele shrugged, not wishing to rub Jensen the wrong way. He didn't want him to change his mind about helping them. "Well," said Steele, "it worked. NATO bombed Serb targets this morning. The country is about to ignite. You achieved your goal."

Staci said, "Jensen, you're a soldier not a politician, right? Isn't your job to observe and report the facts?"

"So, I should have done nothing, so that General Zukić squeezed this town to death?"

"That's why we're here. We want to stop the fighting," Staci said.

"No. The Serbs will never stop. You have heard of the Sarajevo Protocol?"

Steele's eyes widened. "Maybe ..." he said hesitantly. He wondered how much the Dane could possibly know about the Sarajevo Protocol.

Jensen shouted to the driver, "Next right." The APC swerved momentarily, then turned right. "It was written after World War Two—by Tito. It states that the Serbs have a legal and constitutional right to rule former Yugoslavia—all republics—in the event of Tito's death."

Steele said, "How do you know this?"

"Everyone knows. Ask anyone who lives here—Muslim, Croat, or Serb. People have talked about it for decades. It was folklore, but now it turns out to really exist. That's what I hear now anyway."

Steele said, "We need to find Dražen. He knows where it is. That's why we need your help, Jensen."

Staci edged forward. "Captain Jensen, who told you to exaggerate the reports?"

"Things were desperate here. No one was listening."

She pressed him. "So it was *your* idea?"

"I had a little encouragement from my German friend, Klaus Reithoffer."

"EU president?" Steele asked, surprised.

"Yes. We met in Split on vacation many years ago, in another life when I was married and had the time and inclination to enjoy life. We kept in touch over the years. He was just a civil servant in those days."

"And he told you to make false reports?"

"Yes. They killed his daughter, you know," continued Jensen. "Who?"

"He said it was Serbs."

"He gave you proof?" Staci asked.

"Proof?"

"That they killed his daughter? I'm a journalist. I followed the story. I thought it was a car accident—hit-and-run?"

"Honestly, I didn't need proof about his daughter. He was the only one who would listen to me about these people here. I trusted him. He told me to exaggerate the reports. He said it was the only way to secure a peace agreement in Bosnia-Herzegovina."

Steele nodded, biting his bottom lip, trying to decide how much he could trust this story.

Jensen continued. "He called me on our satellite telephone. I have no regrets."

They pulled over outside a small brick house.

Steele said, "You've made the situation a hundred times worse. We all want peace, but not like this ..."

"Like I said, I have no regrets." Jensen pointed to the house. "Dražen's inside."

Near Rogatica, Republika Srpska

Safely through the Rogatica checkpoint, Gen. Brown, who was taking a turn at the wheel, and Yomper continued south toward Goražde. They had spent the last twelve hours at the UNMO Pale house after being turned back at two different checkpoints the day before. Gen. Brown made some calls about the abduction of Klaus Reithoffer, but all he could do for now was to send out his Joint Commission Observers (JCOs) to look for the man. It was unclear at this point if Reithoffer was the victim of more political shenanigans by the Bosnian government or, less likely he thought, the subject of a real abduction or even kidnapping.

At times, they traveled on what was now more dirt track than road, and they proceeded with caution to avoid landmines planted, or merely forgotten about, along that road.

Gen. Brown was glad to be on the ground, on the trail for truth in person. He also urgently needed to talk to the British prime minister again about the Sarajevo Protocol, Jack Steele, and Colonel Boyle. *Who in God's name is Edward Boyle? Is Steele one of Boyle's rookies or minions? Or is Jack Steele also being used?*

After the brief encounter with the BBC's Matt Arlidge, he realized he had much less of a grasp on the entire story than he would have liked. *Not a good feeling.* He didn't mind playing the journalist cat-and-mouse game when he was the cat. But now he felt like the mouse because he simply didn't know the answers to all the questions.

Yomper tried to get through to Downing Street on the

armored Land Rover's satellite telephone. No joy. Then Yomper tried Maj. Small in Sarajevo again without success. Standard operating procedure—SOP—was to establish comms every hour, or every few hours at least, but neither party had done so.

Gen. Brown sighed. Yomper tried London again.

"Hang on, boss," said Yomper, "we've got 'em." Yomper pressed the telephone to his ear and strained to hear the voice at the other end. He glanced at the general. "Here you go, Boss. It's Downing Street."

Gen. Brown took the handset. "This is General Rupert Brown in Bosnia. I need to speak with the prime minister immediately."

"One moment, General Brown," said a female Foreign and Commonwealth Office secretary. "Connecting you to Downing Street now."

Brown thought he'd lost the connection, then, after two more gatekeepers and frustrating silences, Robert Grange, the British prime minister, said, "Hello, Rupert ..."

"Yes, Prime Minister. Can you hear me?"

"How are you, Rupert?"

Gen. Brown paused, almost smiling. He noted how chipper the prime minister sounded no matter the circumstances. "Prime Minister, we need to talk."

"About the Protocol?"

"How—"

"I was expecting your call. I spoke to Boyle earlier. He's concerned."

"He's not alone. Who is actually in charge of that man?"

"I'm afraid I am. Sorry about all this cloak and dagger stuff. Need to know basis and all that ..."

"With respect, Prime Minister—it's time for *me* to know."

"It goes back a long way, Rupert—World War Two, September 1945. The British and American governments decided a Yugoslavia without Tito might serve as an open invitation for Islam to enter the heart of Europe—"

"That's absurd—"

"In retrospect, possibly. Overkill, you might say. But hindsight's a bitch. The truth is they didn't know for sure. But all of them—MI5, MI6, and Big Brother at the CIA—none of them were prepared to take any chances."

"You've lost me. Tito died in 1980."

"The essence of the Protocol was an agreement between us and the Communists of Yugoslavia. Should the country ever go belly up, we would restore order."

"With the Serbs?"

"Yes, but we didn't bargain on Milošević, the maverick, the nationalist fanatic who screwed it up for everyone. And more recently, it became politically incorrect to be, shall we say, distrustful of our Muslim neighbors. So, we did a swift U-turn."

"When?"

"When George Bush Senior got into bed with the Saudis. But that's the simplified version."

"You're telling me that we *want* the Serbs to take Goražde?"

"Let's just say it would make things easier."

"What about innocent civilians being murdered?"

"It's a fine line—"

"*A fine line?* Because of a secret Protocol written half a century ago that no one's ever seen?"

"Its release could be dynamite. We can't take any chances."

"This is absurd. I've never—"

Grange said, "Steady, Rupert. There's more … "

Gen. Brown took a breath and exhaled slowly. "I'm listening."

"We're certain the Protocol exists—our people, the spooks, are rarely mistaken—but we don't know its location. Bottom line is, we want it."

"At any price?"

Silence.

"I'll take that as a yes," said Gen. Brown.

"Yes."

"And you'll allow the Serbs to wipe out Goražde?"

"Then we work on the peace plan in earnest."

Gen. Brown erupted, "With respect, Prime Minister, this is complete bollocks."

"General Brown—"

"I refuse to have anything to do with this."

"You don't have to. The details have been taken care of."

"Boyle and Steele? And the American?"

"They have their orders. Boyle—"

"And so do I, Prime Minister, from the UN Secretary-General. Please ask NATO to back off. I'll sort this mess out myself."

"General, I would prefer you to follow my order—"

Brown pressed the end-call button and resisted the urge to smash the handset on the metal sat phone box "Fuck it."

"Bad news?" asked Yomper.

"If he calls back—"

"Ignore the fucker?"

"Precisely."

CHAPTER THIRTY-EIGHT

Goražde

Capt. Jensen knew Goražde like the back of his hand, which meant he knew young Dražen's precise location. Part of his job was to get to know the locals, especially the important ones.

Steele, Jensen, and Staci entered the house.

"It's one of six secret broadcast studios," Jensen explained. "Luka Rakić used to rotate so he could broadcast every day and not be targeted by Serbs. Now Dražen is the boss."

Two teenage boys wearing green camouflage jackets and carrying AK-47s emerged from the shadows and challenged the foreigners. They held the weapons awkwardly, as if they had picked them up for the first time that morning. Such was the learning-on-the-job nature of this war.

"It's okay," said Steele. "We're friends." The boys recognized Jensen, and his nod removed any doubt they had about the two strangers who accompanied him. They lowered their weapons.

The visitors walked down two steps to the end of a dark corridor and reached a room on the right. Dražen sat behind a primitive radio broadcast console. He wore headphones and was speaking into the microphone in Bosnian:

"Muslim people are invincible. We will survive and win this war. It is God's will," he said emphatically. "Citizens of Goražde … I know that you will honor your brothers and sisters and show the world and our cousins in Sarajevo that we will never surrender."

Dražen looked up.

Steele said, "Dražen, we need to talk."

Dražen pressed a button and faded in some traditional Bosnian pop music. He switched to a less enthusiastic tone: "Come in. I was worried for your safety," he said. "You could have been killed. Serbs were close by when you escaped. It's good you are alive."

"Thanks, Dražen. The Serbs took us. But it's a long story, and that's not why we're here."

"You should have stayed with them …"

Steele moved a step closer. "Dražen, you have great influence in this town—"

"People trusted and respected my father. Now they trust me."

Staci said, "Your father was helping the Bosnian government. Dražen, there are people in your government who want Goražde to suffer. It suits their political goals."

Dražen frowned. "I understand we are in trouble."

"No, you don't understand," continued Staci. "Listen to me carefully. I'm saying it helps their political cause if people die here. Do you understand me?"

"Why you tell these lies? I hate you and your UN peacekeepers. Muslims never harmed your people. Zionist terrorists were more danger to your people than Muslims."

"Zionists?"

"Yes."

"Dražen—"

The boy said, "Yugoslavia fought with you in Second World War. Afterward, your government must fight Zionist terrorists, not Muslims."

It was true, Steele recalled from a history lecture at Sandhurst, that in postwar Britain, Zionist extremists posed a far greater threat to British security than Muslims. The Irgun, under the leadership of future prime minister Menachem Begin, had blown up the British military Palestine HQ in Jerusalem in 1946, killing ninety-one, and later that year had bombed the British embassy in Rome. But now, for Steele, the regurgitation of fifty-year-old ancient history was running thin.

"Dražen, things have changed. That was half a century ago. You must help us find the Protocol. It's the only chance your people have to find peace."

"Why should I trust you?"

"Dražen, the Protocol is an *excuse* for war."

The boy grimaced and thought for a few moments. Finally, he said, "I know where it came from."

"You do?" Steele was shocked. The source of the Protocol would solve many unanswered questions. He could feel his heart beating faster.

"A British man," said Dražen. "His name is … Fitzgerald."

Staci said, "Sir Lawrence Fitzgerald?" She turned to Steele. "He's the one who told *me* about the Sarajevo Protocol. Fitzgerald said he worked for your government. But I thought he was working for Boyle."

Steele said slowly, "It's probably the same thing."

Dražen continued, "Fitzgerald came here a long time ago. UNPROFOR smuggled him through checkpoints. He met with my father. He trusted Luka Rakić."

"Amazing," said Steele, shaking his head in disbelief. He felt as though they had discovered the Holy Grail. *Fitzgerald, the old bugger, has been behind this thing all along.*

Dražen continued, "The Englishman told me people came to his house, searching for the Protocol. They murdered his wife. My father knew this story. Fitzgerald was telling the truth."

"He was a British spy," continued Steele, "during the last war. He was a personal friend of Tito." He eyed Dražen. "What happens here today might decide the outcome of the war in Bosnia."

Staci nodded in agreement and said, "No one wanted this war, Dražen—Muslims, Serbs, Croats—we understand that. The international community didn't do their job. We get that too. They didn't think before they took sides. Or at least they didn't realize they were taking sides."

Dražen stood up and leaned across his broadcast console. "It is too late now. My country's fate is to fight. It is our destiny."

Steele said, "No, Dražen, that's what they want. That's how Milošević and his goons takes advantage of the situation."

"It's okay. My father is dead. I will give Serbs what they deserve."

Steele crossed to Dražen and gripped the boy's shoulders with both hands. He said, "For God's sake, Dražen, let your father's death have some meaning. If you don't help us, the war will never end, thousands more will die, and we will probably all die with them. NATO is going to attack the Serbs, and they will slaughter us."

"Please leave." Dražen turned back to his microphone.

"NATO will attack the Serbs if we cannot find the Protocol. Give us the Protocol and allow us to make a deal with the Serbs. You have to trust us."

Dražen shook his head. "No, Captain. You must leave. I have work to do." He nodded to his bodyguards, who raised their weapons.

"It's okay," said Steele. "We're leaving."

Dražen replaced his headphones and faded down the folk music. "Dear listeners," he continued, "here are the latest casualty figures …"

UNPROFOR HQ, *Sarajevo*

Maj. Small had been trying to establish comms with Gen. Brown all morning. Finally, he got through. Maj. Small took the spare handset, and Boyle monitored on the other.

"General, the situation is critical," Maj. Small said. "NATO has received orders from London and Washington. It's too late to stop NATO—"

"God damn it!" Gen. Brown's voice became a mush of static.

"You have to leave the area." Maj. Small swallowed hard, his cheeks flushed. "There's more … a Bosnian government tank has taken up a fire position here behind UN headquarters. It's a T-55. It's drawing fire from Serbs. Our people are in danger."

"Where did it come from?" asked Gen. Brown.

"Apparently, it's been hiding in the road tunnel all along. Our people suspected it was there, but this is the first time they've provoked the Serbs directly with the tank."

"Tell NATO Ops to take it out if necessary."

Boyle raised his hand and broke in. "NATO won't do it, General. The Bosnians are the prisoners, remember?"

"If the tank is drawing fire, it's a cease-fire violation. Take it out if it fires again."

"It's too close to civilians—collateral damage. The weather's closing in, and the cloud cover is holding up strikes on all targets. Even if they wanted to—"

"Damn it, man, if there's a fucking tank sitting outside our back door, I'll guide them in myself, if necessary."

Boyle said, "NATO is not going to take out a government tank in the middle of besieged Sarajevo. Do you want riots in European capitals?"

The Ops officer entered the room holding up another signal. "Update, gentlemen: There's a British UNMO captain standing in the middle of the footbridge in Goražde—a Serb tank on one side, Bosnian infantry on the other."

The room froze.

Moments later, they heard a voice coming from the receiver. "Brian, can you hear me?" Gen. Brown said to Maj. Small, who then continued.

"Yes, General … we have reports of a British officer standing on the bridge in Goražde. I have no idea—"

"It's Steele," Boyle broke in. "He and the American have their orders. You should return to Sarajevo, General Brown."

"Boyle …"

"Yes, General?"

"Screw yourself!"

The line went dead.

CHAPTER THIRTY-NINE

Pale

Sonja Radovanović looked at the barren fields approaching Pale and remembered how she used to run across them in her childhood, picking flowers, jumping over cowpats.

The Bosnian Serb army Jeep turned off the main road and pulled up outside the Radovanović headquarters, also their home. Sonja had been allowed to go to the market, although technically, her father and Gen. Zukić had ordered her to be on house arrest and that she should remain at the Bosnian Serb leader's residence.

Sonja walked up the steps and was greeted by her father, who had been expecting her; he'd watched her jaunt from the French windows overlooking the town. They stopped a few feet short of each other. They did not hug or embrace. They stared at each other like strangers.

She had always felt closer to her mother than her father. Sonja was never sure why, but perhaps now she had found her answer.

It had crossed Sonja's mind that her father (and certainly her godfather, Gen. Zukić) would have arrested her, and thrown her in prison if they'd found out about Fitzgerald's plan. In their eyes, she would be committing treason, even though she had agreed to help Fitzgerald for the good of all her people, not just Serbs.

Finally, Dr. Radovanović held out his arms. She walked over to him, and he hugged her.

"Please, Papa," she said, "I am your daughter. You can't treat me this way."

"You must forgive me."

She nodded slowly. "I forgive you. But will Serb people forgive you?"

"You are my child."

They walked into the dining room, and Dr. Radovanović closed the door.

Sonja looked out the French windows. She loved the rustic higgledy-piggledy houses and farm buildings that dotted the landscape in Pale. "It feels like we are a long way from Sarajevo. But they are our people too."

"We did not ask for war." Dr. Radovanović scraped his hair back with two hands.

"You should ask mama to cut your hair."

"I know. I will ask her. We are busy."

Sonja said, "This is not about Serb, Muslim, or Croat, Papa. I went to London because of us—father and daughter."

Dr. Radovanović looked at her, puzzled, waiting.

"I left because of *you*," she said. "What *you* have done to this country. I hated you."

Dr. Radovanović, the former psychologist, nodded sympathetically. "This is normal. We did not agree, that is all. All fathers and daughters argue."

"It's not normal. I could not trust you. Now I trust no one." She paused, then said, "It was *those* people who started this war. I can see that."

"The British?"

"British, American … they are all the same. They were afraid."

"Of Serb people?"

"*They are afraid of Islam.* We live with Muslims and we were never afraid. Serb married Muslim and Croat. I was close to so many Muslims. But for British and Americans, for Western countries it is different."

"What happened in London? What did you do there?"

"Nothing. They ask many questions—so many questions. We are stupid … naïve, Papa. Why didn't we see this?"

"You think I did not see this coming? You think your godfather did not see this?" He smiled. "The West promised to help us, but they changed the rules. Just like the Germans deceived the world after the assassination of Archduke Ferdinand. They used us—Gavrilo Princip was *our* Bosnian Serb—for *their* own interests. This is our fate. They lifted the arms embargo for Muslims and threatened our people. We will never surrender. Not to Americans, not to British, or to NATO. We have been tricked."

"But NATO will destroy us."

"They can drop their bombs, but our will is stronger. They do not want Afghanistan in Europe. Muslims break cease-fire, and NATO does nothing … They have a tank in Sarajevo!" He shook his head and raised his index finger. "But God is with us."

"God will not save us, Papa. We must save ourselves. Republika Srpska will die if you attack Goražde."

"You are wrong, dearest."

She felt tears welling. "NATO does not care for Muslims. But they are waiting for an excuse to attack us."

There was a knock on the door. "Enter," said Dr. Radovanović.

A staff officer opened the door and saluted. He stepped smartly forward, shot a glance at Sonja, and gave Dr. Radovanović a JNA-encoded signal.

Dr. Radovanović studied the document. "NATO has destroyed three tanks near Goražde." He looked at Sonja. "General Zukić will never surrender. Even if I wanted to, it is too late to stop him now. I'm sorry."

Sonja stared at her father. She was ashamed of him. He was weak, as she had suspected all along. Gen. Ratko Zukić, her godfather, was really the man in command. She had given up on her father once already, and now she remembered why. He would never be strong enough to stand up to Gen. Zukić.

"I shouldn't have come back from London. Peter Steele was ready to help me. It was a mistake to come back. You will never change."

She turned and hurried toward the door, ran down the corridor, and left the building.

Her driver was waiting.

"Damn Kosta Radovanović!" she said, spitting. "I will stop them myself. I am not afraid of Gen. Zukić."

The driver glanced into his rearview. "Where to, Miss Radovanović?"

"Goražde. Take the Pale Road."

"But—"

"Just do it."

The driver nodded. "Understood."

Slavica Radovanović could not contain herself any longer. She had been eavesdropping on the conversation between husband and daughter from the dining room annex. When Sonja left, she entered the dining room.

Dr. Radovanović replaced the telephone receiver and slouched forward, his head cradled in both hands.

"What have you done?" she said.

"I ordered General Zukić to stop the attack." He looked up. "But it's too late."

"Of course it's too late. But I am not talking about Zukić. Where is Sonja?"

"She is a traitor. If it wasn't for you, I would have had her arrested."

"You taught her to have a conscience. You should be proud."

"Perhaps."

"She has watched as you and your friends destroy her country."

"It is *my* country."

"What country? Sarajevo, Srebrenica, Goražde, Bugojno, and a hundred other towns are destroyed. What kind of country will this be? A land of headstones."

He pushed his chair back, preparing to stand. "Our political masters in Belgrade are responsible ... the Europeans. The Americans."

"You are never to blame. You are never at fault. When you slept with another woman—*a Muslim*—it wasn't your fault. You destroy our daughter's life and our country, and it's still not your fault?"

Dr. Radovanović stood up and approached his wife. "Please, Slavica. We need—"

"No!"

She pulled a pistol from the shawl draped over her arm. "I have lost my country. And now I have lost my daughter."

"Slavica, this is not a game. We must survive. Our country must not die."

"You are right, no game. Enough is enough."

At first, he was shocked, then horrified as she raised the weapon and pointed it at him. Aiming for the heart, Slavica Radovanović shot her husband in the chest. When the bullet penetrated his heart, he smiled, as though death had come as a welcome relief.

He fell to the ground. Then she said, *"Samo Sloga Srbina Spasava."* Only unity saves the Serbs. "Forgive me, Sonja." She placed the pistol in her mouth and pulled the trigger.

CHAPTER FORTY

Goražde

Steele and Staci stood on the north side of the bridge spanning the River Drina. Sporadic tank fire and sniper fire continued nearby, but out of range. The Serbs were closing in on all sides. Dražen had ordered Steele to leave town, but he had not detained them. The boy had made his feelings clear. There would be no more debate about the Sarajevo Protocol. But Steele had another plan.

They reached the embankment, and, as agreed, waited for the UN Russian detachment. Steele pointed across the river and turned to Staci.

"If we walk fifty meters in that direction, we're in the Serb line of fire," he said. "I want Sgt. Tretyakov and his men to spread out on the other side of the bridge and beyond. That should hold off Serb fire. Then we'll show Dražen … He has to believe we can help him stop the Serb attack.

"You think Bosnian Serbs won't shoot their Russian brothers?" asked Staci.

Steele nodded. "I'm certain of it. And the Russians need some good PR. They've had too many black-market stories in too many newspapers recently."

Sgt. Tretyakov approached Steele and saluted. "We are ready, Captain. We await your orders." He even managed a smile, revealing a magnificent set of gold teeth.

Steele said, "I'll walk onto the bridge. Staci, stay here, okay?"

He turned to Sgt. Tretyakov. "Take your vehicle ahead of me, and I'll follow."

"No problem." Sgt. Tretyakov ran back to his APC and climbed aboard.

"Wait for me over there." Steele directed Staci to a building close to the bridge.

Then a deafening whizzing sound ripped through the air followed by a muffled *boom*. A shell landed about thirty meters away next to the APC. Steele and Staci hit the ground.

Flipping onto his back, Steele scanned to pinpoint the Russian APC. Now a deformed black shape of twisted metal and smoke, the APC was destroyed. No survivors. Sgt. Tretyakov and his men had been killed in an instant.

Steele and Staci scrambled for cover.

Staci said, "Now what? This is insane." Her eyes blurred with tears.

"I'm sorry. You were right," Steele replied, breathing heavily. "I guess the Serbs don't like the Russians anymore. We're totally screwed. *Fuck it!*"

They ducked as two more shells landed less than fifty feet away. Staying low—in case of snipers on both sides—they staggered to their feet and sprinted to the nearest house for cover. Steele stumbled a couple of times but regained his balance. They reached the house and ran to the rear for protection. He slammed his back into the wall, and they both slid to the ground with exhaustion and shock. As Steele caught his breath, he glanced at the bridge and could not believe what he saw.

Dražen Rakić was walking away from them *across* the bridge. He was about fifty meters away from direct Serb line of fire. Two soldiers—his teenage guards—ran after him but stopped on this side of the bridge, clearly afraid to follow their young leader.

"What's he doing?" Steele got up, preparing to go after him.

"No," said Staci, grabbing his forearm. "Jack ... think. They'll flatten you. Do you think they care you're trying to help them?"

They stared at the thin, pale boy on the bridge.

Dražen shouted, "SERB BITCHES! BASTARDS! WE WILL NEVER SURRENDER! DO YOU HEAR ME CHETNIK SCUM! WE WILL NEVER SURRENDER!"

Damn it! He's signing his death certificate.

Another shell narrowly missed the bridge, causing a mini geyser to gush from the river. Dražen stood his ground, impervious to the deluge of water that sprayed him.

Steele twisted sharply, shook off Staci's grip, and launched himself toward Dražen. "I'll be back."

Gen. Zukić passed the binoculars to Col. Kostić. "Look."

Col. Kostić said, "There's a boy on the bridge."

"I don't care. Destroy the bridge."

"But General—"

"We will repay them for every Serb life. The Russians have disappointed me. Let no one pass through Rogatica checkpoint. We will cut them off completely while we work."

Col. Kostić shuffled nervously, straining to get a view of the bridge. "There's someone else on the bridge … UNPROFOR."

Gen. Zukić snatched the binoculars. "Captain Steele … and I see the American journalist on the other side of the bridge."

"Shall I cease fire?"

"Execute the fire order."

Steele reached the middle of the bridge and grabbed Dražen by the scruff of the neck. Steele used his superior strength to drag him back across the bridge. Reaching safety, Steele knelt down. "You think you're clever, Dražen, but that was bloody stupid." He glanced down at Dražen's leg, which was bleeding heavily—a stray bullet. Steele pulled out a field dressing he had noticed earlier in Dražen's breast pocket, ripped it open with his teeth, and administered first aid.

Another shell landed and took out a side section of the bridge but left the main structure intact.

"You save my life," Dražen said.

"I won't do it again if you pull another stunt like that." Steele wrapped the bandage tightly around Dražen's leg. "Don't you want to live? Your people need you to live!"

"I am willing to die for my people. I promised my father."

"That's not what I asked. You're not much good to your people dead. Just to be clear, if you die, the Serbs will carry on killing your people. Is that what you want?"

Dražen nodded slowly. "You are right. I was foolish."

Staci gestured across the bridge. She shouted, "I see them. They're up there. Infantry."

Steele said to Dražen, "We need to get you to the hospital."

"I do not know who I can trust anymore."

"That makes two of us. One side launches an attack to provoke another. Your people are so predictable. Your leaders take advantage. They know NATO will not attack government forces."

Steele, with one arm around Dražen, helped him to shelter, and Staci helped Dražen sit down. Steele continued, "Tell me where the Protocol is, Dražen?"

Dražen wiped his face and looked down at the blood-soaked field dressing. "We go to my house. There is a tin for biscuits on top shelf in the kitchen—Princess Diana."

"Where, Dražen?" asked Steele.

"In Princess Diana tin."

Steele nodded and said, "Everything's going to be all right."

"*Inshallah!*" Dražen replied. God willing.

CHAPTER FORTY-ONE

Rogatica checkpoint, near Goražde

Gen. Brown's armored Land Rover approached the Rogatica checkpoint. The checkpoint commander was a small, greasy-looking man in blue camouflage fatigues with a pompous black mustache.

"Just our luck," said Gen. Brown, recognizing the Serb commander with a reputation for holding up UN vehicles and convoys for hours without reason. As a British Army general, it was irksome when some local farmer with an AK-47 could stop his agenda in its tracks. But that was the nature of this very "localized" war in the middle of Europe. This man was known to scrutinize, check, and double-check every item on cargo manifests, retreat to his hut to make lengthy bogus telephone calls, and confiscate as much convoy merchandise as possible for personal use. They didn't have time for this today—not that there was anything in their vehicle that would interest the local commander.

"Shall I ram him, boss?" asked Yomper.

"No, let's get through in one piece."

"Roger that." Yomper eased off the accelerator.

"We're running out of time. Sounds like Admiral Smith and NATO have the green light. I'm surprised we haven't heard aircraft already."

They stopped a few yards short of the barrier. The commander wandered over as if on a Sunday afternoon stroll. "Zdravo!" he said, smiling. *Hello!*

Armored vehicle windows could not be rolled down. Yomper opened his door ajar. "Do-bra dan," he said, mispronouncing one of the few Bosnian phrases he'd learned. *Good day.*

"Dobar dan!" the commander replied.

"General Brown has a meeting in Goražde. We're in a hurry."

Now the guard smiled, revealing a row of teeth in desperate need of dental work. Yomper caught a whiff of slivovitza as the man spoke.

"Hmmm … danas … teško, boga mi! Neće moći … neće moći," said the guard. *Today is tricky. You can't get through … it's too dangerous.* He spoke casually as though bartering the price of meat. "Puca se! Puca se gore!" *They're shooting … shooting up there.*

Yomper rolled his eyes.

"Here we go," said Gen. Brown. Checkpoint negotiation was a fine art, and the game had to be played.

"Fighting up ahead, boss …" said Yomper, turning to Gen. Brown, playing the game.

"The Rogatica Runt—just our luck," Gen. Brown muttered.

"Pucanje! Puca se!" the soldier continued, as if playing charades and they hadn't got it the first time. *Fighting! Shooting!*

Gen. Brown leaned across and said, "It's okay, thank you. We'll be fine." He rapped his knuckles on the bulletproof glass and said, "Look. Armor."

The guard cocked his head to one side and shrugged. "*Saw-ri,*" he said in English. "I must telephone for clearance. You wait here."

"Let's gun it?" Yomper spoke softly.

"Move forward, very slowly. Pretend to pull over. Leave your door open."

Gen. Brown kept the dialogue going as the guard walked away to his hut. "It's very important we get to Goražde. Gen. Zukić will attend this meeting. Quickly, please."

The Land Rover edged forward. As soon as the Rogatica Runt's back was turned, Yomper accelerated.

The commander shouted, "Ej! Sačekaj malo! Kud' ćes, bre?" *Hang on a minute! Where d'you think you're going?* He grimaced and shouted, "Momci! Napolje! Brzo!" *Lads! Everyone out! Quickly!*

Five seconds later, a band of Bosnian Serb militia had gathered in front of the vehicle, forcing Yomper to stop dead. Some of them wore the long Chetnik beard and military forage caps with the nationalistic insignia of four Serb Cs—English S's—on the side. They cocked their weapons, brandishing them aggressively. *Ironic,* Gen. Brown thought, apart from those with long beards, he couldn't even tell who was Serb, Muslim, or Croat.

"Too many of them," said Gen. Brown.

"Only skin and bone, boss. I can crush 'em."

"The last time we came through here, there was a tank around the next bend." Gen. Brown pointed ahead. "Not worth the risk."

Just then, they heard another vehicle approaching behind them. Gen. Brown turned, and Yomper glanced in his rearview mirror. A drab-green Serb army Jeep was speeding toward them—another Bosnian Serb commander?

A soldier moved behind Gen. Brown's vehicle and held up his arm. Even VIPs, it seemed, would pay homage.

The Jeep did not slow down. Serb expletives grew louder, and Gen. Brown heard rounds being chambered. Someone shouted at the hut for more reinforcements. "Napolje! Brzo!" *Come out! Quick!*

"Look out, boss," said Yomper. "On your right. It's gonna be tight."

Gen. Brown had his door open a few inches, one leg on the ground. He ducked back inside and closed the door as the rogue Jeep sped past, missing them by inches.

A lone occupant was driving.

The wooden barrier snapped like a dry twig.

Automatic fire exploded around them. Frenzied shouts failed to hold the checkpoint.

Gen. Brown and Yomper exchanged glances. Words unnecessary. Yomper hit the gas pedal. "Bloody 'ell, sir!"—he was already in third gear—"Guess who that was?"

Gen. Brown reached for his seatbelt. "Friend or foe?"

Yomper swerved to avoid the checkpoint barrier now on the ground. "Sonja Radovanović."

"Impossible."

"Impossible or not, sir, it was her. No fucking shit." Yomper touched the brakes as he approached the first bend after the checkpoint. "Jeez, boss, you were right. That tank you were on about ..."

A hundred yards in front, a T-55 tank was creeping out from dense forest, its turret twitching left as it probed in their direction.

"I've got him, sir," said Yomper. "No wucking furries. We'll get 'round him."

"You've got less than ten seconds to get by." Gen. Brown had every confidence in Yomper's driving, but the Serb T-55 tank would have a clear shot at them as they passed in front and beyond it. The tank commander only needed a few seconds to engage them, and it would be game over.

"They might think twice about a UN vehicle?" offered Yomper, pressing the accelerator to the floor.

"I doubt it."

The tank barrel followed their arc as they passed in front. They heard small-arms fire pinging the side of their armored Land Rover.

A second later, the tank fired. A large boulder on the side of the road exploded to their left and showered the Landover with rocks and stones. Despite the bulletproof windscreen, a small crack appeared in the bottom left-hand corner.

"Cheeky fuckers ..." said Yomper, grappling with the steering wheel. "No worries, boss. Around this bend, and we're sorted." Yomper shouted and gave them the middle finger. *"Armored, mate! We're armored!"*

Another flash-bang from the tank. Not since the First Gulf War in 1991 had Gen. Brown and Yomper been on the wrong side of a tank round firing directly at them. They had served together in the SAS and had both been caught in incidents of friendly fire during reconnaissance missions forward of main allied assault troops just outside Baghdad. That was the last time they had seen a tank firing at them from close quarters.

Just as Gen. Brown thought they were clear, the tank fired again. The Land Rover rose several inches in the air—at least that was what it felt like—and both men were thrown forward into the unforgiving bulletproof windscreen.

"Damn the bastards—"

Gen. Brown missed the end of Yomper's sentence. He opened his mouth to respond, but—

They hit something hard. The Land Rover lurched forward, then to one side and back the other way. It was a miracle, but they kept going a few more seconds before the Land Rover's engine stalled.

"You okay, Yomper?"

"Yes, sir … Bastards!"

"Are you sure that was Sonja Radovanović in the Jeep?"

"I spent time with her in the Chinook and at the safe house. You don't forget a face like that. She's a looker, if you ask me."

Yomper turned the ignition. No joy.

Gen. Brown looked behind. They had passed the tank but were not yet safe. "It's coming," he said.

Yomper turned the ignition again. "The bastards wouldn't dare."

Still looking back, Gen. Brown said, "Let's not wait to find out. Last try or we have to bail."

Gen. Brown tried his door, which was now jammed from the brief but violent collision. Yomper butted his huge frame against the door on his side, but it too was stuck.

Gen. Brown had never seen Yomper looking so worried. In

fact, he suddenly realized he had never seen him looking worried at all.

"The bastard's heading straight for us, sir." Yomper turned the ignition again. The Land Rover's engine fired. Yomper lifted the clutch, but there was no traction. They heard the high-pitched whine like a dentist's drill, their wheels spinning in mud.

"Look, boss." Yomper pointed. The Serb Jeep, which had disappeared around the bend moments before, was reversing.

"She's coming back." Gen. Brown was incredulous.

Seeing the Jeep Sonja was driving, the tank decelerated and slowed to a crawl.

The Jeep reversed past them and stopped in the middle of the road between the UN Land Rover and the tank.

Sonja descended and approached. Yomper was right; it was definitely her.

She tried both passenger doors from the outside without success. She ignored the twitching tank barrel hovering, marking time, uncertain whether to fire at them.

Sonja squatted, and with both hands picked up a rock the size of a basketball. She raised it above her head and slammed it down onto the bottom corner of the windscreen where the crack had appeared. The small boulder bounced off the windscreen, and she skipped out of the way as it landed inches from her feet. She picked it up again and held it even higher before letting it smash down on the weak point of the windscreen.

At the same time, Yomper lashed out at the crack in the glass with the heel of his combat boot. After two kicks, the windscreen fell away.

They pushed out the shattered glass and climbed out.

Gen. Brown said, "Thank you, Sonja."

"Let's go," she replied.

All three climbed into her Jeep. Behind the wheel, Sonja drove off so fast that Yomper grabbed the handrail above the window to steady himself.

The tank did not follow.

Yomper said, "You saved our arses."

She frowned, confused.

"You saved our lives, Sonja," said Gen. Brown. "We owe you big time."

"Don't mention it. You treated me with respect in Ivančevo. The British have honor."

Yomper smiled.

Gen. Brown asked, "Where to?"

"Goražde. I have to meet someone."

"That makes three of us," replied Gen. Brown.

CHAPTER FORTY-TWO

Goražde

The crackle and bursts of small-arms fire got louder. Steele, Staci, and Dražen crouched low as they made their way— Dražen limping—from one half-destroyed house to the next. Three blocks later, they reached Dražen's apartment.

Once inside, Steele helped Dražen to a chair. Seeing her son's flesh wound, Amira turned pale. She stood up and fetched bandages, hot water, and scissors.

"We're here to help, Mrs. Rakić," said Steele. "I promise you Dražen's going to be fine."

Amira gave a weak smile but remained silent as she stripped the field dressing and redressed her son's wound.

Then Dražen made his way to the plastic sheeting covering the windows and pulled it back. Pointing to the pockmarked star in the road outside, he said, "That is where they killed my father."

"I'm really sorry, Dražen," Staci said.

He turned. "You still think the Serbs will stop attacking?"

Steele took a deep breath. "Show us the Protocol, Dražen. Please ..."

Dražen crossed to the kitchen. He opened the pantry door, reached up, and returned clutching a bottle of *rakija*—plum brandy—and a cylindrical biscuit tin with a portrait photograph of Princess Diana on the side. "My father told me, 'Our secret is safe with Diana.'" He smiled and handed Steele the tin and then and poured a glass of plum brandy for his mother. "Here, Mama. This will make you feel better."

Steele opened the tin and took out a couple of pieces of old shortbread fingers. In the bottom he saw an envelope. It didn't look like much.

Steele looked up at Dražen, who nodded his approval.

Steele carefully removed the envelope and started to open it. "A map of Korčula?" Steele looked at Dražen, disappointed.

"It's all I have. I thought you understood this. My father told me this was one part of the puzzle—the Sarajevo Protocol. The other is in Croatia."

Steele read the writing on the map:

BOOT ZIP SIR JOT

"Any idea what it means?" asked Staci.

"A code in English," said Dražen. "My father said anyone who has been there would understand. He was a writer. He loved word puzzles."

"We're looking for a historical document written by Tito, not a treasure map."

"You go to Korčula. It takes a few hours perhaps."

"Not to mention about six confrontation lines, three warring factions, and the sea," Steele said, his tone reflecting his frustration.

"Not if you go with my people. The Bosnian army will escort you."

"There's no time, Dražen." He looked again at the code. "*Boot Zip Sir Jot.* Did your father say anything else that might help us? Anything at all?"

As he waited for a reply, Steele thought about Fitzgerald, who lived on Korčula. Perhaps the old man could help them? If it was true he helped to write the damn thing in the first place, then perhaps he knew where it was now? But then why hadn't Fitzgerald told *them*?

Dražen continued, "My father left me in charge—"

The door opened, and someone entered the apartment:

"Dražene! Dražene! Dodji 'vamo … dodji 'vamo!" *Dražen! Come here!*

A soldier with Bosnian army insignia on his armband approached Dražen and whispered something. Dražen's eyes widened. Then the man said to Steele, "Come with me."

"Who is this?" asked Steele.

Dražen said, "Your General Brown has arrived. He was nearly shot by our troops. He is at the checkpoint across the footbridge."

"Let him through for Christ's sake. If the Serbs know he's here, they'll hold their fire."

"He wants you to meet him on the bridge."

Steele nodded, looking at Staci. They both stood still. *Time to play Bosnian mortar roulette again*, he thought.

Five minutes later, Steele looked across the footbridge. He saw a lone military Jeep on the other side. No movement inside or near the vehicle.

He turned to Staci. "Have you noticed?" he said. "No shelling, no shooting."

"Perhaps they respect the UN after all?" she replied.

Steele frowned. "I don't get it."

A shot rang out behind him from the Bosnian Muslim side of the bridge. Steele shouted, "HOLD YOUR FIRE!" He cursed and turned to Dražen. "Control your men. General Brown can't help us if you shoot him."

Dražen said, "Help us? NATO wants to bomb the Serbs, and General Brown defends them."

"That's not it. That's not why he's here. You're twisting things." Steele walked toward the bridge. "Stay here."

Dražen watched Steele walking away from him. "It's okay," he said raising his voice, "I know that you will leave us with your general, like the rest of the international community."

Steele looked back as he kept walking. "No, Dražen, I'm staying. I'm not like the rest. I keep my promises."

Steele took a few more steps onto the bridge.

"Wait." Dražen slipped off his bulletproof vest. "Take this."

Steele paused for a moment, then walked back and took the vest. "Thank you."

On this side of the bridge, Steele had observed snipers lying in ditches, behind walls and doorways of destroyed houses. Reaching the edge of the bridge again, Steele scanned the hills on the other side and picked out at least four Serb tanks. On the very top of the hill, he saw the tip of a radio mast from the Bosnian Serb army's mobile communications vehicle. It occurred to him that anyone of these fuckers from either side could shoot him at any moment. And quite possibly no one would give a damn, and no one would ever be held responsible.

He could hear the calming sounds of the River Drina just below him. It was almost an out-of-body experience, surreal. He could see himself looking down on the bridge at the jade-green water and the enjoying the most divine sound in such diabolical circumstances.

"Captain Steele," a voice shouted. It was Gen. Brown.

Steele looked ahead and saw Gen. Brown standing with two Bosnian Serb soldiers and a woman in civilian clothes wearing a camouflage jacket. Steele was surprised to see a female form and found himself squinting to get a better look. He did a double take when he realized it was Sonja Radovanović. *Sonja!* After she'd been snatched by the SAS, he had wondered when or even if he would ever see her again. He felt a sense of hope. Maybe Sonja and Dražen could make an agreement?

Gen. Brown shouted, "I'm sending someone across—a friend of yours."

"Understood, General. Send her over." Steele gestured for Sonja to start walking.

What started as a quiet rumble in the distance quickly turned into a deafening roar that filled the sky, but no aircraft was visible due to the low cloud cover. Everyone on all sides looked up. "NATO! NATO!" shouted Bosnian government soldiers from their trenches. "Hurrah! Hurrah!"

They think NATO is coming to their rescue, Steele thought. *I hope they're wrong, or we're all screwed.*

"Sonja?" Steele said in voice loud enough to carry across the bridge. She was walking toward him. His heart was pounding. He was really, really pleased to see her.

He hadn't set eyes on her for several days. But now she was a hundred meters away.

"Jack,"—the velvet timbre of her voice was unmistakable—"I'm coming over."

Oh my God, he thought. *As soon as the Muslims recognize her, they'll shoot her.*

Sarajevo

Maj. Small raised his voice into the telephone. "Let me spell it out, Admiral: If you target the Serbs, they'll retaliate. Our commander is on the bloody ground. Abort the mission."

"I have my orders," replied the Supreme Allied Commander Europe—SACEUR. Admiral Smith commanded NATO's Allied Command Operations on the continent of Europe.

"Who from? Have you told them we have men on the ground?"

"Brussels, London, and Washington are fully aware of the situation. We're waiting on the weather. As soon as there's a window—"

"A window?"

"Cloud cover is not ideal."

"Are you aware that the Russians have orders from Moscow to protect the Serbs if attacked? They also have peacekeepers inside Goražde. Are you trying to start World War Three, Admiral?"

A short pause. Then Adm. Smith said, "Bosnian Serbs are in

direct contravention of the Goražde TEZ,"—the TEZ, or Total Exclusion Zone, was the UN's attempt to force the warring factions to keep away from each other—"not to mention a dozen other breaches in the Sarajevo area. I have my orders."

Maj. Small tried a different approach. "The Muslims launched a major offensive behind the Jewish cemetery yesterday. They're playing us like a cello. They even found a tank to threaten us with for God's sake."

"Can you reach Brown?"

"I can try."

"Tell him to get his backside out of Goražde immediately. Tell him my pilots will get the green light as soon as the weather breaks. We can't wait for him."

The line went dead.

"Damn it," said Maj. Small.

"Shall I try again, sir?" asked a British Army clerk, who had been trying to establish comms with Yomper on the sat phone.

"Yes, Corporal. Where is he?"

"Last radio check was before Rogatica … thirty minutes ago."

"Keep trying."

"Yes, sir."

CHAPTER FORTY-THREE

Goražde

Steele locked eyes with Sonja. She was fifty feet away. *What is she doing here?* The Serbs would go ballistic when they saw her walking into the lion's den. Same for the Bosnian government troops on his side of the bridge. There were observation posts—OPs—in every direction: snipers, artillery, mortars, and tanks. It was only a matter of seconds before she would be recognized and targeted. And shot? Not since Adolf Hitler had there been a more hated man—Sonja's father—in Bosnia, and Europe too, for that matter.

But he was wrong. The exact opposite happened. The closer she got, the quieter it became. Even a firefight on the other side of town dwindled to nothing. Everyone was watching … waiting … listening.

Steele felt an emotional pull toward Sonja. He began walking in her direction. Yes, it was madness. But he needed to protect her. He could not let her be shot like a deer in the forest. How long before one of the government soldiers fired at her?

Ten feet away, he said, "I'd say we have seconds before someone opens fire."

"I agree. They might shoot me … or perhaps they will listen to me."

"Now you want to talk?"

"This is my country, Jack. These are my people—on both sides of this bridge. Where is Dražen?"

"I will ask him to call off his men. They're pointing their weapons at your head right now."

"I take responsibility."

"For what?"

"For my family. For my father."

"Now's not the time." Steele squatted down and took off the armored Kevlar vest Dražen had given him. It was Steele's turn to say, "Take this."

"I don't want your vest. Tell Dražen I want to talk. I'll stay here."

Steele laid the vest at her feet. He looked around him. "Okay."

Then he backed away and headed to the corner building where Dražen had taken cover.

Halfway back, he heard the squeaking and grating of T-55 tank tracks moving from the right flank and taking up a fire position on the other side of the bridge. He kept going.

The tank had moved behind Gen. Brown, who was standing next to Sonja's Jeep. Yomper stood next to him.

Gen. Brown and Yomper stepped onto the bridge and walked toward Sonja.

A few seconds onto the bridge, Gen. Brown cursed the sudden beep of his satellite telephone in Yomper's day sack. The timing couldn't have been worse. "Answer it," said Gen. Brown.

Yomper took out the telephone and passed the handset to Brown. They crouched at the side of the bridge.

"Brown."

"Sir, it's Brian Small. We've been trying to reach you."

"Go ahead."

"What's your location?"

"Goražde. We had some unexpected help from Sonja Radovanović."

A short pause. "Sir, you *must* leave immediately. Admiral Smith refuses to back down. He says he has orders. As soon as the weather clears, NATO will attack—they'll destroy all Bosnian Serb positions in the TEZ."

"We're on the bridge."

"I wasn't sure—"

"Never mind. Tell Admiral Smith we're here, and that I need more time."

"I've already tried to warn him. He's not interested."

"Did you give him our position?"

"Yes, I said you were in Goražde."

"Our exact position? Tell him precisely where—"

"You *must* leave, General. I don't think he's bluffing—"

Gen. Brown pressed the end-call button and looked back at the nearest Serb T-55. It was an obvious target out in the open thirty feet from them. If it were hit, they'd probably go down with it.

"Boss," said Yomper, "no offense, sir, but you look worried?"

Gen. Brown continued toward Sonja, Yomper at his side. "Let's sort this bloody mess out."

⭐　　⭐　　⭐

Dražen stood in the doorway that was once the main entrance to the bakery. Steele reached Dražen and crouched down to catch his breath.

Steele said, "General Brown is here, Dražen."

"I see him."

"And someone else ..."

Dražen studied the woman in the distance. "Sonja?"

"Yes."

"My father knew her mother." Something in Dražen's voice caught Steele off guard.

"You know each other?"

Dražen stared intently at Steele. "Yes. Sonja Radovanović is my half-sister."

Steele felt as though someone had punched him in the gut. He covered his mouth for a moment. "Sonja?"

Staci said, "Wow! Oh my God."

Steele and Staci looked at each other for a moment, their expressions reflecting their shared confusion as they tried to put the pieces together.

Dražen continued, "My father had romance with Slavica Radovanović. They were young. She refused to keep me because I was 'Turk.' She betrayed her own son."

"I don't believe that, Dražen," said Steele. "She wouldn't—"

"People told me this. Eventually, my father left Sarajevo and came to live in Goražde. We lived in both towns for many years. My father was journalist. He went back and forth on business. He met Amira, my mother, and they had my sister. Then he became Mayor of Goražde during the war."

Steele nodded. Now wasn't the time for twenty questions. "Dražen, she's on the bridge. Sonja wants to talk."

Dražen smiled and shrugged. "Why not? She's my sister." Dražen picked himself off the ground and, grimacing, straightened his injured leg. He gestured to his guards to stay put.

Steele and Dražen set off toward the bridge.

The clouds began to clear, and, for the first time since they had arrived, the river began to sparkle, turning a deep shade of jade green. Brown and Yomper stood side by side, halfway between Sonja and the T-55 behind them.

Yomper said, "Not thrilled to see the sun."

Gen. Brown's telephone rang again. He shook his head.

"Better take it, boss. Talk some sense into them?"

Gen. Brown stopped and put the receiver to his ear. "Brown ... "

"Rupert, we have to talk," said Adm. Smith.

"I won't allow it," snapped Gen. Brown. "You'll have to blow me to pieces."

"Don't be ridiculous, Rupert."

"Easy to play God sitting in Naples."

"This is not *your* war, Rupert. You can't wave a magic wand for peace. The warring parties have to want it too."

"Well, I have to do something."

"Everyone agrees on this—Washington, London, and Brussels. Bottom line—Radovanović is in violation of the TEZ. It's over. You must abort. Get the hell out of there."

"What about Bosnian government positions on Mount Igman? There's a bloody tank behind UN headquarters in Sarajevo drawing fire on our people. Are you going to bomb them too?"

"Rupert, listen—"

"UN troops had to clear Bosnian government positions because you wouldn't do your job. Six of our French peacekeepers were killed because you've jeopardized your neutrality. We've lost impartiality."

"Our intel—"

"Your intel is a bag of bollocks."

A short distance away, Sonja turned around.

Gen. Brown continued, "Who in God's name is pulling your strings? A cease-fire violation is a bloody cease-fire violation. Why won't you teach everyone a lesson?"

"We're not going to bomb the Bosnian government, Rupert."

Adm. Smith was right. Gen. Brown understood this. He had been in denial. The international community had taken sides in this war. Gen. Brown's heart sank. His UN peacekeeping mission in Bosnia was almost in a coma. *You can't fight a war in white-painted vehicles.* He had said it to journalists several times. Without trust from all sides, the mission would fail.

Adm. Smith continued, "I can't be responsible for your safety. We have a break in the weather. We're giving the green light."

"I'm standing next to a Serb T-55 on the footbridge in Goražde. I'm not moving. Do whatever you have to do."

Brown hung up and handed Yomper the receiver.

"Didn't go well then, boss?"

"Astute, Yomper. So astute."

"Sir, did you understand what Sonja's plan is?"

"I'm not convinced she has a plan, but we're about to find out."

CHAPTER FORTY-FOUR

Steele and Dražen walked onto the bridge. Dražen slowed his pace as he approached Sonja Radovanović—his half-sister. They hadn't seen each other in person since war broke out.

Steele exchanged a nod with Gen. Brown, who backed off with Yomper toward the tank leaving Sonja alone with Dražen and Steele.

Dražen smiled. "I have made you wrong for many things. But you deserved it."

"Hello, Dražen. How are you?"

"We could shoot you now. With luck your father would die of a broken heart."

"You can shoot me, but my father's heart would survive. His heart is made of stone." She paused. "How are you?"

"I'm fine. Captain Steele says you want to talk."

"Yes."

"You are crazy, Sonja. Why did you come here? Why do you want to die?"

"My life is not important. Our country is dying, Dražen." Her eyes welled. "I believe that you and I can stop this. Stop NATO before they destroy us. We can save lives."

"NATO works for us. They will destroy Serbs."

Steele said, "NATO jets are on their way. We're standing next to a legitimate target." He pointed to the Serb tank on the far side of the bridge. "It's inside the exclusion zone, and if they bomb it, we're all finished."

Sonja looked at Dražen. "I want peace. People in Republika Srpska want peace—"

"Now you come?" Dražen smiled, but with venom in his eyes. "To beg forgiveness before God and NATO?"

Sonja frowned. "My father says I am a traitor, but I know my people. Your people, my people—we were the same our whole lives."

"You think you know what *we* want? Your father tortures my people, and now you tell me what *we* need?"

"Dražen, you are my brother—we can stop this war."

Steele broke in, "I suggest it's time to forgive the past. And now move forward toward securing a real future with General Brown's help." Steele gestured toward Gen. Brown, who had been listening to the conversation thirty-feet away.

Brown nodded.

Dražen said, "And the Sarajevo Protocol?"

"We can use it for peace," said Sonja. "I promise you. It will be our insurance—Serbs and Bosnians—against the West."

"You think it means anything to me that you are my sister?" Dražen said mockingly.

"Yes, Dražen," she nodded. "Yes, yes I do."

Dražen's face tensed. He was also fighting back tears. "So many years, we were nothing to you … my father and me. I did not exist for you—"

"That's not true," said Sonja.

"I grew up without my mother," replied Dražen.

"Luka told me Amira is a good woman."

"But you lived with my real mother. And that monster."

"Yes, that monster is my father. But he is also your biological father. Amira is your real mother."

Everyone looked at Dražen. Steele's stomach dropped.

Sonja continued, "I always wanted to come and find you, but the war … Luka cared about you very much. Our father wanted nothing to do with Amira. That's why you lived with Amira and Luka. I'm sorry, Dražen."

Sonja took two steps forward. They locked eyes, then she cautiously put her arms around Dražen. At first, he resisted, his body stiff. She squeezed him tight.

Steele watched closely. It was the tiniest movement, but Dražen's body relaxed. A moment later, Dražen wrapped his arms around Sonja and reciprocated with a hug, and it seemed as though the bridge itself also relaxed.

When it was finished, Dražen looked up at her. "Luka is still my father. I loved him more than anything. He told me people would come one day. He said to listen. But I never trusted you. I never wanted to speak to you again. Now I understand that perhaps it is my duty. Luka gave me the map."

Steele clutched the map inside his pocket. Dozens, perhaps hundreds of senior British, American, and European government officials, military, and intelligence officers in dozens of countries were waiting for it too.

"We have the map," said Dražen, looking at Steele.

"Let me see," she said.

Steele took it out and, reluctantly, handed it to Sonja. "There's some kind of clue or code. Can you make sense of it?"

Sonja studied the words on the map:

BOOT ZIP SIR JTO

Steele said, "Sonja?"

Then Sonja smiled, almost laughing, as though privy to an inside joke. "It makes perfect sense. This is anagram: JOSIP BROZ TITO."

Steele frowned, ever more confused. "What about him?" asked Steele.

"This tells us the location."

"Of the Sarajevo Protocol?"

"Yes."

"Where?" Steele's eyes widened.

"A safe place," she said.

Dražen took a step back. "Why should I trust you?"

"Because Bosnian Serbs will accept forty-nine percent of the territory, and Muslims and Croats will share the rest. Muslims will have Bosnia-Herzegovina, and Republika Srpska will be ours."

"You accept less than half of the territory? Your … *my* father … the monster has refused this."

"I will guarantee this," said Sonja. "We can show them brother and sister—Serb and Muslim—we are sick of this war."

"Jack …" shouted Staci from the Muslim side of the bridge. "Listen!"

A jet roar returned to clear skies, bringing the conversation to an abrupt halt. The jet made a pass, pulling high and wide and ready to dive back down and attack the Serb tank in open ground.

If the tank was hit, the bridge would be destroyed.

Gen. Brown stayed out in the open and next to the T-55. He effectively made himself a UN human shield for the NATO fighter aircraft. It was a gamble, but he was sure Adm. Smith would have warned the pilots that he was on the ground. In Adm. Smith's position, and despite the bravado, Gen. Brown would have done the same thing. The pilot, Gen. Brown prayed, would not strike without checking the situation on the ground. Adm. Smith would not allow his pilots to attack the UN commander.

Or perhaps it *was* conceivable? Then a voice inside him contradicted: *Anything's possible.*

Gen. Brown estimated twenty seconds to impact. He was disobeying a direct order by refusing to move. But on his first day in Bosnia, Gen. Brown had promised himself never to take sides. He reminded himself of his personal UN mantra: Peace not war. He walked purposefully to the south side of the bridge. "Call Adm. Smith," he said to Yomper.

They reached the T-55. Yomper gave Gen. Brown the handset. "He's on the line, boss."

Looking up at the young Serb tank commander, who looked as confused as anyone to see two UN soldiers standing in front of his tank, Gen. Brown placed the handset to his ear.

Adm. Smith said, "Rupert, this is your last warning. The weather's cleared. My pilots have to do this. Less than a minute."

"I'm standing next to the T-55 your pilots are locked onto. I'm not moving."

"Damn it, man—"

"Remember what you said in Sarajevo?"

"Yes. I promised I would help them."

"Remember when your driver was hit by the sniper?"

"Of course. He'll never walk again."

"What was it all for? The Serbs are bastards, but if you do this, we lose … we're no better than they are. The only way to end this is to find the Sarajevo Protocol."

"Sorry, can't help. Way beyond that, Rupert. Get out of there now!"

"If you bomb these tanks, the Serbs will destroy Goražde."

Gen. Brown pressed the handset to his ear, straining to hear. This was the most important decision of his life. It wasn't too late—they could jump into the Jeep and drive. He thought about his wife and sons, how much he loved them. Then he thought about Dr. Radovanović and Gen. Zukić, and how much he hated them.

Steele waved frantically from the other side of the bridge. "General Brown, sir!" He could just make out Steele's voice over the approaching NATO fighter.

Steele was running toward him. Again, he shouted, "WE HAVE THE PROTOCOL! TELL THEM WE HAVE THE SARA-JEVO PROTOCOL!"

Gen. Brown said, "Jeremy, listen to me carefully. We have the Sarajevo Protocol … I repeat …"

"General Brown, sir!" shouted Steele.

No response.

Steele sprinted as fast as he could. The slats on the wooden bridge creaked and trembled as he pounded across them. "WE HAVE THE PROTOCOL! TELL THEM WE HAVE THE SARAJEVO PROTOCOL!"

Gen. Brown was speaking into the sat phone. Steele couldn't tell if the general had heard him. He squinted into the sky and saw the silhouette of the aircraft bearing down.

Soldiers on both sides took cover. The Serb tank crew leaped down off the tank and ran for their lives. The jet was on them, about to fire. Steele could see the color of the pilot's helmet—it was white.

Steele, Brown, and Yomper closed their eyes.

CHAPTER FORTY-FIVE

The aircraft did not fire.

The deafening roar left a wake of silence. Not a flicker, not a move—the F-16 had flown past and disappeared to a dot in the sky without firing.

Afterward, Steele recalled those moments of silence to be the most peaceful he had ever known. His entire world was still. True peace, quiet, and calm, even if it only lasted for a few moments.

Now he opened his eyes. Everyone was there ... standing, watching, waiting ... in one piece. "Thank God," he said softly. Twice in one day, Steele had thought he was dead. *Please God, I don't need a third.* Gen. Brown had made the right call—Adm. Smith had backed off.

"Nice one, sir," Yomper said to Steele.

Gen. Brown glanced at the sat phone screen. He still had a connection. "You bastard, Jeremy," he said. Then he hung up.

Steele sensed movement from, and in, all directions. Bosnian Serb and Muslim soldiers emerged from cover on both sides of the bridge. Everyone had watched the showdown— UNPROFOR Commander targeted by NATO F-16. Brown had stood his ground.

Now, it seemed to Steele, Serbs and Muslims were waiting for the UN's next move.

"We should probably get out of here," said Steele slowly. "Sonja must tell her people about the agreement with Dražen. We can't trust the military to hold off for long." He glanced at

Sonja, then to Gen. Brown. "Sonja and Dražen agreed the Serbs would not attack Goražde. But she has to show the Protocol to her parliament."

Brown said, "That bloody thing actually exists?"

"Yes, the Serbs can use it as an insurance policy—against further Western aggression."

"Boyle will love that. Not exactly what our foreign policy demagogues had in mind."

"With respect, General," said Steele, "Boyle can screw himself."

Gen. Brown smiled for the first time since arriving at the bridge, raising his eyebrows. "Harsh, but entirely fair, Captain Steele."

Steele turned to Sonja. "Pale?"

"Yes. We must hurry."

"By the way," said Gen. Brown. "Where is it? Can I see it?"

Sonja said, "It's safe, General Brown. Now we have the map." She walked toward Dražen.

Steele said, "Sonja and I will get it. She agrees to share it with us, once she secures the peace deal."

Gen. Brown nodded. Then he whispered, "I hope so. Or we're back to square one. You think you can trust her?"

Steele nodded.

Sonja stepped over to Dražen and kissed him on both checks. She hugged him one last time. Soldiers on both sides lowered their weapons but were still alert. They had been here before—a cease-fire one day, a peace agreement the next, and fighting again the day after. But at least there was a renewed feeling of hope in the air.

Steele sensed they weren't quite ready to throw their guns into the Drina. Both Sonja and Dražen had masters high above them to convince and solidify any kind of peace deal.

★　　★　　★

The T-55 Bosnian Serb commander and his crew appeared from the ruins of a burned-out building. They climbed into the tank, and the commander put on his headset.

Sonja and Steele walked over to the tank. "Return to your base," she told him.

The tank commander saluted. Then, listening intently to a message on his headset, he frowned and raised his hand.

"Stop," he said, looking bewildered. He took off his headset, and climbed down
from his tank to speak to Sonja. "Dr. Radovanović is dead," he said quietly.

"What?"

"Your mother and father are dead. I'm very sorry."

Sonja sank to her haunches, placed her head in her hands but did not cry. Her entire life and memories of childhood, teenage, and adult years reeled through her mind. She regretted her last words to her father. They had not been kind. But Sonja could not help feeling a sense of relief and a kind of release. Not from her mother, but certainly from her father.

Sonja looked at Steele. "How could this happen?"

"I'm sorry, Sonja. I don't know." He glanced up at the commander. "Do you know anything else?"

The commander grimaced and beckoned Steele. "Nothing," he replied. Then he leaned down and whispered something to Steele.

Steele and the commander allowed Sonja a few moments to take in the news.

"Excuse me, Miss," said the commander. "Should we return to base?"

Steele gave his first command ever to the Serb army. "Yes," he said. "Go back to your base now."

Steele and Sonja climbed into the Jeep. Sonja stayed silent.

Pale Road, Republika Srpska

The uneven road took them past fields, forests, and valleys. Without men in uniform, tanks, and military vehicles, the Bosnian countryside was exquisitely beautiful. Steele observed the red-roofed houses and cottages dotted across the terrain. Not as picturesque as Switzerland or Germany, but, unlike dwellings around Sarajevo and much of Bosnian government territory, at least these were intact. Republika Srpska had escaped ethnic cleansing. In fact, NATO had done more damage here than Bosnian government forces.

"I'm sorry," said Steele, "that you've lost him, regardless of what he did."

"Thank you—it's okay. I lost my father the day this war started, and probably long before if I am honest."

"And your mother. It's tragic. I'm so sorry." He placed his hand on hers and gently squeezed. "There's something else you should know."

She sat silently. Her body trembled.

"Apparently, your mother shot your father."

Sonja shook her head and cried.

Then she said, "I had a bad feeling when they announced the referendum. I knew that Serbs could never win."

"Don't say that. Everyone can win."

"I knew war would come. But I didn't know my father would be the demon of this war. I am not surprised someone killed him."

Steele said nothing. A few minutes passed.

"At least we found the Protocol," he offered finally.

She smiled as though thinking about a long-lost secret. "Yes, it was always in a safe place. No Communist apparatchiks came close to it all these years."

Steele said, "What do you mean?"

"Your friend."

"Sorry?"

"Fitzgerald."

"Fitzgerald?"

"Fitzgerald's villa," she said.

His eyes widened. "On Korčula?"

"Yes."

Steele thought for a moment before he said, "You said *was*?"

"I took it. We met in London, and he told me where to find it."

Sonja reached inside her jacket and pulled out an envelope. She looked at Steele, unable to conceal her delight. "I took it with his permission."

Glowing, Steele looked at the envelope. "How do you know this is it?"

"*BOOT ZIP SIR JOT.*"

"The map?" Then he remembered. "Dražen's anagram?"

"JOSIP BROZ TITO—It was hidden behind Tito's portrait in Fitzgerald's villa as Fitzgerald promised. But I needed the map to be sure he had told me the truth. Especially the part about Luka."

"A puzzle in two parts?" Steele was thinking out loud.

"Yes."

"Why *you*?"

"He trusted me because of Luka and Dražen. Flesh and blood."

"He trusted you not to take it straight to your father?"

"I would not have met Fitzgerald in London if I wasn't serious about the survival of my people. I wanted to help."

"And he'd rather you have it than the powers that be from the West?"

"Sir Lawrence knew they would never give up their search. British, Americans, Russians, Serbians, whoever … He knew they would find it eventually. His wife was murdered because of it. But they didn't find it."

"How did he find you?" Steele asked. A lightbulb went off. "Don't tell me … Peter?"

"Fitzgerald contacted me through Peter and invited me to meet him at the Savoy. But he was playing games with me, with everyone."

"I don't understand."

"Fitzgerald told me he worked for MI6 several decades after World War Two."

"Right, he was our main link with Tito—and with the partisans during the war?"

"Correct. But he never stopped working, even *after* the war. I see that now. He told me he would give his life for Yugoslavia. He fell in love with our country. He fought against the Nazis. He believed in us, *all* of us—Serbs, Croats, and Muslims. A Communist utopia worth tolerating, he said. But they killed his wife nevertheless. Yugoslavia was the only thing he had left."

"I'm confused."

"Everything he had lived and worked for would be wasted if our country dies."

Steele nodded slowly. "He was playing you against the British government? He recruited you to help your own people?"

"Yes, for the greater good of former Yugoslavia."

"Okay," Steele said slowly.

Steele was taken off guard by a sharp bend in the road, and he narrowly avoided driving over the edge. He decided to pull over so that he could look at her straight in the eye.

"Where does Dražen fit in? Why did you come to Goražde? How did the map end up in the Princess Diana tin?"

"Fitzgerald told me to take the Protocol to Luka Rakić—they were close friends for many years. Fitzgerald trusted Luka with the secret, and Luka would confirm truth about the Protocol. When the time was right."

"That it was genuine?"

"Yes."

"Fitzgerald knew Dražen is your half-brother?"

"Yes, of course. That is why he told Luka about this secret. Luka, and now Dražen, were the only way to bring us together— Serb and Muslim. One day, if war broke out, he hoped we could come together and make peace for our people. We start with Goražde."

Steele took a deep breathe followed by a slow exhale, trying to piece it all together. "So Fitzgerald preempted the conspiracy? He suspected all along that if your country started falling apart, others might conspire to attack the Bosnian Serbs in favor of Muslims? NATO?"

"In this case, it turned out to be pretext of TEZ violations."

"Right," Steele said slowly, "unless they had the Protocol in their possession to use as leverage—"

Sonja nodded. His gaze lingered on her for a moment. He loved her small but committed gestures. If this had been a first date in London, he would have kissed her.

"So why did Fitzgerald defend Serbs but not Croats or Muslims?"

"Before the war, my country had ethnic utopia. Fitzgerald called it the 'Tito effect.' For decades, Tito united Muslims, Serbs, and Croats. He mixed them together like baking a cake. He wanted Muslims to have their religion but without extremism. When Tito died, it was too difficult to maintain. The West is afraid of Muslim extremism, so they supported Bosnian government to prevent extremism …"

"And they demonize megalomaniac Serb nationalists like President Milošević, your father, and Gen. Zukić? Know thine enemy."

"These men deserve this. They are war criminals."

"This is extraordinary." Steele exhaled again. He felt a surge of adrenaline pumping through his veins. *Fitzgerald. Wiley old, ingenious fox,* he thought. Steele pointed to the Protocol. "You think this will help now? To persuade your people?"

"I will try."

Steele glanced over his shoulder at the deserted country road and drove off. "Without General Brown, we wouldn't be here. The Serbs would be crushed already. He has to help us, finish what we started."

"You think he will help us?"

"I don't know. If he does, he'll have to betray some very powerful political masters. It's a tall order."

CHAPTER FORTY-SIX

Sarajevo, Bosnia

Gen. Brown had ordered Yomper to stay in Goražde with the UN Russian peacekeepers. Their unit was small but sufficient to keep Serb cousins at bay. Yomper would nurture the fragile cease-fire agreement between Dražen's fighters and Sonja and her army's tank firepower on the hills overlooking the town.

"Flatten any bugger who threatens the cease-fire," Gen. Brown had said. "I'll do my best to keep NATO jets at bay."

"Roger that, boss." Yomper seemed confident. "We'll get them sorted, sir."

Gen. Brown returned to Sarajevo. He was prepared to protest and fight like never before in his entire life—first with the British PM, followed by Klaus Reithoffer, the new clown in charge of the European Union. If necessary, he'd call the President of the United States and the UN Secretary-General. And if all that failed, he'd go public, even if it meant throwing his career down the drain. *Some things are more important.*

Or perhaps he'd go public first? There were dozens of international journalists sitting a stone's throw from his office ready to devour any snippet of news he cared to toss their way ... let alone something of this sensational global magnitude.

Gen. Brown insisted that Staci return to Sarajevo with him. He was suspicious of her motives. She had a lot of explaining to do, starting with the truth about her relationship with Boyle. *Who is she? Who does she really work for?*

It took an hour to reach UNPROFOR headquarters in downtown Sarajevo. With Staci close behind—she had not been given a choice in the matter—Gen. Brown stormed into the building and upstairs to his office. The entire headquarters staff was waiting for his next move. Gen. Brown ordered Staci to sit and wait on the bench outside his office.

Maj. Small and Boyle stood up as Gen. Brown entered. Maj. Small covered the telephone receiver he was holding and said, "Dr. Radovanović is dead."

"*What?*" Brown stared incredulously at Small.

"Apparently, Slavica Radovanović shot him in the chest at point blank range this morning. And then she shot herself."

"Do we know why?" asked Gen. Brown.

"We don't," replied Maj. Small.

"Why not?" said Boyle.

Gen. Brown said, "That's the first thing you've said I agree with."

"General Brown," Maj. Small continued, "I have the prime minister for you, sir. He's eager to speak."

"That makes two of us." Gen. Brown hit the speaker button on his telephone unit. He needed witnesses for this, even though he didn't fully trust anyone apart from Yomper. For several days now, it seemed to him, he was one step behind everyone else.

"Prime Minister?"

"Glad you're safe, Rupert," said Robert Grange. "Boyle gave me an update. Nasty business. Glad we're sorting it out."

Boyle broke in, "Prime Minister, it's far from sorted. We should have taken care of Sonja Radovanović in Ivančevo while we had the chance."

"What in God's name are you talking about?" Gen. Brown was seething.

Grange said, "General Zukić's daughter committed suicide a few weeks ago and Zukić was starting to crack. Apparently, he blamed himself for her suicide. We thought it might push Dr. Radovanović to the edge if his daughter went missing."

"You wanted her to commit suicide too?" asked Gen. Brown.

"No, not at all. We wanted to push Zukić and Radovanović to the edge. Make them deal," said Boyle. "If we'd known that his wife was that close to shooting him, we'd have saved our energy on Sonja."

Gen. Brown exhaled. "Why is this Protocol so crucial?"

Grange said, "Our idea, Rupert, was to hoist the Serbs with their own petard, as it were. Intelligence reports have warned of a series of unprecedented attacks across Western Europe by Islamic terrorists. They plan to use bloody conflict in former Yugoslavia as cover and a diversion for their attacks."

Gen. Brown nodded mistrustfully. "You have proof?"

Boyle said, "As much as we needed. But none of it means anything without the Protocol. Do you have it?"

Gen. Brown ignored the question.

Grange continued on speaker, "Understand, Rupert, my job is to protect and safeguard our country and, where possible, our allies. If there's a threat, we take action."

"So, you're saying my little UN peacekeeping mandate is rather inconvenient for the British government?"

Boyle added, "It was in our best interests to create as much turmoil as possible in former Yugoslavia."

"Ignite a war to combat Islamic extremism?" Gen. Brown shook his head in disgust. "You didn't trust the Yugoslavs to look after themselves? They managed perfectly well until we stuck our noses in."

Grange said, "Hardly. I think you have your history mixed up. The ethnic divisions are very real—potentially catastrophic. If Serbs, Croats, and Muslims can't trust each other now, we can never rely on them to neutralize the terrorists in years to come."

"So you just let them fight it out?" asked Gen Brown.

"In a word, yes," replied Grange.

"What does us bombing the Serbs achieve?" asked Gen. Brown. "You're taking sides."

"It shows the Bosnian government we mean business ... if they play the game, we will help them. *Our* game."

"I see." Gen. Brown nodded. "Except for the small matter of the Sarajevo Protocol."

"Precisely, Rupert," said Grange. "First, we had to be sure the Protocol was real—not some wild ruse."

"Send a rookie to Pale to sniff around—Peter Steele?" This from Gen. Brown.

Boyle said, "Not quite a rookie. But I suppose you could argue that his brother *is* a bit of a rookie. We are of course indebted to the Steele brothers."

Gen. Brown said, "Infiltrate the Bosnian Serbs?"

"Correct. Get close to the Bosnian Serb leadership. Find out *everything*," replied Boyle.

"How did you know it existed in the first place?" asked Gen. Brown.

"One of the best spies still alive," said Boyle. "Sir Lawrence Fitzgerald—I believe you know each other."

Gen. Brown weighed every word. "Yes."

"You two go back a long way, Rupert," said Grange on speaker. "I'm sure you wouldn't want to disappoint him."

Gen. Brown frowned. "What's in the document?"

Grange said, "Fifty years ago, albeit misguidedly, the Western alliance made bigoted assertions against Muslims everywhere. If the Serbs decide to show this document to the world, it's a call to arms for every naïve young Muslim with a chip on his shoulder."

Boyle crossed his arms and leaned back on the edge of Gen. Brown's desk. Not for the first time, his crossed arms showed no respect for Gen. Brown's rank. "Where are they? Steele and Sonja Radovanović?" asked Boyle.

Gen. Brown stood up. "Forgive me, but this is the biggest crock—"

"Hard to appreciate," said Boyle, "but it's in the interests of—"

"No, Boyle. It's bullshite."

Grange said, "General Brown—"

Brown leaned toward the speaker: "Gentlemen, you can all go and screw yourselves."

"General, we may be forced to send in NATO after all—"

"Prime Minister, please save your breath." Gen. Brown wanted to resign then and there."

He walked out of the office. He had no idea what his next move was. But he was pleased he had not shared the where-abouts of the Sarajevo Protocol.

Hotel Panorama, Pale

At 3:33 pm, Steele and Sonja arrived at the Hotel Panorama. The safe delivery of the Protocol to the Bosnian Serb parliament session was the next step to peace. It was, after all, *their* peace process—not Steele's. But considering what had just happened, Steele would not leave Sonja alone, even in the heart of Repub-lika Srpska.

The checkpoint guard at the bottom of the hotel driveway recognized Sonja and waved them through. As they passed, the guard leaned toward their vehicle. "I'm sorry for your loss, Miss Radovanović," he said.

She nodded and feigned a polite smile.

Steele drove past the Bosnian Serb headquarters up to the main entrance of the Panorama Hotel and cut the engine. "I'll come with you."

"No, Jack. I do this alone."

"I'll wait."

"It might take a long time. You know what it's like when Serbs discuss politics."

"Okay, I'll wait for you at the UNMO office." He smiled and leaned toward her. "You can do this." He wanted to kiss her, but it felt awkward, so he pulled back. *Timing, Jack. For crying out loud … Timing is everything.* Peter was right. There was definitely something about Sonja …

Sonja smiled. "Thank you for everything you have done for me and for my country. We have a long way to go." She leaned forward and kissed him on the lips.

He smiled like the proverbial kid in the candy store. "Call me on the landline at the UNMO office if you need anything."

The UNMO office was one field down from the Hotel Panorama. UNMOs were located close by due to the dozens of faxes, hand-delivered letters, and documents that went back and forth every day between Bosnian Serb authorities and UNPROFOR HQ in Sarajevo.

"They're waiting for me," she said. "I know where you are."

"Only Unity Saves the Serbs," he said playfully, holding up a fist.

Sonja smiled, genuinely amused by Steele's Chetnik parody. She got out and walked up the steps to the hotel.

Steele called after her, "Good luck!"

CHAPTER FORTY-SEVEN

Two dozen or so black cars with tinted windows—mainly Mercedes, BMWs, and Zhigulis—were parked outside the Hotel Panorama, a ski lodge hotel in peace time. Drivers wearing ill-fitting suits and military uniforms stood next to their vehicles, smoking heavily, looking drawn and haggard.

The Hotel Panorama had become the safest place for the Bosnian Serb parliament to meet. There was an armed checkpoint at the end of the road, and the building enjoyed seclusion from the town center. The municipal building in Pale had become a conspicuous target after recent NATO air strikes. Apart from NATO, the Bosnian Serbs were also understandably nervous about Bosnian government spies and Western Special Forces.

Sonja was shaking. She would never be prepared for this, but she had to do it. Her father was dead—murdered by her mother. With every ounce of mental and emotional super-strength within her, she controlled her emotions and walked up the steps. The circumstances were excruciating, but her duty was to serve her people—*all* her people—at this pivotal moment in history.

A tentative cease-fire in Goražde was one thing, but an agreement with her half-brother that would lead to a lasting peace and an acceptable power-share of sovereign territory in Bosnia was entirely another.

Her mother had shot her father in cold blood. *Today.* She would need to acknowledge this with the assembled politicians. *Can I hold it together? Perhaps Jack should be with me? No, that wouldn't go down well with my people.* Her most difficult task, however, would be to convince the plenum to come to the peace table. On her terms.

Once inside, bodyguards, administrative assistants, and low-level apparatchiks acknowledged Sonja with a sympathetic nod or bow as she moved across the lobby to the banquet and conference room. Others smiled sympathetically to express their condolences.

"I'm okay," she said out loud, aware that everyone was staring at her.

A man in a black suit and open-necked white shirt opened the door to the large room packed with the Bosnian Serb parliamentarians. The hum of expectancy dwindled to a hushed silence as she entered.

In her right hand she held the envelope containing the Sarajevo Protocol.

Steele left the vehicle at the hotel and made the short walk across the field to reach the UNMO house. The office was located in a family home. The owner rented out rooms to the UN—his conservatory and three bedrooms upstairs. It was a win-win for all concerned—the UNMOs lived in comfort and were one minute away from the Bosnian Serb headquarters. The owner stashed the generous UN allowance, which would keep him and his family financially comfortable long after the war ended. Danilo, the landlord, could probably build an entire hotel with all the money he saved.

Steele turned to admire the view of the Hotel Panorama across the open field. *Good luck, Sonja.* He felt sure she could pull it off—convince the entire Bosnian Serb parliament to sign a peace agreement with the Bosnian government. The Sarajevo Protocol would give them the "encouragement" they needed. No deal, and Sonja would show the document to the world and the fighting would continue with the Serbs bearing the brunt of NATO's aggression. It was in everyone's interest to sign.

The UNMO house front door opened.

Capt. Jensen, the Danish UNMO, appeared. "Hello, Jack. I beat you."

"You drive fast, Jensen."

"Come in. I have great news. I am going home tomorrow."

"Congratulations," said Steele flatly, unable to hide his indifference. The man was bonkers. Capt. Jensen had committed gross negligence in his UN reporting duties. He had exaggerated the extent of Serb shells and fatalities inside the Goražde enclave in an effort to draw attention to a diabolical situation. Steele understood Jensen's decisions, actions, and behavior and was not about to judge him. But the man had "gone native" and thankfully, someone had decided it was time for him to leave the theatre.

"I return to Copenhagen," Jensen continued in his Danish singsong cadence. "Jack, you have a message." He handed Steele a sheet of paper from his notebook. "Call General Brown immediately. He has been trying to reach you on the radio here."

Steele snatched the note and hurried into the conservatory office consisting of table, chair, fax, maps and a satellite telephone. He dialed the number Gen. Brown had left.

The UN commander answered on the second ring. "Brown."

"Sir, it's Jack Steele. You left a message—"

"Listen carefully, Jack. Where are you?"

"Pale."

"Where exactly?"

"UNMO office."

"Is Sonja with you?"

"She took the Protocol to the parliament for a cease-fire deal. Everyone's at the Hotel Panorama."

"You need to evacuate immediately."

"Why?"

"The shit's about to hit the fan. A lot of it."

"What about Sonja?"

"Get her if you can, but you don't have much time."

"How long?"

"Probably minutes … I'm sorry, Jack. We did our best. You must leave immediately."

"What happened?"

"I'm relinquishing my UN command and probably saying good-bye to the army along with it. And if it wasn't for you and Sonja, I would probably have lived to regret my part in this fiasco."

"I don't understand."

"No time to explain—NATO is on their way. They intend to take out the entire Bosnian Serb parliament. You must get out of there."

"Sir, we need your help—"

"I've sent Yomper. We'll meet in Sarajevo. Yomper has details."

The line went dead.

Steele walked outside. Capt. Jensen was standing next to his Jeep, packing his kit into the back for the short ride to Sarajevo, then onto Split, Zagreb, and back to Copenhagen.

"I need a ride," Steele said

"No problem," said Jensen. "But make it quick. I'm leaving in ten minutes."

"If you want to live, we leave now. General Brown's direct order!"

"After Goražde, sure I want to live. Let's go!"

Steele quickly explained the situation, and Jensen floored the gas pedal. They reached the main road in seconds, and Steele pointed left to the Panorama Hotel. As they made the turn, another UN vehicle came out of nowhere, narrowly missing them and forcing Jensen to skid to a halt at the side of the road. He blurted a string of Danish expletives.

Steele wound down the window and checked the other vehicle. It was Yomper. Gen. Brown was as good as his word.

"The boss sent me," Yomper said. "Come to give you a hand, sir."

"How long have we got?"

"Time's up, sir. NATO's gonna take them out with or without you."

Jensen revved the accelerator pedal in vain. Their vehicle was literally stuck in the mud.

"I'm not leaving without Sonja," said Steele.

"It's too late," said Jensen. "You said we need to leave now."

Steele gripped Jensen's forearm. "We leave when I say, Jensen. Understand?"

The Jeep's wheels spun aimlessly.

"Wait up, sir," shouted Yomper from his vehicle. He moved forward, then shifted into reverse and nudged back making contact with Jensen's Jeep. The physical jolt allowed Jensen to gain traction and pull away. Yomper made a U-turn and followed.

Seconds later, both UN vehicles—Cherokee and a Toyota 4Runner—swerved left into the Hotel Panorama driveway. Steele's Cherokee smashed through the security barrier, and both vehicles skidded their way up the muddy road to the hotel.

The sentry fired a burst of rounds and began shouting into his handheld radio.

As they approached the second bend, Steele heard what sounded like a sonic boom overhead—NATO fighter making a pass at low altitude. A dark shadow flashed overhead and dropped a bomb in the direction of the Hotel Panorama.

"*Jesus Christ!*" Steele said. "Damn it!" He looked in their rearview mirror and noticed Yomper was right behind him.

They took the next bend and met smoke and flames bellowing from the trees behind the hotel. NATO had missed the target. "Thank God," Steele said, trying to stay calm. But he knew they'd return in seconds. There was a possibility that the fighter jet was only sending some kind of warning, but he wasn't about to take that chance. The more likely scenario was that Reithoffer got his way, and NATO was about to destroy the Bosnian Serb parliament in its entirety.

The Jeep stopped. "Wait here, Jensen," Steele ordered. He jumped out and ran up the steps two at a time. He met screaming and shouting staff and politicians exiting in panic. Head down, he pushed through the throng and forged his way into the hotel.

CHAPTER FORTY-EIGHT

There was pandemonium inside. Steele waded through the crowd. Men and women, politicians and hotel staff alike, were shouting and cursing the UN—most Bosnian Serbs hated NATO and the UN equally and didn't understand the difference anyway. Steele took off his UN blue beret and slipped it into a pocket.

A woman scurried in front of him toward the exit. "Yoshida must burn in hell!" she shouted, referring to Yasushi Yoshida, the UN Special Envoy who had recently visited Pale. Steele knew it was more satisfying to blame individuals than organizations.

As he continued through the building, he hoped that no one would notice his British Army uniform in the melee. He stopped a young waitress, grabbing her arm. "Where is Sonja Radovanović?" he asked in Bosnian.

"I don't know," she replied. She noticed his accent and appeared to make a connection between his foreign military uniform and the attack. "UNPROFOR spy ... UNPROFOR spy ..." she began shouting and then pointing at Steele.

Steele disappeared into the crowd before she could make more commotion. He forged ahead toward the conference room. The swirl of panic-stricken men and women provided good cover. He fought against the current of people surging toward the exits. Making a visual sweep of the room, he caught sight of Gen. Zukić on the far side. Steele sensed that Gen. Zukić—now red-faced and angrier than ever before—had seen him too, but he couldn't be sure. Steele cursed the fact that he, Steele, was unarmed.

Then he saw Sonja.

She was moving away from him toward another exit—a sign over the door read Kitchen. Strain showed on her face, and her eyes were focused intently on the exit. She looked terrified and did not see him.

Then he lost her in the crowd.

"Sonja!" he shouted. It was useless—the stampede was underway, the hysteria had taken root. He continued to fight through the crowd in Sonja's wake. *Somewhere high above, the F-16 fighter must surely strike again.* He pushed and shoved against the sea of people. The adrenaline surged inside him and he sidestepped bodies like an English rugby union center-forward. A large bald officer with thick eyebrows in military uniform collided with Steele and knocked them both to the ground. At first the man looked at him, as though something didn't make sense. But the man's survival instincts kicked in, and he picked himself up, stepped across Steele, and kept running.

Then Steele pushed himself off the ground and continued. He reached the other side of the room and slammed through the set of doors that led to the kitchen. There were fewer people now, but still too much noise, he thought, for Sonja to hear him.

"Sonja! SONJA!"

To his surprise, she stopped and turned around, panic on her face.

Once Steele caught up with her, emotion took hold, and they found themselves hugging. It lasted just for a second, but it just enough time for him to look deep into her eyes and know that she felt something too. For real.

"I was coming to find you," she said. "What's happening? Why are they doing this?"

"Did you have time to show them the Protocol?"

She shook her head. "No time."

Steele froze, taking a moment. Then he said, "This way ..."

He took her hand, and they made their way back into the

conference room. A woman ran past them. "NATO! NATO! They will kill us all!"

As they reached the kitchen swing doors, Steele glanced behind to make sure Sonja was okay. But before he looked forward again, the doors crashed open toward him and knocked him to the ground as a man thundered past.

As Steele lay spread-eagle on the floor face down, a pair of dusty black combat boots appeared inches from his eyeline. He tried to sit up, but a boot slammed down onto his spine; excruciating pain ripped through his body. He looked to his right and saw Sonja lying beside him. She too had fallen and was now stunned. Steele looked up at the man. It was Col. Milan Kostić, chief of staff, the man who had planned to execute them hours before.

Behind Col. Kostić stood the bald officer who had collided with Steele moments before. Col. Kostić pointed his pistol in Steele's face. "So, this is how your people bring us peace?" Then he turned to Sonja. "Or should I start with you, dear Sonja? Interesting that both of you are present every time NATO attacks Serb people." He pulled back the hammer on his CZ-99 pistol. "This is for my people, Captain UNMO."

This is it ... A heightened sensation engulfed Steele's body. He had never imagined life would end so abruptly. He'd spent almost a week in this war zone and seen death and destruction at close quarters. The irony struck him—he and Col. Kostić were trying to help the same people. Oddly, perhaps, he even understood Col. Kostić's point of view. He understood why this man was about to pull the trigger.

Steele said calmly, "I came here to help—" The absurdity of his words stopped him from finishing the thought. NATO warplanes were about to flatten the hotel.

Yomper? Where the hell is Yomper? Sitting beside him, Sonja stared into his eyes. His gaze returned to the small black circle at the end of the pistol. Time slowed. He felt a pulsing sensation in his brain as he tried to comprehend what death might be like.

There was a loud *crack*—not as loud as he had expected a shot to be at close quarters. The glass in the swing doors behind them shattered and covered them with a thousand shards.

Col. Kostić's eyes widened as though he was about to burst. The chief of staff had not pulled the trigger. Instead, he collapsed. A bullet had entered the back of his head and ripped away his face as it exited the front of his skull.

Sonja was speechless, tears streaming down her face. Steele was sweating profusely.

The double doors leading to the kitchen opened and Gen. Zukić entered. The shots had caused another wave of panic inside the building. Steele froze as Gen. Zukić approached, his pistol raised. *Oh God, not again?!*

Gen. Zukić lowered the pistol and said, "It was necessary." He looked at Sonja.

"Thank you," she said.

"Serb people have made many mistakes. Perhaps this will be our last." He looked at Col. Kostić's body.

"You saved my life," said Sonja. "You chose me over Kostić?"

"You have the Protocol. Take it and make peace," Gen. Zukić continued. "We will honor forty-nine/fifty-one percent territory agreement if you can persuade the others."

"You agree to forty-nine percent?" asked Sonja.

"Yes." He studied Col. Kostić's corpse. "You must go. You are my goddaughter, and I have failed you … until now. I am sorry about your father. He used the Protocol as an excuse to fight the world."

"I've got him, sir." It was Yomper's voice, coming from the kitchen doorway. "I can take him out—"

"No. It's okay, Yomper. We're leaving now," said Steele. "All of us."

Yomper lowered his SA80. "OK, boss."

Seconds later, Steele, Sonja, and Yomper were running down the back stairs of the hotel. Yomper said, "Could have saved the war crimes people a load of trouble, sir. Why did you let him go?"

Steele was asking himself the same question. He recalled the numerous articles he'd read about Gen. Zukić the war criminal and the atrocities the man had committed. Then he said, "Simple, he just saved our lives."

But part of him knew Gen. Zukić's victims would never forgive him.

They exited the hotel via the service entrance and found the waiting Jeep. Steele kept a tight hold of Sonja's hand as the fighter jet approached, louder than ever. It was deafening now. The sun was out. *It won't miss this time.*

They climbed into the Jeep, and Capt. Jensen hit the gas.

Seconds later, a huge explosion shook their moving vehicle as the jet roared overhead. Steele looked behind to see the Hotel Panorama engulfed in flames. A huge fireball danced into sky. Luckily, most of the Bosnian Serb parliament had already exited.

Yomper said slowly, "Fuck that shit!"

"You have a way with words, Yomper," said Steele.

"Funny you say that, sir. Gen. Brown was just telling me the same thing."

Jensen said, "I need to stay here now. Check in at the UNMO house."

"We'll drop you," said Steele, nodding. "Are you sure?"

"Yes, hopefully the danger has passed now."

A minute later, they pulled up outside the UNMO house.

Capt. Jensen got out of the Jeep and joined his UNMO colleagues inside.

"Where to, sir?" asked Yomper, climbing into the driver's seat.

"Sarajevo."

"Roger that."

"We've got a press conference to hold."

Steele shivered. His nerves were shot, and all of this was starting to wear on him. He thought he finally understood the Sarajevo Protocol puzzle. But deep down, he hoped he was wrong.

Thanks to Gen. Zukić, however, at least they had made their escape and were en route to Sarajevo. It was Steele's turn to make use of it. NATO had taken the role of aggressor in an ethnic conflict its masters did not seem to understand. Unless Steele acted now, peace in Bosnia-Herzegovina was further away than ever.

CHAPTER FORTY-NINE

UNPROFOR HQ, Sarajevo

On the streets of Sarajevo, people were enjoying yet another cease-fire—a brief respite of café life with cigarette or espresso, or both, a ride on a tram, a loaf of bread purchased without fear of shelling, sniper fire, or Sarajevo roses (the deadly pockmark in concrete sidewalks signifying the point of mortar round contact).

The UN press and information conference room at UN headquarters was packed with journalists—some locals but mainly international. Most of them had not sought access, nor had they obtained clearances to Bosnian Serb territory. But everyone had received word of the two huge explosions less than an hour earlier in Pale. The media pack wanted answers.

Staci Ryan still wanted her story.

Gen. Brown had told her she was forbidden to leave the UN compound. As soon as she heard about Boyle's impromptu press conference, she walked across the courtyard and herded into the stuffy conference room with the other media hounds.

Boyle entered the conference room and sat down in front of the bouquet of wires and microphones. "Good afternoon, ladies and gentlemen," he began. "Thank you for coming at short notice."

Staci stood at the back of the room, melting into the crowd. The hubbub of foreign accents and languages died down as Boyle continued.

"After the repeated belligerence of the Bosnian Serbs in recent days and their refusal to cooperate or comply with UNPROFOR cease-fire agreements, including the return of heavy weapons and armaments to UN collection points, we have been forced to execute NATO bombing raids against the Bosnian Serb leadership in Pale."

The noise level among the journalists flared like the buzzing of a swarm of bees. Heads turned and nodded, pencils scribbled furiously, thumbs dialed editor hotlines across the globe. A phalanx of tape recorders and microphones pointed in Boyle's direction.

"Furthermore,"—Boyle raised his voice and his hand to settle them—"the decision to strike at the heart of the Bosnian Serb parliament reflects our frustration and genuine disappointment with Dr. Radovanović and Gen. Zukić and their refusal to comply with agreements they have signed."

Staci observed the journalists' excitement. No one had been expecting NATO and UNPROFOR to take the iron-fist approach against the Bosnian Serbs. No matter, Staci thought, as long as Boyle handed over the rest of her money and she was able to interview him and publish her inside story.

Two-dozen hands shot up as journalists simultaneously spewed questions. Photojournalists' fingers were glued to their motor drives and video cameramen nestled closer to their eyepieces, all of them focused on today's UNPROFOR spokesman, Col. Edward Boyle.

Boyle held up his hand again. "No questions for the moment. The situation on the ground is volatile, and we are assessing damage to the targets via satellite and our UNMOs and JCOs. Thank you for your understanding."

"Matt Arlidge, BBC. Casualty figures? How many injured?" One man's voice was heard above the rest. The room quickly settled in anticipation of the response, and Boyle was forced to fill the silence.

"No details yet. We'll keep you informed."

Staci wanted her story. Boyle had promised something "sensational." *Now or never*, she thought. The Protocol had to be exposed. Her gut told her to act now. She didn't trust Boyle. She had never trusted him.

Staci pushed between a French and a Danish reporter and raised her hand. Catching his eye, she began, "There are rumors that Captain Jack Steele, UNMO, was on a secret mission in Republika Srpska,"—all heads spun toward Staci—"can you comment? Did he have any part in the NATO action?"

Again, a buzz of anticipation, then hush. The other journalists were excited by her boldness. Knowledge of secret or classified info was traditionally kept close to the chest. It was off limits at a press conference.

Boyle shifted in his seat, biting inside his lip and looking momentarily flummoxed. He stared emptily into the sea of hungry reporters. "Yes," he said slowly, "we do have information about Captain Steele." He paused.

Full steam ahead, thought Staci, *what more does he need?* She'd set him up perfectly. He could tell the world they had found the Protocol. Expose it for what it was, what it meant. She needed the official angle. If she leaked the story herself, no one would believe her. She needed the official line too, but had everything else to write her story.

Boyle said, "Captain Steele was collecting information on behalf of the Bosnian government."

Staci held her breath, eyes narrowing. *NO! Not true!*

"Fortunately," he continued, "we became aware of the situation before it was too late. We believe Captain Steele achieved his goals by nurturing a close personal relationship with Sonja Radovanović."

Another hum of excitement—even the top correspondents couldn't figure this one out.

The BBC's Matt Arlidge raised his hand. "Can you comment on unconfirmed reports that Dr. Radovanović has been assassinated?"

"We're unable to confirm those reports at this time."

Staci said, "Can you confirm or deny the existence of a secret document known as the Sarajevo Protocol?"

Boyle looked daggers at Staci. "No, Miss—?"

"Ryan ..." she said defiantly, pausing for effect. "Staci Ryan. Freelance reporter."

"Miss Ryan, I have never heard of the Sarajevo Protocol." He smiled, as if belittling her suggestion. "If you'll excuse me, I'm afraid we have to wrap up."

Boyle stood up and exited to his right.

Staci froze. *What now? What about her story? What about her money?* The asshole had screwed her.

Matt Arlidge approached her immediately. "Staci," he said. "What was that about? You think Steele is spying?"

"That's what he said, Matt. I don't get it either."

"I don't believe you."

"Fine."

"How about a drink at the Holiday Inn? I'm sure I can think of some useful info to trade you."

"Okay. But I need a ride."

"You got it, Miss USA," said Arlidge, grinning.

"I can't use the main entrance. Low profile. I'll meet you out back in five minutes."

The NATO attack on the Hotel Panorama in Pale meant that Serb checkpoints in the Trebević Hills surrounding Sarajevo were now deserted. *The only problem,* thought Steele as they drove into Sarajevo, *is smuggling Sonja through Bosnian government checkpoints.*

Her father was responsible for the longest urban siege in the history of modern warfare—10,000 Sarajevo deaths, 56,000 wounded by UN estimates, 10,000 apartments destroyed and 100,000 damaged. On average, 329 shells pummeled the city daily, this number soaring to 3,777 on the worst day of the siege.

Even if Muslims knew that Dr. Radovanović's wife had shot him, they might want to take their revenge on Sonja—the daughter would be the next best thing for more revenge. But for Steele's plan to work, he needed Sonja to be in Sarajevo and could not risk her being abducted again.

"They will recognize me," said Sonja.

"Shall we cover her with our jackets?" asked Steele.

"No need, sir," said Yomper. "I know these goons. Leave it with me, sir. They don't mess with me anymore. If we're stopped, Sonja's our interpreter."

"Will they swallow that?" Steele asked.

"Scout's honor." Yomper made the two-finger salute. "I've given these blokes enough cigarettes and sweeties to last a life-time. They owe me. No wucking furries, sir."

Their vehicle cleared all checkpoints into the city. Yomper had been right, and they sailed through.

Today's NATO attack had changed everything. But even though their enemy had borne the brunt of the attack, the citizens of Sarajevo were back in the land of uncertainty about their future.

Steele and Yomper exited the airport road.

Yomper asked, "Holiday Inn, boss?"

Steele nodded.

One of the few advantages of a besieged city was that the world's press gathered in one central location—in this case, the Holiday Inn. Even without electricity and running water most of the time, the eclectic, globe-trotting journalists shared infor-mation and filed reports without Bosnian government or UN censorship.

Sonja said, "Now what?"

Steele said, "We're going to use that …"—he pointed to the Protocol—"it's the only way."

"They will arrest me."

"No one's going to arrest you." He glanced at Yomper. "But we need General Brown to make this work."

"I've been trying, sir," Yomper said. "Last time we spoke, he'd just resigned."

"What happened?"

"He said he'd been set up. Then we got cut off …"

"What exactly did he say?"

"He'd spoken to the PM, got pissed off and resigned. He told me to get you back to Sarajevo, and that he was going to finish what he started."

The Jeep skidded momentarily on the smooth, slippery tramlines running the length of the long boulevard into Sarajevo known as "Sniper Alley." It was so named because it was one of the most dangerous and exposed stretches of road in the city.

At approximately 4:45 pm, they drew up in front of the sand-bagged walls of the most famous Holiday Inn in the world.

The Jeep crunched across a carpet of glass that glistened like a moat around the rear of the building, supposedly the most protected part. But even at the rear, most of the windows were broken, and no one dared to clean up just in case Bosnian Serb snipers were in the surrounding hills.

Steele glanced up at the yellow ten-story building pitted with thousands of rounds of small-arms ammunition and a few tank rounds.

He got out and shouted to a familiar figure also entering the building, "Matt … I've got something for you."

Arlidge, flanked by his Bosnian male cameraman and female producer, was carrying a tripod.

"Go ahead, sir," said Yomper. "I'll park down below for safety."

Steele caught up with Matt Arlidge and beckoned Sonja to keep up.

They shook hands. "I've got a surprise for you," said Steele, turning to introduce Sonja. "Meet Sonja Radovanović."

Arlidge smiled. "And I've got one for you …"

Steele frowned.

"Your American colleague just promised to spill some beans after Boyle's press conference. She's inside."

"Staci?"

Arlidge nodded.

"How did she get here?"

"I gave her a lift." Arlidge smiled at Sonja. "Nice to finally meet you. Brave move coming into the city."

"What did Boyle say?" asked Steele.

"The lowdown on why NATO just attacked the Serbs."

"What reason did he give?"

"He just said some stuff about contravening the TEZ." Arlidge turned to Sonja. The BBC had wanted to interview Sonja for months.

"You're ready to go on record? We can do the interview in my room."

Steele said, "Sorry, Matt. This one's for everyone."

Arlidge shrugged. "You win. Ground floor briefing room?"

"Yes. Can you gather your colleagues?"

"No problem." He nodded to his cameraman, who disappeared into the hotel to rally other journalists.

The female producer said, "I'll get the word out."

Using flashlights, they proceeded along a dark corridor to the briefing room. Electricity was sporadic even for international journalists. Sometimes the hotel was plunged into darkness until the staff managed to get generators going.

"Where's General Brown?" Steele asked.

"He's gone AWOL," said Arlidge. "We came straight here from Boyle's briefing. There was no sign of Brown."

"What else did Boyle talk about?" asked Steele.

"You, Captain Steele. Apparently, you've been a busy little UNMO."

CHAPTER FIFTY

UNPROFOR HQ, Sarajevo

Boyle peered through taped-up office windows. It was 4:51 pm. What a waste, he thought, for Gen. Brown to have given up the game so abruptly. Some people were far too honorable.

Maj. Small hovered nervously outside the office and gave a quick *tap-tap* before entering. "Steele's back," he said.

"Where?"

"One of the Egyptbat LO's"—Egyptian Battalion Liaison Officer—"from Tito barracks saw him enter the Holiday Inn. Yomper was driving him. There was also a local woman he recognized as Sonja Radovanović, if you can believe it?"

"Sonja?" Boyle said. "*Shit.*" He wiped his hand across his cheek, as he weighed his next move. "Send the RMP down there immediately."

"The military police?" Maj. Small looked more nervous.

"Arrest Steele at any cost," Boyle barked back. "General Brown too. Lethal force, if necessary. Do you understand?"

"*Lethal* force?" Maj. Small replied. "On what grounds?"

"Make them up. A hundred journalists at the Holiday Inn are waiting for stories to fall from the sky."

"Don't you think this is over the top? I mean—"

"That's an order. Just do it, would you, Brian ... there's an obedient fellow. We've made a lot of progress. Don't spoil it now." Boyle glowered. "RMP. And get my driver out front immediately. We leave in two."

"We?"

"You're coming with me."

"If you arrest Steele, we'll be the first item on the BBC *Six O'Clock News*."

Boyle did not answer. He squashed his blue beret on his head, then picked up his pistol and holster.

Press briefing room, Holiday Inn Hotel, Sarajevo

Tripods were erected in seconds as though lives depended on them. The makeshift press briefing room on the ground floor of the Holiday Inn was awash with the blinding white light of TV cameras on battery power as cameramen white balanced and checked focus.

Steele sat at the podium. Looking at them, he recognized some of the twenty or so journalists who had quickly gathered—British, American, French, German, Dutch, and more—in the hope of catching a scoop. Word had spread that Dr. Kosta Radovanović's daughter was in the building. Something huge was about to hit. More journalists arrived even as Steele began.

"Good afternoon ..." He paused, checking that Matt Arlidge's crew was up and running. He didn't want anyone—particularly the BBC—to miss a word. He would probably not get a second chance.

Arlidge gave the thumbs-up.

"I'll keep it brief." Steele took a deep breath, his eyes widening as they grew accustomed to the lights. "British and American governments have plotted to stifle, distort, and ultimately derail the peace process in Bosnia-Herzegovina."

Apart from the whir of video cameras, the room was silent. Steele had their full attention. Many had been at Boyle's press conference—and now this. They were all but chomping at the bit.

He glanced at Sonja, who was sitting next to him. She was nervous. He gave her a quick nod of reassurance and a smile before continuing.

"NATO attacks in Pale and Goražde have shown little or no regard for the well-being of the local population—in the most recent case, the Serbs. They have demonstrated zero regard for the lives and safety of UN military personnel—me included. I … *we* were extremely fortunate to escape with our lives at Pale church."

Pens and pencils scratched and scribbled.

Steele continued, "Sonja Radovanović has lost family and friends, including her father and her mother—"

Steele was bombarded with questions. *This* was breaking news!

"Are you saying—?" "Who's behind this?" "Where's the proof?" "Is it true that Radovanović was murdered today?" "Does the Bosnian government know Miss Radovanović is in Sarajevo?"

Steele held up both hands. "If I may … " For the first time in a long time, he felt empowered and in command of the situation. Adrenaline flowed. This was the end of his army career, no doubt. But something much bigger than his career was at stake. He felt sadness and betrayal, but also a keen sense of exhilaration. He felt a clarity he'd never known before.

The truth was coming out.

He pointed to the BBC.

Arlidge said, "If what you say about NATO is true, what's behind it?"

Steele nodded. "This war is not about Bosnians—Muslims, Serbs, *or* Croats. This conflict is about the fear of Islam and the threat of terrorist attacks on the heart of Europe. It is also about one man's effort to save a country he loved and risked his life for."

More rapid-fired questions across the room.

Steele continued, "Sonja Radovanović is holding a secret document called the Sarajevo Protocol. It is a signed agreement between Josip Broz Tito and Western allies ratified at the end of World War Two. It was drawn up by a very clever, brave man named Sir Lawrence Fitzgerald."

The frowns and twisted faces of the journalists turned to whispers and suppressed exclamations. Like an orchestra conductor holding a pause at the end of a movement, Steele milked the silence. It wouldn't be long, he thought, before his revelation spread to UN authorities and they came to arrest him.

Arlidge shot back, "Where does Sonja Radovanović fit into this?"

"Sonja has been fighting for her people. *All* her people. And I don't just mean the Bosnia Serbs. She disagreed with her father's politics, his actions, and certainly his methods. I am ashamed to say our security services have tried to exploit this. I'm embarrassed to say I was duped into this mission unaware of the wider consequences of my actions."

"In what way?" countered Arlidge.

"I was sent to infiltrate the Bosnian Serb leadership to find the secret document. My superiors *knew* I would eventually find it because, with Sir Lawrence's help, they planted it in the middle of this conflict."

Again, the questions exploded.

No one inside the press conference heard the rotor blades of the Army Air Corps twin-engine helicopter landing on rough terrain near the Holiday Inn. Gen. Brown had called in a favor from a pilot he had served with in the Grenadier Guards a decade before.

Gen. Brown knew this was going to be his last military flight. He had disobeyed direct orders from the British prime minister and the Ministry of Defense.

But he wasn't going down without a fight. He knew Steele was inside the hotel, and he knew it wouldn't be long before Boyle tried to silence both of them.

"Thanks, Jamie." Gen. Brown took off his headset and patted

his old friend on the shoulder. "Don't go anywhere." The pilot responded with a wave of the hand, followed by a thumbs-up.

Gen. Brown sprang from the helicopter accompanied by his VIP companion, and they both jogged away from the roar and backwash of rotor blades. They reached the corner and entered the side entrance of the Holiday Inn.

A Britbat RMP sergeant, SA80 assault rifle jammed in his shoulder, blocked his path. The RMP sergeant pointed his weapon at Gen. Brown.

"Sorry, sir," he said politely but firmly, "I have orders to arrest you."

Gen. Brown slowed from a jog to a walk, hands out to the side. The RMP took aim. "Don't come any closer, sir."

"Why not, sergeant?" Gen. Brown called the RMP's bluff and kept going, looking him in the eye, weighing if the man would pull the trigger? He had a split second to decide—

"Safety catch," said Gen. Brown, pointing.

The sergeant glanced down. Gen. Brown seized the advantage by stepping into a forward assault. He punched the sergeant in the face followed by a sharp jab with the tip of his elbow to the man's throat.

The RMP dropped to the floor, writhing and choking, hands gripping his neck.

"You'll live," said Gen. Brown. He picked up the man's SA80 and continued inside the building. He had come to Bosnia to broker a peace deal, and he wouldn't leave until he had achieved his personal mission.

CHAPTER FIFTY-ONE

Steele looked at Sonja, then, in front of everyone, said, "I love Sonja Radovanović." He surprised even himself.

Sonja stared incredulously, eyes misting. It was as though he had released some kind of emotional block inside her. She smiled.

Puzzled by this revelation, most of the journalists smiled too.

"What I mean by that is that I love Sonja's courage, her spirit, and her sense of loyalty to her people no matter the personal cost."

Arlidge said, "So we shouldn't save the date just yet?"

Chuckles filled the room.

Steele smiled. Everyone was enjoying the light relief. "You'll be the first to know, Matt."

"But that's not why we're here," Steele went on, pulling himself together. "Like everyone else, Sonja Radovanović wanted to find the Sarajevo Protocol. Unlike her father, who wanted to use it *against* Muslims, Sonja believed it could actually stop the war. But the Sarajevo Protocol was used by Western security agencies to derail the peace process."

Sonja looked at Steele. Among the journalists, heads turned and brows furrowed.

Steele continued, "The threat of Islamic extremism and terror attacks in Europe is very real. Some believed that the Sarajevo Protocol would help neutralize the threat. By helping the Bosnian government win this war, some in the West believed they could influence and even control Bosnian government policy. But they needed an enemy—the Bosnian Serbs. In a short time, the Bosnian Serbs aided the conspiracy, albeit unwittingly, by committing outrageous atrocities and war crimes. The international community was forced to take sides."

One of the Danish journalists shouted, "Slow down please!"

Steele paused, allowing journalists to make notes, then continued, "Under the guise of UN and NATO authority, Western governments obstructed General Brown's genuine peace efforts to end hostilities. They used any and all means necessary—including NATO air strikes—to rewrite history, bringing death and destruction to the good people of former Yugoslavia—Muslim, Croat, but mainly Serb."

"Can you tell us more about this Sir Lawrence?" asked Arlidge. "Who is he?"

Steele nodded, as though anticipating the question. "Sir Lawrence Fitzgerald wrote the Protocol. Some of you might have heard of him."

"The spy?" asked a British reporter at the back of the room.

"First Baronet of Strachur and Glensluain?" asked another British voice somewhere in the room. I wrote a feature on him for *The Telegraph* a few years back?"

Steele concurred with a nod. "Yes, that's him. Fitzgerald's expertise and background convinced those in former Yugoslavia of the Protocol's authenticity. Fitzgerald and Tito were great friends during the Second World War. Fitzgerald thought his actions would benefit Yugoslavia. Alas, the opposite turned out to be true."

Steele placed both palms on the table and drew himself up tall.

Staci asked, "What was Fitzgerald's motive? You said he loved this country?"

"Correct, Ms. Ryan," Steele replied. "You only knew part of the story. If you'll forgive me, not as much as you thought you did." He smiled sympathetically and without a hint of condescension. "Fitzgerald couldn't bear to watch the country he loved—the one he risked his life for against Nazi

Germany—disintegrate. He told both Sonja and me on separate occasions that he had wanted to help Western authorities *unite* Yugoslavia, not destroy it. With close ties to the British security services for half a century, he was the most qualified person to reveal the plan. And everyone was taken in."

"You're saying that he was using it as a kind of insurance policy?" asked Arlidge.

"Fitzgerald realized he'd been tricked, or rather, that the Protocol was going to be used for nefarious purposes. He decided to share it with two trusted people, one on each side of the Bosnia conflict: Luka Rakić, the journalist and mayor of Goražde, and Sonja. He had told Luka Rakić, his former trusted journalist friend from Sarajevo, about the secret Protocol in case the peace process didn't work out. Luka moved to Goražde to help his people when the war began, not realizing the importance of the document. Unfortunately, it was almost impossible to make contact with him directly when Fitzgerald needed to, given the sensitive nature of the document and his location in Goražde." Steele paused to allow the print journalists catch up. "Meanwhile, rumors spread. The Serbs wanted the document. The Russians, Brits, and Americans wanted it. Assassins were hired to find it. Unknown actors even murdered Fitzgerald's wife during the hunt for it at his family villa on the island of Korčula when the rumors surfaced a year ago."

"You have evidence?" asked a French journalist. "How did you find out? Why *you*, Captain Steele?"

"I'm still asking myself the same question." Steele smiled. "It's a long story. And it began in Hyde Park a couple of weeks ago. But I can assure you"—he prayed Gen. Brown would arrive soon—"that General Brown will corroborate my story. We're expecting him at any moment."

But there was still no sign of Gen. Brown. *Without Brown, we're screwed,* he thought.

Instead, Steele noticed another British uniform entering from the back. He immediately recognized Boyle's silhouette moving through the crowd of journalists, cameramen, producers, and tripods. *What's he doing here? He's supposed to be at HQ. Is he here to arrest me?*

"Except," said Boyle, "that General Rupert Brown is no longer UNPROFOR commander. He has resigned and been RTUed, back to the UK. And you, Captain Steele, forgot to mention to the good men and women of the international press corps that you are wanted for espionage by the Bosnian government. He's 'gone native,' ladies and gentlemen."

Boyle beamed, swanning across the room like a courtroom prosecutor certain of victory. "It's time to stop the charade, Captain Steele. We're taking you into custody—for your own safety."

Steele said nothing. *This is not part of the plan.*

Boyle drew his pistol, aiming at Steele. As he drew parallel with the TV cameras, they panned onto him. "Reporters, you should treat any information you've heard today with a healthy skepticism. Check the facts, ladies and gentlemen, before you make fools of yourselves, your readers, your viewers, and your editors. My office at UNPROFOR headquarters will be happy to answer questions."

Steele searched the crowd. *Where the fuck is Brown? Where the hell is Yomper?* Without their corroboration and collaboration, this whole thing came across as an insane rant of a rookie British Army captain whose emotions had got the better of him. They'd say he'd fallen in love with the daughter of an insane mass murderer. Without Gen. Brown, Steele's story was absurd. No one would believe him.

"Let's go," said Boyle, steadying his pistol with both hands. He glanced behind. "The RMP are outside. Please, Captain Steele ... no need for any more drama."

Steele stood up slowly. His chair scraped the bare floor. *How can I buy some time?*

"One moment, Colonel Boyle," said a voice from the other side of the room. "This UNMO is not going anywhere. And neither are you ..." Gen. Brown strode down the center aisle of the briefing room with his eyes on Boyle. "I have brought a VIP guest who contradicts your story and would like to set the record straight once and for all."

Gen. Brown walked a few paces in front of a tight scrum of Bosnian government soldiers surrounding the VIP. They had been waiting inside the Holiday Inn hotel. Steele craned his neck to identify the person inside the scrum. Yomper was at the rear, giving orders.

Boyle began to twitch, looking one way then the other. He aimed his pistol at Gen. Brown, then to the TV cameras, then to the scrum of soldiers, then back to Steele. He looked more pathetic than Steele had ever seen him. He lowered the pistol and was immediately surrounded by Bosnian government guards.

That is when Steele identified the VIP. Wearing a disheveled gray suit, Klaus Reithoffer had returned. Steele assumed that Reithoffer had been abducted or held by Bosnian government soldiers, but now Yomper or Brown had somehow brought him here.

Steele's eyes flicked back and forth between Brown, Yomper, Reithoffer, and Boyle as they made their way to the podium.

Shrugging off his bodyguards, Reithoffer smiled warily and stood next to Steele in front of the microphones and cameras.

Flashes popped, motor drives clattered and whirred, and the TV cameras kept rolling. *Now what?* thought Steele.

"I am to blame for this travesty of international justice," Reithoffer began. "And I have paid a heavy personal price ... My wife *and* my daughter have been taken from me—assassinated." He pouted, holding back tears. "But I take full responsibility for my actions."

Again, silence.

"Today, I have good news," Reithoffer continued slowly. "Thanks to the heroic acts of Captain Steele, General Brown, and Ms. Radovanović, monumental progress has been made toward a lasting cease-fire. Thanks to Ms. Radovanović, a tentative, but I believe substantive, cease-fire agreement was reached in Goražde between the Bosnian Serbs and representatives of the Bosnian government and military."

Jesus, this is news to me, Steele thought.

The journalists broke out into spontaneous applause and cheers. They had never seen or heard anything like the drama taking place in this press conference. Many had covered the war for several years, and this end-in-sight moment produced a spontaneous surge of emotion.

More questions pinged across the room.

"Matt Arlidge, BBC. Mr. Reithoffer, is it true you were abducted by the Bosnian government?"

"No, this is false. I was their guest. For the last twenty-four hours, we have been engaged in constructive peace talks. I had a lot to learn. They helped me to understand the perspective of all parties in this tragic conflict. I came here with certain ... prejudices, but I am pleased to say that they have been erased."

"What evidence do you have your wife and daughter were assassinated?" asked Arlidge. "Why do you say you were responsible?"

"Unfortunately," Reithoffer said, "I may never find those responsible. This war is complicated, and there are many different interests and players. I may never be able to forgive myself for putting my personal views before what was best for my family and for the peace and security of Europe. That is why I have decided to resign my EU presidency before you here today."

More shouts, more questions, and the flurry of camera shutters on rapid fire. Journalists jumped on their cell phones to break the extraordinary news from the siege of Sarajevo. Boyle did not know which way to turn. He did know that he was finished. All he had worked for had been destroyed in a few seconds and a couple of sound bites.

A CNN cameraman shouted to his producer, "We got a live feed."

Boyle snapped. *Live feed?* His family, friends, colleagues, and neighbors would see him like this … a lifetime's reputation and respect destroyed in a minute. *God damn Jack Steele! But who do I blame most for this monumental fuckup?*

He pointed his Browning at Steele, then Gen. Brown, then back to Steele. Red-faced and sweating, he was incapable of settling his eyes on a target. The cameras panned to Boyle. He squinted at the lights and began trembling. His index finger went to the trigger. His arms straightened and locked on Steele.

No, this is an easy choice. Steele's the one. Steele and his brother. They failed their mission. They can't obey orders. The Steeles are to blame. I finished one. Now the next …

His brain sent a message to his index finger. The electrical signal set off from his brain and rushed along the tiny fibers, one neuron to the next, toward his finger.

Everyone froze at the crack of the bullet. Boyle fell to the floor clutching his chest. The cameras panned down to him. Camera operators tore their machines off the tripods and went handheld to get close-ups of Boyle.

"Medevac!" someone shouted.

Gen. Brown said, "Come with me, Jack. We need to move fast. Transport's waiting."

Steele glanced at Sonja.

Gen. Brown said, "Yes, of course. Sonja comes with us."

They barged their way to the exit where Yomper joined them and created some time and space between his boss and unwanted observers and their cameras. Flummoxed journalists continued to shout their questions in vain. Hotel employees administered first aid to Boyle.

As they ran down the corridor, Steele said, "Thanks, Yomper."

"Perfect timing," added Gen. Brown.

"I didn't have a choice, sirs," replied Yomper. "It was you or him."

Steele asked, "Is he dead?"

"Best not worry about it, sir. Above my pay grade."

Outside, Steele heard the sound of helicopter rotor blades.

CHAPTER FIFTY-TWO

Primrose Hill, London

Three days later, Steele and Sonja reached the top of Primrose Hill, a public park in one of the trendiest parts of North London. They would have gone to Hyde Park in Peter's honor, but circumstances—that is, British security services—dictated otherwise.

Unusual for London, the sun was shining, clouds sauntered across a canvas sky. Less than a dozen people were in the park, most of them walking dogs. A handful of people jogged along the footpaths in various directions. It was Monday, and most of London was at work.

Between them—the British Army, the EU, and the UN—it had been decided at the highest level that a bolt-hole in North London was the safest place for Jack Steele and Sonja Radovanović. Officially, Steele and Sonja were ordered to remain at the smart, well-furnished, two-bedroom garden flat in St. John's Wood—just across the park from Primrose Hill village—until further notice. A full investigation was underway. Events, locations, personalities, claims and counterclaims—and, of course, the Sarajevo Protocol—had to be fully examined, deliberated upon, and put to bed before Steele and Sonja would be safe and free to go about their business and their lives. But contrary to safe-flat rules that demanded occupants remain there at all times, Steele had decided they needed fresh air. This was not the first time he'd made up his own rules, something that usually got him into trouble.

Anonymity was their only security, but neither of them cared. They sat down on a park bench overlooking London Zoo surrounded by Regent's Park, to take in the stunning panorama of the London skyline. Steele always liked to pick out Big Ben all the way down by the River Thames four miles away.

"Who shot Boyle?" asked Sonja.

"As far as I know, Yomper … But I wouldn't lose any sleep over it."

"You think Boyle was going to shoot you?"

Steele nodded. "And you were probably next. He's nuts. As soon as Reithoffer walked in, Boyle knew it was all over. Black Cobra needed a fall guy, and Boyle knew it would be him. Yomper told me Boyle was working with Reithoffer all along."

"Boyle and Reithoffer? What are you saying?"

"They had the same goal—different perspectives perhaps. They both wanted the Bosnian Serbs to set things off. Boyle probably thought he'd end up with lots of friends in very high places."

"Like Reithoffer?"

"Correct. But Black Cobra went to his head."

"*Black Cobra?* Will they be held accountable?"

"Probably not. They were effectively outsourced by … the government? MI6? CIA? Who knows? Can't touch 'em. They'll melt into oblivion if they haven't already."

"So will they arrest Boyle?"

"Good question. Crazy Boyle—the madman who wanted me dead. They'll probably say he blamed himself for the NATO bombing or some such bullshit and make him disappear. Perhaps send him abroad? He's a convenient fall guy for the security services."

"Reithoffer gave the order for my abduction?"

"No. It was probably our boys. MI6 wanted to keep an eye on you. You were a valuable asset."

"What about Peter?"

"What about your mother?" countered Steele. They had both lost close family members.

"What do you want me to say? It breaks my heart. I still cannot believe it. A friend once told me you never get over your parents' death. But it gets a little easier each day. I understand why she took her life." Sonja turned to Steele. "And who killed Peter?"

"I'm very sorry about your mother." Steele exhaled. "As for Peter, I'd say it was the Russian security or intelligence services—FSB or SVR. They support your people. Everyone was after the Protocol, and they didn't want Peter to get there first. They probably assumed Peter was working *for our* security services. But I still don't even know the truth. Do you? Did he say if he was working for someone else? Fitzgerald?"

Sonja stared straight ahead for a few moments. Steele assumed she was just enjoying the magnificent London panorama.

"I'm sorry, Jack. I lied to Peter in Hyde Park the day he was murdered. I told him I loved him and that if he came to Bosnia with me, we could be together. I was not in love with him."

"You lied?"

"Yes."

"For your people?"

"Yes."

"And I conveniently took over?"

"Correct."

"Wow ... that's a lot."

"I'm sorry."

"It's okay. I understand. Thanks for the honesty." Steele nodded slowly, biting his cheek.

A few moments later, Sonja continued, "Why did Yomper take orders from Boyle? He was with me in Ivančevo."

"Yomper's allegiance was always to General Brown—they'd served together in the SAS. General Brown told Yomper to find out as much as possible ... get close to Boyle, so Yomper had to make it look good, which, I suppose, included whisking you off in a Chinook. General Brown did his homework on Boyle before he left for Bosnia. He never trusted Boyle. General Brown was the one who made sure Yomper was with you from the moment you were taken from Pale. He never hurt you, right?"

"No, he didn't. You are correct."

They enjoyed a few moments of silence. Steele glanced down the hill at his mother's flat overlooking the park. For the time being, he wasn't even allowed to call or communicate with her.

"And who ordered you to fall in love with me?" Sonja squeezed his arm with both hands.

"Who says I'm in love with you?"

"I think you are."

"I told you, I only work alone." Steele smiled. "At least they're keeping us 'safe' together." Steele leaned over and kissed her on the lips.

A small terrier approached the bench, slobbering and panting, a red rubber ball in his mouth. Halfway down the hill, a young woman shouted, "Justin! Heeeeere, Justin!"

Steele took the ball, shook off the saliva, growled like a dog, and threw it back in the direction of Justin's owner. Justin scampered after his ball, which hurtled past Justin's owner and toward the railings at the edge of the park.

Steele sat back down on the bench.

"How do we know Fitzgerald wrote the Protocol?" asked Sonja.

"Apart from the fact that he told you he did?"

Sonja nodded. "Yes."

"Dražen's father warned him to expect Fitzgerald one day. He described Fitzgerald in detail. There was no one else it could have been. Dražen's story fitted perfectly with Fitzgerald's."

"Why did he attack you in Split?"

"*Attack?* The old sod tried to scare me, I think. His wife's death left him a bit … I don't know, he was 'out there.' I think he was trying to test my mettle. I don't think he was out to kill me."

"Are you sure it was him?"

"It had to be him. He was the only one who knew I was in that café. And he was the one who found me when his guy chased me halfway around Split."

Sonja frowned and laughed at the same time. "This whole thing is crazy."

Steele said, "He really is on your side, you know."

"Where is he now?"

"Korčula. He said to drop by any time."

"You want to have tea with him?" Sonja raised her eyebrows.

"He's not one to bear a grudge. Neither am I. Sir Lawrence is an amazing gentleman,"—he paused—"and MI6 operative, and he served our country well. He had his reasons for using me. It all got a bit beyond him, I think."

"What about Boyle? Who was really in charge of this man?"

Steele took a deep breath, exhaled, as if sifting the truth in his own mind. "Black Cobra, Yomper explained to me, is a private security firm under the watchful eye of the US and British authorities, but completely untraceable back to them. That's the point. They asked Yomper to join a few months ago. General Brown told him to go along with it and see what he could find out. Unfortunately, there's nothing concrete to tie Black Cobra to any of this." Steele twisted up his mouth. "It's as if the bastards never existed."

"But who controls them?"

"We'll never know precisely who. But I'm confident that the Bosnians will sign a peace deal, and the international community will hunt down war criminals—Bosnians, Serbs, and Croats. But Black Cobra gets off scot-free."

"What will they do to my godfather?"

"General Zukić is a war criminal. He can say good-bye to the rest of his life if and when they catch him. He saved our lives, yes, but we can't change what he did. And I wouldn't recommend giving him a character reference."

Sonja stared out over London. "I feel sorry for Reithoffer."

"Me too. He lost everything."

"Why did he hate the Serbs?"

"I don't know. He lost touch with reality on the ground in Bosnia. He was living in the past, like Fitzgerald, trying to revive his own former Yugoslavia—his visits to Dalmatia, his love for Croatia. He took sides, used the atrocities to blame the Serbs, and began to convince himself he could control the outcome of the war. I'm guessing Serb paramilitaries—maybe Arkan's Tigers—killed his daughter. Maybe the Russians killed his wife in Paris? In some ways, I can understand the assassinations. He did a heck of a lot of damage."

Sonja sighed. "My father probably asked Arkan to do this. He hated Reithoffer."

"General Zukić was probably involved too."

"Do you think they will find my godfather?"

"Is he good with disguises?"

Sonja shrugged.

"They'll find him. But we have to make sure you don't become the scapegoat."

They sat still and calm and allowed the Primrose Hill breeze to caress them.

"Peace in Bosnia. Is it possible now, Jack?"

"If anyone can do it, General Brown's the man. I'm glad they let him stay on. We're close to peace."

"I hate this bloody Sarajevo Protocol."

"Not so bloody," Steele said quickly. "You found Dražen because of it. So long as the Sarajevo Protocol leads to peace."

"Perhaps you are right." Sonja smiled and looked deep into his eyes.

Steele touched her cheek with the back of his hand and took a deep breath. "My faith in human nature is returning ..." He took Sonja's hands, leaned in, and kissed her again. "When I passed out from Sandhurst—"

"Passed out?"

"Graduated ... When I graduated from Sandhurst, I came here for a walk. I made a promise to myself: one day I would sit here with the most beautiful woman in the world." He paused. "And maybe I would ask her to marry me one day."

Holding hands, they stood up. Steele pointed and said, "You can see Big Ben from here. Look …" He moved behind her, taking her hand and pointing it toward Big Ben. He nuzzled into the side of her neck and hair and inhaled.

"You are very confident, Captain Steele."

They laughed.

A single gunshot shattered the gentle rumble of North London traffic. It wasn't a loud bang like a car backfiring, or even a firework banger let off by local kids, Steele recalled afterward. It was more of a *fizz-bang*.

Steele looked across to Regent's Park Road. He saw nothing. He scanned Primrose Hill Road, a steep incline, which ran up the northeast side of the park. Then he remembered. It was the crack of a high-velocity sniper's rifle, just like the sound he had heard and experienced firsthand on Sniper Alley in Sarajevo.

A white British Telecom van was speeding away down Primrose Hill Road toward Regent's Park Road and Camden Town. Someone inside was trying to close the sliding door. Steele caught sight of a rifle with a telescopic sight being covered inside the van. Inside the park railings, Justin the terrier was chasing the van down the hill. His owner was screaming hysterically for her dog to heel.

Nothing about the last five seconds made any sense.

What the bloody hell just happened?

Sonja?

Then he understood.

Sonja had fallen against Steele, her weight almost knocking him over. He looked down and saw blood seeping through her shirt. *No, Jesus Christ, please!*

They had shot Sonja.

After all that had happened, all they had discovered and survived together in Bosnia, they had shot her in the middle of a London park a few hundred yards from his mother's flat.

He sat down on the bench and laid her head on his lap. He began stroking her hair and examining her wound at the same time.

"It's okay, it's okay, Sonja ... You're going to be okay, I promise ..." He looked around for help but saw no one. Cradling her in his arms, he tore off his jacket and used it to stem the flow of blood. He checked his front jeans pocket for his cell phone. Nothing. He'd left it at the safe house so they could not be disturbed.

Then he saw the dog's owner. She had taken out her mobile phone and was waving it at him to show she was calling for help.

Sonja stared at Steele, as though seeing him for the first time. She smiled, her eyes full of life and love despite the pain. "Thank you ..."

"*Thank you?*"

Sonja tried to smile. "Jack, you are beautiful."

He smiled. "It's okay, my darling. You're going to be fine."

At that moment, Steele knew he had fallen in love.

CHAPTER FIFTY-THREE

March 2001, Amsterdam, Netherlands

E ven now, seven years later, as the British Airways Embraer E170 glided to a halt at Schiphol Airport, Amsterdam, Steele thought back to the tenacious terrier that six years before had nearly saved Sonja's life, and certainly saved his.

One week after the shooting, the stolen van used by the assassins had been found abandoned. A detective inspector from New Scotland Yard told Steele that the shooter would probably have fired again and finished the job if it hadn't been for the dog.

Witnesses had reported the terrier barking and growling at a man pointing a weapon from a British Telecom van parked next to Primrose Hill Park. Whether the dog had really saved him was a moot point. He had lost Sonja, and he would miss her for the rest of his life.

Now Steele nodded good-bye to the BA flight attendants. He felt a draft of cold air as he passed from the aircraft along the gangway to the airport interior. He was nervous. He had watched a puzzling and disturbing news item on Sky News before boarding the flight in London. There were unconfirmed reports of an escape earlier that day of an unidentified war criminal on trial at the International Criminal Tribunal for the former Yugoslavia—ICTY—in The Hague.

Who the hell has escaped? If it was General Zukić, have they recaptured him yet?

Steele spotted his escort/driver immediately. The young man was an ex-military type with a short haircut and wearing a jacket and tie with jeans and casual shoes. He was waiting for Steele at the end of the walkway just inside the airport building. The man had a wide, honest face and seemed to recognize Steele immediately. He held up a card that read *2552*, Steele's number (for identification and security purposes), which Steele had been told to look for on arrival.

Steele made eye contact. "Hello," he said. "Jack Steele."

They shook hands.

"My name is Kurt. I will take you to your hotel."

"Thank you," said Steele.

Kurt walked briskly through the airport. No attempt at small talk. Kurt flashed his ICTY ID card at passport control, allowing them to skip a long line of international passengers without Steele showing his passport. *This is the first time in my life I haven't shown my passport to enter another country.* After passing effortlessly through customs, they waited in the baggage hall for the carousel to eject Steele's suitcase.

The first item on the conveyor belt was a red suitcase with a rubber fish head and tail stuck to the case, one on each side. A large sticker read:

ANYTHING TO DECLARE?!

"Dutch customs …" Kurt said with a shrug.

"I like it," replied Steele. "Sense of humor."

They both smiled. Steele spotted his suitcase and grabbed it from the conveyor belt.

They left the building and climbed into a navy-blue minivan with tinted windows parked on the police/diplomatic bay. Minutes later they were en route to the ICTY in The Hague.

They reached the outskirts of Amsterdam and the wide-open fields.

"Who escaped today, Kurt?"

"I have not heard."

"But you wouldn't tell me anyway, right?"

"Perhaps ..."

Steele put his questions on hold. He looked out the window and admired the clichéd scenery—windmills, farms, and bicycles by the dozen.

A few minutes later, Steele said, "You served in Bosnia?"

Kurt nodded. "Seventeenth Dutch Infantry Regiment, Srebrenica."

"How did you get this job?"

"I applied for ICTY when the war ended." Kurt spoke near-perfect English with a slight Dutch accent.

"We were in Goražde at the same time ... February 1995?"

"Yes, it's possible. Captain Jensen was my commanding officer. Danes and Dutch served together."

Steele hoped this coincidence might help him glean some information. "I knew Jensen. He did me a big favor once, helped me locate a friend—"

"Many crazy things happened in Goražde." Kurt kept his eyes on the road.

Steele nodded. "How's this job?" he asked, changing the subject. "Probably interesting?"

"I drive Bosnian Serb, Croat, and Muslim generals from Scheveningen prison to the court, and witnesses from the airport to their hotels. Yes, it's interesting. Part of history."

"You drove Milošević during his trial?"

"Yes, every morning he refused to leave his cell until he'd had a strong black coffee."

"Did you meet any Muslim generals?"

"Of course. General Orić never missed his five hundred squats before leaving his cell."

"They found him not guilty?"

"On all counts."

The van reached the outskirts of Scheveningen town, and Kurt pointed to a bleak gray building with an older facade on one side, which reminded Steele of HM Prison Wormwood Scrubs, London. "Scheveningen is a maximum security, state-of-the-art facility, a prison within a prison," Kurt said. "They built a wing especially for ICTY war criminals."

Kurt is opening up, Steele thought. *Good news.*

Steele said, "I read that the inmates walk freely into each other's cells. They have internet access?"

Kurt nodded. "Muslims, Croats, Serbs. One happy family."

"Ironic."

Kurt nodded. "Very."

"Any news on Gen. Zukić? Did he escape?"

"The media is confused. You know what they do. A new VIP arrived today, and they got their information mixed up."

Steele shot a glance at Kurt. "It's not true?"

"Don't worry, if he escaped, we will find him." Kurt smiled so that Steele couldn't tell if he was joking.

For the first time during the drive, Kurt looked Steele in the eye, one former UN peacekeeper to another. "Mr. Steele, the trial begins tomorrow. Everyone has waited a long time for your testimony. You are the key witness. Everyone is counting on you. There is nothing to worry about."

Steele bit his cheek. He had been summoned to testify against Gen. Ratko Zukić, Sonja's godfather, the man responsible for thousands of deaths in Bosnia. It had taken six years to catch Gen. Zukić and bring him to trial.

It had also taken Steele an enormous amount of energy and soul searching to make the decision to come to The Hague. But he concluded that Sonja would have wanted him to testify. He hoped and prayed the rumors of Gen. Zukić escaping were unfounded.

A few minutes later, they reached the center of Scheveningen town and stopped outside the Hotel Kurhaus, a popular weekend destination on the seafront. Kurt carried Steele's case inside and nodded at Saeed, an ICTY witness protection officer, who was sitting in a corner near the hotel bar.

"Please," said Kurt, "Saeed will take care of you. I will check you into the hotel. Use this number if you need anything." He jotted down the number "0507" on a Post-it Note. "Yes, another number, names not necessary."

"Thanks for your help."

Steele sat down, and Saeed, an Albanian refugee, introduced himself and handed Steele some ICTY information sheets with telephone numbers in case of emergency.

"I don't understand what's going on," said Steele. "Did Gen. Zukić escape today?"

"You are safe here, Mr. Steele. Trust me."

Steele always felt uneasy when someone asked him to trust them. Invariably there was a reason why he shouldn't …

"He did not escape. He was transferred to another prison."

"That doesn't make sense. The trial begins tomorrow."

"You are tired, Mr. Steele," said Saeed. "Please rest. There is room service if you are hungry. Kurt will pick you up at eight am. He will drive you to ICTY to meet Stefan Rast, ICTY chief prosecutor. Remember, no one knows you here. You are safe. We have security watching the hotel."

"I have questions about my testimony—"

"Of course, this is normal. Mr. Rast will answer all your questions in the morning. You will meet with him tomorrow to prepare."

Kurt returned from the reception desk and handed Steele his room keycard. "Use your number at reception if you need anything."

"Zero-five-zero-seven?" Steele held up his hand as he spoke. Kurt nodded.

"Okay."

Steele took the lift to the nineth floor. His room was located directly opposite the lift doors. Good, he thought, I can see who comes and goes. He slipped his keycard in the slot. Then he entered, closed the door, and flipped over the metal lock bar on the back of the door. He felt safe, but somehow, he didn't feel completely secure. Being anonymous in some ways was more unnerving, he decided, than people knowing who he was and why he was in The Hague.

Looking around the room, he concluded it was adequate for his, hopefully short, stay. As well as the normal curtains, he was pleased to see a thick, heavy blackout curtain, which would help him nap during the day if necessary. Who knew how long he would be here. He walked to the sliding door, opened it, and stepped out onto the balcony.

The railing was chest height. Safer that way, if you'd had one too many. He took a few breaths of salty sea air and enjoyed the sea view. Then he went back inside, drew the thick blackout curtains, and crashed out onto the bed.

He was exhausted but couldn't fall asleep.

Twenty minutes later, he flicked on the television and scrolled down to CNN International, then the local news channel. He lowered the volume, hoping to watch the images and lull himself to sleep. He set the timer for thirty minutes, but the thirty minutes came and went several times, and he had to switch the television back on. Steele kept watch for news on Gen. Zukić's transfer, which never came.

He lay awake, turning the volume up when stories piqued his interest, but became bored of the news items as they were repeated.

He thought about Bosnia: Zukić, Radovanović, Brown, Staci, Dražen, Small, and, of course, Sonja. It felt like a lifetime ago. And now, on the eve of his testimony, he relived every moment as though it were yesterday.

Apart from Gen. Zukić being Sonja's godfather, Steele was greatly troubled that Gen. Zukić had saved his life (when Col. Kostić was about to pull the trigger at the Hotel Panorama) and now Steele was about to give testimony that might put Gen. Zukić away for forever.

Six years on, Steele yearned to put Bosnia behind him and get on with his life. Yes, he had every right to be nervous. But he had promised himself for many years to tell the truth one day about the Sarajevo Protocol, about everyone and everything connected to it. He would name names, point fingers, and, if necessary, defend his own role in the conspiracy …

At 3:15 am, Steele heard the lift doors open. Odd, he thought. This was the first time he had heard the heavy metal lift doors clunking open since midnight. The hotel did not seem particularly full. He got up and looked through his spy hole. The hallway was dimly lit, but someone was standing directly outside *his* door.

Fuck. Now he was worried. His heart beat faster.

He walked back to his bedside table where he was about to reach for the telephone. *They had men watching the building,* Saeed had said. *Steady, Jack,* he muttered to himself. *For God sake's calm down … No need to overreact.*

Before he could pick up the receiver, there was a knock on the door and an envelope pushed underneath it.

"Jack?" the man said in an English accent and knocked again. "Jack, it's Brian Small."

What the fuck?

Steele walked to the door, shaking his head in disbelief, rubbing his face to make sure he was as awake as possible. He peered through the spy hole. No mistake. The man outside his door was Maj. Brian Small, former UN Chief Ops Officer. Even after all these years, Steele recognized him immediately.

He didn't know why, but his heart sank. Somehow, he knew this wasn't good news.

CHAPTER FIFTY-FOUR

03:16 am

Steele said nothing. He felt sick. This doesn't feel right. What is Brian Small doing outside my door, here, now, at three am? I haven't seen him for six years. How does he know I'm here? Instinctively, he stepped back from the door for a second, shaking his head.

No one knows I'm here …

Again, Small tapped on the door. Steele peered through the hole.

"I know it's late," Small said. "I need to talk. It's urgent. Look in the envelope." He moved away from the door, smiling, arms outstretched. "Unarmed."

Then it occurred to Steele that this might be the perfect opportunity, the answer to a humble prayer, to find out what on earth was going on with Gen. Zukić. Perhaps Small had news about the escape? There was no reason for concern. I'm overreacting. It's Brian Small, for God's sake, ex-British Army, General Brown's staff officer. Perhaps Small is working for ICTY?

Steele said, "Hang on, Brian." But he thought, This still feels wrong.

If this had been a movie, Steele would have grabbed his pistol from the nightstand just to be sure. But it wasn't a movie, and he didn't have a pistol anyway. Brian Small is on our side, Steele reassured himself. The ICTY security people who were watching the hotel would have intercepted him if he was a threat.

Steele swung back the safety latch and confidently opened the door.

Before he had a chance to say anything, Small forced his way inside, suddenly producing a pistol from nowhere. He hammered the butt of his pistol onto the bridge of Steele's nose, knocking him backward onto the bed. Small shut the door and placed his index finger to his mouth. He pointed the pistol with silencer at Steele's face.

"Nothing personal, Jack ... Hard times, I'm afraid."

"You're insane. What do you want?" Steele grabbed the hotel towel lying next to him and held it to his nose to stem the flow of blood running down his face and hands. "What the fuck are you doing?"

"Sorry, Jack. Just helping out an old friend of ours. An offer I couldn't refuse. I'm just the hired gun, you might say."

"I don't know what you're talking about?"

"They didn't tell you why you're here?"

"I'm here to testify against Gen. Zukić."

Small laughed.

"What's so funny?"

"They kept you in the dark. It's not Zukić you're here for. It's Boyle."

"Boyle?" Steele couldn't believe what he was hearing.

"You're here to testify against Boyle."

"What?"

"And I can't let you do that."

Steele raised his voice. "Why are you here?"

"Ssssh ... Keep it down, will you, Jack." Small aimed the weapon at Steele's head. "We need to talk, but we don't need to wake the other guests, do we?"

"I don't understand. I thought Boyle was dead," Steele continued. "What are you saying?"

"Apparently, not as dead as everyone thought." Small smiled. "It was touch and go. He was on the edge for a few hours, but he pulled through, bless him. He actually made a full recovery, then disappeared, only to be arrested years later for his role in the Sarajevo Protocol debacle. But you know all about that."

Steele stared down the barrel of the pistol. *This makes absolutely no sense.*

"What do you want?"

"I'll explain, Jack. You deserve that much."

Slowly, Steele began to recall events from six years ago and started putting the pieces together. After Sonja's murder on Primrose Hill, Small had called Steele to offer his condolences. Steele thought it was a decent gesture. During the call, Small had told him that Boyle had died of the gunshot wound in Sarajevo. That's what the press had reported too.

"You lied."

"That's right, Jack," Small continued, "your little trip to The Hague has nothing to do with our old friend, Gen. Zukić. You're here to—"

"They need me to put him away?"

"Bravo, Jack. Correct on both counts. You always were a bright little UNMO. And as much as I hate to speak ill of the dead, Sonja wasn't quite the peace angel you thought she was. Take a look." Small pointed to the envelope.

Steele picked up the envelope and took out the document inside written in Bosnian. It was some kind of military fire mission. Then he noticed the date: 5th February, 1995—date of the Sarajevo Market Massacre. At the bottom was Sonja's signature and her position as "Chief of Staff, Army of Republika Srpska."

Steele said, "I don't believe it."

"Like I said, very sorry to burst your bubble. You two were close. The good news is that Sonja's dead, so they can't prosecute her."

Small moved to the end of the bed, creating distance between himself and Steele. "Tomorrow, our old friend will be the first Westerner tried for war crimes in former Yugoslavia. They can't get Black Cobra, so Boyle, poor sod, is the next best thing. And who better to nail him than a respectable ex-British UNMO with impeccable service to Queen and country? You're an unsung hero, Jack, and they're giving you a chance to sing."

Steele stared back, his mind reeling, trying to work out the implications of Small's revelation and, more importantly, his presence in Steele's room. He wasn't sure which bombshell was worse—the fact that he might be testifying against Boyle or the fact that Sonja, the woman he wanted to marry, might somehow be implicated in the Sarajevo Market Massacre. "Jesus Christ, Brian. This is absurd."

"Not really, Jack." Small wagged his pistol at Steele. "Think about it. Washington and London want accountability. The latest buzz word. The twenty-first century is all about accountability ... Personally, I agree. Banks, insurance companies, pharmaceuticals, even the food industry. They're all greedy fucking bastards if you think about it, aren't they? But our political masters are cleaning house, going after everyone, including former corrupt spies and regime change infidels like Boyle. It's a popular move. US president's polls are through the roof. He's even talking about universal healthcare."

Steele glanced at the white towel now soaked with blood. "Why Boyle? He was no worse than anyone else in Black Cobra."

"Precisely, Jack. But that's not how they see it. They want blood." Small screwed up his mouth. "Boyle is fucked if you testify. They kept him around all these years waiting for the right moment to nail the poor bugger."

"Where was he?"

"They gave him a new identity, promised him immunity. But after the likes of Bush and Cheney shook up that squeaky-clean image Americans are in love with, London and Washington want to make amends. Someone changed their mind about Boyle. And what better place to officially finish him than The Hague? They completely reneged on all their promises to him."

Steele understood. "Boyle goes down with my help?"

"Precisely. They say this is the first of many indictments."

Small leaned back on the dresser. "Except, as you might imagine, old boy, Boyle is not terribly happy about the idea. I'm sure you can appreciate his predicament."

Steele felt a cold chill run from head to toe. He had reached the logical conclusion of Small's visit. There was only one reason Small was standing in front of him, with a pistol and silencer—

Small had been sent to assassinate him.

Steele's mind raced. "Brian—" He didn't know what to say.

Shouting wouldn't help—he was on the nineth floor; the walls and doors were thick. One cry and Small would pull the trigger. And besides, Steele hadn't seen or heard anyone in adjacent rooms. The staff weren't exactly patrolling the corridors.

Steele said, "He must be paying you well?"

"Like I said, hard times. Sorry, Jack."

"Boyle must have saved wisely."

"Old money. He never really needed to draw his salary. Plus Black Cobra took care of him too, of course." He lowered the pistol for a moment then re-aimed. "Life's not fair, is it, Jack? I want you to know this is nothing personal."

"Thanks, Brian." He set down the bloody towel and locked eyes with Small. "You're better than this."

"Too late for the high ground. Are you any better? Why did you really want to marry Sonja? Boyle told me you begged him to send you to Pale. You wanted your fifteen minutes of fame like everyone else, Jack. Anything for Queen and country, isn't that right?"

"That's not true. I wanted to help."

"Of course, you did, Jack."

"Boyle's lying."

"No one really cares about Sonja's reputation anymore after all those nasty things her father did. Water under the bridge. Bloody water."

Rage surged through Steele's mind and body at the same time. It was now or never, he had to make—

Steele retched violently. "I'm going to be sick."

"Don't move, Jack—"

Steele rolled across the bed. "I'm going to throw up!" He stumbled away from Small toward the balcony making retching noises. As he moved to the partially open sliding door, he saw himself flying to his death nine floors below, a bullet in the back of his skull.

But this was his only chance. He had to get Small to the balcony. Roles reversed, Steele wouldn't shoot outside even with a silencer.

Steele dove for the blackout curtain that was opaque and thicker than a usual curtain.

Small fired.

The curtain broke his fall as Steele fell onto the balcony. He smashed his elbow on the concrete. An excruciating pain seared his forearm, but for a split second, he couldn't tell if it was from the fall or a bullet.

The curtain separating them, Steele looked up at the stars. The contradiction of death, his life flashing before him again, the dawn sky and the sound of waves in the near distance struck him as ironic. Enough with the poetry, he thought. There was nowhere to go but down. He'd have to stay and fight. But with what?

The curtain was flung to one side, and Steele saw the pistol. Then he looked up at Small.

Another shot.

It was loud … this is it. But something didn't add up … Then he realized the shot had come from behind him, not from Small's pistol.

Everything stopped.

Steele turned slowly and looked around. He saw a hole in the curtain and Small's foot and lower leg on the floor inside—motionless.

Small had been shot from the outside. But by whom?

He turned and scanned the apartment building opposite, every window from top to bottom. He saw nothing.

Then he heard sirens.

The hotel staff quickly arranged for Steele to move to another room a few floors below. Two armed Dutch policemen with pistols and semiautomatic weapons patrolled his floor. Saeed, the ICTY protection officer, arrived shortly after and issued a thousand apologies and a thousand more reassurances that nothing else would happen.

Steele accepted the apology but wasn't convinced about the reassurances.

He *was* thankful to be alive. He spent the next couple of hours thinking about Bosnia and Boyle. What would happen in the courtroom? Did he even want to testify? Could they *force* him to testify?

Somewhere deep down inside, he felt relief. He would rather deal with Boyle than Gen. Zukić and his band of crazies.

Kurt telephoned at 7:00 am sharp. Steele hadn't slept, but he was pumped with adrenaline. For the past six years, he had wanted the world to know how, in his opinion, the West had messed up in Bosnia. Today was his opportunity to tell them.

Kurt met Steele in the lobby and apologized for the incident. As they drove from the hotel in convoy—flanked by three Dutch police vehicles—Kurt said, "This was unacceptable, Mr. Steele."

"Why didn't they tell me why I'm really here?"

"Stefan Rast, the prosecutor, will explain. It was easier this way. We told you the minimum information for your protection."

"What protection?" Steele shot Kurt a look that said, *Give me a break.*

"This was our first security failure in eight years, Mr. Steele. It was too close. We messed up, and I apologize for that."

"Not everyone screwed up, Kurt ..." Steele half smiled. "Where were you last night?"

"I was asleep at home," said Kurt, straight faced. "But Captain Jensen (retired) says hello. He apologizes for the inconvenience."

Steele saw the twinkle in Kurt's eye.

At that moment, he confirmed what he had suspected all along. The Dutch security services had fulfilled their remit. Steele said, "Tell Jensen from me, *Boom, boom!* Luka would be proud."

"Jensen told me he would keep an eye on you. He said you deserve a medal for your service in Bosnia."

"Thanks, Kurt."

"By the way, why didn't your queen give you a medal?"

"She did," said Steele. "It was a private ceremony."

They both smiled.

CHAPTER FIFTY-FIVE

ICTY, The Hague

Twenty-five minutes later, they arrived at the ICTY, a large gray building sandwiched between Eisenhowerln and Johan de Wittln in The Hague. The official address was Churchillplein 1. The side street of Churchillplein was jammed with all shapes, sizes, and colors of satellite television trucks and vans from many different countries.

Steele had never seen so many media vehicles in one place, even in Sarajevo. Between them, cables and generators were scattered like the tubes of a life-support machine providing oxygen to each vehicle.

Kurt said, "They don't know it yet. But they are waiting to see you. You are mystery VIP witness."

"I'll try not to disappoint."

Now it all makes sense. The secrecy, the vagueness, the importance of me being here in the first place.

"You are the number one news story in homes all over the world tonight. Boyle is the first private security firm officer to be indicted for war crimes. You open the case for the prosecution."

Steele marveled at the ICTY building, an art deco monstrosity. The water fountain in front made the ugly building look more elegant and impressive than it was. But the history and accomplishments of ICTY were impressive enough. Established as an *ad hoc* court by the UN Security Council in 1993, the ICTY building had been adapted for maximum security, high-profile cases of war crimes and atrocities committed during the conflict in former Yugoslavia. It was the first international war crimes tribunal since the Nuremberg and Tokyo trials, and the first set up by the UN. *This place is a big fucking deal*, thought Steele. Many years later, Steele discovered that of the three hundred or so war criminals indicted, only two international arrest warrants remained outstanding. In other words, the ICTY, somewhat miraculously, had caught nearly everyone on their war criminal list.

Kurt drove past the media circus and the main entrance into the ICTY underground car park. He continued around the one-way system and pulled up in front of the staff entrance. No mistake which country they were in—at least one hundred bicycles were neatly stacked in bike racks next to the building behind the bulky iron gates of the ICTY premises. The electric gates opened quickly and closed behind them with the same efficiency.

"Follow me, Mr. Steele," said Kurt.

He escorted Steele through a double layer of Star Trek-like transparent walk-in security cylinders. Steele said, "I definitely feel safe in here."

"I'm pleased." Kurt did not smile.

A minute later, they had passed through security.

They stood at the bottom of a grand staircase. "Which way?" asked Steele.

"Please …" Kurt led the way.

They walked up several flights. Kurt pointed out three main sections—Chambers, Registry, and Office of the Prosecutor. "The building is equipped with maximum security entry pods, gates, holding cells, and three state-of-the art courtrooms with TV and internet broadcast capability. All proceedings are interpreted into English, French, Bosnian, and Macedonian."

"Bloody amazing. I'm impressed." It was an ultrasafe environment to spill your guts.

"I will take you to the prosecutor's office. He will explain everything."

Steele sat in the Victims and Witnesses Section—VWS—waiting room inside the Registry. He tried to imagine the pain and suffering of the countless witnesses, men and women—Bosnian Muslim, Serb, and Croat—who had sat and would continue to sit in this room over the years. But he concluded that this was not his war and that he would never truly understand what Bosnians—all of them—had suffered.

Steele sat down in a large blue armchair. On a bookcase to his right, separate volumes of English, Serbian, and Croatian dictionaries were on hand. Serbian and Croatian were virtually the same language, but the ICTY had to cater to all parties and be politically correct with language.

A well-thumbed pile of magazines from different regions of former Yugoslavia were neatly stacked on a coffee table in the middle of the room. Two hardback books sat next to them—*At Some Disputed Barricade* by Anne Perry and *Girl from the South* by Joanna Trollope.

He plucked a tissue from a box on the coffee table and stared at a yellow rose in its tall, thin vase. He blew his nose and cleared his throat and thought about the many tears that had almost certainly been shed in this room.

There was a knock on the door.

A tall, fit, healthy-looking man with a gray beard, flushed cheeks, and a receding hairline entered. He looked like a mixture of Christopher Lee and Peter Cushing. Wearing black robes with a pristine white judicial ruff, he was smiling and holding out a large, confident hand.

"Thank you for coming, Mr. Steele. My name is Stefan Rast. I know your journey hasn't been easy. I apologize for last night."

"I'm in one piece. That's what counts." Steele nodded, and they shook hands like warriors about to join forces against a common enemy.

Kurt had told Steele that Stefan Rast was one of the most successful prosecutors in Swiss legal history. He spoke perfect English but with a slight German-Swiss accent.

"It was better this way," Rast continued. "We could not tell you the truth. We are about to make history. The less you knew the better. I apologize again." He placed his hand on his chest.

"It's fine. I'm glad to help. I want to help."

"We had to make it look as though you were coming here for Gen. Zukić."

"And Maj. Small? He showed me the Bosnian Serb army fire mission signed by Sonja? The Market Massacre?"

Rast frowned. "I don't understand."

"Brian Small gave me a Bosnian Serb fire order document with Sonja's signature on it."

"We had no part in that, but we can help you investigate its validity if you wish. I doubt it's authentic."

"OK, thank you. I'll let you know." Steele reflected for a few moments.

"Forgive me, Mr. Steele. But time is short."

"Okay, I'm ready. How does this play out?"

"In court, you may speak freely. We will ask you everything you know about Colonel Edward Boyle, his position in the UNPRO-FOR command structure, and detailed accounts of your contact with him—names, dates as best you can recall, conversations, places. We can work on more details in the coming days. In court today, we will dissect the Sarajevo Protocol, your part in General Brown's peace plan, and the murder of Jimmy Broadbent—"

"Who?"

"The dispatch cyclist in London … Our investigators believe Boyle was also responsible."

Steele shook his head. He felt guilty. He had forgotten the name of the slain cyclist. "Poor bastard. It was my fault he got involved in the first place."

"What happened happened … Do not go there, Mr. Steele."

Steele nodded, unconvinced. "Thanks. I'll try not to."

"We have not indicted any Western ex-military, nor anyone from a private Western security firm. This is a first. Until now, the Americans would never allow it. But a new age of accountability and transparency is upon us. We can thank the American president.

"Bush balls, someone called it."

Rast chuckled. "Very good. I like it."

"How long will you need me?"

"Difficult to say. Weeks possibly, but—fingers crossed—not months."

"No problem. They already warned me to put my life on hold."

"One more thing, Mr. Steele. You have the right to decline to help us, and you also have the right to ask the judge for anonymity if you think you or your family's lives are in danger."

Steele thought about his mother. He'd already made sure someone was keeping a close eye on her.

"From what you and others have told me about the threat level, that won't be necessary," he said confidently. "What about the media? How do I handle them? We saw at least thirty satellite dishes parked outside."

"None of them knows where you are staying. We managed to keep last night's incident confidential. You may not speak to them during the trial. After your testimony is over, however, I would ask you to use your discretion if and when you decide to speak to the media. We have no jurisdiction over you after the fact."

"Understood."

They shook hands. "Thank you again, Mr. Steele. The clerk will come for you shortly. See you in court three."

For the next four minutes, Steele watched the red seconds hand of the clock on the wall circle the clock face four times as he reflected on all those who had died in Bosnia.

Wearing a judicial wig and black robes, the clerk of the court knocked firmly and entered. She introduced herself and asked if Steele had any questions.

"No."

"Thank you for being here. The judge is ready. Good luck, Mr. Steele."

He followed her down a maze of corridors to court three. Armed ICTY security officers in pale blue shirts stood at the entrance to the court.

Steele entered and walked over to the witness stand. Behind the desk was a tinted glass window, back-lit and with enough light to see into the crowded gallery full of journalists from all over the world. So much for anonymity ... but at least he'd have privacy at the hotel.

TV news cameras were not allowed inside the ICTY, but the entire proceedings would be streamed live on the internet courtesy of the ICTY.

Steele sat down and made himself comfortable at the witness stand. He adjusted the microphone and poured himself a glass of water. Behind and to his left and right were small booths with more tinted windows. Highly skilled interpreters would simultaneously interpret all proceedings into the official languages of the court—English, French, Bosnian, and Macedonian.

"All rise," the clerk announced crisply. The judge entered, and Steele recognized him. He had presided over the Slobodan Milošević case Steele had followed in the press.

The judge acknowledged the court with a majestic nod.

Steele glanced across to his left. Behind two rows of British defense team barristers wearing wigs, Boyle was staring at him.

Steele nodded and smiled victoriously.

Boyle kept staring, expressionless.

The judge said, "Would the clerk of the court swear the witness in?"

The clerk nodded at Steele. "Mr. Steele ..."

Steele picked up the oath printed on the card in front of him. "I swear to tell the truth, the whole truth, and nothing but the truth."

The clerk said, "Thank you, Mr. Steele. Please sit down."

Then he remembered the choirboy who he later found out had died after the Pale church shelling. Steele knew how lucky he was to be alive. More than anything else, after this was all over, he wanted to move to the Cotswolds and raise a family. But with all that was going on, his simple desire now seemed further away than ever.

Prosecutor Rast stood up. "Good morning, Mr. Steele," he began.

"Good morning."

"Can you confirm for the court that you are Mr. Jack Steele, formerly Captain Jack Steele, and that you served as an UNMO during the Bosnia conflict in 1994.

"Yes, that's correct."

"Thank you, Mr. Steele. And can you also confirm you were sent to Bosnian Serb territory, and more specifically to the town of Pale, on the orders of an officer you believed to be your British Army superior by the name of Colonel Edward Boyle?"

"Yes, that is correct."

"And can you tell the court if you see that man in this court?"

"Yes, I do."

"Can you point to him, please?"

Steele pointed across the court.

The prosecutor leaned down and searched in one of the many thick files on his table. "Thank you, Mr. Steele."

Steele picked up his glass and drank some water. His throat was already dry.

"Mr. Steele, can you begin by telling the court what you know about a secret document known as the Sarajevo Protocol?"

"Certainly," said Steele, clearing his throat and adjusting the microphone. "It's a little complicated …"

THE END

ACKNOWLEDGMENTS

Karen Ross for keeping me going during the first few drafts of Book 1 and beyond. Christopher Dawson for his love and kindness. Margaret Bramford for showing me how it's done. Beverly Swerling for mentoring, patience, and believing. Frank Freudberg for fun, frivolity, and facts. Sophie Jenkins for inspiration. Marvlus Mav for always picking up the phone. Candace Johnson, the most fun, thorough, and talented editor an author could wish for. Sara Lukens for countless hours of attention to detail and hard work. Steve Sklair for a fantastic book trailer. Carol & Gary Rosenberg, The Book Couple, for endless good-humored interior book design patience. Jae Song for his inimitable cover designs. Vanja Sikirica and Zdenka Sajko for blast-from-the-past translation consultation. And for the thousands of readers and supporters along this amazing journey ...

ABOUT THE AUTHOR

Richard Lyntton was born Richard Bramford in Highgate, London. He attended William Ellis School, Exeter University, Moscow State Linguistic University (formerly Maurice Thorez Moscow State Pedagogical Institute of Foreign Languages), and Sandhurst. Richard served as a Captain and tank commander in the British Army in the First Gulf War; European Community Task Force Humanitarian Liaison in Russia; UNHCR Liaison Officer, and United Nations Military Observer (during heavy shelling and NATO airstrikes) in Sarajevo, Bosnia; and was a United Nations Television producer in former Yugoslavia. He was called to testify at the International War Crimes Tribunal in the Hague after witnessing and filming human rights atrocities and abuses in Bosnia. His films are archived at the Imperial War Museum, London.

When he's not writing, Richard is a film & television actor. He lives in Philadelphia with his wife, interior designer Michelle Wenitsky, and their two sons.

Thank you for reading

HYDE PARK DECEPTION

The audio book is also available.

✪   ✪   ✪

If you enjoyed the book, I would very
much appreciate it if you could leave
a review on the platform you used.
Reviews make a big difference for the author!

✪   ✪   ✪

CLICK on the richardlynttonbooks website link
to sign up for VIP news, events and updates for Book 3:

https://richardlynttonbooks.com/